'*Love is Blind* has a beautiful sense of the power
and charm of music' *Irish Times*

'He makes it look easy: he's a pro' *New Statesman*

'*Love is Blind* wins you over with infectious charm' *Daily Mail*

'I guarantee *Love is Blind* will grip you, and after
you've finished, haunt you' *Daily Express*

'Thoroughly involving with beautifully realized characters
and an unexpected sting in its tail' *Woman and Home*

'Expertly engineered to produce chords of feeling'
The Times Literary Supplement

'Gripping and rather gorgeous' *Scotsman*

'Heart-rending and compulsively readable' *Herald*

By the same author

NOVELS

A Good Man in Africa

An Ice-Cream War

Stars and Bars

The New Confessions

Brazzaville Beach

The Blue Afternoon

Armadillo

Nat Tate: An American Artist 1928–1960

Any Human Heart

Restless

Ordinary Thunderstorms

Waiting for Sunrise

Solo

Sweet Caress: The Many Lives of Amory Clay

SHORT-STORY COLLECTIONS

On the Yankee Station

The Destiny of Nathalie 'X'

Fascination

The Dream Lover

The Dreams of Bethany Mellmoth

PLAYS

School Ties

Six Parties

Longing

The Argument

NON-FICTION

Bamboo

Love is Blind

The Rapture of Brodie Moncur

WILLIAM BOYD

PENGUIN BOOKS

PENGUIN BOOKS

UK | USA | Canada | Ireland | Australia
India | New Zealand | South Africa

Penguin Books is part of the Penguin Random House group of companies
whose addresses can be found at global.penguinrandomhouse.com.

First published by Viking 2018
Published in Penguin Books 2019
001

Printed and bound in Great Britain by Clays Ltd, Elcograf S.p.A.

A CIP catalogue record for this book is available from the British Library

ISBN: 978-0-241-29592-2

www.greenpenguin.co.uk

Penguin Random House is committed to a sustainable future for our business, our readers and our planet. This book is made from Forest Stewardship Council® certified paper.

For Susan

During the last year of his life Anton [Chekhov] thought of writing another play. It was not quite clear in his mind, but he told me that the hero, a scientist, loves a woman who either does not love him or is unfaithful to him. The scientist goes to the Far North. He pictured the third act thus: a ship is icebound; the sky is ablaze with the Northern Lights. The scientist stands, a solitary figure, on the deck amidst the utter silence and grandeur of the night, and against the background of the Northern Lights he sees the shadow of the woman he loves.

Olga Knipper-Chekhova, *The Last Years*

Falling in love is the one illogical adventure, the one thing of which we are tempted to think as supernatural, in our trite and reasonable world. The effect is out of all proportion with the cause.

Robert Louis Stevenson, *Virginibus Puerisque*

Prologue

Port Blair
Andaman Islands
Indian Empire

11 March 1906

Dear Amelia,

There was an attempt to escape from the jail last night and a small riot ensued. Most unusual. Three of the prisoners were killed but a number managed to flee. Consequently we have a twenty-four-hour curfew imposed on the town so here I am in my house at luncheon writing this long-overdue missive.

All is well, my leg is much better (Dr Klein is very pleased, he says, though I'm walking with a stick – very elegant) and the new tribe we've found is slowly becoming accommodating. Colonel Ticknell, the British superintendent here, is most helpful. 'Your every need, Miss Arbogast, is mine. Please don't hesitate, the merest trifle, etc., etc.' And I don't hesitate (you know me). Transport, bearers, diplomatic postal facilities – even a firearm – have been supplied. I think Col Ticknell has a soft spot for me and he imagines diligent concern will win my heart. No harm in thinking, I suppose. You will call me a calculating minx, but needs must out here.

And, mirabile dictu, *the advertisement I placed in the local newspaper and that I personally affixed to the wall in the post office has been answered. I have a new assistant – finally!*

A policeman is knocking on the door. The curfew is over, I suspect. I will write again, later.

In the meantime, with my love as always, your sister,
Page

PS. By the way my new assistant is a tall young Scotchman, about thirty-five years old, called Brodie Moncur.

PART I

Edinburgh

1894

I

Brodie Moncur stood in the main window of Channon & Co. and looked out at the hurrying pedestrians, the cabs, carriages and labouring drays of George Street. It was raining – a steady soft rain driven slant from time to time by the occasional fierce gust of wind – and, under the ponderous pewter light, the sooty facades of the buildings opposite had darkened with the water to a near-black. Like velvet, Brodie thought, or moleskin. He took off his spectacles and wiped the lenses clean on his handkerchief. Looking out of the window again, spectacle-less, he saw that rainy Edinburgh had now gone utterly aqueous. The buildings opposite were a cliff of black suede.

He replaced his spectacles – hooking the wire sides behind his ears – and the world returned to normal. He slipped his watch from his waistcoat pocket. Nearly nine o'clock – better start. He opened up the glossy new grand piano that was on the display dais, propping up the curved lid with its inlaid mirror (only for display purposes – his idea) the better to present the intricate machinery – the 'action' – inside a Channon grand. He removed the fall from over the keys and undid the key-block screws. He checked that no hammers were up and then drew the whole action forward by the flange rail under the front. As it was a new piano it drew out perfectly. Already a passer-by had stopped and was peering in. Drawing out the action always compelled attention. Everyone had seen a grand piano with the lid up but having the action on display somehow altered every easy assumption. The piano no longer seemed familiar. Now all the moving parts were visible beyond the black and white keys – the hammers, the rockers, the jacks, the whippens, the dampers – its innards were exposed like a clock with its back off or a railway engine dismantled in a repair shed. Mysteries – music, time, movement – were reduced to complex, elaborate mechanisms. People tended to be fascinated.

He untied his leather roll of tools, selected the tuning lever and pretended to tune the piano, tightening a few strings here and there, testing them and resetting them. The piano was perfectly tuned – he had tuned it himself when it had emerged, pristine, from the factory two weeks ago. He tuned F a modicum on the sharp side then knocked it in – back into tune – with a few brisk taps on the key. He supported a hammer-head and needled-up the felt a little with his three-pronged voicing tool and returned it to its position. This pantomime of tuning a piano was meant to lure the customers in. He had suggested, at one of the rare staff meetings, that they should have someone actually playing the piano – an accomplished pianist – as they did in showrooms in Germany, and as the Erard and Pleyel piano manufacturers had done in Paris in the 1830s and drawn huge crowds. It was hardly an innovation – but an impromptu recital in a shop window would surely be more enticing than listening to the mannered repetitions of a piano being tuned. *Donk! Ding! Donk! Donk! Donk! Ding!* He had been overruled – an accomplished pianist would cost money – and instead he was given this job of display-tuning: an hour in the morning and an hour after luncheon. In fact he did attract spectators, although he had been the single beneficiary – he wasn't sure if the firm had sold one more piano as a result of his demonstrations, but many people and not a few institutions (schools, church halls, public houses) had slipped into the shop, pressed a calling card on him, and offered him out-of-hours piano tuning. He had earned a good few pounds.

So, he played A above middle C several times, to 'get the pitch', pointedly listening to the tone with a cocked head. Then played a few octaves. He stood, slipped some felt mutes between strings, took out his tuning lever, set it over a wrest pin at random and gave it some tiny turns, just to deliver torque, then eased the pin slightly to 'set the pin' and hit the note hard, to deliver a cast-iron tuning, feeling it in the hand through the lever. Then he sat down and played a few chords, listening to the Channon's particular voice. Big and strongly resonant – the precision thinness of the sounding board (made from Scottish spruce) under the strings was the special Channon trademark, its trade secret. A Channon could rival a Steinway or a Bösendorfer when it came to breaking through an orchestra. Where the spruce forests were in Scotland that Channon used, what trees were selected – the straighter the tree, the straighter the grain – and what sawmills prepared the timber, were facts known only to a handful of people in the firm. Channon claimed that it was the quality of the Scottish wood they used that made their pianos' distinct, unique tone.

Brodie's feigning over, he sat down and started to play 'The Skye Boat Song' and saw that the single spectator had now been joined by three others. If he played for half an hour he knew there would be a crowd of twenty looking on. It was a good idea, the Continental idea. Perhaps, out of that twenty, two might enquire about the price of a baby grand or an upright. He stopped playing, took out his plectrum, reached into the piano and twanged a few strings, listening intently. What would that look like to anyone? A man with a plectrum playing a grand piano like a guitar. All very mysterious—

'Brodie!'

He looked round. Emmeline Grant, Mr Channon's secretary, stood at the window's framing edge, beckoning at him. She was a small burly woman who tried to disguise how fond she was of him.

'I'm in full tune, Mrs Grant.'

'Mr Channon wants to see you. Right away. Come along now.'

'I'm coming, I'm coming.'

He stood, thought about closing the piano down but decided against it. He'd be back in ten minutes. He gave a deep bow to his small audience and followed Mrs Grant through the showroom, with its parked, glossy pianos, and into the main hall of the Channon building. Austere unsmiling portraits of previous generations of Channons hung on olive and charcoal-grey striped wallpaper. Another mistake, Brodie thought: it was like a provincial art gallery or a funeral parlour.

'Give me two minutes, Mrs G. I have to wash my hands.'

'Hurry along. I'll see you upstairs. It's important.'

Brodie went through the back, through a leather, brass-studded door into the warehouse area where the workshop was located. It was a cross between a carpentry shop and an office, he always thought, the air seasoned with the smell of wood shavings, glue and resin. He pushed open the door and found his number two, Lachlan Hood, at work replacing the centre pins on a baby grand – a long job, there were hundreds of them.

Lachlan glanced at him as he came in.

'What's going on, Brodie? Should you no be in the window?'

'I'm wanted. Mr Channon.'

He slid up his roll-top desk and opened the drawer where he kept his tin of tobacco. 'Margarita' was the brand name: an American blend of Virginia, Turkish and perique tobacco, made by a tobacconist called Blakely in New York City and to be found in only one retailer in Edinburgh – Hoskings, in the Grassmarket. He took one of the three cigarettes he had already rolled and lit it, inhaling deeply.

'What's he want you for?' Lachlan asked.

'I don't know. Darling Emmeline says it's "important".'

'Well, it was nice knowing youse. I suppose I'll get your job, the now.'

Lachlan was from Dundee and had a strong Dundonian accent. Brodie made the sign of the evil eye at him, took two more puffs, stubbed out his cigarette and headed for Ainsley Channon's office.

Ainsley Channon was the sixth Channon to head the firm since it had been established in the mid-eighteenth century. On the landing was a 1783 Channon five-octave spinet – the first Channon model to be a true success and which began the firm's fortunes. Now it was the fourth-largest piano manufacturer, some said the third, in Britain, after Broadwood, Pate and – possibly – Franklin. And, as if to confirm the length of this lineage, Ainsley Channon dressed in a style that had been fashionable half a century before. He wore luxuriant Dundreary whiskers and a stiff wing collar with silk cravat and pin. His receding grey hair hung down long behind his ears, almost touching his shoulders. He looked like an old musician, like a stout Paganini. Brodie knew he couldn't play a note.

Brodie gave a one-knuckle knock and pushed open the door.

'Come away in, Brodie. Brodie, my boy. Sit ye down, sit ye down.'

The room was large and gloomy – the gas lamps lit even though it was morning – with three tall, twelve-paned windows looking out over George Street. Brodie could make out the high, thin spire of St Andrew's and St George's West Church through the still-falling smear of misty rain.

Ainsley stepped round from behind his partners' desk and pulled up a chair for Brodie, patting its leather seat.

Brodie sat down on it. Ainsley smiled at him as if he hadn't seen him for years, taking him in.

'You'll have a dram.'

It was a statement, not a question and Brodie didn't bother to reply. Ainsley went to a table with a clustered, light-winking collection of decanters, selected one and poured two generous glasses, bringing Brodie's over to him before taking his place behind his desk again.

'Here's how,' Ainsley said and raised his glass.

'Slangevar,' Brodie replied and sipped at his amber whisky. Malt, peaty, West Coast.

Ainsley held up a puce cardboard dossier and waved it at him.

'The Brodie Moncur file,' he said.

For some reason Brodie felt a little heart-jig of worry. He calmed it with another sip of whisky.

Ainsley Channon had a somewhat dreamy and disconnected air about him, Brodie knew, and so was not surprised at the meandering path the meeting took.

'How long have you been with us, Brodie? It'll be about three years now, yes?'

'Actually six, sir.'

'Good God, good God, good God.' He paused and smiled, taking this in. 'How's your father?'

'Well, sir.'

'And your siblings?'

'All fit and well.'

'Have you seen Lady Dalcastle recently?'

'Not for a while.'

'Wonderful woman. Wonderful woman. Very brave.'

'I believe she's very well, also.'

Ainsley Channon was a cousin of Lady Dalcastle, who had been a close friend of Brodie's late mother. It was through Lady Dalcastle's good offices that Brodie had been taken on by Channon's as an apprentice tuner.

Ainsley was looking at his dossier again.

'Aye. You're a clever boy, right enough. Very good grades . . .' He looked up. 'Do you parley-voo?'

'Excuse me?'

'Speakee zee French? Ooh la-la. *Bonjour monsieur.*'

'Well, I studied French at school.'

'Give us a wee whirl.'

Brodie thought for a moment.

'*Je peux parler français*,' he said. '*Mais je fais les erreurs. Quand même, les gens me comprennent bien.*'

Ainsley looked at him in astonishment.

'That's incredible! The accent! I'd have sworn blind you were a Frenchie.'

'Thank you, sir. *Merci mille fois.*'

'Good God above. How old are you now, Brodie? Thirty? Thirty-two?'

'I'm twenty-four, sir.'

'Christ alive! How long have you been with us? Three years, now?'

'Six,' Brodie repeated. 'I was apprenticed to old Mr Lanhire, back in '88.'

'Oh, yes, right enough. Findlay Lanhire. God rest him. The best tuner ever. Ever. The very best. Ever. He designed the Phoenix, you know.'

The Phoenix was Channon's bestselling upright. Brodie had tuned hundreds over his six years.

'I learned everything from Mr Lanhire.'

Ainsley leaned forward and peered at him.

'Only twenty-four? You've an old head on your shoulders, Brodie.'

'I came here straight from school.'

Ainsley looked at the dossier.

'What school was that?'

'Mrs Maskelyne's Academy of Music.'

'Where's that? London?'

'Here in Edinburgh, sir.'

Ainsley was still computing numbers in his head.

''88, you say?'

'September 1888. That's when I started at Channon's.'

'Well, we've got a Channon challenge for you now . . .' He paused. 'Top us up, Brodie.'

Brodie fetched the decanter and topped up their two glasses and sat down again. Ainsley Channon was staring at him over his steepled fingers. Again, Brodie felt vague unease. He sipped whisky.

'You know we opened that Channon showroom in Paris, last year . . .' Ainsley said.

Brodie admitted that he did.

'Well, it's not going well,' Ainsley confided, lowering his voice as if someone might overhear. 'In fact it's going very badly, between ourselves.' He explained further. Ainsley's son, Calder Channon, had been appointed manager in Paris and although everything was in reasonable shape, seemed well set up, contacts made, stock warehoused, regular advertisements in the Parisian press placed, they were losing money – not worryingly – but at a steady, unignorable rate.

'We need an injection of new energy,' Ainsley said. 'We need someone who understands the piano business. We need someone with bright ideas . . .' He paused theatrically. 'And we need someone who can speak French. Calder seems incapable.'

Brodie decided not to confess how rudimentary his grasp of the French language was and let Ainsley continue.

'Here's the plan, Brodie, my boy.'

Brodie was to go to Paris as soon as possible – in a week, say, once his affairs were in order – and become Calder Channon's number two. Assistant manager of the Paris showroom. There was only one thing to have on his mind, Ainsley said: sales, sales, sales – and more sales.

'Do you know how many major piano manufacturers there are in Europe? Go on, have a guess.'

'Twenty?'

'Two hundred and fifty-five, at the last count! That's who we're competing with. Our pianos are wonderful but nobody's buying them in Paris – well, not enough of them, anyway. They're buying trash like Montcalms, Angelems, Maugeners, Pontenegros. They're even starting to make pianos in Japan! Can you believe it? It's a fiercely contested market. Excellence isn't enough. It's got to change, Brodie. And something tells me you're the man for the job – you know pianos inside out and you're a world-class tuner. And you speak fluent French. Good God above! Calder needs someone like you. Stupid old fool that I am for not realizing this.' He sat back and took a gulp of his whisky, pondering. 'Calder was too confident – overconfident, I now see. He needs someone at his side, help steer the ship, if you know what I mean . . .'

'I understand, sir. But, if the language is a problem, why not employ a Frenchman?'

'Sweet Jesus, no! Are you losing your reason? We've got to have one of our own. Someone you can trust absolutely. Member of the family, as it were.'

'I see.'

'Can you do it, laddie?'

'I can certainly try, sir.'

'Try your damnedest? Try your utmost?'

'Of course.'

Ainsley seemed suddenly cheered and assured him he'd have a significant increase in salary, and his position – and his salary – would be reviewed in six months, depending on results.

Ainsley came round from behind his desk and poured them two more drams, the better to toast the new Parisian enterprise. They clinked glasses, drank.

'We'll meet again, afore you go, Brodie. I've a couple of wee tips that might be useful.' He took Brodie's glass from him and set it on the desk. The meeting was over. As he showed Brodie to the door he squeezed his elbow, hard.

'Calder's a good boy but he could do with a staunch lieutenant.'

'I'll do my best, Mr Channon. Rely on me.'

'That I will. It's a great opportunity for us. Paris is the centre for music, these days. Not London, not Rome, or Berlin. Apart from Vienna, of course. But we could be number one in Europe – see them all off: Steinway, Broadwood, Erard, Bösendorfer, Schiedmayer. You'll see.'

Back in the workshop Brodie smoked another cigarette, thinking hard. He should be pleased, he knew, incredibly pleased – but something was bothering him, something indeterminate, naggingly vague. Was it Paris, the fact that he'd never been there, never been abroad? No, that excited him: to live, to work in Paris, that would be—

Lachlan Hood sauntered in from the shop.

'Still here?'

'Not for long,' Brodie said.

'I knew it. Tough luck, Brodie. Hard cheese, old pal.'

'No. I'm to go to Paris. Help Calder with the shop there.'

Lachlan couldn't conceal his shock, his disappointment.

'Why you? Fuck! Why not me? I've been to America.'

'*Mais est-ce que vous parlez français, monsieur?*'

'What?'

'Exactly.' Brodie spread his hands, mock-ruefully. 'The benefits of a good education, sonny boy. I happen to speak excellent French.'

'Liar. Fucking liar. You speak opera French.'

'All right, I admit it. The key thing is I speak *enough* French. Which is about one hundred per cent more French than you do.' He offered Lachlan a cigarette, and smiled patronizingly.

'If it all goes well, maybe I'll send for you.'

'Bastard.'

2

Brodie hailed a cab that was trotting by Channon's and asked to be taken up to Charles Street by the university where the Bonar Concert Rooms were. He sat back in the cab and drew the curtains a little, enjoying the darkness and the reassuring clip-clop of the nag and the squeak of the springs over the cobbles as the cab took him east through the city. Some woman had been in the cab before him, he realized, smelling her scent – rosewater or lilac – masking the odour of old leather and horse shit. Now he had some time alone he thought further about Ainsley Channon's proposition, aware that he had accepted that proposition without thinking. Should he have asked for some time to reflect? But who would have thought for more than a second? To swap Edinburgh for Paris. To swap being senior piano tuner for assistant manager. To swap four guineas a week for eight. It was hardly a difficult decision.

He paid off the cab and went looking for the stage door. The management that night had asked for an old Channon concert grand and stipulated that it be regulated to the maestro's requirements, whatever they might be. The house manager of the Bonar Concert Rooms – a solemn, bald fellow with an odd smell of mildew about him, Brodie thought – led him through dark passageways backstage towards the concert hall itself.

'Who's the artiste?' Brodie asked, forgetting.

'Georg Brabec.'

'Never heard of him.'

'Aye. He's the talk of Prague and Budapest. So he keeps telling me. A big cheese in Leipzig, and all.'

'God protect us.'

Brodie felt a slight dulling of the spirits. It was the second, third and fourth level of concert pianist that gave the most trouble to a tuner; problems ascending pro rata as the rank diminished. He had tuned a piano for Gianfranco Firmin himself when he came to perform at the Assembly Rooms, Firmin, who was one of the most famous piano virtuosos in Europe, yet a humble, charming, self-deprecating man. Every request preceded by 'If it isn't too much trouble' or 'Might it be possible for' – no arrogance, no assumptions of overweening genius. Brodie had a bad feeling about Georg Brabec.

Brodie climbed the short flight of stairs to the stage and wandered through the crowded seats and music stands already in place for the orchestra towards the Channon, set before the empty amphitheatre. Georg Brabec stood beside it. Long hair to his shoulders, Brodie saw, with a dramatic streak of grey. A downy moustache. School of Liszt, Brodie reckoned, it did not bode well. Brabec was smoking a cigarillo.

Brodie shook hands and introduced himself. Brabec interrupted before he could mention his surname.

'The piano is not tuned,' he said in a somehow dubious, thick Mitteleuropean accent. Brodie couldn't place it.

'And very echo in treble register.'

'I tuned it this morning before we sent the piano over, sir,' Brodie said politely and patiently.

He sat down and played a few chords: C major, F sharp minor, E flat diminished. He had played in octaves. The piano was perfectly tuned.

'And I asking for old piano.'

'This is an old piano, sir. Forty years old.'

Brabec banged some keys with one hand, loudly.

'Listen: here is thin. The hammer is . . .' he searched for the word. 'The hammer is not hitting true. Truly.'

Brodie sighed inwardly. Smiled, outwardly.

'Let me have a look at it, sir.'

He opened his little Gladstone bag and took out his canvas roll of tools.

Brabec pointed the ashy end of his cigarillo at Brodie's chest, aggressively, almost touching his jacket lapels.

'And the keyboard is clean. I didn't not ask for clean piano.'

'Let me deal with that, sir.'

Brodie removed the fall, and pulled the action out. Most concert pianists he knew – 99 per cent of them – had absolutely no idea what happened between their striking a key and the note being produced. The vital factor was to reveal the arcane complexity of the moving parts. Brabec stared at the action for a moment, blinking.

'Let me work on it, sir,' Brodie said. 'I'll inform you when everything is in order.'

The manager reappeared and led Brabec off to his dressing room.

As soon as they disappeared Brodie pushed the action back in and put away his tools. In his Gladstone bag he had a small glass bottle containing a thin solution of honey and water. With a fine badger-hair brush he painted the keys with this solution then wiped them down with a rag. He checked the merest trace of tackiness that was left. Accumulated finger grease was what some pianists wanted when they demanded an old piano – the tiniest hint of something sticking so the palps of the finger would grip ever so slightly. All was well: the Channon perfectly tuned and regulated. Georg Brabec would be even more pleased with himself.

Brodie went in search of the manager and found him in his office with a small glass of port and water on the go.

'Not the most accommodating of fellows, our Signor Brabec,' Brodie said.

'Aye. Total bampot,' the manager said flatly. 'And he now tells me he wants you in attendance for the recital, in case he needs you to retune at the interval.'

'Tell him I'll be here,' Brodie said. 'But in fact you probably won't be able to find me . . .'

'Right enough.' The manager actually smiled and held up his port and water. 'Will you have a wee snifter?'

Brodie – carrying his glass of thinly acidic claret – followed Senga up the stairs to her room. She kept looking back over her shoulder as if she couldn't quite believe he'd actually come to see her. Brodie had left the Bonar Concert Rooms as soon as Brabec had marched on stage and taken his bow and had gone directly to Mrs Louthern's 'house' in its side street off the Royal Mile down towards Holyrood Palace. He had sat in the small parlour for ten minutes with two of the other girls while he had waited for Senga to come free. The girls silently played bezique and paid him no attention although he was the only man waiting in the house.

What he liked about Mrs Louthern's establishment was that there was a rear exit into a close behind the tenement. You didn't leave the way you arrived, through the parlour, and so he would have no idea who Senga's last client was. He was under no illusions – she had a job to do and the busier she was the better for her. Still, it was all the more welcome not to have to encounter some grinning, flush-faced farmer up for the agricultural fair fresh from her bed and, thereby, become pointedly aware of his own place in the queue.

Mrs Louthern topped up his glass of inferior claret and suggested that if he was in a hurry either Ida or Joyce here could happily oblige. No thank you, Brodie said, I'd rather wait for Senga. And Senga duly arrived.

In her bedroom upstairs Senga kissed him on the cheek and said she'd missed him. He hadn't been to Mrs Louthern's in over two months so it may have been true. Brodie put his glass down and began to undress. Senga undid her skirt and hauled off her frilly blouse, standing there in her cotton shift and ankle boots watching him strip off his clothes down to his vest and drawers.

'I'll be wanting the shift off, Senga,' he said.

'It's another two shillings,' she said. 'Even for you.'

He didn't care, he wanted them both to be naked. Senga was from South Uist, a girl who had come to Edinburgh to work as a housemaid in a big house in the New Town. She had become pregnant, had been promptly sacked, and had ended up at Mrs Louthern's establishment earning another, somewhat more profitable, living. She was younger than him, twenty or so, he supposed, and there must be a child cared for somewhere, he supposed further. He hadn't asked: it was Senga who provided all the information about herself.

She was fair, slim and heavy-breasted – which was why she was so popular – though he had heard some clients say they didn't want the 'squinty lassie'. Her right eye was a so-called 'lazy eye' and it obviously put some people off. Brodie, with his own acute eyesight problems, didn't care. She still affected the good manners she had learned at the New Town house – despite the straightforward carnal nature of their encounters – and was always polite and she genuinely seemed to like him. More to the point, she aroused him. Maybe it was the lazy eye, he sometimes wondered.

Both naked now, Senga drew him to the narrow cast-iron bed and they sat beside each other while she gently worked at his penis with both hands, making it hard.

'Why have ye no been to see me, Brodie?'

'I've been busy,' he said, watching her breasts sway.

'Busy doing what?'

'Writing.' He had told her he was a composer.

'Writing a song for me?'

'Maybe.'

Seeing him ready, she rolled onto her back, spreading her legs and Brodie eased himself on top of her, resting his weight on his stiff arms.

'Can I kiss you?' he asked.

'I don't like kissing,' she said. 'You know that.'

'I'll give you a shilling.'

'I don't want another shilling. I don't like kissing.'

'All right. Have it your way.'

He eased the weight off his arms and she reached for him and guided him into her – so easy, he thought. How many times has she done that?

'Take your specs off, Brodie.' She had a lilting Highland accent.

'No.'

'Go on.'

'I want to see you Senga. You're a pretty girl. I like to see the pretty girl I'm fucking.'

She eased her knees back. She was familiar with the routine and the banter.

'You say that to all the girls. A handsome bastard like you with your enormous big graith on ye, like a shinty bat. You want to see us girls as you take your pleasure, don't you, fine sir? Like to see us shidder, don't ye?'

'I certainly do.'

Brodie sent down for a bottle of claret. A ridiculous, overpriced five shillings but he didn't want to leave just yet. As long as you were spending then Mrs Louthern's house never closed. Sometimes he'd walked out of Mrs Louthern's into a refulgent Edinburgh morning, all sharp-angled sun and scouthering breezes, and gone straight to Channon's, stinking of drink, tobacco and fornication – or so he thought – unshaven and greasy-haired and then ducked out at lunchtime to a barbershop for a shave and slap on some pomade before Mrs Grant could complain to Mr Channon about his staff's debaucheries.

He poured Senga a glass and she drank the wine avidly. They had both dressed after their exertions. She was called Agnes McCloud but she didn't like the name Agnes and so had simply reversed it.

'I'm going away, Senga.'

'No! Where's better than Edinburgh?'

'Paris.'

'Ah. Right.' She looked sad for a moment. She couldn't compete with that.

'What'll ye do in Paris?'

'Write a symphony or two, I suppose.'

'And there'll be lots of they French girls for you to dally with.'

'I'll always think of you, Senga.' He poured more wine.

'No ye won't, you'll forget me in a flash.'

'No I won't, I promise. You're very special.' He touched her cheek below her right eye. 'That's why I want to tell you something.'

'What's that, then?'

'You know your funny eye? Your right eye. You can get it fixed.'

This had never been brought up before and it made her seem suddenly discomfited, vulnerable. The strange unspoken decorum of their transaction – her trade with him; money for services rendered – was suddenly present in the room. She had been objectified, somehow, and Brodie felt obscurely ashamed for mentioning the matter, trying to be helpful.

'What's wrong with my eye?'

'It's just "lazy", so they describe it. But they can fix it, nowadays.'

He took out one of his calling cards and wrote the name and address of his optician on the back.

'I'll pay. Just go and see this man – show him this card and he'll know it's from me – and he'll sort you out.'

'Will I have to wear spengtacles like you? Those awfy bottle-bottoms.'

'For a while, and maybe a patch, till your eye gets stronger . . . But life will be better, Senga, believe me.'

'Life will be what life will be, Brodie. Nothing much we can do about it.'

'I'll be back one day. Have some more wine.'

He poured more wine into their glasses. She looked at him – winnel-skewed – harder somehow.

'Aye. Maybe. Maybe not. Well, I wish you luck,' she said, standing and going to the door. 'Thanks for the wine. I'd better be getting on with things.'

3

Brodie paid off the rest of the month's rent he owed to the landlord of his lodging house in Bruntsfield. The landlord, a surly fellow called McBain, was irritated to lose a long-term lodger at such short notice and wanted to penalize him further, Brodie realized. He searched Brodie's room diligently for signs of damage or neglect but could find none.

'It's so sudden because I'm off to work in Paris, you see,' Brodie said, keen to make McBain envy him.

'Rather you than me. It's a sink, Paris. A sewer.'

'So, you've been there, Mr McBain. To Paris.'

'I don't need to step in a sewer to know what a sewer is.'

Brodie lugged his cabin trunk to the end of the road and waited for a cab to come by. Paris was the great opportunity of his life, he realized, but it provided its own set of concerns. One in particular was beginning to stand out – Calder Channon. Brodie knew him a little from the short time he had spent in the George Street show-room before the Paris opening beckoned. A flighty, complicated individual had been his assessment, and very pleased with himself, moreover. Still, Paris was Paris – Calder Channon couldn't ruin an entire city.

He caught the 10.45 train from Waverley station to Hawick and sat in the window seat of a smoking compartment looking at the rolling countryside of the Borders as they headed south out of Edin-burgh. *Vallonné* was the word the French used for this type of landscape, he suddenly remembered. The hills were softly rounded, not jagged or rocky, carpeted with tough blond grass and heather. Nothing forbidding or awe-inspiring – just nature at her most pleas-ing and easy on the eye. And between the hills at their foot were swift shallow rivers, woods and copses, small fields of corn and bar-ley, sheep and cattle grazing in pastureland. Clouds slid to reveal the sun and for a moment the valleys were exposed in a perfect fanfare of light. Brodie felt his heart give a thud of applause. It was beautiful countryside but he was heading homeward.

At Peebles station he threw his trunk into the back of a dog cart and told its driver to take him to Liethen Manor, a village some three miles away from town off the road to Biggar. The driver, a boy in his teens, gladly accepted Brodie's offer of a cigarette, broke it in half and lodged the half he'd smoke later behind his ear.

'I think I ken you,' the driver said after twenty minutes, the rest of Brodie's cigarette now smoked down to his fingernails.

'Well, I've lived in Liethen Manor most of my life.'

'You're a Moncur. That's it – you're Malcolm Moncur's son.'

'I am, for my sins.'

'Aw, no! No, no – he's a great man.'

As they turned off the Biggar road, crossed the three-arched bridge over the Tweed river, Brodie felt that sinking of spirits that returning home always seemed to engender. They headed along a single-track metalled road between drystone walls running between farmland and woodland, meandering up the Liethen Valley towards the small village that was Liethen Manor. The village sat snug on the north bank of Liethen Water, a small, fast-flowing tributary of the Tweed. Brodie looked about him at the round hills that framed the valley and duly recalled his many ascents of them – Cadhmore, Ring Knowe, the Whaum. This was his home – there was no denying it. And he thought of a new definition of the word. 'Home' – the place you have to leave.

They arrived at the outskirts of Liethen Manor. An abandoned tollbooth and then a few low, slate-roofed, small-windowed workers' cottages. On this side of the village there was a shop, a public house, a livery yard and blacksmith, an agricultural supplies depot, a dame school and a post office. In between these establishments was an untidy assortment of cottages and larger houses set in their vegetable gardens. The village was made important by its unusually large church and manse, both built only thirty years before, further down at the end of the main street, such as it was, on the western side. These were imposing buildings of red sandstone, somehow out of scale for this modest hamlet in its gentle valley. The big church and its grand four-storey adjoining house seemed more suited for a prosperous suburb in a big city.

The dog cart clip-clopped through the village and led them past the church, St Mungo's, still looking new – pure Gothic Revival with flying buttresses, finials wherever a finial could be placed and a tall bell tower with no steeple. Its rowan- and yew-dotted cemetery was crowded with ancient graves, former parishioners, the late, good folk of the Liethen Valley. Then they turned into the gravelled carriage drive of the manse, set in a wide dark garden filled with ornamental conifers – monkey puzzles, larches and cedars – and beech trees. Beeches grew well in the Liethen Valley soil.

Brodie's mood slumped further as the dog cart pulled up outside the porticoed front door of the manse and he glanced back at St Mungo's, built on the site of the old Liethen Kirk that had been completely demolished to make way for the new church. The church and the manse had been constructed to his father's design and financed through a complicated Tontine scheme. The Reverend Malcolm Moncur had put Liethen Manor on the ecclesiastical map and these dominant, inappropriate buildings were brash evidence of his power and sway.

Brodie paid the lad his sixpence and gave him another cigarette.

'Is Moncur preaching this Sunday?' the boy asked.

'I'm sure he is,' Brodie said and, thus reminded, told the boy to come back and collect him at 6 a.m. prompt on Sunday. As the dog cart turned round on the gravelled sweep, the front door opened and two of Brodie's six sisters rushed out to welcome him. He turned to greet his family with the broadest smile he could manage.

Brodie sat on the bed in his old bedroom on the third floor under the eaves of the manse. He had gathered up the few belongings he had left there – a pair of heavy boots, a tweed overcoat, some photographs, some books – and had already packed them away in his trunk. Two nights at home, he thought to himself, surely it can't be that bad . . .

There was a knock on the door and his brother Callum appeared. They looked at each other, blankly.

'Are you a stupid, miscreant bastard or are you a terrible, poor lunatic fit for the loony bin in Penicuik?' Callum said, apparently not joking.

'Well, I'm here,' Brodie said. 'So, you're probably right. I am insane. But, then again, so are you.'

They shook hands warmly and Callum punched him on the shoulder and Brodie punched him back. It was what they did when they saw each other.

'I'll have one of your fancy American cigarettes, thank you very much,' Callum said. Brodie dug out his tin of Margarita from his trunk and they lit up.

Callum was two years younger than Brodie, shorter and more muscled, with a soft blond moustache. He worked in Peebles as a clerk to a Writer to the Signet. He lay back on Brodie's bed and crossed his ankles on the bed-end, smoking histrionically, blowing smoke rings at the ceiling.

'Your telegram informed us you were going to Paris,' Callum said.

'I am. I'm here to pack up my things and say goodbye to my stupid brother – and the rest of the Moncurs, of course.'

'Oh, yes, you'll be fucking French girls, lucky dog.'

'I've got a very serious job to do. Where's Malky?'

'Malky has gone to Glasgow. He'll be back tonight.'

'Glasgow . . .' Brodie thought. 'Why does he keep going to Glasgow? Has he a woman there?'

'Because nobody knows him in Glasgow – he's safe. And there's no particular woman – he just goes a-whoring with his cronies, I'll wager. Incognito.'

Callum talked on, salaciously denigrating their father. Only between the two of them was he referred to as 'Malky'. Brodie walked to the small dormer window and looked down over the garden spread below him. Three of his sisters sat on wicker chairs darning and sewing. Doreen, Ernestine and Aileen. The three oldest Moncur children, all in their thirties, and all unmarried. He and

Callum referred to them as the 'Eens'. He looked at the Eens as they worked and chatted. It was like a moment from a Russian novel, he thought: Tolstoy or Turgenev. He had six sisters, four of them older than he was, yet none was married. Why, he wondered? He turned away. Come to that, he wasn't married either, nor was Callum – and the third Moncur son, Alfie, was only nineteen. Perhaps they'd all be married in the fullness of time . . . The key factor was to put as much distance between yourself and Malcolm Moncur, he knew. That was why he so wanted to go to Paris, he suddenly realized – Edinburgh wasn't far enough away. Of all the Moncur children he was the only one who had fashioned and made good his escape. Perhaps he'd be an inspiration to the others.

Brodie came down to dinner promptly at six. He had shaved, and had oiled and combed his hair flat. He wore his charcoal-grey suit, a white soft-collared shirt and his Channon & Co. bow tie with its jocular symbols of musical notes, like polka dots. A bow tie made him feel older, somehow. He remarked to himself that he felt unusually nervous for someone who was meant to be welcomed to the bosom of his family.

He stepped into the big drawing room. Callum was there and five of the sisters.

'Where's Electra?' he said. 'And Alfie?'

'They'll be here,' Doreen said sharply. 'We'll all be here to greet the Prodigal Son.'

'What's prodigal about him?' Callum said. 'Prodigal Idiot, more like.'

Aileen came over and took Brodie's arm. Perhaps he liked Aileen best, he thought.

'He's prodigal because he went away and now he's home,' she said.

'And how long will you be gracing us with your company?' Doreen asked. She was the oldest and occupied a position somewhere between housekeeper and surrogate wife. Certainly Malcolm Moncur talked to his eldest daughter as rudely as he had talked to his wife when she was alive, Brodie remembered.

'Two nights,' Brodie said. 'I leave for Paris at dawn on Sunday.'

'You have to stay for the sermon,' Ernestine said, shooting worried glances at Doreen. 'Papa will want you to stay.'

'Alas, alack – I don't control the steamer timetables.'

Brodie could hear voices and laughter – men's voices and laughter – coming down the corridor from his father's sitting room. His 'receiving room', as he sometimes termed it.

'Who's with Papa?' he asked Doreen.

'The mayor of Lyne and some friends who've come up from England for some sport.'

'And what sport would that be?' Callum said. 'Not fish or fowl, I bet you.'

'Callum!'

They listened to the laughter growing louder from the sitting room and heard Malcolm Moncur's booming voice shouting: '. . . and he's not fit to wash my shoes!'

Brodie felt briefly nauseous, turned away and walked over to his sisters.

'Any chance of a preprandial drink? A sherry or Madeira?'

'Papa has locked the pantry and has the key.'

All alcohol in the manse – and there was a copious supply – was locked in a large walk-in butler's pantry off the drawing room. Only Malcolm Moncur had the key; only he dispensed liquor in his house.

'There'll be something to drink in the receiving room,' Callum said. 'If they haven't finished it already.'

'Sneak in and grab a bottle,' Brodie said to Isabella, the second youngest. She was a quiet girl who wore spectacles like him. 'He's never cross with you. Tell him we're all dying of thirst out here.'

'I don't dare, Brodie. He'll belt me.'

'You're seventeen years old, Isabella!'

'He still belts me when he's roused.'

'Sweet Jesus. Are we allowed to smoke?'

He took out his pewter cigarette case with his pre-rolled cigarettes and passed them around. All his older sisters – the Eens – smoked, he was glad to see. Small acts of rebellion in this household were important. He lit their cigarettes, then Edith, his fourth older sister, decided she would like one as well and, when he and Callum lit up, they were all smoking, all six of them (only Isabella declining), as they made small talk, creating quite a fug, so that Electra, when she came in, followed by Alfie, opened the French windows onto the back lawn to provide a bit of air, she said. They greeted Brodie shyly, as if he were a stranger.

'I hear you're leaving us,' Electra said. She was petite and the prettiest of all the Moncur girls.

'Aye. Off to Paris.'

'You'll never come back,' she said.

'Of course I will,' Brodie said. 'It's just a job. I'm not emigrating.'

'I'd emigrate,' she said, lowering her eyes.

'And where would you emigrate to?' came a loud voice from the doorway. 'Darkest Africa? You'd be chicken soup in a second, my darling. Best to bide with your old papa. Eh? Eh?'

Electra slid behind Brodie as Malcolm Moncur stepped into the room and scanned his large family as all the women severally stubbed out their cigarettes.

Brodie glanced at Callum. They knew the signs, the descending stages, of Malcolm Moncur's intoxication – four-fifths drunk, Brodie calculated: it could be a difficult evening.

The Reverend Malcolm Moncur was a short, burly man – going to fat – with a big strong-featured head, almost out of proportion to the rest of his stocky body. He was sixty years old but his light reddish-brown hair was just greying at the temples and he had a dense well-shaped moustache, like something cut from coir matting, a darker gingery red. Callum thought he had some barber colour-tint it.

Malky Moncur, Brodie thought, in your cups as usual, waiting for his father's eyes to settle on him, as they duly did.

'Talking of Africa – look! The darkie's come home. Well, well, well.'

'Hello, Papa,' Brodie said, his voice staying calm.

'How's my wee mulatto?' he said coming up to Brodie. Brodie was a head taller than his father and the pointed height difference always seemed to agitate Malky, Brodie had noticed, as if it were some kind of personal genetic affront. Brodie was very dark – his hair ink-black, his eyes brown, his skin sallow – alone in this family of fair-haired, light-eyed, pale-faced Moncurs. His father had commented on this discrepancy all his life. Brodie rather hoped that he was the result of an affair his mother had enjoyed with some olive-skinned Latin visitor to Scotland. It was a fantasy, he knew.

'You're as black as ever, I see. Black as the day you were born.'

'Thank you, Papa,' he said, levelly. 'You seem well. Glasgow must have been invigorating.'

The two of them looked at each other. Brodie kept his features impassive, his eyes dead. You may control the others but you do not control me, Malky Moncur, he thought: I am my own man.

'Agonizing Christ!' Malky Moncur turned on his oldest daughter. 'Are we going to eat or starve, Doreen? I'm dying of hunger!'

And at this the Reverend Malcolm Moncur marched into the dining room, the Moncur sisters and brothers silently following, looking sharply at each other, unspoken messages darting between them.

The dinner passed off relatively well, Brodie thought. Doreen carved a big side of mutton – boiled potatoes and carrots as supplements – served by the Moncur housekeeper and cook, Mrs Daw. A short grace was said (by Alfie) before the family picked up their knives and forks and ate with hungry enthusiasm. Jugs of water were served as drinks and Brodie, for once, was glad of his huge family – there were ten of them round the table – therefore many conversations took place outwith Malky's orbit. Doreen and Ernestine flanked him and on the whole managed to confine him to his end of the table. But from time to time Malky would rise to his feet and leave the room for a couple of minutes; or he would wander down the table and affectionately squeeze the shoulders of one or other of his daughters and whisper in her ear; or, if he needed it, he would personally go in search of the salt cellar or water jug and carry it back to his seat. He seemed to like this perambulating way of dining: his mood improved – he seemed mellow, almost paternalistic, Brodie thought, as the meal progressed.

But it all changed with pudding – blancmange with raspberry jam – an offering that prompted Malky to expostulate that, 'I may be a confirmed bloody fool but I will not eat that shite!' and he strode out of the room leaving the rest of the family to their dessert. The mood lightened, instantly.

After dinner the women all slipped away to their bedrooms but Brodie, Callum and Alfie decided they might confront Malky in his den if there was the prospect of something to drink. When they wandered into the drawing room the door to the butler's pantry was open and Malky was inside.

'Anything to drink in this pub?' Callum called out and Malky appeared, jacket off, braces hanging round his rump.

'Is that the donsie loun clerk of a third-rate Peebles notary speaking?' Malky said aggressively, swaying slightly, brandy bottle in hand. Five-fifths drunk, now, Brodie thought.

'We're away to bed if there's no drink,' Callum continued, bravely.

Malky grudgingly provided them with small tumblers of brandy and they sat down on armchairs facing him as he sprawled on the Chesterfield.

'Here's how, Papa,' Brodie said, raising his glass.

'*Slàinte*,' Malky replied. 'And I'll have none of your Anglo-Edinburgh, pretentious claptrap in this house.'

'I'm allowed to wish you "good health", I assume.'

'Weeping God!' he said theatrically. 'Weeping God that I should have three such sons.'

Brodie passed round his cigarettes and Malky reached forward to take one.

'And how is Ainsley Channon?' he asked Brodie. 'The fornicating bottle-washer.'

'He's very well,' Brodie said. 'He asked me to convey his very best wishes to you.'

'He can shove his best wishes up his narrow arse, I say.'

Callum now had the brandy bottle and was refilling everyone's glass.

'Ainsley Channon is a good friend to this family,' Callum

said, keen to provoke more profanities. 'Look what he's doing for Brodie.'

'He's an Edinburgh counter-jumper,' Malky said, 'who had the good fortune to inherit a family business when his cousin died young. He sits on his bum in George Street and counts the money coming in.'

Brodie covertly signalled Callum to drop the topic but Malky spotted the gesture and turned on him.

'Just because he's sending you to Paris doesn't change a thing,' Malky said, coldly. 'You black bastard.'

Brodie drained his brandy.

'Goodnight, Father dear.'

He left, not closing the door and not listening to the imprecations following him and climbed the stairs to his bedroom on the top floor. He didn't feel angry – he felt strange. Why did his father – a complicated man, admittedly – resent him so? He went to the small oak bureau set opposite his bed and opened a drawer and took out the cameo of his mother that he kept there. Moira Moncur, 1842–1884.

She had died in childbirth when he was fourteen years old so at least he had strong fixed memories of her: a wan, loving but harassed figure burdened by her many children and constant pregnancies. From 1861 to her death twenty-three years later, Brodie had recently calculated, she had given birth to fourteen children, five of them stillborn or dead within days of their parturition. He wondered what his father thought about this woman, his wife. Was she just some sort of child-factory, a breed-cow? First came four daughters in five years, then the initial two stillbirths, then his, Brodie's, arrival in 1870. She was twenty-eight years old. Two other boys followed (Callum and Alfie, with a dead brother between them) before the female cycle resumed again with the appearance of Isabella and Electra, also on either side of a dead infant. The stillborn child that hastened her death was another son, unnamed. Nine children living and she was dead at forty-two years old.

He looked intently at her face in the oval cameo but the dated formalities of the pose, the exposure's long hold denied any sense of the real person emerging from the portrait. It was a mask, this image, really, not any depiction of a living, breathing human being. What was she like? What if she were alive now? She would have been fifty-two. How would things have been different? It seemed unimaginable: how could she have lived alongside the monstrous, self-obsessed spectacle that was Malky Moncur today? And he thought, not for the first time, that her premature death may have unleashed some devilry in her husband. Though that was too charitable, he corrected himself – Malky Moncur was a dark singularity, unique. He had always known which direction he was heading in: his destination was fixed.

Brodie put the cameo away safely in his trunk, wondering vaguely about his five dead siblings. He wasn't entirely sure of their sex, he had to admit – they had been boys and girls, some named – a Hector, he recalled; a Marjorie – some just anonymous foetuses, as far as he was concerned. He felt guilt over his ignorance. There must be a parish record somewhere, he supposed. Maybe he should do their tiny memories a modicum of justice by finding out whatever bare facts there were about these lost children. But the prospect suddenly seemed overwhelming, futile, and he slumped on his bed, weary, exhausted by the multiple tensions of coming home. Think of Paris, he told himself – that is the gift that the gods of chance have given you. Paris was waiting.

4

The next morning, Saturday, Brodie – freshly shaved, nails cleaned with his penknife's point, smoking his first Margarita of the day – walked the mile or so up the Liethen Valley to Dalcastle Hall to meet Lady Dalcastle. He had had a note delivered to her on his arrival and she had suggested by reply that a rendezvous at eleven o'clock in the morning would be ideal. She was 'looking forward with anticipation' to seeing him again.

Dalcastle Hall was a strange hybrid of a manor house. Brodie walked through ornamental gates past a neo-Gothic lodge with polygonal chimneys, ridge tiles, gingerbread eave-trim and wheel-windows and then down a potholed drive through an avenue of ancient beech trees towards the hall. The first glimpse through the trees revealed what seemed like an old fortified tower, thick-walled, castellated, with small high asymmetrical windows. It was in bad repair. Moss and small ferns grew from the pointing of the stones and some of the windows were boarded up. But as he approached, the Georgian wing came into view – white stucco, three storeys, symmetrically placed sash windows and, adjoining that, was the extensive stable block and beyond the stables the high grey walls of two gardens, one for a lawn, flowerbeds and glasshouses, the other for fruit and vegetables. Lady Dalcastle lived here alone – alone with her staff, that is. Her husband, Hugo Dalcastle, had died in his thirties ('Of drink and debauchery,' Malky said) and their only child, Murdoch, a captain in the Scots Greys, had perished ten years later of yellow fever in Ashanti in West Africa in 1870 aged twenty-four. In her grief Lady Dalcastle had found solace and company with the minister's wife, Moira Moncur, and the two of them had become fast if unlikely friends.

Brodie was born in the year Murdoch Dalcastle died and Lady Dalcastle had taken a special interest in him, as if somehow the soul of her dead son had transmuted into the infant Brodie. She singled him out for treats and presents and he was regularly sent to Dalcastle Hall to 'play'. When it was discovered that he had perfect pitch and he began to sing in the St Mungo's Church choir it was Lady Dalcastle who had paid for further lessons and, as the pure integrity of his voice was recognized, it was she who had come up with the fee for him to be sent to Mrs Maskelyne's Academy of Music in Edinburgh when he was nine years old. There was talk of a foreign conservatoire; prospects of a brilliant operatic career beckoned. But when, at the age of thirteen, Brodie's voice broke it became clear that the incandescent treble had mutated into a mediocre baritone. Brodie switched to the piano but although perfectly competent – he tried hard – he had no special gift. He could have taught the piano but the world was full of moderately talented piano teachers, he swiftly realized. His perfect pitch – his ear – was still there, however. It was an asset that could be cultivated. Lady Dalcastle spoke to her cousin, Ainsley Channon, and Brodie was taken on, after his leaving certificate examinations – he was a bright, intelligent boy – as an apprentice piano tuner at Channon & Co. It was a steady job that quickly became a vocation. He was eighteen, it was 1888.

All these memories clustered around him as he approached the front door of the hall, as familiar as the manse in its way, and with happier associations – he owed Lady Dalcastle almost everything, he acknowledged, including whatever good manners and gentility he possessed. There was a family joke that Brodie was destined to inherit the Dalcastle estate but every time the idea was entertained Malky would mock him, vigorously. 'She's in debt up to her oxters,' he would sneer. Hugo Dalcastle had drunk and gambled away the family fortune. The estate was mortgaged ten times over. 'Ask your dunderhead notary-public brother. He knows all about it. You'll not get a brass farthing, laddie!'

This information made Brodie relieved rather than cast down. He didn't want to live in the Liethen Valley under an insuperable burden of debt a mile away from his family home and Malky Moncur. What a circle of hell that would be! He liked Lady Dalcastle and would be forever grateful to her that she had provided the means for his escape. The only aspect of her life that troubled him was that she was a constant attendee of his father's Sunday sermons. She never missed a single one; she thought Malcolm Moncur was inspired and inspiring. Malky in his turn became atypically demure whenever he spoke to her. Brodie found this very amusing and, at the same time, somewhat repulsive.

He knocked on the front door and was admitted by Broderick, Lady Dalcastle's butler, and led upstairs to the small drawing room. Broderick was an elderly man, he'd been in Dalcastle service for over fifty years and had a slight stammer. He paused on the landing.

'Lady D-D-D-Dalcastle is not well, Mr Brodie.'

'I'm sorry to hear it.'

'She mustn't get tired.'

'I understand. I won't tire her. Ten minutes – just to pay my respects.'

'Ten minutes maximum, Mr Brodie. She mustn't be fffffffatigued.'

'Consider it done.'

Broderick led him into the drawing room and left him there. Brodie wandered about, suddenly craving a cigarette. The room was panelled in a very light wood – ash? Walnut? – and there were small dark landscapes hanging on the panelling from a picture rail. Two windows looked out over the walled garden. To Brodie's eye it appeared somewhat neglected. A tree had fallen. The herbaceous borders were full of weeds, willowherb and nettles. There was a whitewashed glasshouse and a couple of tethered sheep grazed on the lawn – it was well cropped.

Brodie heard a polite cough behind him and turned to see that Lady Dalcastle had crept silently into the room. She offered her hand to be kissed. Since Murdoch's death she had decided to wear only the gayest colours. Today she had on a cerise velvet jacket over a wide plum-coloured skirt. Her grey hair was tied back with a yellow silk scarf. She wore her hair long like a girl's.

She was pleased to see him, she said, though it had been – what? – two years now, he was a scoundrel for neglecting her.

'But I'll forgive you, come and sit beside me.'

They sat down together on a small sofa and Broderick brought in a tray of tea. He set the fine china cups and saucers out with such a rattle that Lady Dalcastle dismissed him and poured from the silver teapot herself, chatting away, talking about replacing Broderick but she hadn't the heart, it would be the death of him, so she had to do more and more herself, *c'est la vie*.

She was incredibly thin, Brodie saw, thinner than ever, as if her wrists might snap from the weight of the full teapot she lifted. But she was bright and eager, eyes shining, a little lip rouge applied, her scent – of lime-tree flowers, Brodie thought – subtle yet pungent.

The tea was tepid; the shortbread biscuits crumbled under his fingertips like damp sugar.

'Do please smoke if you wish, Brodie. I know you like a cigarette.'

'No thank you, Lady Dalcastle. I'm trying to give up – it's an expensive habit and I've foolishly developed a taste for American tobacco. There's only one shop in—'

'Have you seen your father's advertisement?'

'No. What advertisement?'

'In the *Scotsman*, no less.' She reached for a folded newspaper on the side table and handed it to him. There was a black-framed square advertisement in the bottom right-hand corner. 'The Reverend Malcolm Moncur will preach on Sunday at St Mungo's Church, Liethen Manor. Transportation available at Peebles railway station. The text is from the Book of Baruch (Apocrypha). Admission free.'

'Callum told me about these advertisements,' Brodie said. 'Sometimes they get five hundred in the church, I hear. Folk coming from Edinburgh, Selkirk, Biggar—'

'There are dozens of carriages. Dozens. The streets of the village filled. Charabancs at Peebles station. He's quite the draw. Oh yes.'

'Well, he always wanted to attract—'

'I wouldn't miss it,' Lady Dalcastle said firmly, in case there was any doubt about her zeal. 'It can be quite fascinating – his interpretations of these very obscure bits of the Bible. Very intuitive what he digs out.'

'Alas, I'm going to miss it, I'm afraid. I have to leave very early tomorrow morning.'

She wagged a skinny finger at him.

'You're not an atheist, are you, Brodie?'

'To be honest . . . I do have doubts, Lady Dalcastle. I find my father's faith . . . a paradox.' Brodie was happy to let her know he might be saved. But he was the son of Malky Moncur, therefore his atheism was devout, implacable.

'Do you know the poetry of Swinburne, Algernon Swinburne?'

'No, I don't. I know his name but—'

'Very beautiful verse. He is an atheist, I believe.'

'Right. Aye. No. It's just that—'

'Paris, Brodie, Paris! The city of light. *La ville lumineuse.* How I envy you!'

'It's a rare opportunity. I'm excited to be going, I admit.'

'But is it an opportunity? Truly?'

'I believe so, yes,' he said. 'I have to help Calder Channon with—'

'Or is it a trap?'

Brodie felt the cigarette craving come upon him again. He drank some of his cold tea.

'How could it be a trap, Lady Dalcastle?'

'Ah, Paris, Paris. She can be a difficult mistress. Hugo – my late husband – spent a lot of time in Paris. Yes, he was often there, towards the end.'

'Really?'

'It was his undoing.'

'I see.'

She wagged her finger at him again.

'Don't let it be *your* undoing, Brodie. Promise me.'

'I won't. I promise.'

'Have another cup of tea. I'm so enjoying our conversation.'

She showed him to the front door herself, half an hour later, making Brodie swear he would write to her from Paris and she would do the same by return. She squeezed both his hands and looked up at him, saying, 'Bless you, dear boy, bless you. Your darling mother would have been so proud. So tall and handsome.'

Then she dug in the small reticule hanging from her belt and gave him a gold sovereign, pressing it into his palm and reminding him, in a whisper, as if it was their secret: 'I await all the news from Paris.'

Brodie wandered up the pitted drive away from Dalcastle Hall feeling exhausted, a puzzle of conflicted emotions. The sun was breaking through a sky that had seemed full of lumbering, cumbersome clouds and the June day now appeared set fair. Back at the manse he went into the kitchen and drank three glasses of water.

Mrs Daw was peeling potatoes, and a scullery maid was stirring a steaming cauldron on the range.

'I hear ye're off tae Paris, Brodie,' Mrs Daw said.

'That's the plan, Mrs D. I've been given a job there.'

'So we'll ne'er see you back here again, like enough.'

'Of course I'll be back. Why does everyone assume I'll be gone forever?'

'Oh no. You willnae be back,' she said confidently. 'No, no. You'll get a taste for that life. I've seen it afore.'

'What life?'

'Foreign life. It's nothing like our life here. Simple, strong, God-fearing.'

'So what's it like there, Mrs Daw? In Paris?'

She pointed her knife at him.

'It's dangerous. It'll make your head reel!'

'Maybe that's good. Maybe it's good to have your head reel from time to time.'

'Not for the likes of you, Brodie Moncur. I know you. If your mother was alive she'd be agreeing with me.'

Brodie assured her he had an important and responsible job to do in a piano shop. There was nothing head-reeling about that. Mrs Daw shook her head and smiled sadly.

'Mark my words, my bonny boy. Mark my words.'

Brodie wandered into the hall, bemused, and found Callum there.

'I think we need to go fishing,' Callum said.

Brodie and Callum sat on the high bank of the Liethen Water in the shade of a big old willow tree looking down on one of the largest pools that the small river possessed. This was where they would come to swim or plunge when they were children on the rare hot days of summer. Callum had filched two slices of veal and ham pie from Mrs Daw's kitchen and they ate this hungrily, washed down with handfuls of cold Liethen Water. They had fished upstream, away from the village – wet fly – and had been successful. There were a dozen half-pound brown trout in Callum's wicker fishing basket, covered in wet dock leaves.

They had started off fishing on the edge of the meadows around Liethen Manor then followed the river as it flowed through a kind of Scottish wilderness, the banks dense with hazel and alder where casting was tricky. The grass was thigh-high, full of teazles, willowherb and thistles, unmown, uncropped for years. The Liethen Water was shallow and brown, like unmilked tea, fast-flowing over its pebbled, stony bed, but, where the river swerved, the current cut deep, narrow pools and Brodie knew that if you carefully floated your fly into them then the Liethen trout often took the bait.

Brodie had been fishing this small river since he could remember – Callum also. They knew every bend and pool, every potential crossing point, every placid, midge-hovered eddy. It had a calming effect on him, walking up the Liethen Water, casting his line; memories skittered through his mind, came and went like butterflies or sun dapples beneath breeze-shifted branches; he saw himself as a little boy with his first rod, remembered the charge and thrill of his first catch. Maybe this small river in its wilderness should be 'home' to him, he thought, not the manse or the village. He should carefully store the memories of this day away and recall it whenever he felt lonely or homesick. Sick for home . . .

He threw the last of his dry pie crust into the gloomy tangle of the big pool and offered Callum a Margarita. Callum lay back on the turf and looked up at the dusty sunrays angling through whippy branches of the willow, drawing on his cigarette. Upstream a heron yanked itself skywards. Brodie turned to watch it beat slowly up the valley. He felt the moment cohere, solidify. A breeze fingered his hair. Remember this, remember this. Callum was saying something.

'What'll become of us, Brodie? You and me?'

He turned back. 'I'll go off to Paris and meet a beautiful French countess who'll set me up in her chateau. You'll become a Writer to the Signet and marry an ugly rich Peebles lassie. Buy a big house in the country and have ten bairns.'

'I'd rather die.'

'Well, you know there are other options.'

'Run away to the circus,' Callum said with a dry laugh.

'That's the general idea. Head out of town. Go anywhere.'

Callum turned on his side, resting his weight on an elbow.

'All very well for you. You've made the break.'

'We're lucky,' Brodie said. 'The girls are stuck. And Malky seems to have Alfie dancing to his tune.'

'Are you coming to church tomorrow?'

'Am I hell. I'm being picked up at six in the morning.'

'Malky will be furious.'

'Malky can boil his head.'

Brodie stood up and dusted the grass seeds off his trousers.

'Let's head back to the village and have a pint at the Howden.'

'Maybe I'll come to Paris with you,' Callum said, clambering to his feet. 'But I'll want a mysterious beautiful countess of my own.'

'Paris is full of them. You'll be fighting them off.'

They walked off downstream, the Liethen Water on their right side, the tilted fields on their left, their rods easy in their hands, talking of possible futures for themselves, then, when the bell tower of St Mungo's came into view, they cut across some pastureland towards the village. The lukewarm June sun shone on their backs when it appeared between the scudding clouds and Brodie recalled his injunction to himself – remember this, remember this almost perfect day: he and Callum at the end of an afternoon's fishing, striding home together through the wind-combed meadows of the south of Scotland. Store it away, he told himself, it would be a salve whenever his soul needed some consolation.

The Howden Inn was on the Peebles side of Liethen Manor, at the opposite end of the village from the church and the manse. It was a low slate-roofed cottage, whitewashed, the stone dressing of its windows painted black – a drinking den for the drovers, shepherds and farm labourers of the Liethen Valley. It was the only public house between Biggar and Peebles, was its particular boast, and it was often busy.

Callum pushed open the low door and Brodie followed him into the bar-room. Low-ceilinged and smoke-foxed, it had a curious smell: part beer, part cold fireplace ash, part pipe tobacco. Two old men sat in a window booth playing dominoes and drinking whisky. A young girl was washing down the flagstones with a mop. No fire burned in the fireplace as it was June and the sun was shining.

Brodie and Callum found a table in a corner, placed their broken rods behind their chairs and ordered two pints of Ethelstane pale ale from the young innkeeper. His name was Campbell Wishart – the brothers knew him. He was a burly fellow with a broad wild beard, already greying, even though he was still in his twenties. He had grown a beard to disguise a badly repaired harelip that gave him a lisp and that made him sound almost effeminate sometimes.

'Brodie Moncur,' he said. 'By God, I havnae seen you in a year or two. More. Where've you been?'

'I'm a busy man in Edinburgh, these days, Campbell.'

'Aye, I heard. Tuning pianos, I'm told, isn't it?' He pronounced it 'fianoths'.

'Pulling pints, tuning pianos – we all have to make a living.'

'Aye, right enough.'

'And I'll have a wee half of whisky,' Callum said, 'seeing my brother's doing so well. He's away to Paris, you know.'

'Aye and I'm away tae Rio de Janeiro,' Campbell said, unimpressed.

They sat down and drank their beer, Callum downing his whisky in one go, and idly watched the young girl swabbing the floor. Brodie felt a contentment spread through him and he wanted to prolong the pleasures of the day.

'Here's an idea,' Brodie said. 'We've got a dozen trout in that basket. Give six to Campbell and ask him to fry up the others for us.'

'We're wanted at the manse for dinner,' Callum said. 'We'd better be on our way.'

'What if we've been detained?'

'What will Malky say?'

'Callum, Malky isn't our lord and master.'

Brodie went to the bar with the wicker creel, showed the fish to Campbell and made his suggestion. Food was to be had at the Howden, pies and bridies, the occasional roast fowl, a stew of mince and carrots. Campbell's wife did the cooking.

'I think we can do that,' Campbell said. 'I'd want a shilling or two, mind.'

'Of course. Have you potatoes?'

'No, but we've bread – and vinegar.'

Brodie and Callum ate their fried trout with slices of bread and butter, washed down with another pint of Ethelstane. Callum ordered another whisky chaser. Brodie looked at him knowingly.

'Christ, man, it's the weekend,' Callum protested. 'And I've got bloody church the morrow.'

Brodie scribbled a note on a scrap of paper and summoned the young girl who had mopped the floor.

'What's your name?' he said.

'Constance.'

'Well, Constance, I'm going to give you a penny and ask you to deliver this note to Mrs Daw at the manse. Can you do that for me?'

'Aye. I'm no stupid.'

'Make sure she gets it and I'll give you your penny when you come back.'

'I want my penny now. Else you'll be gone when I get back.'

'Fair enough.' Brodie gave her a penny. 'I trust you, Constance. You've an honest face. Give it to Mrs Daw, now.'

Constance skipped out on her errand.

'I've excused us from dinner,' Brodie said. 'Unavoidably detained. Drink up and have another whisky.'

5

Brodie wrote another note for his father early the next morning.

Dear Papa –

I greatly enjoyed my stay. It was grand to see you again in such fine form. My apologies for missing the service and your sermon but I have to catch the evening packet to Antwerp. I will write once safely installed in Paris.

Ever your affect. son,
Brodie

He folded the paper, scribbled his father's name on the outside flap and propped it on the hall table next to his father's homburg.

He opened the front door quietly – no one else was about, only the two housemaids were stirring in the kitchen – and hoicked his cabin trunk out onto the gravel of the driveway. It was cool and the rising sun was intermittently visible through the hurrying clouds.

There was no sign of the boy with the dog cart from Peebles. Brodie swore and looked at his watch. Ten past six. Where the hell was he?

'He was here half an hour ago but I sent him on his way.'

Brodie turned slowly.

His father, in a long black greatcoat, was walking across the back lawn between the conifers. He was smoking a small cigar and Brodie remembered it was Malky's habit to rise early on a Sunday and collect his thoughts before his sermon. He decided to remain calm.

'Why did you send the boy away?' he asked. 'You had no right.'

'Because I want you in church.'

'I have to catch a boat to Antwerp this evening.'

'You can catch another bloody boat any day of the week.'

Malky stepped up to him. Brodie closed his eyes, smelling the acid reek of his father's cigar – unpleasant, sour, fouling the sweet early-morning air.

'Look,' Brodie began. 'I don't want to be—'

'No, you look. Just be in church – then you can go to Paris and be damned, you blackamoor.'

'It's just a fucking job. I'm not descending to hell.'

'Keep your filthy profanities to yourself. I want my family in church. All ten of my children.'

'Nine, actually, at the last count.'

'Nine, ten, eleven, twelve. I don't give a fig. I want you all there.'

'You can whistle for it, Malky.'

They stared at each other, the mutual hate in their eyes entirely candid.

'You've forgotten what day it is, haven't you, Brodie?'

'It's a Sunday. Malky Moncur does his preaching act.'

'It's the day your mother died, you Hottentot! Show some respect. Pray for her immortal soul in your parish church. Your family church. Lay some flowers on her grave before you go on your merry way to your own dissolution. Shame on you!'

This information had taken Brodie aback. He had forgotten – and he felt sudden unfamiliar tears salty in his eyes.

'I feel no shame,' he said quietly. 'I had nothing to do with her death, but you did. You're the one who should be praying for forgiveness. I'll see you in church – but that's the last favour you'll ever get from me.'

Malky allowed a brief look of triumph to animate his face then turned and strode off back into the garden. Brodie lugged his trunk into the hall and stood it by the door, feeling confused and upset. Malky knew how to rile him, how to work on his feelings, and he was annoyed that he'd let him see his emotion. And a pin-scratch of conscience nagged at him. He had forgotten about his mother . . . And he had no choice, anyway, now his transportation had been dismissed. He would go to church with his brothers and sisters and hear the great man in his pulpit.

Callum was surprised to find Brodie at the breakfast table, drinking tea – he had no appetite.

'I thought you'd be long gone,' Callum said, helping himself to scrambled eggs from the chafing dish on the sideboard.

'I should have been but Malky had other plans. He wants his entire family in attendance.'

'Jesus. It must be fire and brimstone today, then.'

The sisters began to arrive for breakfast, dressed up primly for Sunday and the kirk. The mood was subdued as the family gathered. Brodie had made his farewells the night before, returning late from the Howden, and everyone was surprised – and pleased – to see he was still present. Brodie told them he'd decided spontaneously to stay for the sermon – he hadn't heard his father preach for two years, after all. It all sounded rather hollow but everyone happily went along with the pretence.

As they filed out of the dining room Doreen tugged at Brodie's elbow and drew him aside.

'What did you say to him?'

'Nothing out of the ordinary. Nothing I haven't said before. It was what he said to me that was shocking.'

'I've never seen him in such a mood. You must have said something to him, Brodie. You know how you get under his skin. You should apologize, calm him down.'

'I won't apologize. And I do my utmost not to get under his skin. Why do you think I stayed away from dinner last night? He just . . . reacts to me. I don't need to do anything.' The idea struck him. 'I believe he can read my mind – he knows what I'm thinking about him. I don't need to say a thing. That's what angers him.'

From ten o'clock onwards the carriages, traps and dog carts started arriving – and the charabancs from Peebles station bringing the railway passengers from Hawick, Melrose and Galashiels. Slowly the throng grew on the churchyard lawn in front of the main entrance, people chatting quietly to each other, greeting acquaintances. It was more like the crowd at a ball or a prize fight, Brodie thought: there was nothing devout about the mood; it was more one of expectation, little tremors of excitement apparent, occasional laughter.

Ten minutes before the start of the service the rest of the family wandered over from the manse. Seven of them. Alfie and Electra were required in church as ushers. As a group, the brothers and sisters took their reserved places in the second row from the front to the right of the aisle. The Moncur boys and girls, in their dark clothes and neat hair, a credit to their father and the memory of their mother.

Brodie let the others slide in and took his seat at the end of the pew and looked around. It wasn't beautiful, St Mungo's – strong and austerely confident in its faith, Brodie would have said. The walls were cream plaster with one row of polychromatic tiles at head height being the only gesture at decoration, the pointed nave windows were clear glass. The organist was playing a fugue by Buxtehude and the choir was in place on either side of the altar. St Mungo's was Church of Scotland, but it was Malcolm Moncur's version. On the altar was a half-life-sized, wooden, painted Christ on the Cross – commissioned by Malky – and as detailed as a Grunewald crucifixion. Real nails were hammered through the wooden palms and feet, the body was a flat greyish white, the better to contrast with the lurid blood, raised globules of scarlet paint dripped from the metal crown of thorns onto the chest, and the white flash of a rib could be glimpsed through the wide spear-wound in Christ's side. The simple wooden pulpit was set unusually high on the nave wall to the left of the chancel. It was hung with a backdrop of crimson velvet that hid the steep stairs leading to it from a small anteroom behind the wall. It looked more like a small balcony than a pulpit. It contained a brass lectern with a vast black Bible, six inches thick, open at the text for the day. There was no sign of the Reverend Moncur.

Brodie turned and looked as the church quickly filled. It was a big crowd – the whole gallery was occupied and there were a few dozen people without seats gathered at the back of the nave. It was a 500-day, he reckoned, full house, standing room only. The organist came to the end of the fugue and on an invisible cue the choir began to sing 'The Lord is my Shepherd' and the congregation grew quiet. There was a choirmaster, Brodie now saw, half-hidden by a pillar, a young bald man who conducted with histrionic vigour.

Brodie's own musical career had begun here, singing in the St Mungo's choir under the direction of old Kenneth McGilchrist. He closed his eyes and listened to the music, trying to let the growing agitation in him subside. The choir was good but there was an alto singing a semitone flat.

The hymn ended and an apprehensive, rustling, half-silence ensued. There were a few nervous coughs and some audible whispering. Regulars turned the pages of their Bibles looking for the verses that Malky had chosen as his text for his sermon. It was, Brodie saw, very obscure, even for Malky. From the Apocrypha, the Book of Baruch, chapter six, verses ten to twelve. He could see people vainly flicking through their Bibles, searching for it. Not every Bible contained the Apocrypha, he realized.

Brodie remembered what was due to happen next. After a minute or so of this anticipation, Malcolm Moncur would appear, as though miraculously, in his pulpit, sliding through the crimson curtains, arms spread in benediction. And, sure enough, he was suddenly there, in a black surplice with a white linen stock with two long bands at his throat. There was a distinct gasp from the congregation before Malky boomed out in his deep bass voice, 'Let us pray!'

The prayer was a form of warming up – extemporized, treating of events in the world at large and garnished with the odd 'In the name of the Lord' or 'In the memory of suffering Christ', and so forth. Brodie could sense Malky's inspiration growing as he considered the mishaps and calamities of contemporary history. He was like a boxer sparring in the gymnasium before the championship bout or a thoroughbred doing a few furlongs on the downs before the big race. Today he covered the opening of the Manchester Ship Canal, the occupation of Bulawayo, Matabeleland, the French anarchist whose bomb had gone off outside the Royal Observatory at Greenwich, expressed his regret at the absence of William Gladstone from the political arena, combined with mockery of Lord Rosebery's performance as prime minister, then, scarcely concealing his glee, contemplated the shocking death toll – over a thousand – of last year's hurricane in Mississippi. Implicit in all this, as he admonished governments and statesmen, deplored conflicts far and wide, gave advice to kings to be prudent, presidents to think twice, emperors to restrain their imperial ambitions, was the sub-theme that, somehow, St Mungo's Church, Liethen Manor, Peeblesshire, Scotland, was the centre of the turning world – it was from here that all wisdom was dispensed and the deity urged to take note and intervene. So, when Malky's long prayer ended, the congregation was poised and ready. He said 'Amen', blessed them all, made the sign of the cross several times and looked them in their collective eye.

'Our sacred text this morning will not be found in every Bible.' He turned the page. It was to be found in his huge Bible, however. 'From the Apocrypha. The Book of Baruch, chapter six, verses ten to twelve.'

He paused. Then began to read – slowly, stentoriously.

'Now, whereof Nerias knew that his son Sedacius was caught in the snares of harlots and indeed had lusted after his brother's wife, Ruth, and his brother's daughter, Esther, and showed no remorse, yet Nerias suffered his son to live in his own house, yea, and fed him and his servants also. For Nerias, the Levite, was a righteous man. And the people saw the wisdom of the righteous man and Sedacius was spurned by the Levites, they spake not of him. There was a void, thereof. He was forgotten as a cloud melted by the force of the noonday sun, as smoke dispersed by a breeze. He was shadowless, a nothing, less than a mote of dust.'

Malky paused again, then launched into his exegesis and why this forgotten text from a forgotten book of the Bible had relevance to the lives of the good folk gathered here in St Mungo's Church. Brodie sat back, listening. He had heard dozens of these sermons over the years and had come to regard them as Malky's own brand of vaudeville or end-of-the pier variety turn. It was a way for Malky to unleash the showman in him. He no more believed what he said than any mountebank or street shiller. For him it was an exercise in power and acclaim. He would tell them a few home truths and send them back to their dreary lives shriven and enlightened – and often titillated and even shocked. The texts Malky chose were often about sins: adultery, sexual envy and concubinage, or of wars, murder, mutilation and fratricide. There had been a memorable sermon on the Sin of Onan. And at the mention of semen being spilled on the ground a dozen people had walked out, offended by the subject matter. But like any barker at a fairground Malky knew that licentiousness was a powerful draw, especially when it had the protective gloss of religiosity.

Brodie raised a hand to conceal a yawn. Malky was rambling on about Nerias and the poisonous ingrate that was his son Sedacius. He looked at the front row of pews, reserved for the great and the good. Lady Dalcastle was there in lemon yellow and Lincoln green, rapt. And so were the mayors of Peebles, Innerliethen and Melrose. And somebody from the Ministries Council of the Church of Scotland, he had been told. There were Edinburgh lawyers and their wives, aldermen and magistrates and a few adventurous socialites who had heard of this firebrand preacher in the Borders and were keen on a bit of diversion on a boring Sunday.

He turned his head to study his brothers and sisters sitting along the row from him, all with their heads bowed, contemplating their clasped hands. Malky's sway in his church was absolute. To pass the time, Brodie began to think of Paris – where would he stay? Perhaps a small hotel, first, then find some lodgings or a boarding house near the showrooms. He'd need to take some French lessons also. But then at the edge of his hearing he registered a tonal change in Malky's delivery.

Normally Malky spoke in a resonating bass monotone – he had a fine, powerful voice, effortlessly captivating, avoiding inflection, whimsy, irony – allowing the sheer weight of his seriousness to ram the words home. But now there was an air of the histrionic. Most unusual. Brodie looked up to the pulpit.

'But this is it, I tell you, my friends, dear friends. This is the key distinction. "Nerias was a righteous man" the Book of Baruch tells us. Therefore, therefore what was his son, Sedacius? Sedacius was a *self-righteous* man. It doesn't seem too severe an appellation, does it? Self-righteousness, what can be so wrong with that? But I tell you, my friends, it is the threshold to the vilest sins. The primrose path to vainglory, to arrogance, to intolerance – this is the sin of SELF-LOVE!' He almost shouted, now. 'This is the sin of Narcissus, so we might term it. To be enraptured by your own self, your own wonderful self to the exclusion of the rest of the world. Me! Me! Me! This is the sin of the self-righteous man. The sin of Sedacius who had fallen into the snares of harlots!'

And, on cue, Malky turned his eyes on Brodie. He might as well have pointed his finger at me, Brodie thought, feeling a kind of lucid panic. Even Callum glanced at him.

Malky was now in full rhetorical flow.

'The righteous man believes in the rule of law, in the love of God, in the fundamental honesty and good nature of his fellow human beings. But the self-righteous man believes only in himself. Everything in the world exists only for him and his greater glory. But the sin of self-righteousness is a cancer, it devours all that is good and noble. The self-righteous man is a hollow man. The self-righteous man is a husk. Empty. Worthless.'

Brodie had to lower his head – people were aware of this staring contest going on between father and son and were beginning to turn their heads to see who was the object of Malky's wrath and disdain. Brodie let the tide of vituperation wash over him. Now he knew why Malky so desperately wanted him to be in church, present at his sermon. It was his act of revenge; his public castigation of his errant son. The only member of his family who dared to confront him, to disobey him and go his own way.

'And what will be the fate of this self-righteous man, this scarcely human being?' Malky continued, his vehemence unabated. 'He will be damned, damned by his corrupt self-love. As the holy text declares: "He was shadowless, a nothing, less than a mote of dust."' Brodie was aware of pages being turned as people searched vainly for the text and he suddenly realized that these last words were Malky's own interpolations to the Book of Baruch. He looked up at the pulpit again but Malky had gone. His exits from the pulpit were as sudden as his entries: like a hint of magic, he slipped back through the crimson hangings. There was a steep wooden stair that led down to the anteroom and he was never to be seen after his sermons. The silence in the congregation was eloquent, Brodie thought, as if the men and women gathered there in St Mungo's sensed the extra-textual personal element to the wrath they had witnessed. There were glances right and left. Were they blissfully righteous or horribly self-righteous people, they wondered nervously? Brodie closed his eyes and breathed deeply as the choir broke into a rousing oratorio – the prologue to Sullivan's *The Light of the World* – and the whispering among the congregation grew louder.

Callum accepted one of Brodie's Margaritas and Brodie lit their cigarettes. They watched the congregation file out of the church through a gauntlet of choirboys, each one holding long, deep, crimson velvet collection bags. This was the principal object of the exercise. Money. Alfie was entrusted with the collection of the collection, Brodie knew. After all donations had been made, the collection bags were brought to the vestry, locked in a cupboard and the key was handed to Malky. Callum had once asked Alfie how much money they gathered in after a big crowd had attended a sermon and Alfie had told him it was usually over £20, cash – occasionally close to £50. Malky gave around forty sermons a year. Brodie did the calculation: forty times twenty equals 800. So around £1,000 a year, give or take. Brodie thought: I earn approximately £400 a year as an expert piano tuner. He remembered something Malky had once said to him, in all seriousness: 'Religion is a splendid way of getting on in the world.'

'What do you think he does with all that money?' he asked Callum.

'He must be paying off someone with some of it, that's for sure. He can't be pocketing it all himself.'

'It's a kind of extortion. Like a reverse simony,' Brodie said. 'Suppose he gives this person a hundred a year to keep quiet, to let the Malky pantomime continue . . . What does he do with all the rest?'

'I wonder,' Callum said. 'But he only really started making real money a few years ago, that's when he became famous and the big crowds started coming, not just the locals. That's why he advertises, now.'

Brodie watched people leaving, chatting, smiling, exhilarated, climbing into their waiting carriages like a first-night crowd. Now they were off to their Sunday lunches.

'It's very clever the way he disappears like that,' Brodie said. 'He doesn't stay around to lap up the applause. Keeps his mystery.'

'What was all that shite about the "self-righteous" man?'

Brodie felt a thin silt of resentment gather in him. He dropped his cigarette on a flagstone and stepped on it.

'That was his particular message to me. Now, how do I get out of here?'

Three days later, Brodie stood on the quayside at Leith docks. There was a light drizzle falling through the night air and the gas lamps on the dockside wore shining haloes of luminescence. His trunk was aboard the steamer to Antwerp and his cabin secured for the crossing but he wanted to spend these last moments with his feet on the ground, as it were, before taking to sea. From Antwerp he would catch a train to Paris, to the Gare du Nord, and thence to Channon & Cie on the avenue de l'Alma, where the new life of the 'self-righteous man' would begin.

He lit a cigarette, thinking back to that last Sunday at Liethen Manor. He had left – securing a ride to Peebles in a cart from the Howden Inn – without seeing his father again. The same note he had placed on the hall table would have to suffice as a farewell. It was a bitter parting, he supposed, but all the bitterness and resentment flowed from the paternal side of the equation. Anyway, he said to himself, who gave a bean – a hoot, a brass farthing – for Malky Moncur? He, Brodie Moncur, had his life to lead and he owed nothing to that scheming, manipulative, self-fabulating monster that was his father.

He told himself to calm down. He had used his three days wisely. He had had his conference with Ainsley Channon where various fiscal objectives had been made plain to him and his authority in certain matters confirmed. He had managed to see Senga for another carnal farewell. He had been to his optician, Mr Fairchild, to buy and assess his new Franklin spectacles. He was wearing them now – two thick lenses of different strengths set above each other in the same oval metal frame: the higher one for long distance; the lower for closer matters. They seemed to work well and he was growing used to the thin line where the lenses met at the lower edge of his vision – he barely noticed it, now. He took out his fob watch and looked through the lower lens to confirm the time. Ten minutes to departure – he felt his chest swell with excited anticipation – and the markings of the watch face were admirably sharp and clear.

He had a lot to be thankful for, he told himself: a solid profession that he could travel with worldwide, should the inclination take him – or at least anywhere there were pianos – good health, apart from his eyesight, and a good education, thanks to the generosity of Lady Dalcastle. So what did he owe to Malky Moncur? A lifetime of grievances, unpleasantness and potent irritations. And the death of his mother, possibly . . . No, he was well rid of him, St Mungo's and Liethen Manor. Too bad about his siblings – though he would miss Callum – they had to make their own way in life, make their own choices and live with them as best they could. He was off to Paris and the future.

The packet's steam whistle tooted breathily, signalling the time for final boarding. Brodie flicked his cigarette into the wharf's oily black water and strode up the gangway. He stayed on deck to watch the sailors cast off the thick ropes round the mooring bollards as the steamship's engines thrummed loudly into life and it began to wheel away from the quayside. Somewhat self-consciously – the self-righteous man that he was – he bade a formal, silent farewell to his native land. For the first time he had a powerful conviction he would never see Scotland again.

PART II

Paris – Geneva – Nice

1896–1898

I

'Non, non, c'est beaucoup mieux, Monsieur Moncur. Vous avancez vraiment bien. Vraiment. Impeccable.'

Brodie's French teacher, Monsieur Hippolyte Lorette, gave his usual stiff little bow and showed him to the door of his small apartment high under the eaves of a building on the rue Saint-Dominique. To the east, such was the height of the block, there was a good view of the new railway station at Les Invalides. Consequently many of their educational conversations were about transport and railway journeys as Brodie essayed some of the harder tenses and complicated locutions of this elegant language he was attempting to master. Monsieur Lorette was a bachelor, a retired teacher from the Lycée Henri IV. He was thin and stooped and had a grey pointed beard and no moustache, an omission Brodie found odd and made him think that Monsieur Lorette was a member of some strange religious order. His manners were immaculate and rigidly formal – Brodie had no impression at all of Hippolyte Lorette, the man, behind this impregnable facade. He spoke his perfect French slowly and clearly as if talking to a child. Brodie had been studying French with him now for many months – they were both familiars and absolute strangers.

But Brodie was pleased with his progress. They met three times a week at eight o'clock in the morning for an hour's conversation, except in the months of July and August when Monsieur Lorette returned to his family in Rheims, and Brodie felt, more than eighteen months on from his arrival in Paris, that he could justifiably say he spoke a fluent though error-littered French. Masculine and feminine nouns and agreements still defeated him – was it '*le*' or '*la*'? '*Un*' or '*une*'? – but Monsieur Lorette assured him, sadly, that *'C'est normal chez les Anglais.'* He felt conversationally at ease in French, nonetheless; comprehension virtually 100 per cent; with expression hovering around 90, he would have calculated.

Brodie stepped out onto the rue Saint-Dominique and hailed a victoria, asking to be taken over the river to the Channon showroom on the avenue de l'Alma, just off the Champs-Elysées. It was a cold February day with a cloud-packed sky and he was glad of his old tweed greatcoat and the tawny woollen scarf Doreen had knitted for him. Brodie unreflectingly glanced at the Tour Eiffel – he wondered how long you had to live in Paris to ignore it, to take it for granted, like Notre-Dame or the Arc de Triomphe – and noted its summit was obscured by unmoving clouds. It seemed a shame that the whole thing was going to be dismantled in a few years' time, but maybe it was too much of a monstrosity for any city to cope with. The highest man-made structure in the world! *Incroyable! Magnifique!* He had been up to the top, twice.

He fished in his pocket for Callum's letter, glad of some distraction before he faced the complications of the morning ahead. He was apprehensive. Ainsley Channon was in town and today, Monday, was designated as being reserved for 'a review of the business'. A lunch had been booked at a nearby restaurant. There had been clear successes since Brodie's arrival in Paris. Successes that were all down to him. And there were ongoing problems, seemingly unsolvable, all down to Calder Channon. It had every sign of being an uncomfortable encounter.

He took Callum's letter out of its envelope.

Dear Brodie, brother mine, O wise one,

Married life is bliss, isn't that what they say? You half-predicted it – but not a Peebles lass, a Galashiels one. Why weren't you at the wedding – scoundrel, ingrate? Sheila longs to meet you as I talk about you all the time. We've just moved to a big new house called Edenbrae on Venlaw Hill (thank you father-in-law) and a little Callum Moncur is on his or her way, I'm delighted to report. Can you believe I will furnish Malky with his first grandchild? The baby's imminence seems to have unsettled him – your mortal clock is ticking loudly, Malky Moncur. By the way, he still talks foully, evilly of you – turncoat, traitor, bottle-washing émigré. I know you've asked me this before but I still have no answer. Malky seems obsessed with you for whatever perverse reasons and he—

Brodie folded the letter away – all this talk of Malky wasn't helping his mood. Callum had married a young woman called Sheila Anstruther-Kerr, the only daughter of a wool merchant in Galashiels. They had been married – by Malky – in St Mungo's in October 1894, a few months after Brodie's arrival in Paris. He had thought about returning home for the wedding but it was too soon. He wanted a long stretch of time to intervene before he revisited Liethen Manor. And now there was a child on the way – perhaps he'd go home for the christening.

He called for the driver to stop the victoria, paid him and walked the rest of the way to the showroom, gathering his thoughts.

Channon & Cie was an imposing shop with two wide windows giving on to the street on either side of an ornate, pillared, arched *porte d'entrée*. Above the glass of the cartwheel transom was an angled flagpole flying the Saltire. Another of his ideas – flaunt the Scottishness, reference the 'auld alliance'. Brodie paused across the street so he could prepare himself and imagined how things might look to Ainsley. This was only his second visit to Paris during Brodie's sojourn but he would have been pleased with what he saw, Brodie surmised. There was Dmitri in the left-hand window playing away on a baby grand (new model). In the other window on a canted dais was a semi-dismantled Channon grand, all the intricate workings of the action on display: the fall removed, the action extended, the hammers and strings perfectly visible to the curious onlooker. Like a corpse on an anatomical table, was the comparison Brodie had made. It was a prize specimen and stuck here and there were printed cardboard notices in French and English explaining some of the finer points of the Channon – the wood used, the number of miles of wire that made the strings, the astonishing seventeen tons of tension of said strings, the cost of ivory and ebony for the keys, and so forth. Both educational and fascinating, Brodie had claimed, when he'd suggested the idea. It lured passers-by all day, many of whom then wandered into the shop to look at the pianos on show. Calder Channon had strongly opposed the idea – a waste of space, he claimed – as he opposed every idea Brodie advanced. Brodie would then write and complain to Ainsley;

Ainsley would write back and overrule Calder and so the relationship between manager and assistant manager of the Paris showroom steadily diminished; currently running, so Brodie estimated, at 'cool', on a good day, to 'icy' on a bad.

Brodie urged himself across the street and into the shop, striding through the large showroom space behind the picture windows and on into the workshop area at the rear. This was his demesne – Calder rarely ventured in – and where the tuning side of Channon's Paris business was flourishing. Brodie had interviewed, tested and hired two accomplished tuners (*accordeurs*) – René Dujardin and Romain Lebeau – and was training up two apprentices to supplement them, such was the increasing demand. They were constantly busy, the days and rosters filled, and Brodie found he had to help them out himself from time to time as the workload increased. Yesterday he had left the office and gone out of town to Neuilly and Fontainebleau to tune – word was spreading. All monies from the tuning side of the business were of course paid into central accounting at Channon & Cie, a department run by a curious little man called Thibault Dieulafoy, closely supervised by Calder. Brodie knew the tuners and the workshop were making a significant contribution to the firm's turnover but he had absolutely no idea of the amount. Calder was extremely secretive when it came to financial matters.

Romain had already left and René was about to leave when Brodie arrived. None of his tuners and apprentices spoke English so Monsieur Lorette's lessons had been vital. They greeted each other and shook hands. Brodie enquired about René's wife (eight months pregnant), was reassured that she was in excellent health and so went into his little office. Through the glass panes he could see Murray Dodd (also shipped over from Edinburgh) showing the two new apprentices how to fix the pedal rockers on a Channon Phoenix. Murray ran the small workshop at the back of the avenue de l'Alma showroom. More serious restoration required the Channons being crated up and shipped back to Edinburgh to the factory. Brodie's latest suggestion was that they acquire and set up an interim warehouse and larger repair shop somewhere on the outskirts of Paris where the rates were lower and substantial buildings were to be easily had. Calder had vetoed the idea.

After ten minutes, having verified that all was well with his world, Brodie decided it was time to face Calder Channon. No point in prevaricating. He slipped up the back stairway to Calder's office on the first floor and knocked on the door.

Calder Channon was about ten years older than Brodie and twice his size. For a youngish man not yet in middle age he was surprisingly corpulent but his height – he was almost as tall as Brodie – disguised the real extent of his increasing obesity. He was dark and had grown a dense soup-strainer moustache that almost covered his lower lip and had the effect of making him look permanently doleful. It was as if his face could muster no other expression, so dominant was the moustache in its middle. He was married to a young, timid English woman called Matilda – whom Brodie liked – and they had a small son, Ainsley junior, who had just turned two.

Calder ushered Brodie into his office.

'There's no need to knock so hard,' Calder said.

'I didn't knock hard.'

'I'm surprised your knuckles aren't bleeding.'

'I just rapped on your door, Calder. No more, no less.'

'What's that saying? "A loud knock, false friend".'

'I'm not familiar with it. Sounds very unlikely.'

'Think about it,' Calder almost sneered.

'Or, "Loud knock – deaf neighbour". That makes more sense.'

Calder looked at him.

'Take a seat. My father will be here presently.'

Calder's office on the first floor had three large windows that looked out onto the avenue de l'Alma. It should have been light and airy but it was dimmed by black velvet curtains hung half-drawn at the windows and there was a darkly patterned Persian carpet on the stained parquet floor. The room was dominated by an enormous wide desk – more like a dining table than a desk – and there was a complicated compressed-air tube system to one side of it for delivering messages throughout the shop and the offices behind.

Lithographs of Edinburgh scenes – the Royal Mile, Arthur's Seat, St Andrew's Square – decorated the walls. The tone was rich, solid, sumptuous. Channon & Cie was doing well, the decor seemed to whisper.

Brodie offered Calder a cigarette but he declined, lighting a small pipe instead, and the two of them sat and smoked in silence – Calder studying some papers on his desk – while they waited for Ainsley to arrive.

'You know what this meeting's all about, don't you?' Calder asked eventually.

'A progress report, I assume.'

'That's the sunny optimistic view. More like: do we close down the Paris showroom?'

'Surely not. I thought we were doing well.'

'We're just about breaking even. Just about.'

'We've sold eighty-seven pianos in the last six months. I can't keep up with the tuning. I don't see how we—'

'Of course you don't see how,' Calder said, irritated, pluming a thin stream of pipe smoke at an engraving of George IV Bridge. 'How can you see the greater scheme of things? Only I can see the whole panorama.'

'Perhaps if you let me talk to Monsieur Dieulafoy I could see the whole panorama as well.'

'That's not your responsibility. Only the manager confers with Monsieur Dieulafoy.'

'Which is my point. We're meant to be working as a team.'

'This is going nowhere, Brodie.'

'Fine, fine. Let the matter stay in its limbo.'

The conversation ended as Ainsley Channon was shown in. Ainsley dressed up for his Paris visits, as if he were a young blade out on the town. He wore bright silk waistcoats and patent shoes, his whiskers were trimmed, his hair oiled. He greeted Brodie with a warm two-fisted handshake and a brisk pat on the shoulder.

'Take me on a tour,' he said to Brodie and Calder. 'We'll talk business over lunch.'

*

They lunched at the Laurent on the Champs-Elysées, a five-minute walk from the shop. It wasn't busy and they were given a table at the window with a fine view of the wide boulevard. Brodie flapped out his napkin and looked around, feeling a familiar sense of well-being flood through him – despite the fact that business was going to be discussed. The Laurent was an excellent restaurant – he knew they would eat well, drink well and be served well. The napery was crisp and dazzling white, the silverware winked and glinted, reflecting the bulbs of the electric chandelier above their heads, elegant ladies in the latest fashions were seated right and left. This was Paris, the culinary centre of the world. It was just a shame he wasn't more hungry.

But Calder clearly was. He ate two bread rolls before his consommé with poached eggs arrived, followed by calves' brains with brown sauce and a purée of potatoes. Ainsley ordered a plate of radishes and a fillet of pike. Brodie picked at a cucumber salad and an oyster vol-au-vent. Calder called for a bottle of Château Gruaud-Larose but Brodie said a glass of Apollinaris would be sufficient for him – he wanted to keep a clear head.

They paused after their main course to consult the menu again. Calder requested another bottle of Gruaud-Larose and a plate of lentils to keep him going while he decided on dessert. Brodie picked some pith from his bread roll and chewed it slowly.

Ainsley looked at the two of them and smiled.

'Well, lads, there's good news and there's bad news. I'll take another drop of that wine, Calder.'

Brodie sipped his water. Calder lit his small-bowled pipe. For some reason the smallness of the bowl irritated Brodie in the same way as Calder's unnecessarily large moustache did. What was the point? The pipe's bowl was the size of a thimble and could contain only a finger-pinch of shag. Ainsley accepted a proffered cigarette.

'The good news,' Ainsley said. 'Turnover up sixty per cent. Bad news. Profits of less than one hundred pounds. What's going on?'

Calder pointed the stem of his pipe at Brodie.

'Ask him, Father. Four tuners, three pianists on shifts, Monday to Saturday. Do you know how much that costs?'

'Do you know how much money the tuning brings in, Monday to Saturday?' Brodie responded, calmly. 'When you can't sell a piano you can always tune a piano.'

'When you can't sell a piano doesn't mean you must play a piano. Those three pianists you hired are—'

'Boys, boys,' Ainsley interrupted. 'We know the problem. Let's see if we can come up with a solution.'

They ordered dessert – *tarte du jour* for Calder, ices for Ainsley and Brodie – and talked about possibilities. Brodie raised his idea about warehousing in Paris, not Edinburgh. A proper repair workshop would save shipping costs and increase revenue. If they had more stock in or near Paris it could be highly advantageous, he argued.

Calder ordered a supplementary *omelette au rhum* as they pondered the pros and cons. Calder was vehemently against – why introduce expensive new systems when the old ones worked efficiently? Ainsley, Brodie could sense, was warming to his Paris warehouse idea. Brodie kept quiet as father and son debated. He noticed that Calder had a gaudy jewelled ring on the little finger of his left hand. That must be new – he hadn't seen it before, and the unwelcome thought crept into his mind – as Calder shovelled omelette into his mouth, leaving eggy deposits on his moustache – that Ainsley's son might just be defrauding him . . .

As they left the Laurent, after coffee and brandy, nothing resolved, Calder having abandoned his pipe for a cigar, Brodie chose his moment (Calder was walking behind) and asked if he might come and see Ainsley privately at his hotel.

'I'm at the Hôtel du Rhin, place Vendôme,' Ainsley said. 'Why do you want to see me alone?'

'I've an idea, sir. It may make every difference. But I'm sure Calder won't agree.'

'Come by tomorrow at nine,' Ainsley said. 'And I'll not mention it to Calder.'

Calder took his father off to look for a barber's shop and Brodie wandered back to the showroom mulling over his embezzlement supposition. If true it would explain the firm's baffling, poor performance. But how to prove it? And what and how was Calder embezzling?

When he arrived at the shop, Dmitri, the young piano player, was packing up for the day, sliding his sheet music into his thin case. His name was Dmitri Kuvakin and he was a Russian student at the Paris Conservatoire. Brodie had placed an advertisement at the conservatoire offering ten francs an hour for piano demonstrations in the showroom windows and had received over two dozen applications. He chose Dmitri and two other French students and worked out a simple rota system so there was always a piano being played during the shop's opening hours. Once again the idea had been popular and successful. Over the weeks he and Dmitri had struck up a good friendship. He was a couple of years younger than Brodie and seemed to have a genuine talent – at least one that could provide him with a career as a concert pianist. He was a slim wide-eyed young man who had a permanent air of being startled, somehow. An enthusiast who knew Paris well, he took Brodie out on the town, visiting restaurants and theatres and, when the appetite took them, to various *maisons de tolérance*.

'What're you doing on Saturday night?' Dmitri asked. He spoke good French and German but little English. He and Brodie spoke French to each other. Brodie said he had no plans.

Dmitri lowered his voice. 'I've found this new place – not in Clichy – nice girls, cheap.'

'I don't think "nice" and "cheap" go together somehow.'

'Ah, but they're not French. They're Spanish – that's the difference. Come and see.'

They made a date to meet up.

'Where is this place?' Brodie asked. 'Montmartre?'

'Close by. You'll be surprised. It's a real discovery.'

Brodie shaved in his room at the Pension Bensinger. There was a flushing lavatory with a plumbed-in sink at the end of the corridor but he preferred the privacy of the chamber pot and the jug and ewer. He considered, as he always did while shaving, leaving his upper lip untouched and growing a moustache. But then he thought it was more 'modern' to be clean-shaven these days, more in tune with the rapidly approaching twentieth century. And, besides, most of the people he admired were clean-shaven – or so he thought – but, annoyingly, no clean-shaven idols came biddingly to mind. Thomas Hardy – no. Randolph Churchill – no. Walt Whitman – no. David Livingstone – no . . : Perhaps he should recast the prejudice: people he *didn't* admire tended to sport facial hair. Calder Channon for one. The tsar of Russia. Kaiser Wilhelm with his absurd W-shaped moustache . . . Brodie cleaned his razor and put it away in its leather case – there would be plenty of time to grow a moustache if he wanted to, one day.

The Pension Bensinger – situated on rue d'Uzès, near La Bourse – was very reasonable, 120 francs a month with half board and, when he'd chosen it, he imagined staying only a few weeks until he found rooms of his own. Yet here he still was well over a year later, one of Madame Bensinger's *habitués*. It was ideal for him, and, whenever he decided to dine in, he found the food was copious and tasty. His fellow lodgers were discreet and perfectly friendly and he was saving money.

He combed his hair, put on a clean shirt and his navy-blue suit and, forgoing breakfast, he decided to walk to the Hôtel du Rhin on the place Vendôme – it would take him only twenty minutes.

He discovered Ainsley Channon taking breakfast in the dining room, eating a plate of soused herring accompanied by a glass of hock. His waistcoat this morning was caramel-coloured with little royal-blue embroidered squares superimposed. He had had his moustache waxed also. It was as if, once free of Edinburgh and temporarily installed in Paris, another Ainsley Channon was cautiously allowed to emerge and thrive before being chased back into his lair for the return to Edinburgh.

Brodie ordered a coffee with hot milk and waited while Ainsley ate a soufflé and then various small cakes from a stand in the centre of the table.

'I don't know how you stay so damned skinny, Brodie,' Ainsley said, reaching for a final *chocolatine*. 'There's something about Paris and food. I seem to have a terrible hunger all day.'

Ainsley suggested they walk off their breakfasts so they sauntered across the place Vendôme to the rue Saint-Honoré and turned left towards the Palais-Royal. The business was back on the agenda.

'We've got to come up with something, a plan, a scheme,' Ainsley said. 'I can't understand why we're not making money hand over fist. We're in the business of selling pianos and, God's blood, we *are* selling pianos. Lots of them. But . . .' He glanced at Brodie. 'What about this fellow Dieulafoy who does the accounts?'

'I've met him,' Brodie said carefully. 'But I'm never shown any figures.'

'Why not?'

'Calder likes to keep things, you know, close to his chest.'

Ainsley grunted, then frowned.

'So what's your big idea then?' he said.

Brodie counted to three and launched in.

'It's simple. We need a famous pianist to play a Channon at his concerts and recitals. We will then publish this fact and he will endorse the Channon. But – it has to be someone of the very top rank. The very top.'

'Like who?'

'Like Pabst or Arensky or Sauter.' He paused, thinking of other names. 'Or de Pachmann or Paderewski.'

'Good God! I see what you mean by the very top. But how in hellfire do we get someone like that to play our piano?'

'We pay them.'

Ainsley stopped. Theatrically, he leaned against a lamp post, hand to brow. A man in shock.

'Why do all so-called "good" ideas ending up costing more and more money?' he asked, pleadingly. 'We're trying to make money, Brodie. Not spend it.'

'There's more,' Brodie said. 'We not only pay them to choose a Channon, we make them a Channon to their precise specification. I can supervise all that. And we ship that piano – at our expense – to the concerts wherever they happen to be. France, Germany, Austria, England.'

'Oh, yes, of course. We'll pay for his hotels as well.' Ainsley shook his head and started walking again.

'How much do you suggest we pay this maestro?' he said.

'Fifty pounds a concert.'

'Sweet suffering Jesus!'

'It makes sense, Mr Channon,' Brodie's tone was insistent. 'That's how we move up to Steinway, Bösendorfer level. And if one great virtuoso is playing Channon, why, then others will follow. It'll make our name.'

'Have you mentioned this "bright idea" to Calder?'

'No. He'll reject it. He's rejected all my ideas, as you know. The French tuners, the display piano, the pianists in the windows, the need for a Paris warehouse. It's almost like a reflex.'

'He's very cautious, Calder. It's in his nature. Too cautious. That's why I knew I needed you here, Brodie. Someone with vim.'

'I tell you, Mr Channon, it'll work. Imagine. Just imagine if Liszt had played a Channon . . . What renown. The éclat.'

'The what?'

'It's a French word. No, if we have one of these giants playing a Channon then the Channon name will spread without us doing anything. We just have to find the right genius . . .'

They had reached the little square with the Théâtre-Français opposite them. Ainsley Channon was thinking hard. He rested his hand on Brodie's shoulder, gave a squeeze.

'You may be on to something, Brodie. Start making investigations and I'll have a quiet word with Calder. And mind, no more than fifty pounds per concert. Daylight robbery though it is.'

2

Pension Bensinger
23, rue d'Uzès
Paris

5 October 1896

Dear Lady Dalcastle,

I was thinking of you last Sunday as I walked the entire length of the avenue des Champs Elysées and then on to the avenue du Bois de Boulogne. These new boulevards must be the finest streets in Europe. When the trees are fully grown they—

Brodie stopped writing. His eye had been caught by the recent telegram from Ernst Sauter rejecting his Channon proposal. He added it to the file that contained the six other rejections. Arensky had declined, as had Palomer and de Pachmann. Several had not even replied. Even Constant de Villeneuve, a man in his late sixties and at the very end of his professional career, had said no – or rather some managerial underling had said no on his behalf. It was humiliating: months had gone by since he'd made his proposal to Ainsley Channon. These virtuosi took an age to reply – weeks. In the case of de Pachmann it had been three months. Brodie had been patient – feeling he needed a reply from one, even in the negative, before he could approach another. That had been a mistake, also, he now realized, ruefully: he should have sent all his offers out simultaneously, scattered his Channon bread on the waters.

He was sitting at his desk in the small glassed-in cubicle that was his office in the workshop. 1896 was in its last quarter and it seemed as if nothing had changed. He was still living in the Pension Bensinger; Channon & Cie was still making a nugatory, insignificant profit despite the burgeoning success of the tuning side of the business. He now had four full-time tuners and another two new apprentices. His new warehouse and repair shop in Saint-Cloud was up and running and already making significant savings. Piano sales were steady but the profit margin remained very small, not to say minuscule. However, Brodie was now convinced that Calder and Dieulafoy were embezzlers. There could be no other explanation for this consistent underperformance. The clever aspect of it all was the very modest profit – Channon was not in deficit – for if there had been years of loss the shop would have been closed by Ainsley, surely. Somehow Calder and Dieulafoy were siphoning off the majority of the profits that should have been registered – Brodie just couldn't understand how it was being achieved.

He lit a cigarette and wandered out into the showroom. The gleaming new pianos stood there on the parquet under the electric lights – the grands, the baby grands, the uprights – precision machines, glossy and black. In the window Dmitri was playing something familiar yet modern – Debussy, Brodie thought, or Fauré – and went to take a look. The usual small crowd stood on the pavement looking in, marvelling, enjoying the free concert. He felt a sudden bitterness as he watched Dmitri play, feeling that all his efforts had been wasted because of clever, covert larceny in high places. Channon should have been a triumphant success in Paris, a success amplified by his own shrewd innovations, but it limped along, just surviving – only Calder and his henchman enjoying the dividends.

He looked at his watch. Six o'clock, time for Dmitri to finish and, on cue, Dmitri played his final chord, stood, took his bow, closed the fall and the lid and stepped back into the showroom where he spotted Brodie watching. They shook hands and went back to the workshop office where Brodie opened the cash box and paid Dmitri the thirty francs he was owed. Dmitri slipped the notes into his wallet.

'Are you all right, Brodie?' he asked. 'You seem a bit, I don't know, cast down.'

'I've had a frustrating day. Very.'

'So we should go to Number 7 and have some fun, don't you think?'

Number 7 was a *maison de tolérance* that they patronized – 7, rue des Ardennes up by the large abattoir in Villette. Brodie went there with Dmitri, and sometimes on his own, once a month or so. There was another 'house' near the Pension Bensinger which he and one of the other long-term lodgers – a Belgian engineer called Didier Neuchâtel – sometimes visited. But Number 7 was his favourite and he had a favourite girl there, Encarnacion, a sometime dancer – so she said – from Pamplona. It seemed like a good idea.

'Yes, let's go,' Brodie said, with new enthusiasm. 'I owe myself some amusement.'

Encarnacion did her best to rejuvenate his low spirits but sensed nothing much had changed. She said – in her heavily accented French – as he was dressing after their swift and unsatisfactory coition, '*Toute la tristesse du monde ce soir, Brodie?*' He said he'd had a difficult day and she reminded him that all days were difficult when you thought about it. He admitted the truth of the statement.

She put on her tight little bolero jacket, tied her sash around her waist and walked down the stairs with him to the salon. Brodie tipped her the usual five francs extra and she wandered away to join the other waiting girls. Brodie looked around for Dmitri but there was no sign of him so he ordered an absinthe from the bar and picked up a newspaper.

The distinguishing feature of Number 7 was that the 'girls' waited for their clients in the salon naked or semi-naked. Brodie noticed that the plumper and less attractive girls seemed to elect to wear nothing but others had realized that partial nakedness was more titillating than complete nudity. That was why he had been drawn to Encarnacion that first night. Her dark brown nipples were fleetingly exposed by the tiny jacket she wore, unbuttoned. The red sash she tied round her waist was another sign of Iberian exoticism and served somehow to emphasize her dense pudenda. She waved at him now from the banquette where she was sitting and opened her jacket to show him her breasts – to cheer him up, he supposed.

Triste est omne animal post coitum, he said to himself, feeling his self-pity and melancholia return as he waited for Dmitri – where was he? What was taking him so long? – but he knew his mood wasn't caused by his unsatisfactory ten minutes with Encarnacion. It was deeper and darker than that. He looked around to distract himself. The salon was busy: payday at the Marché aux Bestiaux next door – auctioneers and managers, stockmen and farmers all eager for some Parisian hospitality. He saw Encarnacion heading back upstairs with a new customer and felt the usual illogical spasm of jealously and resentment that another stranger was about to enjoy her favours.

He had no moral objection to going to these houses and paying for prostitutes. Number 7 was a licensed brothel, after all, licensed by the city of Paris. He was a young, virile man, also, and how else was he to satisfy sexual urges and rid himself of sexual frustration? Pleasuring yourself was all very well but sometimes you needed to hold another naked body in your arms – flesh on flesh, breast to breast, thigh to thigh. That was another reason why he liked Encarnacion – she let him kiss her for an extra five francs. Lip to lip. Usually, kissing seemed to make a difference to the simple commercial transaction of money for sex, but not tonight.

No, his mood was caused by the job at Channon – it was beginning to wear him down: the constant war of attrition with Calder; the sense of stasis, the failure of his 'grand plan'. Even Paris's beauties were beginning to lose their power to inspire and cheer. Sometimes he found himself hankering for cold austere Edinburgh with its black castle on its rainy crag.

Finally Dmitri appeared and they wandered out into the night. Dmitri's girl had been Japanese, he said, and he had wanted to linger as it was all so different, happily paying for an extra half-hour.

'She was very polite,' Dmitri said. 'Very attentive. Not like the French girls. Are English girls polite? I would imagine so.'

'I only know Scottish girls, in fact,' Brodie said. 'They're polite enough, most of the time. I've never been with an English girl, now you come to mention it.'

They strolled southwards, keeping to lit streets, heading towards the Parc des Buttes Chaumont, looking for a café or a bistro that was still open. They found one on the rue Secrétan and hurried inside – the night was cold and dark with a persistent light rain. Brodie ordered a hot rum and water, Dmitri had a glass of red wine and they found a corner table near the stove.

'You still don't seem so happy,' Dmitri said. 'It's Friday night. I thought you liked Encarnacion. We're meant to be out on the town having fun.'

Brodie apologized. He ordered another rum and water and told Dmitri of his grand plan and its months of frustrating rejections.

'I've approached seven,' he said, 'seven famous pianists.' He listed their names. 'They've all turned me down.'

'Even for an extra fifty pounds a concert?'

'Do you think it's not enough?'

Dmitri thought for a while.

'Do you know John Kilbarron?' he asked.

'John Kilbarron? Of course. The "Irish Liszt" – what about him?'

'He came to the conservatoire last month to give a recital. It was amazing.' Dmitri raved on – the incredible speed, the emotion. The most difficult pieces effortlessly mastered.

Brodie was thinking hard. John Kilbarron – a bit passé, perhaps, but one of the real old-school *klaviertigers* ten or twenty years ago. He remembered a few details – Kilbarron had been a child prodigy; his great years were the 1870s and 80s. Perhaps he was perceived as a bit old-fashioned today but the reputation had endured. Everyone knew the name of John Kilbarron – an astonishing virtuoso on the piano, hence his nickname of the 'Irish Liszt'.

'It's not a bad idea,' Brodie said. 'But I thought he was based in Vienna.'

'No, he lives in Paris now.'

Brodie thought further. Maybe an Irish virtuoso might look more favourably on a Scottish piano manufacturer . . . Yes, it might be worth a final try.

'Do you know where he lives?'

'I can find out. I can ask at the conservatoire.'

Brodie pressed Dmitri for more information. Dmitri said Kilbarron must be in his late forties. He still seemed to be playing with miraculous panache, evidently.

'I mean,' Dmitri said, 'he played the "Rondo Fantastique" as if it was a one-finger exercise. I've never seen anyone play like that. I wouldn't even attempt that piece. I just can't do it,' he shrugged. 'I'm not bad, but compared to Kilbarron I'm just a beginner.'

'No. You're good, Dmitri. Very gifted.'

'You see Kilbarron play like that and you wonder why you bother.'

Now it was Dmitri's turn to be cast down while Brodie's mood was improving as he thought on. John Kilbarron, here in Paris . . . Yes, maybe this was the gift of good fortune he was owed. He would write to him – the letter of all letters – and what a bonus that he could write to him in English. He had a sudden premonition – John Kilbarron plays Channon. It already had a ring to it and, in his mind's eye, he could see the advertisements they would take in the newspapers. Everything was going to change.

3

Dmitri found Kilbarron's address through the office of the conservatoire. Brodie wrote his letter of letters outlining his proposal – hinting that all terms were potentially renegotiable – and had it hand-delivered to Kilbarron's address. He was living in an apartment on the ground floor of a *hôtel particulier* on the boulevard Saint-Germain on the left bank. Dmitri also told Brodie that Kilbarron was participating in a concert – a *soirée russe*, as it was advertised – taking place in two weeks at the Théâtre de la République. Brodie bought a ticket – eight francs in the *fauteuils d'orchestre*, as close to the stage as he could manage, and waited impatiently for the day to come around.

Brodie stood outside the Théâtre de la République reading the poster. The orchestra – L'Orchestre de l'Académie de Musique – was one he'd never encountered before. They were playing Tchaikovsky's Symphony No. 3 and a tone poem by Panin with one Lydia Blum (soprano) as soloist. Then there was the interval, after which John Kilbarron ('Le Liszt irlandais') would perform Rimsky-Korsakov's Piano Concerto in C sharp minor followed by variations and *fantaisies* on themes by Borodin arranged by Kilbarron himself. All very Russian, apart from the Irish Liszt, Brodie thought.

It was a cold grey day, darkened by rain, on and off, so Brodie took his seat early, feeling an unusual apprehension. He had left his calling card for Kilbarron at the stage door with a note scribbled on the back – 'It would be an honour to meet you and discuss our mutual interests' – but he was beginning to sense this potential encounter was somehow misguided. Had Kilbarron received his letter, delivered a fortnight ago? If so, why had he not replied? If he hadn't received the letter what would he make of the note on the calling card? Why, after a gruelling recital, should he receive a complete stranger in his dressing room? The questions continued clamorously as he sat there staring at the stage, with its empty seats and music stands, trying and failing to make out the manufacturer of the piano that was set to one side. Women weren't allowed in the *fauteuils d'orchestre* as the seats were too close for them to slip decorously by, unbrushed-against, so he found himself surrounded by men, men whom he recognized as the so-called *chevaliers du lustre* – the 'knights of the chandelier' – a claque of paid applauders. He wondered if Kilbarron had spent money to obtain this noisily enthusiastic crowd. Even after the concert had begun they talked quite loudly amongst themselves, uninterested in the Tchaikovsky or the tone poem.

Annoyingly, the soprano, Lydia Blum, stood at the very limits of both the lenses in his Franklin spectacles – move his head and squint as he might, he still couldn't quite bring her into focus. That she was unusually tall and fair-haired was all he could distinguish from the indeterminate blur of her figure. Her voice was good but a bit underpowered, he thought – she must have been almost inaudible in the higher galleries. The applause at the interval as she took her bow was muted – everyone was waiting for the Irish Liszt.

Brodie stepped outside and was surprised to see how dark it had become. He had a glass of wine at the next-door café trying to ignore his mounting trepidation. Trepidation was the wrong word, he decided. It was a sense of something impending, unsure if it was good or bad. *Impendingment*, would do as a nonce word. He sipped his wine and tried to ignore his feeling of impendingment. He did sense that here was a chance, an opportunity, if only he could handle the situation adroitly enough. He felt, impendingmently, that what happened in the next hour or two might change his life, either for good or for bad.

He took his seat again, dry-mouthed. The piano had been moved to centre stage – there was no dais for a conductor. The piano was a Pate, he now noticed, and felt pleased. Pates were good – good for the salon, not for the theatre – no match for Channons.

The orchestra players slowly took their seats and tuned up – and then John Kilbarron suddenly strode on stage at an unusually brisk speed, taking everyone by surprise, even the *chevaliers du lustre*. But they quickly began their bellows of approval and rose to their feet, clapping energetically. Kilbarron didn't look at his claque as he took his dramatic low bow and moved to the piano.

Kilbarron was closer so Brodie could see him clearly. He had long dark hair combed back from his forehead and tucked behind his ears, and there was a sunken, somewhat ravaged handsomeness to his features. Clean-shaven. Medium height. Deep lines on his face cutting through his cheeks. He was impassive as he sat there waiting to start, allowing the applause to engulf him. He was wearing a tailcoat and a white tie of unusual looseness and volume. The style was brooding romanticism. A cold person – Brodie thought – almost menacingly arrogant in demeanour. But this impression may have been purposefully manufactured for the stage, he realized.

The crowd quietened, the audience was ready and so Kilbarron gave the upbeat to the first violinist and launched into the Rimsky-Korsakov. Brodie sat back and closed his eyes, listening. After about five minutes the piano began to lose its tuning – but of course he was the only person in the theatre who noticed. He doubted if Kilbarron was even aware he was playing a piano that was slightly out of tune.

Still, the Rimsky-Korsakov was good – albeit surprisingly short – and Kilbarron played with exemplary control and interpretation. It was when he started on the Borodin arrangements that the full Kilbarron genius was revealed. Brodie now had his eyes open, marvelling. Astonishing speed and dexterity; intense concentration and great dramatization – a lot of head-tossing, eyes-closing, vivid expressions, arm-raising, swaying on the stool. One of the variations was in the so-called 'three-hand technique' popularized by Thalberg in the 1830s. Left and right fingers played swooping arpeggios and other complex figurations while the thumbs of both hands played the melody – hence the illusion that the pianist had three hands not simply two. It was phenomenally difficult but Kilbarron spent most of the variation not even looking at his hands on the keys. A hank of his hair fell over his brow and he left it there. His face soon had a glaze of sweat. Kilbarron ended the third Borodin variation with a series of keyboard-length black-note glissandos. When he stood to take his bow – the audience rapturous, yelling, baying – Brodie could see drops of blood falling from the fingernails of his right hand. The audience had no need of the paid-for claque to encourage them: they were on their feet shouting, bellowing their appreciation, clapping their hands sore. Flowers were thrown on stage. Kilbarron ignored them, not even smiling his thanks. He wiped his face with a handkerchief and then wrapped his broken fingernails in it. He left the stage without a backward glance.

Brodie had to admit he was somewhat stunned. In Edinburgh he had been to countless concerts and recitals and seen many virtuosi but this was a . . . He searched for a word: this thunderstorm was something new, and he wondered if this was what it had been like at a Liszt recital or a Thalberg concert. You could be a fine and talented piano player, like Dmitri, but artists such as John Kilbarron were at another, unattainable, near-superhuman level.

Brodie stepped out of the theatre and lit a cigarette. Concentrate, concentrate, he told himself – now it's your turn. He wandered down the side of the theatre towards the stage door where he found a crowd of about a hundred gathered, so he quickly reckoned. He pushed his way through to the harassed doorman and explained he had left his card earlier and was expected by Maestro Kilbarron. He was let through and found himself following two dozen excited people down a corridor, all heading for Kilbarron's dressing-room suite, he supposed. He stopped – this was pointless. How could he introduce himself properly and privately with all these admirers milling around? He saw a sign – *'Artistes'* – pointing up a flight of stairs. The two dozen Kilbarron aficionados had reached a dead end and were now retracing their steps. Brodie saw his opportunity to go to the head of the queue and dashed up the stairs to find himself in a corridor on an upper floor. There were no names on the doors that flanked the passageway, just numbers. He made his way to number 1 and knocked, pleased by his subterfuge. Surely this would be where— The door was opened.

A young woman stood there in a Japanese-style dressing gown.

Black scaly dragons, large pink flowers, it reached to her ankles. Brodie took in tousled curly blonde hair. In one hand she held a cigarette; her other hand held her kimono-robe closed at the neck. He knew – his male senses told him – that she was naked under her lurid gown. And somehow this knowledge changed everything.

'Yes?' she said. 'Can I help you?'

She spoke French with an accent Brodie couldn't place.

'Excuse me,' Brodie said. 'But I'm looking for Maestro Kilbarron.'

'One floor up,' she said, pointing with her cigarette. As she raised her hand Brodie registered unthinkingly the clear shift and rearrangement of her small breasts beneath the silk. He was stirred. He swallowed, his throat dry.

'My apologies,' he said as other details crowded swiftly in. Heavy-lidded eyes as if she were half-asleep. A strong pointed chin. It was a Russian accent, yes. Ah. This would be the out-of-focus soprano, Lydia Blum. Brodie stood there trying to think of other words to utter. Blue eyes. Pink lips. Full pink lips. Cigarette now placed between full pink lips. Strong inhalation. Slight head turn, eyes still on him. Powerful exhalation through side of mouth. Shred of tobacco picked from tip of tongue.

Brodie said: 'I thought your solo was remarkable.'

'Thank you. One floor up. Follow the crowds.'

She closed the door on him before he could apologize again for the interruption.

He wandered back to the stairway, feeling confused and conscious of a trapped bubble of air in his chest, in his oesophagus, like a fist. So that was Lydia Blum . . . He felt his sphincter loosen and the bubble of air expand to fill his lungs. He exhaled and became dizzy for a second. What was going on? Forget Lydia Blum – find Kilbarron.

Brodie had to wait twenty minutes in Kilbarron's crowded sitting room until the admiring fanatics thinned. A waiter stood at the door with a tray filled with green-stemmed glasses of wine and Brodie helped himself to one – and then another – as he watched Kilbarron receive the plaudits of his madly overenthusiastic admirers. Men and women.

He was indeed a handsome man, Brodie saw, but – now he was just feet away – he noticed the bags under his eyes and that the skin of his face was slightly pocked, giving his handsomeness a coarser, less refined look. He had combed his hair and his face was pale as he nodded and smiled fleetingly at the extravagant compliments that were being paid him. For a moment or two he stood alone as a group left and Brodie seized his opportunity.

'Mr Kilbarron, sir. I'm Brodie Moncur. I sent you a letter from my firm.'

Kilbarron turned his eyes on Brodie.

'A letter?'

'A letter hand-delivered – with a proposal. I work for Channon, the piano makers.'

'Oh, yes. I seem to remember, now. What do you want?' Kilbarron had a pronounced Irish accent.

'Might I pay you a visit? It's an important and complicated matter. Now's perhaps not the best time. You must be exhausted.'

Kilbarron looked bored. He took a glass off the waiter's tray and drained it.

'There is a significant financial element to the proposal,' Brodie added swiftly, quietly.

'You sent me a letter so you must know where I live.'

'I do indeed, sir.'

'Come and see me on Monday morning. Eleven o'clock.'

'I'll be there.'

'Not any earlier.'

'Prompt. Eleven o'clock, Monday morning.'

'Where are you from?'

'Scotland. Edinburgh.'

'As long as you're not English.'

Then an elderly woman swept in and embraced Kilbarron and Brodie realized, to his amazement, that he had achieved all he could have hoped for. He stepped back. Monday morning, eleven o'clock. Excellent. But why did his contrary mind turn to thinking of Lydia Blum and not John Kilbarron?

4

On Monday morning, five minutes before eleven o'clock, Brodie presented himself at John Kilbarron's apartment in the *hôtel particulier* on the boulevard Saint-Germain. He went through a small door in tall green double doors and found himself in a capacious courtyard, finely gravelled. Two bay trees in terracotta pots stood on either side of an ornate front door with a half-shell pediment. A maroon, dying Virginia creeper, clinging to the sandstone walls, shed its few remaining leaves. He knocked on the door and was admitted by a dozy, unshaven manservant who hung his coat on a stand in the hallway and showed him into a sizeable drawing room.

'I have an appointment with Mr Kilbarron,' Brodie said.

'What? Right. Are you sure?'

'Yes. At eleven o'clock.'

'Mmm. Yes. I'll tell him,' the manservant said uncertainly and left him alone.

There was a fire lit, though barely, just a flame-twitch through orange embers. Brodie allowed himself to rake it into life with a poker. The curtains – thick olive-green damask – were drawn and there was a smell of stale tobacco smoke in the air. Bottles and glasses stood on the tables, some still filled with wine. Brodie parted the curtains to let some light in and saw that the tall windows of the drawing room gave on to a small formal garden of gravelled paths and clipped box hedges leading to a feature of two curved stone benches flanking a fountain – Cupid in a lead basin. No water flowed.

Turning back, Brodie saw there was a grand piano at the end of the room and he went to investigate it. A Feurich, interestingly, not a Pate. He opened it and quietly played three octaves on A, C and D sharp. Badly out of tune. He began to wonder about Kilbarron's ear . . . Then again, maybe he never played this piano.

He sat down on a creaking cane armchair and smoked a cigarette. Ten minutes later he opened the windows onto the garden and strolled around the pathways several times, feet crunching. There was an empty wine bottle in the Cupid fountain, he saw. He left it there and went back inside, feeling cold.

Fifteen minutes later he was leafing through the sheet music he'd found in the piano stool – Brahms, Mozart and someone called John Field – when John Kilbarron came in. He was looking ill, Brodie thought, white-faced and red-eyed, two days' stubble, his thick hair lank.

'Top of the morning,' he said. 'And who may you be, my good sir?'

Brodie reintroduced himself. 'We met at your recital at the République. I had written to you about a proposal from Channon, the piano manufacturers.'

'Excellent pianos,' Kilbarron said. 'Yes, indeed. Excellent . . .' He began to roam about the room as if looking for something. He was wearing an embroidered floor-length charcoal-grey gown over an open shirt and trousers. His feet were in unmatching leather slippers, Brodie noticed.

Kilbarron found what he was looking for – a carafe half-filled with red wine. He chose an empty glass and poured some wine into it.

'Can I tempt you to a glass of wine?' he asked. 'Strangely, it sometimes tastes better the morning after.'

'No, thank you.'

Kilbarron emptied his glass in two gulps and pulled at his nose. He topped himself up and crossed the room towards Brodie, now seemingly focussed on him and his mission.

'Where are you from? Where's that accent from?'

'I'm Scottish,' Brodie said. 'I was working in Edinburgh before I came to Paris.'

'A Scotsman, eh? Never trust a Scotsman with a proposal. That's what my pappy told me, may he rot in eternal hellfire.'

'You can trust me, sir.'

'Remind me of your famous proposal.'

Brodie outlined the plan – the new, bespoke piano, shipped to every concert at Channon's expense; the £50 supplementary fee for every concert or recital; the use of Kilbarron's name in all advertisements. And the contract to be renegotiated after six months by both parties – this being a new clause Brodie thought it wise to be introduced.

Kilbarron drank his wine in silence, thinking.

'Fifty pounds per concert – on top of the fee I'm already being paid?'

'Yes . . . Initially.'

'What's in it for Channon?'

'The best kind of advertisement. An endorsement to be dreamt of. "John Kilbarron plays Channon pianos". And you would have a wonderful piano, sir – precisely adapted and regulated for your playing style. I would see to that myself.' Brodie added that he was Channon's senior piano tuner.

'A piano tuner? You're a piano tuner? Now you tell me. Are you any good?'

'I'm also the assistant manager of the Paris showroom.'

'You can find assistant managers in every street but a decent piano tuner is a rare bird,' Kilbarron said, topping up his glass. 'Assistant manager, you say. Why didn't they send the manager? I'm insulted.'

'He's not a musical man.'

'And you are.'

'After a fashion. I am a very good tuner – in all modesty.'

'You mean, "in no modesty". It's one of those slippery self-promotional phrases. Like "my humble opinion". My arrogant un-humble opinion, don't you know.'

Brodie said nothing. Kilbarron was appearing livelier by the second, fuelled by his overnight-stewed wine.

'And are you a good assistant manager, in all modesty?'

'I do my best for the firm.'

'A good company man. Solid as a rock. Steady as the day is long.' He turned away.

Brodie sensed his contempt and thought he had an opening.

'By the way,' he said, 'your piano at the République, your Pate, went out of tune after ten minutes.'

Kilbarron whirled round.

'Fuck you, Scotsman, whatever your name is!'

Brodie pointed. 'And that piano there is completely out of tune.'

Kilbarron advanced on him and Brodie smelt the miasma of wine, sweat and tobacco clinging to him. He braced himself. Then Kilbarron smiled – both rows of teeth exposed. It was oddly disarming.

'I thought there was something wrong with that piano. Now you tell me. Jesus Christ on the Cross.'

'For example,' Brodie continued, 'that last black-note glissando you played. I can weight and lighten the keys precisely for you. Your nails wouldn't bleed. It would be like . . .' He thought. 'It would be like running your fingers through soapsuds.'

'Is that right?' *Roight*. The Irish accent. 'I'll be damned. Soapsuds, eh?'

He showed Brodie his right hand. Perfect undamaged nails.

'I'll tell you a secret, Mr Scottish-man,' Kilbarron said. 'I have a little pocket in my waistcoat lined with oil cloth. I just tip in a splash of red poster paint. Nobody notices when I slip my fingertips in at the end of the concert but the audience does like to think you've damaged yourself in the name of art. Blood dripping. Drip, drip, drip. Works like a charm. Always.'

He ranged around the room again, his long robe widening and billowing in the draught he created. He stopped at the fireplace and shook the coals with the poker so that the flames rose.

'Fifty pounds a concert or recital. On top of the establishment's fee?'

'Yes,' Brodie said. 'Guaranteed.'

Kilbarron stood up from the fire and smiled his smile.

'Well, I've thought about it, young fella, whatever your name is – and the answer is no.'

Brodie stood in the hallway and put his coat on slowly. Had he said something wrong? Had he been too bold, too bumptious? No, surely not . . . He felt a depression settle on his shoulders like a heavy cape. Who next? Francobelli? Or Klinger? He was advancing into the second tier, now, lower – hopeless. Nobody would care or pay any attention to the piano they were playing. He had to have the *crème de la crème*, nothing else would—

'Excuse me?'

He turned.

Lydia Blum was coming down the stairs.

She was wearing a white blouse with a pie-crust neck and a cameo at her throat. Her long cherry-red skirt was cinched at the waist with a thick, diamanté-buckled black belt. Her curly blonde hair was held up in a loose bun secured with two long wooden pins. He took all this in immediately in a split second as other questions began to yammer in his brain.

She stepped on to the chequerboard marble of the hallway. She was tall for a woman, he thought, almost lanky. Nearly as tall as he was. He felt his throat tighten and wondered if he'd be able to form words. Her heavy-lidded blue eyes scrutinized him.

'Can I help you?'

'I . . . No, honestly. Just. I was just . . .'

'What?'

'I just had, ah, a . . . Ah, a meeting with Mr Kilbarron. Thank you. I'm leaving. About to leave. Now.'

She cocked her head, puzzled. Her lips were full, almost as if she were pouting. Strong pointed chin.

'Have we met before?' she asked. 'You seem familiar.'

'I knocked on the door of your changing room at the Théâtre de la République. A few days ago.'

'Are you English?'

'Scottish.'

'You speak excellent French.'

'Thank you. Most kind.'

'I remember now. You were looking for John.'

'Yes. I was.'

Silence. They stared at each other. She smiled.

'Well, you obviously found him.'

Brodie felt now as if his innards were molten – as if he might melt in a puddle of sizzling magma on the floor. What was it about this woman? How could a tall, Russian, mediocre opera singer be having this effect on him?

'Lika!' Kilbarron roared from the drawing room. 'Are you there?'

'Yes!' she shouted back.

Lydia – so diminutive 'Lika'. Right. More information – Lika Blum.

'Where are my cigars?'

'Where they always are!' she called back. 'In the humidor on the bookshelf.'

'Someone has moved them.'

'Excuse me,' she said to Brodie. Then added in English. 'I wish you very good morning.'

Then she went into the drawing room to search for her lover's cigars.

5

January 1897 seemed an exceptionally, cruelly, perversely cold month, Brodie thought – blood-freezingly cold – though nobody else to whom he voiced this opinion appeared to concur. It was winter, therefore it was cold and damp like all winters, but nothing exceptional, was the general opinion. It must be my mood, Brodie thought, my black mood making me feel the cold.

He had travelled this Wednesday morning in mid-January to the Théâtre du Gymnase on the boulevard de Bonne-Nouvelle to tune their grand piano for a comic opera based on a play by Scribe. The piano was in poor condition – there was bad hammer block and he had to replace the felt and reposition the rails – and it had taken him a full morning's work to restore it to playability. The manager popped out of his office from time to time to see how the work was progressing and tut-tutted at Brodie's exertions.

'You should get a new piano,' Brodie said and handed him one of the printed Channon flyers (another of his ideas) that he carried with him. It showed small photogravures of a range of models and prices and various ways of purchasing a piano with a deposit down and monthly payments. 'If you come by the showroom I'm sure we can manage a modest discount.'

The manager seemed intrigued and said he might indeed pass by. Another potential sale, Brodie thought as he shoved the action back in place, and what do I gain? He closed the fall and sat down on the stool for a moment, his mood darkening again. He must try not to feel bitter.

He heard his name called and he looked round to see Benoît, the office boy from the showroom, walking down the aisle between the stalls.

'Benoît? What're you doing here? What's happened?'

'A man came into the shop looking for you. He said it was important. Monsieur Dmitri said I should come and find you.'

'What man?'

'His name is . . .' he consulted a scrap of paper in his hand. 'Monsieur Kilbarron.'

Everything changed in an instant. It was extraordinary how that could happen, Brodie thought, getting to his feet, exulting. Boulevard de Bonne-Nouvelle indeed! It was astonishing how everything could alter in a day, an hour, a minute, a second. He would never forget that – never let his pessimism get the better of him again. He said goodbye to the manager, urging him to purchase a new piano and promising a 20 per cent discount, such was his new generous mood, and he and Benoît jumped in a cab and raced back to the avenue de l'Alma. There a calling card had been left on his desk. 'John Kilbarron' and, scrawled on the back, a note: 'Please come to the Saint-Germain apartment tomorrow at 6 p.m. K.'

This can only mean good news, Brodie calculated. A change of heart. The initial 'no' had been so final, so unpleasantly final. But the Channon offer was generous – a lot of money – so obviously second thoughts had begun to gather. He went through to the front of the shop and signalled Dmitri to stop playing so he could relate this fantastic turn in his fortunes to him. Kilbarron wanted to see him again. Perhaps there might even be a chance for a reunion with Lika Blum . . .

The next evening, promptly at six o'clock, Brodie was back at the Kilbarron apartment in the *hôtel particulier.* The manservant – smarter, less dozy – took his hat and coat and showed him into the drawing room. It was far tidier than his last visit with no traces of wassailing visible and a good fire burned in the grate. Brodie stood in front of it as he waited, enjoying the spreading warmth on his thighs and buttocks.

The manservant reappeared. 'Monsieur Kilbarron,' he announced.

Another man came into the room. He was handsome but heavy, a strong-boned man and swarthy with a grey-flecked, dense, black goatee. He had bags under his brown, watchful eyes. He was dressed in a dark grey suit with a crimson waistcoat whose buttons were straining from the considerable belly they had to retain.

'Malachi Kilbarron,' the man said in a deep, raspy voice and strong Irish accent. 'I'm the great man's little brother.'

They shook hands and Malachi Kilbarron offered Brodie a glass of port. Brodie accepted. Drinks poured, Malachi lit a long, thin cheroot; Brodie lit a Margarita.

'You should never talk business with my brother,' Malachi said, taking a seat. 'He considers "money" a dirty word – even though he thinks about it all the time like most artistes.' He used the French word as if to underline the feckless, pretentious aspect of the profession. He chuckled. 'John has a dirty mind, anyway, so everything is smirched and degraded, consequently.' He seemed to find this idea amusing and chortled again to himself as he drew on his cheroot. They had the same accent but otherwise the resemblance to his brother was a displaced one – skewed. John Kilbarron was handsome in his haggard, debauched way. Malachi – handsome enough, even-featured – looked far heftier and, if it were possible, more sinisterly debauched. John was lean; Malachi broad, muscle going to fat. John clean-shaven, Malachi bearded. It wasn't that unusual, Brodie supposed: two brothers similar but dissimilar. He and Callum didn't really look like brothers either, now he thought about it.

'No, if John hadn't mentioned your meeting in a casual, throwaway manner, like, I'd never have known. John says: Sure, I was offered a brand-new piano by some young Scotch fella, he says to me last week. Oh, yes, says I, and how did that come about? And so he told me the story of your encounter, plus your interesting offer. Refused only by John Kilbarron's pig-headedness, I should say. It's the story of my life. I go around and put the broken pieces back together again.' He poured more port wine into their glasses.

'So you, on the other hand, do find the offer interesting,' Brodie said, cautiously.

'I'd find the offer more interesting if there was more on offer. If you catch my drift.'

'I'm authorized to offer up to sixty pounds per concert and recital,' Brodie said spontaneously, knowing he was authorized to do no such thing, but he was a desperate man. 'Subject to a review every six months,' he added, as a cautious rider. Malachi didn't respond to this, fortunately. 'Everything else is on the table. The new Channon grand, all shipping and transportation costs to be met by the company.'

Malachi puffed vigorously at his cheroot, looking at the smoke he made as if it were some wondrous apparition.

'And what if you sell a thousand pianos as a result of John's endorsement?'

'That's our risk and our dividend. We would be paying a great deal in advance.'

'And if you sell two thousand pianos, what then? We'll look a right couple of eejits.'

'What're you trying to say?'

'We want a royalty on every piano sold after the first concert.'

'It might be possible. Every grand piano, though, no uprights.'

'That seems fair enough to me.'

'I'll have to consult Mr Channon, of course.'

'Let's say twenty pounds for every new grand sold.'

Brodie concealed his relief. 'I'm not authorized to settle on that. But I'm sure Mr Channon will take everything into consideration.'

Malachi stood and hitched up his trousers which had slipped below his belly.

'I'm sure you'll do your best, Mr Moncur. Let's not allow a few pounds here and there come between us and our enterprise.'

The meeting was over. Malachi walked him to the door.

'You have a chat to your Mr Channon and draw up a contract. Then we can meet again and set the whole wonderful show in motion.' He clapped Brodie on the back, quite hard. 'I'll await your earliest communication. We will be here in Paris for at least another month.'

Brodie stood in the hall putting on his coat, experiencing that strange sense of life repeating itself – the same situation but altogether different. He picked up his bowler. Now, if Lika Blum would only come down the stairs again then everything would be perfect. But she was never going to appear, of course. Brodie stepped out into the courtyard to confront Paris in January. It seemed decidedly warmer.

6

Ainsley Channon came back to Paris to sign the Kilbarron contract himself. Matters had been resolved relatively swiftly, letters and then telegrams whizzing to and fro finalizing terms. To Brodie's surprise and relief Ainsley had quickly conceded the rise in Kilbarron's concert fee though the royalty on piano sales was reduced to £10 per grand piano, initially, with an ascending scale as sales mounted up. The crucial clause about a six-month period had been retained. The Kilbarrons seemed unconcerned by this, though Calder maintained a sulky resentment throughout all discussions, objecting to every suggestion and counter-proposal almost as a matter of reflex. He particularly disapproved of Malachi Kilbarron's insistence that Channon & Cie's accounts could be audited by the Kilbarrons so they could determine the exact number of piano sales. Ainsley was again unperturbed, remarking that they had nothing to hide and that if they happened to sell another 1,000 pianos on the back of Brodie's excellent idea then what could possibly be wrong with allowing the brothers to see for themselves?

'We're honest brokers,' Ainsley said. 'We're not trying to cheat them. It's a joint enterprise – the better we do the better he does, and vice versa.'

'It's a matter of principle,' Calder snapped back.

'It's something entirely new – therefore matters of principle don't apply, yet,' Ainsley said. 'I'm sure you agree, Brodie.'

'I do,' Brodie said. 'John Kilbarron is our golden goose. We don't want to trim his wings.'

'Hear, hear!' Ainsley said. 'Let alone kill him!' He seemed to find the idea very amusing.

John and Malachi Kilbarron came to the showroom and signed the contract. A bottle of champagne was opened and the Channons and the Kilbarrons toasted each other and the success of this unique collaboration.

'Now, about my own new piano,' John Kilbarron said. 'I have some particular requests.'

'I suggest you speak to young Brodie, here,' Ainsley said. 'I'll leave you in his very capable hands.'

'Why don't you come and see me tomorrow morning,' Kilbarron said, turning to Brodie, 'and we can make a start?'

Brodie sat on the piano stool beside Kilbarron in the drawing room of the Saint-Germain apartment. Kilbarron's hands rested on the keys.

'There are three things you need to be a pianist of my standing,' Kilbarron said, with no trace of arrogance. He seemed more thoughtful, more subdued, today, Brodie thought. Kilbarron hit a key with his forefinger, as if to punctuate his statement.

'Sensibility, difficulty and speed,' he went on. 'If you have mastered all three you can become a true *klaviertiger*.' He paused, played another note. 'Now, "sensibility" is easy. It's just acting. A tear, a grimace, a head shake, a backward lean.' He leaned backwards and held his right hand up, poised dramatically. 'Then "difficulty". I can play anything – the most complex pieces. But "speed" . . . I used to be so fast.' He flexed the fingers of his right hand. 'But now I have pain in the hand, in the arm and the shoulder.'

He played a series of arpeggios with his right hand, running up the keyboard, his fingers a blur of movement. He turned his face to Brodie, wincing. 'It's sore. I'm slowing down.' He paused. 'And if I get slower then "difficulty" begins to become an issue. That's why I'm writing my own adaptations now, paraphrases, variations, fantasies. They may seem difficult but they're not. Well, not to me, that is.'

'I can solve the problem,' Brodie said, bravely. 'When we come to voice and regulate your own Channon I can do things to it that'll make a huge difference.'

Kilbarron looked sceptical.

'Can you fix a piano for me so I won't feel pain?'

'I think so,' Brodie said. 'I can make it so much easier to play, certainly. It'll be unlike any other piano you've ever played. I use weights, tiny ribbons of lead weights, dry lubrication. The contact will seem minimal, the pressure you use will be hugely reduced.'

'Like soapsuds.'

'Exactly.'

Kilbarron gave him his big two-rows-of-teeth smile.

'Well, if you can do that, my lad, then you may just get the job as my guardian angel.'

'I thought that was my role.'

They both turned to see Malachi saunter into the room.

'He can be your assistant guardian angel, then. Brodie, here, is going to work some magic on our new piano, he tells me.'

Brodie stood. 'I'd better be away,' he said.

Malachi came up to him and cupped his cheek – roughly.

'Are you going to be our saving grace, Mr Moncur?'

'Depends what you mean by "saving grace", I suppose.'

'Just make sure you are,' he said and gave his odd barking laugh, looking at his brother. 'We like saving graces, don't we, John?'

'Sure, we like anyone that makes our lives easier.' There was more fraternal laughter.

The dozy manservant showed Brodie out, holding the front door open for him and, as a matter of course now, Brodie looked up the stairs in case Lydia/Lika might descend. But no.

'Is Mademoiselle Blum in town?' Brodie asked.

'No, sir. She's in Dresden singing in an opera.'

The new Channon warehouse and workshops were situated on the rue Gounod in the centre of Saint-Cloud. Brodie met Kilbarron at the Gare Saint-Lazare and they caught a stopper the ten miles or so to Saint-Cloud and walked to the warehouse from the station along the northern edge of the huge park.

Kilbarron seemed somewhat astonished to be in a building that contained over one hundred pianos. They were parked in tight lanes with corridors between, and as he and Brodie wandered through the maze of uprights Kilbarron looked about him in obvious wonderment.

'It is a business, isn't it?' he said to Brodie. 'We forget that, we piano players. A factory for piano-making. And all over the world there are other factories making hundreds and hundreds more. You could be churning out galvanized iron buckets.'

'I hardly think so,' Brodie said. 'Think of these pianos as Swiss chronometers, as the most intricate machines designed to produce melodious sounds. Not buckets, no, no.'

They had arrived at the row of grand pianos. Brodie quickly removed the dust sheets. A dozen grands stood there on their solid three legs: wide, pristine, gleaming.

'Should we go for the latest model?' Kilbarron asked.

'Can I suggest this one?' Brodie said, walking towards an older model and resting his hand on it. There were scuff marks on the legs and the lid creaked as he opened it.

'This piano is twelve years old and was one of the last to be designed and built and supervised in production by the man who taught me everything I know: Findlay Lanhire.' Brodie played the C major chord. 'It's a beautiful thing,' he said. 'Findlay Lanhire's finest. I'll just tweak it for you. Personalize it.'

Kilbarron stood above the keyboard, leaned forward and played a few bars of Mozart's Piano Sonata No. 9 in D.

'The treble register,' he said. 'That's where the pain kicks in. The left hand is fine.' He played a continuous five-finger tremolo in the higher octaves. 'I can feel it,' he said. 'Already. The pain starting to come up my arm.' He stopped and flexed and unflexed his fingers, massaged his palm.

'People think you sit down on your stool and twiddle your fingers and the music comes out,' he said. 'But every muscle in your body's in action. It's a very physical business playing the piano at my level. Your back, your shoulders, your thighs, your feet on the pedals.' He paused. 'Not to mention your nerves and your guts.' He looked at the keys. 'And I've been doing it since I was six years old.' He cracked the knuckles on each hand. 'Every day, almost, for decades . . . There's wear and tear. It takes its toll.'

'I can make those keys feather-light, sir,' Brodie said.

'Oh, yes. Soap bubbles.'

'Goose-down.'

'Dandelion fluff.'

'The air that we breathe.'

Kilbarron leaned forward and played a series of loud chords – *bang, bang, bang* – the sound echoing through the steel rafters of the warehouse.

'All right, young Brodie. This is the one for me. Now, can we get a decent lunch in this godforsaken town?'

They found a restaurant, Le Pavillon Bleu on the place d'Armes. Kilbarron asked for a table at the back and they studied the menu. Kilbarron said he wanted only a *plat du jour*. He lit a small cigar and ordered a brandy and iced water, insisting Brodie joined him in a toast to the new piano. Kilbarron was wearing a dark grey tweed suit, a white shirt with a high stiff collar and a cobalt-blue tie. With his long hair brushed back and falling to his shoulders he looked very much a personage, Brodie thought, a person of consequence, even if you didn't recognize him. Brodie was aware of fellow diners looking curiously at them. Who is that man? A woman timidly approached and asked if Monsieur Kilbarron would sign her menu. Kilbarron put down his cigar and obliged. He was very charming.

Kilbarron was served veal kidneys but barely touched them, being more interested in the wine he ordered. Brodie ate a skate wing with black butter and, when Kilbarron called for a second bottle, realized he was not going to remain compos mentis for much longer. While Kilbarron had his wits about him, Brodie asked after Mademoiselle Blum.

'She's in Dresden,' Kilbarron said. 'Singing Inès in *L'Africaine*.'

'She has a very . . .' Brodie chose his words carefully. 'Pure voice.'

'Her voice is all right. That's not a problem. The problem is her height – she's too tall.'

'Too tall?'

'She towers over most tenors and they don't like that. And her voice may be pure enough but they can't hear her at the back.'

He forked a chunk of kidney into his mouth, chewed and washed it down with a gulp of wine. He topped their glasses up, brimful.

'I can get her work for now but it won't last long.' Kilbarron pushed his plate away, half-eaten. 'The law of diminishing returns will kick in.'

'Really? I didn't realize—'

'Why are you so interested in Miss Blum, Mr Moncur?'

'I'm not. No.' Brodie tried to disguise the fact that he was suddenly flustered, feeling his cheeks burn. 'Rather I'm curious, you know, having heard her sing.'

'Right. I'll buy that for now.' He looked shrewdly at him. 'Are you a married man, Brodie, my fine fella?'

'No.'

'Steer well clear of it, I'll tell you that for nothing. It's a waste of time – a waste of everything. And there's no need, either, in this day and age.'

'I suppose so. But what if you fall in love?'

'Love?' Kilbarron said, blankly. 'What's that? Can you eat it? Can you drink it? Is it of any use to man or beast?'

Brodie called for the bill.

'Have you any idea of your concert programme?' he asked, trying to bring the conversation back to work. 'When might you start?'

'Malachi deals with that side of things. I just show up and play.'

'Are you thinking of a full orchestra – or just solo piano?'

'I leave that up to Malachi. And the hall, of course. They have their own ideas of how to get the people in.'

'Fine. I'll wait to hear from him.'

'But I will tell you one thing, young Brodie.'

'Yes?' He felt a distinct sense of foreboding.

'I'll be wanting you with me along the way. Your wonderful, personally regulated piano – and including your good self.'

'I'm not sure I can—'

'Oh, I'm sure you can. I want you there tuning my intricate machine.'

7

Hôtel de l'Europe
Rue Auguste Bottin
Genève
Suisse

15 May 1897

Dear Married One, Callumius Rex, Imperator –

Is it bliss? Still bliss? I hear it is reputed to be. Kilbarron thinks it an unnecessary state in this day and age. All very well for him with forty fine ladies swooning in his dressing room after every concert. Once everything has calmed down I will be home to meet Mrs Callum Moncur though to tell you the truth I'm not sure when that might be. As you can see from my writing paper I am in Geneva, our last stop on a six-city tour. Brussels, Berlin, Vienna, Milan, Rome. The Kilbarrons are making a small fortune but so are we. The news from Paris is that piano sales have already doubled – so the great Brodie Moncur scheme appears to be working. My concerns are all to do with shipping the Channon itself hither and thither. I have to hire a gang and a wagon to take it to the station and load it on a train. Then when we arrive another gang and a wagon has to take it to the theatre. Then I pay the stagehands there to unload and set up. And I have to retune, of course. My days are filled and I've seen very little of these beautiful cities we've visited. But Kilbarron is pleased, playing well and to large crowds. The pain in his hand and arm is negligible so his mood is affable. His brother, Malachi, is a less congenial travelling companion – always complaining about something: the compartment, the hotel, the food, the weather – but I don't allow myself to get over-bothered by him.

*Last concert tonight. Pack up piano, ship to Paris and then I'll see where we stand. Malachi Kilbarron is booking more dates for a second tour in the summer. I think he knows time may be running out. We renew everything contractual after six months. I have a feeling Ainsley Channon will call a halt if he thinks we've achieved all we can (*id est*: made lots of money).*

Give a respectable brother-in-law's kiss to your lovely spouse.

Ever your affect. bro.,
Brodie the Wanderer

Brodie sealed the envelope and wrote Callum's address down, feeling a little pang of nostalgia as he wrote 'Ecosse'. He had been away for nearly three years now. He never thought he would hanker to be back in the Liethen Valley – maybe it was all this travelling that was causing this fleeting homesickness. He looked at his watch – half-past five – he should make his way to the theatre for the final checks. He slipped on his coat, picked up his hat and his Gladstone bag and walked down the corridor to knock on the door of Kilbarron's suite.

'Come in. No, wait,' came the call. 'One minute.'

Brodie waited until he heard a key turn in the lock and Kilbarron let him in. His jacket was off and the left sleeve of his shirt was rolled up to the bicep. On the desk Brodie saw a saucer, a leather strap and a hypodermic syringe.

'Brodie, my good companion, what can I do for you?'

'Are you all right?' Brodie pointed to the hypodermic syringe.

'It's just a painkiller. Remarkably efficient. So, yes, I am all right. In fact, more than all right.'

'Has the pain returned?'

'A twinge. So I thought it better to act now.'

'Right . . . I'm off to the theatre. See everything's in order.'

'I think Malachi wants a word. After the show.'

'Of course. See you about six thirty.'

The theatre – the Théâtre des Ducs de Savoie – was a ten-minute walk from the hotel and Brodie headed straight there, taking the back streets. The manager met him and led him to the stage. Findlay Lanhire's Channon stood there, opened, ready.

Brodie enjoyed being in empty theatres. He had fine-tuned the Channon that morning but, just to ensure all was in order, he sat down and – to the empty seats – played the little ditty that he used to check all was well as far as the tuning was concerned. It was a folk song that he remembered his mother used to sing to him and he had adapted and embellished the simple melody so that every octave and almost every note was played. The Channon was perfectly tuned and he noticed once again how his little artifices were working smoothly. The keys in the treble register were incredibly light – the slightest touch made the note sound truly. He had glued thin strips of lead below the front of the keys – out of sight – a measure that had reduced the up-weight to less than half an ounce – a third less than was normal. Findlay Lanhire would have been proud. He pulled out the action and, with some fine-grade sandpaper, minutely sanded the hammer-heads on the top two treble octaves. He played his little tune again on these high notes and, seeing it was the last concert of the tour and everything had gone so perfectly in a musical sense, he went through his final checks once more. He knew Kilbarron was finishing tonight's recital with an encore of ferocious difficulty, one of Liszt's Transcendental Etudes, 'Mazeppa'. Brodie had looked at the sheet music with its dense clusters of black notes, like ripe bunches of grapes hanging from the staves. He had tried to play a few bars but had given up – he felt he would need four hands just to manufacture these sounds, let alone play them with any competence or flair. He thought again – maybe that was why Kilbarron was administering a pain-killing injection. He knew what demands would be made on his fingers tonight.

Brodie stayed for the concert as he had done every night of the tour. Kilbarron played Beethoven's Piano Concerto No. 3. Then after the interval he played his party pieces as he called them – *fantaisies* and paraphrases that he had adapted and arranged himself, the better to show off his astonishing technique. Brodie closed his eyes and listened as Kilbarron ended with the Liszt. Flawlessly good, he thought, also noting the Channon's rich sound as it flooded through the large auditorium. Kilbarron bowed deeply, receiving the obligatory standing ovation, thanked the conductor, shook hands with the first violinist and strode off stage. Tour over.

Brodie hurried round to the dressing room and knocked on the door.

It was opened by Lika Blum.

Silence. Consternation. Her smile of welcome.

'Mr Moncur, how lovely to see you. Come in, come in.'

Brodie stepped in, feeling a faint sheen of sweat breaking out on his face already, brain empty. They were in a small oak-panelled sitting room, a little shabby but with dim electric lighting in sconces that hid the shabbiness somewhat. A door led to the dressing room. On a central table was an ice bucket with a champagne bottle and half a dozen glasses. No sign of Kilbarron. Sometimes he dozed after a concert, stretched out on a divan.

'Can you open this for me?' Lika held up the champagne bottle. 'I broke my nail.'

Brodie was glad to busy himself with a simple task.

'I had no idea you were coming,' he said. 'I didn't see you in the audience.'

'I was in a box,' she said. 'All very last minute. I was in Nizza. I mean Nice. Do you know Nice? Full of Russians – and English, of course. But I decided to come up here and escort John back to Paris. I hear it's been a wild success.'

Brodie agreed and summarized the events of the tour as he poured champagne. He and Lika clinked glasses.

'*Za vashe zdrovie*,' she said in Russian.

'*Slangevar*,' he replied in Scottish.

She was wearing black, top to toe. A jet-beaded dress, alive with winking lights, with a little black fur capelet and a five-row collar of pearls around her throat. Her hair was held up by two jewelled ebony combs. Ravishing and vaguely Spanish-looking, he thought ineptly.

'Oh, yes,' she said. 'You must meet César.'

She crossed the room to her bag and returned with a small puppy in her arms. The dog – white with brown patches – blinked at Brodie and licked its chops. It was very small – small as a baby rabbit, he thought.

'John bought him for me,' she said. 'Isn't he adorable?'

'What kind of dog is it?' Brodie said, feigning interest – dogs meant nothing to him. 'The breed, I mean.'

'He's an English dog, called a "Jack Russell". Am I saying that right?'

'Russell – not Roussell.'

'Thank you. I decided to call him César, for some reason. Spontaneously. Nothing to do with César Franck, by the way. John can't stand Franck.'

'It's a good name – for a dog,' Brodie said, lamely. He was pleased to see her put César back in her bag and pick up her champagne glass again.

'Are you planning another tour?' she asked. 'Do you have a cigarette?'

Brodie found his cigarette case in his jacket pocket. She took one and he lit it for her.

'There is talk of another tour – in the summer – yes. Mr Malachi is keen to capitalize on the success of this one. Indeed.' He wondered why he was speaking with such ridiculous formality, like a functionary being interviewed for a superior position. It was a measure of the disturbance going on inside him – he had indigestion also, the champagne burning – this was the effect of being alone with Lika Blum.

But not alone for long. There was a rap on the door and Malachi Kilbarron entered, big-chested and flushed, cigar on the go.

'Talk of the devil,' Lika said. 'I'll go and see how John is getting on.' She flitted into the dressing room, closing the door behind her softly.

'Talking about me, eh?' Malachi said, helping himself to champagne.

'I was just telling Miss Blum how well the tour had gone – and that you were keen on another.'

'Very apposite – because I wanted a private word with you,

young Brodie. So you can whisper in that wily rascal Ainsley Channon's ear with confidence and clarity.'

'Right.'

'We do want another tour. Yes. But not on the same terms. It'll be a hundred guineas. Guineas, mind. Per performance.'

Brodie realized that such an increase would mean the end of the Channon–Kilbarron association but said nothing, other than, 'I'll certainly pass that information along.'

'And talking of information,' Malachi said, stepping closer, 'we have our own. We know how well the piano sales are going – hence our new negotiating position.'

'Then you know more than me,' Brodie said. 'I'm not au fait with sales.'

'And I wouldn't expect you to be,' Malachi said. 'I just want you to let that old buzzard Ainsley know that we are "au fait", as you put it.'

He smiled and turned away as Kilbarron and Lika emerged from the dressing room.

'Ah, Brodie,' John Kilbarron said. 'I thought the old Channon was in fine voice tonight.' He looked tired – just as well the tour was over.

'Impeccable,' Brodie said. 'The "Mazeppa" was stunning.' He knew Kilbarron liked praise. 'I've never heard it better. Never – I swear.'

Kilbarron nodded sagely in agreement. 'Yes . . . Have you had your quiet word with Malachi, here?'

'I have. Fully informed.'

'Excellent. Final task of the evening – will you walk this young lady back to our hotel? Malachi and I have other business to conclude.'

Brodie and Lika opted to return to the hotel by the lakeside. The night was cool and the street lights of the promenade wriggled and shimmied in the still, tideless water as they walked back to the hotel along the quai des Eaux-Vives. Brodie tested various possible conversational openings but none felt right. The sound of their footsteps seemed enough, filling the silence down by the lakeside.

Out over the black water the night appeared vast, immeasurable, he thought, meriting silence. Lika, in any event, was preoccupied with her puppy in her bag, talking to him in Russian. Eventually the dog settled and Lika took Brodie's arm, a gesture that made him feel he might fall over. He remembered something he could say.

'Any luck with your audition?' he asked. He knew she had gone up for Laura in *Luisa Miller* at the Palais des Beaux-Arts in Monte Carlo, hence her presence in Nice.

'Pretty compliments, but I know nothing will happen.'

'Surely not?'

She asked for another cigarette so they paused to light up. As she shifted her bag, concerned her little dog might tumble out, it actually fell to the ground. She managed to grab the puppy but the bag clunked heavily on the pavement. The hard ring of metal.

'Oh dear, I think you've broken something there,' Brodie said. He picked the bag up and handed it to her. Lika took out a small drawstring maroon velvet purse. From it she removed a tiny pistol – two short barrels, no more than three inches long, one set above the other, and a curved mother-of-pearl handle, like a baby goat's horn.

'It's my hotel-gun – at least that's what John calls it. He gave it to me.' She handed it to him. It was small but surprisingly heavy – its weight seemed to confirm its lethal potential. He gave it back and she put it away. They resumed lighting their cigarettes.

'Why would he give you a gun?' he asked.

'For when I'm on tour alone, to protect myself. In case someone tries to rob me, or breaks down my door and tries to ravish me.'

'Is it loaded?'

'Of course. Two barrels, two bullets, two triggers. It's called a Derringer.'

She put her cigarette in her mouth and resettled her puppy in the bag, then puffed smoke into the night sky. They resumed their promenade.

'I know it's very bad manners for a young lady to smoke in the street,' she said. 'But I don't think I'll be recognized, somehow.'

'You were saying: why will nothing happen?' Brodie felt the warmth of her palm in his elbow crook. 'You have a wonderful voice,' he added gallantly.

'Because I'm too tall to be an opera singer, so they tell me. All the tenors are short and they don't want a tall soprano standing beside them, making them look small.'

'But that's ridiculous, Miss Blum,' Brodie protested.

'You must call me Lika, Brodie – but only when we're alone, if you don't mind. I don't think John would approve of such familiarity.'

'Thank you . . . Lika.' It was wonderful to say her name out loud. 'As I was saying, Lika, that's preposterous. What has a person's height to do with the quality of their voice? It's like saying no one with a beard can play the piano.'

'Ah, but you talk as a tall man, Brodie. If you were a little, short, vain tenor you would think differently. You're taller than me so you don't see it as an issue. The little tenor doesn't want to stand beside a Russian giantess.'

They both had to laugh at this. Brodie felt a level of happiness invade him that he thought he had never experienced before. To be walking with this mesmerizing, beautiful woman – this tall woman – arm in arm, beside the lake in Geneva, talking as equals, as friends. He felt tears smart in his eyes.

'If only you were a tenor, Brodie,' she said. 'Then we could sing together.'

They had arrived at the Hôtel de l'Europe. Lika threw away her half-smoked cigarette and they separated, walking inside together, greeting the doorman, who doffed his hat, familiarly.

Brodie lay in his bed, an hour later, the lights switched off, thinking about Lydia Blum. Lika Blum. Lika. What was she doing consorting with someone like Kilbarron? Did she think it would help her career, he thought, unkindly? And then he rebuked himself. Who knew what attracted one person to another. It was a mystery, something entirely individual and personal. What had attracted his mother to Malky Moncur? Maybe there were aspects of John Kilbarron that he would only reveal to a lover. The ignorant spectator's guesses were futile and irrelevant. Love, mutual attraction, sexual obsession were all fundamentally personal, utterly private evocations of an individual's desires and innermost longings. He should know that. Look how he desired Lika Blum, already, a woman he'd met only three times . . .

He imagined her naked. He imagined himself in bed with Lika, naked, entering her, staring down at that face surrounded by its unruly blonde hair. Those lips. Those hooded, sleepy eyes.

He reached down and touched himself. Gripped himself. He looked at the ceiling then closed his eyes and thought of Lika.

8

Ainsley Channon had cut off most of his Dundreary whiskers and appeared ten years younger, Brodie thought. With that great spread of grizzled beard gone the features of his face were properly revealed and one could see that father and son did actually resemble each other, to a significant degree. The comparison was made all the easier as they were sitting beside each other – opposite him across Calder's vast desk.

'No, it's an unequivocal, not to say raging, success,' Ainsley said, beaming. 'And we won't forget it was your idea, Brodie. No, no. Brodie's Smart Idea . . .' He looked at papers in front of him. 'Sales compared to last year are up two hundred and seventy-eight per cent. We're actually thinking of opening a branch of Channon in Vienna. Take the battle to Steinway and Bösendorfer on their own ground. Why not? If we can do it in Paris—'

'We're only thinking about it,' Calder interjected coldly. 'Nothing's been decided.'

Ainsley continued, regardless. 'We've had approaches from Door and Julius, and others. They all want to play Channons.'

'Aye. For cartloads of money!' Calder scoffed.

Ainsley ignored him. 'It couldn't have gone better, Brodie. *Bravissimo*.'

'Thank you,' Brodie said. 'My other news is that the Kilbarrons are looking to do another tour as soon as possible. Ten cities, maybe twenty concerts.'

Calder gave an incredulous, screeching laugh.

Ainsley nodded his head, judiciously. 'Mr Kilbarron is free to play as many concerts as he wishes, wherever he wishes. The fact is . . .' he blinked a few times. 'The astonishing fact is that if we contract with the likes of Julius, Door and Stimmer and whoever else, then the services of John Kilbarron are no longer really required. He's rather . . . What's the French phrase?'

'*Passé*,' Calder said. '*Fini*.'

'No. *Vieux jeu* was the one I was thinking of. How would you translate that, Brodie? Colloquially.'

'Old hat.'

'Exactly. John Kilbarron is now rather old hat.'

Brodie felt the familiar shawl of foreboding envelop him. He interlocked the fingers of both hands and leaned forward, as though almost at prayer, to emphasize his seriousness.

'The thing is, I had a conversation with Malachi Kilbarron – he's the financial, manager-figure, as you know. What he says is more important than John Kilbarron's opinions. He said he would be happy to continue the association with Channon – on condition the concert fee is raised.'

'Oh, would he indeed?' Calder said, indignation colouring his plump features.

'To a hundred guineas. He insisted on guineas.'

Ainsley smiled, sadly. 'Now *that* is what I call killing the golden goose. Do you mind how we talked about that, Brodie? We were worried about it and now Kilbarron has put the knife to his own throat.'

He stood and went in search of a decanter of brandy and poured three glasses. He toasted Brodie.

'It was a brilliant stroke, Brodie. Well done. Costly – but it paid off, royally. You watch the other piano manufacturers – they'll be running to catch up . . .' He looked thoughtful for a moment. 'Calder and I want to recognize your contribution. We want to create a new department in the company that you will lead. You will continue your efforts – recruiting piano virtuosi who will play Channon pianos. You'll run the whole show – supervise the tours, shipping, the travel arrangements – and all the tuning required, of course.' He paused. 'And you will benefit financially, of course.'

Brodie smiled back as though in perfect accord, noting that the precise financial benefits of running this new department were not actually mentioned. He saw his life changing in a way he'd never envisaged and he wasn't sure if it was the best turn in his fortunes.

'What do I say to Malachi Kilbarron?' he asked, casually.

Ainsley frowned and scratched his new trim sideburns, thinking. Then said, firmly, 'It's very simple. He can stay on at the same rate for another six months. Take it or leave it. It wouldn't be seemly to dispose of him too abruptly. Then it's over.'

Calder reached for the decanter. 'And you can tell Malachi Kilbarron to put that in his pipe and smoke it.'

Brodie kept his distance from the Kilbarrons for a week until a note was delivered to the Channon showroom asking him to come and tune the piano in the Saint-Germain apartment. He could hardly refuse.

John Kilbarron answered the door himself. He looked somewhat unkempt, even by his standards. He had a small, scabbed sore on a corner of his lower lip; he needed a shave and had one of his thin cigars in his hand. But he seemed pleased to see Brodie and confirmed that there was no other motive than to get the wretched piano properly tuned.

'I know, I know,' he said. 'You've been telling me for months that it's horribly out of tune. But I need it now – I'm trying to write something ambitious, damn my eyes. And I can hear how off it is.'

He showed Brodie into the drawing room and Brodie set his Gladstone bag down, opened the piano and went to work. At lunchtime the dozy manservant said a meal was to be served in the dining room. Brodie went through to find only one place set. Where was Lika? Or Kilbarron, come to that? He was provided with a bowl of cauliflower soup and a mushroom omelette. He declined the offer of wine.

It took him another two hours after lunch to finish the tuning. He slid the action back into the piano and played his usual Scottish folk song several times in different keys, listening hard for the hammer strikes and the dampers working properly.

He felt a hand come to rest softly on his shoulder and turned to find Lika standing there, a tear running down one cheek, wordless.

Brodie jumped to his feet. 'Lika! My God, is everything all right?'

'That music. That tune . . .' she said, wonderingly. 'What is it? I heard it. I was standing in the doorway, listening – and it made me cry. Look.' She wiped her tears away, smiling. 'How strange. It was like an instinct, a reflex. I heard you playing and the next thing I knew my eyes were full of tears.'

Brodie explained. 'It's a folk song from Scotland. My mother used to sing it to me when I was young. I've changed it a bit – but I use it when I'm tuning. At the end, you know, just to see if everything is fine. If the piano's ready.'

'But it's beautiful. Play it again, will you?'

'Of course.'

Brodie sat down and played the song through, all two minutes of it.

'What's it called?'

'It's called "My Bonny Boy".' He said the title in English and translated it. *Mon beau garçon*. 'There are words to the song – just three verses.'

Lika frowned. 'It's most extraordinary. There's one bit of it – one transition. Is it a key change? It makes me want to cry, instantly. How can that happen?'

Then they heard the front door open and Kilbarron appeared, having handed his hat and coat to the manservant.

'Well, hello, hello,' he said. 'All done, Master Brodie?' He looked at Lika. 'Are you well, my sweet?'

Lika, in some excitement, explained about the effect Brodie's folk song had had on her. A completely new, unheard piece of music that seemed to provoke a direct attack on her tear ducts.

'Good Lord above. What miraculous music is that?'

Brodie recounted the story once more. 'It's just an old Scottish folk song that I've adapted,' he added. Kilbarron was intrigued and asked him to play it again. So Brodie sat down at the piano and ran through the song once more, Kilbarron listening intently.

'See! There!' Lika exclaimed. 'That moment, those few bars. Don't you feel it? So much emotion.'

'I do – in a way,' Kilbarron said and asked Brodie to play it again.

'Yes,' he said when Brodie had finished. 'It's very simple but effective. An interrupted cadence on a rising scale – accented passing notes. Play it again if you will, Brodie, old man.'

Brodie did so.

'You expect the tonic, you see. Every instinct is telling you which way the music will go,' Kilbarron said, almost to himself. 'But it's unresolved – that's where the emotion springs from.' He smiled. 'An old trick. But old tricks are the best.'

He budged Brodie away from the piano and sat down at the stool and played the song himself.

'See?' he said to Lika. 'Rising sevenths, falling fourths – suspensions, passing notes . . . There! A falling sixth, a rising ninth.' He took his hands off the keys. 'G flat major to D flat major then – this is what you don't expect – D flat minor ninth. The unexpected chord . . .'

He played the three chords and seemed untypically thoughtful, suddenly.

'An old folk song, you say,' Kilbarron stood and moved away from the piano.

'It's as much an act of memory,' Brodie said. 'I've fiddled around with it so much over the years. I suppose I've invented half of it. I needed more range . . . My mother used to sing it to me – but she died when I was thirteen. So . . .'

Kilbarron stood by the fireplace, frowning. 'Still, very effective. Nice little melody, also. That's important – then you can fiddle around with it, as you say.' He opened a silver box and took out a cigarillo and lit it. 'D'you know who wrote it?'

'Traditional. Nobody knows. Somebody wrote words to the old tune and it entered the folk-song repertoire. I remembered the tune and so I took it and made some—'

'We have the same kind of songs in Ireland,' Kilbarron said. 'These Celtic songs use the same tricks. You expect a tonic resolution but it's held back in various ways, deliberately unresolved. The unexpected chord,' he repeated. He pointed his cigarillo at Lika. 'But it made you want to cry. Astonishing. All very visceral and nothing to do with the intellect – which is where the tear ducts come into play.'

Brodie stepped forward, closed the piano and gave it a pat. 'Well, it's in fine tune. And about time.'

'I'm very grateful,' Kilbarron said, vaguely – his mind seemed to be on other matters. 'Charge it to Channon *père et fils*.'

9

Brodie wandered into the workshop and hung his boater on the hook to the side of his desk. He blew his nose for the hundredth time that day. He had a chest cold that seemed unusually tenacious. It was warm, the sun was shining and he had a cold. He was returning from the Saint-Cloud warehouse where he'd been helping Karl-Heinz Nagel select a piano. Nagel was now the third virtuoso to be signed up by Channon since the arrival of John Kilbarron – Ernst Sauter had been the second (having suddenly changed his mind) – and after Kilbarron and Sauter now Nagel was joining the team. Others were interested but Nagel was a real coup. And the others would follow, now.

Nagel was a small grey-haired man in his fifties, charming and reserved, and he had seemed very happy with the piano that Brodie had steered him towards. He had also insisted that Brodie accompany him on tour. He had grand ambitions – a sequence of German and Scandinavian cities in 1898 and then a whole series of concerts in Berlin for the turn of the century. Brodie had kept his affirmation very vague. Everyone now under contract to Channon wanted him to tune their new pianos, as if he were some sort of accessory that came with the instrument – like a stool or a music stand.

Brodie lit a cigarette and felt his life disappearing under an avalanche of work. Simply co-ordinating these dozens of concerts and recitals was more than enough for one man; but then there was the crating, the shipping, the administration, the training of new tuners to his own exacting standards . . . It was going to be impossible, he now saw, and Ainsley had raised his salary by five pounds a month. It wasn't enough, in fact it was—

Dmitri knocked on the door frame.

'Somebody to see you out front,' he said. Dmitri now worked three days a week as a junior manager for Channon as well. Brodie stubbed out his cigarette and strolled through to the showroom.

Lika Blum stood there looking at a Channon Phoenix covered in tortoiseshell inlays. She had her little dog with her on a lead. What was it called? Brodie felt that inner somersault of gut-spasm, the heart-swell.

'Lika,' he said, smiling blandly. 'Good afternoon. How lovely to see you. What can I do for you?'

She came over to him tugging her little dog behind her.

'Brodie – is there a café or a tea room near here? I need your advice.'

La Loge des Dames Légendaires was a small tea room a fifty-yard walk down the avenue de l'Alma at the corner of the rue Pierre Charron. There was glass everywhere. It was panelled in smoked glass and the metal tables had glass tops. A huge Venetian glass chandelier dominated the small salon. It felt a very fragile place – you entered it with care, Brodie thought, feeling large and clumsy – and it boasted that it served over a hundred varieties of teas, tisanes and infusions.

Brodie and Lika found a table with a view of the street. A child was running up and down the pavement spinning a metal hoop with a stick that made a rather irritating, grating noise. Brodie drew the muslin curtain to obscure it. He blew his nose.

'Apologies,' he said. 'I've a chest cold. A hot tea is just the thing.'

They ordered their teas – a rose-petal infusion for Lika; a Darjeeling with honey for Brodie – and a plate of pastries. Lika was wearing a severe charcoal-grey suit with a tight skirt that came down to her ankle boots. It had bottle-green lapels and many silver buttons and looked vaguely Germanic, militaristic. Her straw hat had a matching green feather in its band. As usual he thought she looked almost unbearably beautiful as she talked – perhaps because she was so animated, he wondered: there was clearly something on her mind and he was touched as well as pleased that she had come to him for advice.

Their teas and pastries arrived. She ate a tiny chocolate éclair, the size of her little finger; he said he wasn't hungry and sipped his soothing, honeyed tea, feeling its sweet warmth spread through his chest, easing the constriction. He began to sense an unusual relaxation, sitting there, seeming to lose all sense of himself as a person with needs, bodily functions and a demanding job to be done. He would happily have stayed in this tea room with Lika forever.

'. . . because, you see, I think you can help me, Brodie,' she was saying.

'What? Yes, anything.'

She explained: she was going for an audition for an oratorio in English. Handel's *The Triumph of Time and Truth*. She was up for the role of 'Truth'.

'It's more of a mezzo-soprano but John says I can do it easily. In fact I sing mezzo roles all the time.'

'I don't think I know it,' Brodie said. 'The *Messiah*, yes, of course, *Alexander's Feast*. But this is—'

'I thought it would be good to sing something in English for them. For the audition.'

'Excellent idea.'

'So I thought of your Scottish folk song.'

'Yes . . . Yes, it might be perfect. It's very short, easy to learn.'

'Exactly,' she said, then added in English, 'for my English is not so good. Approximately.'

'It's a very simple song. You can do it, easily.'

'Do you know the words?'

'Yes, I think I can remember them. Three verses. My mother sang this song to me all the time.'

'Can you write them down for me?'

'Of course.'

'Then we can practise together – I can be word-perfect.'

Brodie said yes to every proposal. Lika set a date for the rehearsal – Thursday afternoon.

'I'll be there.'

'And the music?' Lika asked. 'Can you transcribe that? So I can give something to the accompanist.'

'I'll jot something down. We'll run through it.'

'And if I could make them cry, Brodie. Do you see? Melt their hearts. And they'd have to give me the role . . .'

'Ah-ha! Very cunning. I see your plan.'

They chatted on – Lika bemoaning the impossibilities, the endless difficulties of her chosen career, wondering if there was any way of disguising her height. Brodie listened and made the odd remark, entranced, looking at her face as she expostulated and gestured across from him. Was it the lips or was it the eyes? Or was it some more subtle equation of the face? The distance between eyes equalling distance between nose and top lip. Or the precise setting of the lips between nose and chin . . . How did such fascination occur? One saw a thousand women's faces in a month, say. Why was your eye – your heart, your loins – enthralled by just one?

It was an unusually warm day, even for early summer, Brodie thought, wishing he'd worn a lighter suit. He felt he was perspiring and worried that he'd smell of sweat. The streets of Paris were pungent with horse shit decomposing in the hot sun. Every crossing meant parting a way between thousands of hovering black flies. He thought of hot summer weather in all the large cities of Europe with their hundreds of thousands of horses defecating in the streets. A Sargasso of shit. It was a relief to step through the doors of the Kilbarron *hôtel* and find oneself in the quiet courtyard. As he crossed the gravel parterre to the front door he checked again that he had his music with him.

Lika opened the door, a virginal vision in white cotton and lace. White billowy blouse, a lace shawl, a wide cream flannel skirt, her hair tied up loosely. For the first time Brodie really took in the Russian woman in her.

'So hot!' she said. 'I've made some lemonade.'

They went into the drawing room where the glass doors were open to the small garden so they could hear the sound of the Cupid fountain plashing. There was a jug of lemonade and a dish of sweet biscuits set out on a round table and Lika poured them each a glass. Brodie asked where John Kilbarron was.

'He's gone to Dublin with Malachi – some family business about a house – he'll be back next week. Oh, yes, they both want to talk to you about the new tour. They're full of plans.'

Brodie munched on a biscuit to suppress the sudden shiver of worry he was experiencing. 'Full of plans . . .' He had no idea at all how he was going to deal with John Kilbarron, let alone his sinister thug of a brother. Concentrate on the here and now, he told himself. He took out his sheaf of papers – the words of the song and the simple melody he had written down on a sheet of manuscript paper – a melody simple enough to be picked out by one hand but there was enough there for any tolerable pianist to work out a left-hand accompaniment. He handed the words of the song to Lika and she read them out slowly in her heavily Russian-accented English. It sounded both strange and enchanting to Brodie – his country's folk culture rendered through the lens of another.

'My Bonny Boy' (trad.)
Arranged by Brodie Moncur

My bonny boy has gone tae sleep
He dreams of worlds he cannae know,
I watch him and I want tae weep –
He has a journey far to go.

My bonny lad has gone tae sleep
Our bairns are sleeping too.
We live our lives and try to keep
Our bearings as we journey through.

My bonny man has gone tae sleep,
His journey o'er – he's heard the call.
Birth tae death is the shortest leap,
The grave is waiting for one and all.

He explained the Scottish dialect words – bonny, tae, cannae, bairns. He had memories of his mother singing the song but they were imprecise – he had written down the words as best he remembered. No doubt there were some lines of his own composition – just like the melody. The crucial melodic change – the unexpected chord, as Kilbarron called it – took place between lines three and four in each verse. This was the transition that had brought tears to Lika's eyes.

'Shall we give it a go?' he said.

She took her position by his side, standing, one hand resting on the piano, the other holding the lyrics, and together, slowly, he played through the song and she sang the three verses. Her voice was very soft, he remarked to himself again, pure but with no projection – fine for the drawing room but inadequate for a theatre of any size. He wondered if those impresarios who said she was too tall to be an opera singer were simply being kind.

After three goes she seemed to lose confidence.

'Perhaps it's not such a good idea,' she said. 'My English is so bad and I can hear my accent. So Russki.'

'Nonsense,' he said. 'You just need to practise it more. We can do it together any time. You tell me when.'

She sat down beside him on the wide piano stool and picked out the melody with her right hand.

'Yes, it's that bit here,' she said. 'That change. Lines three and four.'

'What did John say? You expect a kind of affirmation—'

'The tonic.'

'And you get that different chord. The unexpected chord. D flat minor ninth.'

He played D flat major then the D flat minor ninth.

'That's what makes it sad,' she said. 'And that's why you get tears in your eyes.'

'And it's a sad story, I suppose. But true. Sadly true.'

'Life is sad,' she said, softly, thinking. 'And complicated.'

He could feel a warmth on his left-hand side, where she was sitting, an inch away from him, as if some sort of force – electric, magnetic – was emanating from her, like these X-rays he'd read about. He had never been so close to her for so long, except for that walk along the lake that night in Geneva when she had taken his arm and he had felt the heat of her palm in his elbow crook.

'Take your spectacles off, Brodie.'

'What? Why?'

'I want to see what your face is like without them.'

He slipped his spectacles off, feeling his throat contract. He swallowed.

'You're just a blur,' he said.

'Close your eyes.'

He did. And then he felt her face press gently up against his. Like the palm of a hand set softly on a cheek. Very deliberate but soft. A coming-together of two faces. Her nose was next to his nose, on the left; he could feel her eyelashes batting on his; her chin touching his chin. And her lips were on his lips, touching.

He froze, not breathing. It was just contact – the ultimate proximity. And everything about that ultimate proximity was possible, implicit. The unfolding, tactile moment seemed unending, blissful.

How long did they stay like that, face to face, lips to lips, he wondered later? Ten seconds? Twenty? He could hear her breathing in and exhaling, levelly, calmly, and of course the softness of her full lips was a constant small pressure on his own. Then she pouted slightly – lips tightening – and he responded. The pressure increased. He breathed in deeply. Then he felt the tip of her tongue probe. He opened his mouth and the kiss was conceived and fully executed. Her arms went round his neck and he slipped his free arm round her waist to pull her to him.

They broke apart and he put on his spectacles. She was in focus again, smiling, lovely, lips shining.

'Did you like that?' she asked.

'Yes, very much.'

'It's my invention. I call it the Lika-kiss.'

'Well, it's a pretty damned amazing damn invention. I would say. Yes.'

She reached for his hand and stood up.

'Shall we go upstairs?'

Brodie decided to walk home after his three hours in bed with Lika Blum. Dusk was gathering as he walked along the boulevard Saint-Germain and turned to cross the Seine on the Pont de Sully. He walked like an automaton, a slight smile on his face, bemused, exultant, astonished at what had come to pass. He stopped in the middle of the bridge, deliberately, to collect his thoughts, looking downstream to Notre-Dame then upstream towards the Pont d'Austerlitz and the Jardin des Plantes.

But he saw nothing of Paris – only images of Lika. Her thick curly hair down and unrestrained; her small heavy breasts with near-invisible pink nipples. Her long limber body squirming beneath him. The way she grabbed her knees and pulled them towards her so he could go deeper. How she slipped out of bed and walked across the room to find his cigarette case and lighter in his jacket on the floor and stood there, naked, one haunch cocked, clicking the recalcitrant lighter – *click, click, click* – until it caught.

Later she went downstairs to fetch a bottle of wine and they drank, smoked and talked until they became aroused again. Lika bit his shoulder, not so gently, as he orgasmed. Then they lay in bed as the afternoon sun squeezed through the gap in the curtains and sent its vertical bar of horizontal gold on a slow clockwise patrol of the wall beside them. He didn't ask any questions. Where were the servants? Had this been planned? How long had she known that Kilbarron would be away? Stay with these precious moments, he told himself as he stood on the bridge over the Seine as the dusky light thickened. Store them away in your memory's treasure house. It was entirely possible, he realized, that they may never happen again.

10

'Think of it this way,' Brodie said to Malachi Kilbarron, in as convincing a tone of voice as he could muster. 'You're a victim of your own success.'

They were sitting in the office of Thibault Dieulafoy, the firm's accountant, who happened to be away visiting his aged mother in Vichy. Brodie sat in Dieulafoy's chair behind the desk, a desk that was immaculately tidy. Three paper knives parallel with the desk edge; a rectangle of blotting paper in its leather border, virgin white; steel-nibbed pens ranked like soldiers on parade; a glass inkwell, empty and gleaming. Brodie did not dare touch a thing.

Malachi took in Brodie's last statement and frowned. Then he stood and went to the three wooden filing cabinets against the wall, testing their top drawers, as though absent-mindedly. They were all locked tight.

'There you have it,' Malachi said, in his rasping, hoarse-sounding voice. 'The thing is, Brodie, me old china, that I don't want to be the *victim* of my success – I want to be the beneficiary. What's the point of success, otherwise? That's how the world works: you're a success and you benefit thereby.'

'The trouble is you're too successful for us, now.' Brodie persisted, feeling weak. 'We can't afford you.'

'But you're successful, also. As successful as we are. You've sold hundreds of pianos. Hundreds since the tour began in February. Two hundred and twenty-three grand pianos, to be precise.'

'How do you know that?'

'I just happen to know, Mr Moncur. The point is we want to continue this . . . this story of success. Another tour: forty concerts in ten cities. We will all emerge winners, don't you see?'

'There is another problem – a direct consequence of your success – in that we have now contracted with three other pianists.

All playing Channons, all with long tours in mind – but not at the rates you're demanding.'

'So, you're saying that we, the Kilbarrons, the instigators of this lucrative scheme, should be penalized for making Channon all this money?'

'One firm cannot bear this large burden.'

'I could take you to court.'

Brodie closed his eyes for a moment. This was going as badly as he feared. He sensed Malachi's growing animus.

'Mr Kilbarron,' he said. 'This is a business. We have a contract. I suggest you look closely at our contract with you. There is a clause in it that states everything is renewable, or not, after six months. We are within our rights. Litigation would be pointless, costly and, ultimately, the worse for you and your brother.'

Malachi sat down again opposite him and, unthinkingly, reached for one of Monsieur Dieulafoy's paper knives that he then twiddled in his fingers as he pondered. Brodie thought: he is capable of stabbing me with that knife.

'We will gladly renew your contract for six months on the old terms. That's the best I can do,' Brodie said.

'That is unacceptable.'

'Well, then . . .'

'What are you saying?' Malachi asked quietly.

'If you refuse, then our contract is terminated. You have been paid in full. Well paid. You may keep the piano. Gratis.'

'You are a horrible Scottish bastard of a whoreson cunt.'

'There's no need for that, Mr Kilbarron.'

'After everything we've done for you.'

'It was a business arrangement. Not a favour.'

'You travelled with us, Moncur. For weeks, months. We were a team. We counted on you. You saw the notices, the adulation. We made the name of Channon in Europe.'

'I hope you realize that, at the end of the day, it's not my personal decision.' Brodie had a sudden urge to defecate – this was getting very much out of control.

Malachi put the paper knife down.

'You'll regret this, you and your Scottish cunting usurers.'

'Accept the old contract, Mr Kilbarron,' Brodie almost pleaded. 'You'll have another six months. It's very generous. It's a lot of money.'

'Hell will freeze over before I do that.'

Then he spat at Brodie. A gobbet of phlegm hit the left lapel of his jacket, like a soft badge. Malachi Kilbarron walked out.

Brodie tore a strip off Monsieur Dieulafoy's virgin blotter and removed Malachi's parting gesture. He felt unmanned, trembly, almost tearful.

The rear door of the office opened and Calder Channon appeared.

'How did that go?' he said. 'Is he clear of the shop yet?'

Brodie sat in the small glassed-walled cubbyhole that was his office in the workshop, the electric light off, happy to be in the gloom, smoking a Margarita, calming down. That had been possibly the most unpleasant half-hour of his life – and he felt anger building. Why hadn't Calder dealt with Malachi Kilbarron? He was the damn bloody manager – and it had been his father who had signed the contract, not him, Brodie Moncur, the company scapegoat.

There were other concerns nudging into his mind, personal concerns. This bitter rift with the Kilbarron brothers might make it impossible for him to be with Lika again, he realized. He hadn't seen her since that unforgettable afternoon . . . He tapped ash off his cigarette into the ashtray. Perhaps he should write to her. He made a mental effort and called her to mind, called to mind the intimate details of that afternoon, trying to remember everything, what they had said and done, her naked body. Yes, he would write to her and explain what had occurred, how it was not his fault. He drew on his cigarette and coughed harshly. That cold had never properly left him. He reached for his pen.

It was a sensation of drowning – he thought later – as he felt his throat fill with fluid and then his mouth. His lips parted and he sensed the gush of vomit burst out. Except it wasn't vomit – it was dark blood, splashing on his desk and the books ranked on the far side against the wall. Like a breakwater against the blood-tide. A break-blood against . . .

He stood and reeled back. Blood dripped from his chin onto the floor. He saw a slowly spreading puddle of his blood pool on his desktop and ease over the sides, pattering. He staggered and fell to the ground feeling another wave coming, cascading out of his mouth, this time wetting the floorboards and the square of carpet that lay there. A huge whooshing, uncontrolled surge. He was on all fours now, spitting, his mouth rank with the salty, metal taste of his blood. Stay calm, he told himself. Some kind of brutal vomiting, an ulcer, something he'd eaten poisoning his innards, rotting them. He spat again.

Jesus. Bloody hell . . . he sensed it had passed, this fit, this seizure. He clambered to his feet, using the back of his chair as a support. So much blood. He was breathing fast, like a man who'd run a mile. He felt sweat pouring from him, his face slick, his armpits a swamp. Jesus Christ, what's happening? He went to a wicker basket where they kept yards of cotton waste and threw the thick shreds of cloth on the floor and the desk in an attempt to mop up all the awful gleaming redness that was congealing there. He felt light-headed, terrified. What if it happened again? He should go to a doctor, take a day or two off. He was being worked too hard – like a dog, like a slave – and there was all the terrible tension associated with terminating the Kilbarron contract. It wasn't fair.

II

Dr Maisonfort frowned, looking at Brodie's dossier, and the few pages of notes it contained. He was a small bald man with pince-nez spectacles.

'No, it's certain, I'm sorry to have to tell you – but you have developed tuberculosis.'

Brodie sat in his dressing gown and pyjamas, his chair facing the doctor across his desk, feeling his body shrink, as if he had suddenly become a smaller person.

'Am I going to die?' he said.

Dr Maisonfort laughed airily. 'We're all going to die, Monsieur Moncur – we just don't know where, when or how. You speak excellent French, by the way. The accent is charming.'

'Thank you. Let me put it this way – am I going to die soon?'

'No, no, absolutely not. No, no, no. We have many cures.'

Brodie felt his body regain its natural size. His sphincter eased and he farted, silently.

'It was a terrible shock,' he said. 'So much blood. Like a fountain.'

'Yes, haemoptysis, we call it – it can be quite spectacular.'

Dr Maisonfort explained, though Brodie sometimes thought he wasn't entirely sure of his own diagnosis.

'You have this tubercle in your lung. Possibly several. Think of it like a small abscess growing slowly, and, as it grows, filling with necrotic cells.'

'What're they?'

'Dead cells. Caseatic cells is the precise name. Slowly, they—'

'Caseatic?'

'Like "cheese", so to speak. The dead tissue looks like a kind of crumbly cream cheese. The caseation reaches the artery branch, "consumes" it, erodes it – hence the haemorrhage you suffered.'

'I have a tubercle?'

'In fact you may have more than one, quite conceivably.'

'Have I?'

'I think so. Anyway, slowly they begin to consume the lung tissue. Your lung capacity diminishes. Which is why the disease is sometimes called "consumption".'

'But why all the blood?'

'The tubercle has grown and reached a branch of the pulmonary artery – or a vein in the lung. It ruptures. And the haemorrhage occurs and fills the cavity. It has to exit, to overflow, if I may put it like that. It can be very distressing. It depends on how large the vein or the branch is and the aneurism that has formed, and the pressure of the blood, of course. There is some evidence that a sudden increase in pressure provokes the rupture.'

Brodie thought: the meeting with Malachi. The tension; the pressure.

'What causes it? Tuberculosis, I mean.'

'There are new theories. It's a bacteria, we think, a microbe that lodges in the lungs or other parts of the body. The gut, the spine, the brain. I think it's better for you that it's in the lungs.'

Brodie half-listened, not very reassured. He was twenty-seven years old and, despite the shock of the haemorrhage, his crucial death-question having been answered – 'No, no, absolutely not' – put an end to the subject as far as he was concerned. The tuberculosis diagnosis was a setback, an inconvenience, but he felt reassured: it was simply a matter of time, and whatever medication was required, before he felt his old self again, surely.

A porter led him back to his room. He was in the Maison Municipale de Santé in the rue du Faubourg Saint Denis in the third arrondissement. It was now ten days since his attack. It had been Dmitri who had found him lying unconscious on the floor of his blood-hosed office – whence he'd been rushed by cab to the hospital. For some days he felt feverish and an incredible sense of weakness and had been strictly enjoined not to leave his bed – bedpans and chamber pots ensuring that he stayed put. His diet was heavily milk-based: either a kind of porridge or rice cooked in milk, or fish cooked in milk – then milk puddings, milk jellies and blancmanges. He was beginning to crave red meat – which he took to be a positive sign.

He had had many visitors. All his pianists from the shop – Dmitri came every day – and even Calder had passed by for ten minutes, pointedly mentioning that they had been obliged to employ a specialist cleaning service to remove the bloodstains from the floorboards of his office. While he lay in bed waiting for visitors, Brodie read newspapers. He read about the continuing animosities of the Dreyfus Affair, the celebrations being organized around Queen Victoria's Diamond Jubilee, the economic tribulations facing President McKinley, and a review of a shocking new novel called *Dracula*. He slept a lot, ate his three milky meals a day and wrote letters. After the first week the visits diminished, though Benoît, the office boy, was sent round every day to see if there was anything he required. Dmitri seemed to have all the impending touring business under control. And, as he began to feel better, stronger, his thoughts turned to Lika.

He gave Benoît a note for her – saying that he was in hospital – and precise instructions. Benoît was to wait outside the Saint-Germain *hôtel* and hand the note to Lika but only when she was alone. Brodie made him repeat the instruction and then repeat it again. Benoît protested: I'm not stupid, sir. But Brodie wanted to minimize the risk of interception absolutely and was taking no chances. A day later Benoît reported that the note had been delivered and that the mademoiselle had been entirely alone apart from a little dog. Brodie relaxed somewhat; at least now Lika knew where he was and what had happened. He fantasized about her visiting his bedside. Perhaps she might slip her hand under the sheet and . . .

The shock was all his, however, when – three days after Benoît had delivered the note – unannounced, John Kilbarron knocked on his door and sauntered in. Lika followed a second later, making alarming faces and incomprehensible gestures behind Kilbarron's back.

Wooden folding seats were unfolded and they sat by his bedside. Brodie buttoned the top button of his pyjama jacket.

'So, what the hell's wrong with you?' Kilbarron asked, cheerfully.

'They think an ulcer, some sort of rupturing,' Brodie lied. For some reason he didn't want Kilbarron to know the real diagnosis – he would tell Lika himself at the right moment.

'Spitting blood?'

'Yes. Quite a deal of blood. All very disturbing.' He glanced at Lika, hearing a kind of panicked keening whistle in his head. It was difficult having her here in his room with Kilbarron – he couldn't help remembering the last time they had been together.

'You know we've sacked Channon,' Kilbarron said. 'We're having nothing more to do with your cheapskate firm.'

'I didn't know, in fact,' Brodie said. 'I'm sorry to hear that. I thought we had a very good—'

'We're negotiating with Pate and Bösendorfer for the next tour.'

'As I said to your brother—'

'He sends his best wishes.' Kilbarron leaned forward, as if confidentially. 'We've nothing against you, young Brodie. You've always been fair and square.'

'Thank you.'

'And I may be calling on you, privately, like, on piano business. Can you tune me a Pate or a Bösendorfer like you did the Channon?'

'Of course. Any piano in the world.'

'It's a rare gift – lucky you. Is one allowed to smoke a cigarette in here?'

'Yes. Please have one of mine.'

Kilbarron took Brodie's cigarette case from the bedside-table drawer and lit it. While he was engaged Brodie and Lika stared at each other, eyes full of messages. Lika pouted, blew him a kiss, and Brodie thought he might faint.

Kilbarron exhaled smoke at the ceiling.

'You know all my little foibles, you see. And they will remain something entirely between the two of us, young Brodie, on the quiet, like. Understand? No need to let those bastard Channons know.'

'I understand, Mr Kilbarron. Anything I can do to help.'

He stood and patted Brodie on the shoulder.

'Hurry up and get well, now.'

Lika stepped forward and they shook hands.

'Very happy to see you making such a good recovery, Mr Moncur.'

'Thank you, Miss Blum.'

He slipped the note she had palmed him under the sheet. She followed Kilbarron out and, as she left the room, she turned to him and smiled. Conspirators again.

My dear Brodie,

I think of you all the time but if you wish to contact me be very careful. Write to me at Poste Restante, Paris VI, and please don't send any more messages to the Saint-Germain apartment. We will meet soon.

With all my friendship,
Lika Blum

Brodie lay back against his pillows, tears in his eyes. Tears of gratitude, he thought. He was in love and his love was being reciprocated. Maybe that was enough? Maybe one couldn't ask for more in an individual life. Simply to know that Lika was in the world and that she thought fondly of him and wanted to see him . . . He folded the note carefully and slipped it between the pages of his copy of Algernon Swinburne's *Poems and Ballads*, a gift from Lady Dalcastle.

Dr Maisonfort studied him through his pince-nez spectacles. Brodie stood – dressed in his suit, shirt and tie – in his consulting room. Dr Maisonfort left his chair and circled Brodie twice.

'Do you know you have lost more than four kilos of weight? You look very thin.'

'I feel not too bad.'

'And there lies the danger, sir. You feel "not too bad"; you feel you can return to your old life, your old habits. No, no – not with tuberculosis. In your case I recommend at least six months of convalescence. At least. You're young, you're strong. If you were a man in your forties I would advise a year or more.'

'Right.'

'To try and return to your normal life – now, after such a big haemorrhage, would be very, very dangerous. Suicide.'

'Perhaps I could do an hour or two a day – back at my work, I mean – until my strength returns.'

'It would be catastrophic.'

Dr Maisonfort sat down and began to write something on a sheet of paper.

'I've spoken to your employers and they fully understand.'

'Really?'

'They will give you leave of absence. Unpaid, of course.'

'Of course.'

He handed Brodie the sheet of paper. There was an address on it – in Nice, Alpes-Maritimes.

'I send all my tuberculosis patients there – a wonderful establishment. It's a medicinal boarding house. The diet is correct, there is nursing supervision and they monitor your progress. Every week they send me a written report.' Dr Maisonfort smiled and removed his pince-nez. 'Think of it as a forced holiday, an obligatory vacation. You eat, you rest, you do nothing. It's warm; the Mediterranean is at your feet. In six months or so, I assure you, you will feel that all this shock is behind you.'

'I assume this boarding house is not free.'

'Your employer has volunteered to contribute half the expenses. Have you the wherewithal to cover the rest?'

'I think so,' Brodie said, hopefully.

'Then bon voyage,' Dr Maisonfort said. 'Do you know Nice?'

'Only by reputation.'

'A charming town. The season will start soon, but it will be peaceful – full of invalids and the English. Come back and see me in the spring.'

*

Calder Channon looked more than unusually surly, as Brodie sat patiently opposite him across his vast desk. Calder was having difficulty lighting his small pipe but finally he got it going and he leaned back in his chair, snorting thick smoke from his nostrils onto his dense moustache where it seemed to be momentarily trapped and then filtered forth to be whisked away by the forceful exhalation from his mouth. Brodie thought it was all rather disgusting: pipe-smoking was not for him.

'It wasn't my idea, I have to tell you,' Calder said.

'I'm not surprised.'

'It was my father's. He seems to have a soft spot for you, for some reason.'

'Well, whatever the reason, I'm grateful.'

'We'll not pay your salary until you return.'

'Of course. That seems entirely reasonable.' Brodie kept a faint smile on his lips while silently cursing, as foully as he could, the want of human charity in Calder Channon. Fucking horrible, ugly, fat, self-satisfied, shit, bastard evil fat fucking fat bastard shite of hell.

'I'm most grateful for everything,' Brodie said, his slight smile fixed. 'Luckily I have some savings.'

'You've left us in a difficult position. Sauter's tour begins in a week. Julius starts in a month.'

'Dmitri has everything under control – he's more than capable. And we have six tuners now. I can always be written to or telegrammed in an emergency. I'm in the same country, after all, not in Timbuktu.'

'There's no need to adopt that cynical tone.'

'I'm using the same tone as you. I'm adopting nothing.'

Calder had no riposte. He put his pipe down in the wide glass ashtray on his desk and thought for a few seconds.

'Have you seen anything of the Kilbarrons?'

'John Kilbarron visited me in hospital – for about five minutes.'

'I had a most unpleasant encounter with Malachi Kilbarron. At one stage I thought I might have to call the police.'

'He's a violent man, I believe.'

'He insisted we pay his brother two hundred guineas per concert. I told him to go hang.'

'They seem to have come to another arrangement with Pate.'

'Good luck to him. And them. Anyway, we don't need John Kilbarron any more. God rot him.'

12

Pension Deladier
73, rue Dante
Nice, Alpes-Maritimes
France

19 February 1898

Dear Lady Dalcastle,

Having spent a few months here I now feel myself a passable Niçois, so familiar have I become with the town. Yesterday, I went to a marché aux cochons *in a village to the north, keen to have a change of scene – the sea and its horizon after all these weeks afford decreasing stimulation.*

I couldn't have wished for greater contrast. The small square was strewn with hay and the pigs lolled and grunted as the black-suited peasant buyers wandered around. Pigs are much bigger than one imagines, and there were over 200 of them, washed and pink, unbesmirched by mud. Many of the peasants selling their pigs, men and women, were barefoot, a few wore heavy wooden clogs. They spoke an incomprehensible patois that my French – very good now – couldn't penetrate. I felt I had travelled back in time to the middle of the century or even further. So, after my adventure, I was pleased to catch the diligence back to Nice, an agreeable small city of almost 100,000 inhabitants, with every modern convenience. Fine hotels and casinos, museums, bathing establishments, tramways and a sophisticated international population during the season. The Promenade des Anglais that fronts the wide Baie des Anges is full of the most elegant and rich crowds of visitors. Yet, apparently, in the summer months it's deserted. The only disappointment is the strand – a few yards of large pebbles – called the 'beach' but one searches in vain for a patch of sand.

It is a quiet life, however diverting. I've made a few acquaintances amongst my fellow pension-*dwellers. We are all, to a man and a woman, ill in some way, and it's somewhat dispiriting as all conversations quickly diverge to a discussion of symptoms. I leave the* pension *after breakfast and walk down to the Promenade des Anglais and read my newspaper, look at the Mediterranean and watch the world go by until lunchtime. I have a 'siesta' in the afternoon, then go for another stroll while I wait for dinner (served promptly at six). More reading time in the* pension's *comfortable, well-lit salon and then it's time for an early bed. I seem to have slept for years but it is working – I do feel better and stronger and have regained most of my weight. All being well I'll return to Paris and my old life in a month or so. But only Dr Maisonfort can secure my release – we exist in a form of benign imprisonment. I will write again from Paris when I return.*

Sending my sincere good wishes, affectionately,
Brodie Moncur

In fact, everything about the Pension Deladier suited Brodie – its situation, the food, the service, his large room. The other guests kept to themselves – everyone was convalescing – except for one other occupant, an Englishman. Normally the pension was filled with French invalids – consumptives in the main – but Monsieur Deladier had taken to advertising in English journals – the *Illustrated London News*, the *Athenaeum*, *Bart's Weekly* – in order to exploit the English enthusiasm for Nice and the Côte d'Azur. And, as if to spite Brodie, his publicity had snared one Cuthbert Leache who, inevitably, gravitated towards the only other anglophone in the establishment. Leache – a former surveyor in the Royal Engineers – was also a consumptive. A man in his forties, he seemed to make his living from various family properties that he rented out in London, Birmingham and Cornwall. 'I'm not a landlord,' Leache insisted to Brodie. 'I'm simply managing the properties I inherited. What else is a chap to do?' Leache didn't look ill – he had a square face with a large nose and a thick bull neck. His greying hair was low-browed and curly, parted in the middle. He was always touching his hair gently with his fingertips, as if he wore a toupee and it might have slipped. His other habit was to spell out his name on being introduced. 'How do you do? Cuthbert Leache. L,E,A,C,H,E. Very pleased to meet you.' It was as if he wanted swiftly to distance the Leache family from the bloodsucking homonym.

Brodie made every effort to avoid Leache but, as the weeks in Nice progressed, contact was inevitable. Brodie would be in the salon, quietly reading the latest *Hearth and Home* or the *Savoy*, and would hear a polite cough and there would be Leache. 'May I join you, old fellow?'

A typical Leache anecdote usually moved along the following lines.

'Have you ever been to Manchester, Moncur?'

'No.'

'I go there regularly. And I always stay in the same hotel. The manager there is a fascinating cove. Jack – no, James. No, Jimmie, he calls himself. Or is it Johnnie? . . . Let's call him James. Anyway, this James, most amusing chap, told me this story about a time he went to Stoke-on-Trent. No, not Stoke. I think it was Macclesfield. I forget exactly where it was but he went to this place on business and before he left on his journey back to Manchester he decided to buy himself a . . . what do you call those things, you know? Now I remember, it was Stockport, that's the place. He wanted something to eat – not a sandwich, not a pie. A pastry, yes, but folded over, half-moon shape. What are they called? Dialect name . . . A pastie? That's Cornwall – now there's a lovely spot. Long story short, he bought himself something to eat on the journey home. He decided to go by train. But when he looked at the timetable he saw it was cheaper if he changed trains at . . . What's the name of that place? Between Manchester and Stockport? That place where they make that kind of pottery . . . Is it Doncaster? No. Derby. Could it be Derby? In any event it doubled the time of his journey but it was half the price. Can you believe it? Extraordinary, isn't it? Most amusing fellow, James. Yes, delightful company, full of stories like that one. You'd like him, Moncur.'

Consequently Brodie began to avoid the salon after breakfast and luncheon. He tipped the staff to tell him if Monsieur Leache was in the vicinity and he'd slip away to his room. In the mornings he'd take his book or his newspaper down to the Promenade des Anglais and find a bench facing the Mediterranean and sit and read undisturbed, pausing to watch the crowds go by. Nice was exceptionally busy in the winter months of the 'season' – October to March – and there were always interesting sights to be seen along the Promenade. Old men with young women; old women with young men; ancient, just-living creatures in wheelchairs pushed by exotic-looking servants in turbans, tarbooshes and fezzes. Yachtsmen strolling in their caps and boating coats looking for carnal distraction; painted ladies looking for yachtsmen. Life in all its strange variety was here on the Promenade, Brodie came to realize, glad to be free of Cuthbert Leache.

After a week or so, Brodie became aware of another man also absorbed in his newspapers and journals of a morning, usually sitting on a bench a few yards away. It was curious, Brodie thought, given the hundreds of benches available on the Promenade des Anglais, how you always wanted to return to your familiar one. On the few occasions when 'his' bench had been occupied by others he had felt almost affronted.

Slowly, the familiarity and regularity of their almost-encounters during these many tranquil mornings – the sun shining just warmly enough, the shift and rattle of the pebbles on the narrow beach as the modest waves hit the shoreline – meant that after a while the two of them began to acknowledge each other's presence with a smile or a nod or a finger to the hat brim, a near-imperceptible bow. Yes, here we both are again, was the implication, but we are so respectful of our individual privacy that nothing will extend beyond this, the very slightest formal greeting. Brodie both understood and welcomed the unspoken rules and so did the stranger. If only the ghastly Leache had a similarly circumspect bone in his burly body . . .

And then one day in March the stranger on the other bench suddenly put down his newspaper, put his hat on the newspaper, and walked down the concrete steps – somewhat abruptly – that led to the beach. Brodie couldn't quite see what he was doing but it seemed as if he had recognized someone and had gone to meet them.

Suddenly a gust of wind tipped the man's hat off the bench and the newspaper went flying. Brodie raced to retrieve it before it blew to shreds, gathering up the pages and folding them together. A Russian newspaper, he noticed. He picked up the hat also – a pearl-grey homburg – that was beginning to bowl along the Promenade, and he was about to replace them discreetly on the bench when the man appeared up from the beach.

'Excuse me,' Brodie said in French, 'but the wind blew your hat and newspaper away. I managed to catch them in time.'

'Thank you so much,' the man replied. His French was thick with a Russian accent, much stronger than Lika's. He was older than Brodie – late thirties, early forties, Brodie calculated – well dressed in a long-jacketed dark suit and a stiff collar, and quite tall and slim with a full, pointed beard. He took back his hat and newspaper and asked if Brodie would care to join him for a coffee by way of recompense, to thank him for saving his possessions.

They crossed the Promenade and walked towards the Hôtel West-End that had a roomy glassed-in café on the front. They found a table and ordered two coffees with hot milk. Brodie introduced himself and the Russian did so as well, but Brodie couldn't pick up his exact name as his Russian accent was so thick. And he must also have used his patronymic as all that Brodie could hear was a rush of mashed syllables. 'Archibald' was as close to any name as he could make out, but this man was clearly not called Archibald.

Their coffee was served and they added milk and sugar.

'Are you here on holiday?' the Russian asked in his somewhat faltering French.

'I'm convalescing,' Brodie said. 'At least six months' rest, my doctor insisted, somewhere warm.'

'I am the same. May I ask your condition?'

'Tuberculosis.'

'Yes. I too have the same problem.' The Russian gave a sad smile. 'May I ask your age, sir?'

'Twenty-seven.'

'How many haemorrhages?'

'Just the one. Severe.'

'I had my first haemorrhage at the age of twenty-three. And now I'm thirty-eight. So you see you have a long life ahead of you.' The Russian peered at him. 'May I ask your profession?'

'I'm a piano tuner.' This took some further explanation as the word *accordeur* was not familiar.

'How fascinating,' the Russian said. 'I'm sure you must have some interesting stories to tell.'

'Oh, I certainly do. What about you, sir?'

'I'm a doctor,' the Russian said. 'But this doctor is sick. Where are you staying?'

'The Pension Deladier.'

'I hear it's very good. Naturally, I'm staying at the Pension Russe. Full of Russians. Sick Russians. Annoying Russians.'

They talked further about their mutual disease and the doctor mentioned a particular Russian cure – a constant diet of *kumys*, which was fermented mare's milk. He had tasted *kumys* once and knew about its effect.

'It looks like a kind of milk but has a somewhat strange taste – but the good thing is you put on a huge amount of weight, apparently. And of course getting fat makes you feel better – you think it's working: you think, how can I die when I'm getting so fat?' He shrugged. 'We all have to die some day and who's to say when that day will come?'

'That's exactly what my doctor in Paris told me.'

'So you live in Paris. An Englishman in Paris.'

'A Scotsman, sir.'

'A Scotsman. I'd like to go to Scotland. Somehow I doubt I'll ever get there.'

They talked a bit about Paris – the doctor had been there once – and the mention of the city gave Brodie an idea.

'Would you be so good as to write something down for me, in Russian?'

The doctor took a fountain pen from his pocket and a small notebook. He tore out a page.

'It's a bit personal,' Brodie said, 'but would you write "I miss you and I love you"?'

The doctor wrote it down and handed the page over.

'I have very bad handwriting so I have written it as clearly as I can,' he said.

Brodie looked at the extraordinary letters: 'Скучаю по тебе, люблю тебя'.

'I'm no detective,' the doctor said, 'but I assume this isn't for your grandmother.'

'No . . . I . . .' Brodie considered and then said, candidly, 'I've fallen in love with a young Russian woman, you see, an opera singer.'

'Oh my God! Actresses! Russian actresses, even worse! Don't go near them, I implore you.'

'No, sir. This is different. This is a real passion.'

'Yes, yes, of course it is. I always said the same myself, always. "But this time it's different." At least for the first ten actresses I knew – and then I stopped saying it.'

'There are, it has to be said, complications.'

'Naturally – she's an actress.' He laughed wryly to himself. 'Complications. Oh, yes.' The doctor reflected and then said, 'I always think a life without complications isn't really a life, you know. In life things go wrong, nothing stays the same and there's nothing you can do about it. Friends betray you, family is a nightmare, lovers are fickle. This is the norm, no?' He smiled to himself, as if remembering something pertinent. 'What kind of a world would it be where nothing ever went wrong, where everything stayed the same, life followed its designated path – family was adorable, friends and lovers were faithful and true?' He paused. 'You know, I don't think I'd like that kind of a world. We're made for complications, we human beings. Anyway, such a perfect world could never exist – at least not on this small planet.'

Unusually, Brodie felt he could unburden himself to this amiable, cynical, melancholic doctor. He had tired, kind eyes.

'What would you say to me, sir? There are many obstacles between me and this young woman, this young singer. Am I wasting my time?'

'Is she free to be with you?'

'Ah . . . She's living with another man.'

The doctor nodded and smiled.

'I could give you lots of excellent, sensible advice, based on long experience,' he said. 'But what would be the point? You'll do exactly what you want to do. Nothing I say will make any difference.'

They fell silent and sipped their coffee, Brodie pondering the brutal wisdom of the statement. Yes, he needed Lika – she was the only one for him. Ever. To hell with Kilbarron – there was obviously no love left between the two of them.

'S'il vous plaît, monsieur.'

Brodie looked round. A young woman was standing at their table looking intently at the doctor. She was very young and quite pretty in a simple rose-coloured dress with a fringed, darker rose shawl. He saw a small oval face with a retroussé nose. *Gamine*, the French would say. How old? Nineteen? Twenty? He noted that the dress was cheap and the shawl had a stain. She looked like a housemaid on her day off. The doctor looked at her intently, almost angrily, and stroked his beard, pulling at it with his right hand. The girl's eyes were red, as if she'd been crying.

Brodie felt he should do something so he stood and introduced himself. But before the girl could reply the doctor stood also.

'This is Margot,' he said. 'And she is going to leave us. Now.'

He led her off a few steps and tersely instructed her, Brodie could see. The doctor fished in his pocket and slipped her some money, notes and coins. She gave Brodie a brisk curtsey and hurried off out of the café.

The doctor sat down.

'You were talking about complications,' he said, with a vague smile. 'I have a great many of my own. I'm an expert.'

*

Pension Deladier
73, rue Dante
Nice, Alpes-Maritimes
France

23 March 1898

Brother!

Bonjour! Are you still in the land of the living? Now this is the fourth letter I've written to you and still no reply. Stir yourself, O lazy one. Think of your poor brother languishing in this beautiful, sunlit Mediterranean city with nothing to do but wander down to the sea, read his newspaper, eat a delicious lunch, drink some wine, take a nap, then go out and find a café for an aperitif, all before another excellent dinner. What torments! You see how I suffer but you never correspond.

Last week, I was so bored I went to Monte Carlo – to the casino. I took a brake along the Grande Corniche (10 fr – 8 shillings). The views of the coast are spectacular. We stopped for lunch in Beaulieu and arrived in Monte Carlo in the afternoon. I only played roulette – you know what a hopeless gambler I am. I played a simple martingale system: doubling my stake (2 fr) when I lost and pocketing my winnings when I won. You only bet on 2 to 1 odds. Red or black, odd or even. By the law of averages you will win at some stage. The only strange thing – if you double your stake each time you lose – is that sometimes you can be betting 40 francs to win 2 – so you need a substantial float. I cashed in 50 francs but I never needed more than 10 that day – it was a lucky day. To my surprise after an hour and a half (I moved tables from time to time) I had made 180 francs, just over £7. I suddenly saw how I could live down here on the Mediterranean. Gamble for a few hours per day in the martingale style while living in a simple hotel. You could make, I calculate, going hard at it, maybe £20 per week. Even gambling for two hours a day, five days a week (the casinos are open most of the year) I think I could earn over £200. It's not very exciting – there is no thrill of a big win – just a steady accumulation of 2 francs – but it would be a living, an independent living, and no taxes to pay, just the odd tip to give to the croupier. Something to think about. I left the casino feeling liberated, walking on warm Mediterranean air. I treated myself to an excellent dinner in Les Frères Provinciaux and bought myself a £2 bottle of wine. Then I took the rest of my winnings back to Nice – by train, first class.

Write, brother, or you will inherit nothing!

Yours affectionately,
*Brodie (*le gagnant*)*

*

Brodie sat, his shirt off, in Dr Roissansac's consulting room, breathing in and out as requested, feeling the cold, then warming steel circle of Dr Roissansac's stethoscope range over his back listening to his lungs. Dr Roissansac – a young, serious man with a toothbrush moustache – was the recommendation and colleague of Dr Maisonfort. Brodie sensed there was a financially useful quid pro quo going on.

Brodie dressed himself as Dr Roissansac wrote down his notes.

'Well you have regained the weight you lost so we should interpret that as a good sign. There's no significant congestion, as far as I can judge.'

'I feel well,' Brodie said. 'Full of energy.'

'Ignore your energy. Everything must proceed very cautiously, in the case of tuberculosis. Cautiously, carefully.'

'Yes, I know, Doctor. I will be cautious.'

'Then I think you can go back to Paris, Monsieur Moncur.' Dr Roissansac's wide smile made the bristles of his moustache flip up for a moment, touching his nose.

Brodie walked down the rue Halévy to the seafront at the big Jetée Promenade with its small casino. For a moment he was tempted to go in and see if the good luck of his health might extend to a quick martingale session, but he decided it wasn't the moment. He wandered westwards – a few brave souls were bathing in the sea, the sun was shining weakly – and felt happy: I can go home,

home to Paris and Lika. He called her to mind, as he did constantly, regretting he had no photograph of her. What was she doing right now? Was she with Kilbarron? Dmitri had written to him saying Julius's tour was underway and they were preparing Door's. Sales were very good indeed. The 'Channon Recitals' already seemed almost established through the key cities in Europe, as if they'd been taking place for years. Ainsley Channon had authorized increased expenditure on newspaper advertising. René was with Sauter; Romain would travel with Door. All was more than well.

Brodie was pleased that his months of absence hadn't seemed to hold the Channons back but he slightly resented the fact that he was clearly not as indispensable as he thought. Why, despite Malachi's aggressive bluster, had Kilbarron not signed up for another six months with Channon as he had been offered? It seemed vainglorious to throw away so much money, so easily earned . . . To hell with Kilbarron, he thought, as he climbed aboard an electric tram that would take him close to the rue Dante. The only person he cared about in this wide world was Lika.

Pension Deladier
73, rue Dante
Nice

28 March 1898

My dearest Lika,

I hope you received my letters and postcards – I have written to you once a week, at least, to the Poste Restante. Don't worry, I know how difficult it must be for you to reply.

My good news is that my health is stable and my doctor here in Nice – Dr Roissansac – has declared me fit to return home. All being well I should be back in Paris next week when I'll resume my old job at the Channon showrooms. Obviously I want urgently to see you. Where and how shall we meet? We must find a way.

Скучаю по тебе, люблю тебя.

A Russian doctor who I met here wrote this down for me. I hope I have transcribed it correctly. Its message is absolutely sincere. I long to see you and hold you in my arms.

Your Brodie Moncur

*

Brodie posted his final letter to Lika at the central post office in the place de la Liberté as if, somehow, it would arrive sooner having been deposited centrally rather than locally. He felt light-headed as the letter slipped from his hand into the slit of the postbox, a lover's insane fantastical joy invigorating him for a few seconds, making him shiver. Love was indeed a kind of madness, he realized, it defied all logic – a naked flame of illogic – the intensity of the feeling you experienced was the only vindication necessary. Despite these long months without seeing her he knew with absolute conviction that not only was he in love with Lika Blum, but that state of affairs was the only significant fact about his life.

He called to mind some lines from a poem by Algernon Swinburne that he had memorized, from the book Lady Dalcastle had given him. They fitted his mood perfectly:

We shone as the stars shone, and moved
As the moon moved, twain halves of a perfect heart.
Soul to soul. You loved me, as I thee loved,
And our dreams began, dreaming our life would start.

He wandered back to the *pension*, repeating the lines to himself as if they were some sort of votive incantation. The streets were busy, the sun was shining, Nice's season was drawing to a close. Dinner was served promptly at 6 p.m. – an hour Brodie had always thought was irritatingly early – but this evening he was happy to join the other diners (glad to see no sign of Leache in the room) because (a) he was leaving Nice for Paris the next day, and (b) he would never see Cuthbert Leache in his life again. Leache was booked in for another three months – he had suffered a minor haemorrhage and had been taken to the Clinique Sturge, a private hospital connected to the *pension*. Again Brodie sensed wheels within wheels – ill health meant money to healthy people. He was sorry for poor Leache but pleased he was going to miss him on his final night as an invalid.

Brodie ate fillet of turbot in a cream and caper sauce followed by an *île flottante*, all washed down with several glasses of mineral water (the Deladier was teetotal). He was waiting for his coffee when Madame Deladier crossed the dining room towards him, a frown making her already severe face even more severe.

'There is someone to see you, Monsieur Moncur,' she said disapprovingly. 'The message I have to deliver to you is that it concerns a "Russian doctor" – if that makes sense.'

'Yes, it does,' Brodie said and hurried to the *pension*'s large hall by the front door where visitors were received. He hadn't seen the Russian doctor since their shared coffee in the Hôtel West-End. What could have brought him to the Deladier, he wondered?

But it wasn't the Russian doctor waiting for him in the hall – it was the young French girl who had approached them that day. What was her name? Marie? No, Margot, that was it. Brodie greeted her, puzzled. She had changed, colouring her fair hair a rather harsh auburn and she was wearing a black suit piped with gold. She wore a little straw bonnet pinned rakishly to the side of her head. Everything seemed garish and cheap and the scent of her perfume seemed to fill the *pension*'s hallway, farinaceous and powerful – spikenard, musk – it could almost be tasted.

'Do you remember me?' she said, obviously very nervous.

'Yes. You're Margot – aren't you? I met you with the Russian doctor. How did you find me?'

'My friend – the Russian doctor – told me you were staying at the Pension Deladier.'

'Did he? Oh . . . Right. Does he need help?'

'No. It's I who need help. Or, rather, I was wondering if I could be of some assistance to you, monsieur. I could keep house for you. I'm a good cook. I can do laundry and sew. And, of course . . .'

She looked down at her cracked leather boots. 'I would be there . . . At night.'

Brodie felt his mouth dry.

'What about your doctor friend?'

'He has to go back to Russia. I can't go with him, he says.'

'I see.'

'So, he thought that maybe you would . . .' She didn't finish her sentence.

'How old are you, Margot?'

'I'm nineteen.'

'Where are you from? Are you from Nice?'

'I'm from Biarritz. I came here with the doctor from Biarritz when he moved to Nice.'

'I think you should go back to Biarritz. Go back to your family.'

'My family won't receive me,' she said. 'I can't do that,' she added gravely, as if he were asking her to climb Mont Blanc.

'Well, I'm so sorry, but I can't help you,' Brodie said. 'I'm going back to Paris tomorrow.'

Margot's eyes opened wide and she stiffened with a kind of suppressed glee.

'I long to go to Paris! I could come with you. I could look after you, monsieur.'

Brodie fumbled in his pockets and found some coins – a twenty-franc gold coin and a silver five. He handed them to her. She took them.

'It's impossible, Margot. I'm engaged to be married. I'm going back to Paris to marry the woman I love.'

He watched her recoil at this – this lie – as if it were the cruellest news in the world and he saw tears form in her eyes, all faint hopes gone. She clenched her fist around the coins, knuckles blanching.

'I wish you and your fiancée every happiness, monsieur,' she said, adding quietly, 'You're a very lucky man.'

13

It was as if Brodie's months of convalescence in Nice had never happened. He felt well in himself, not unduly tired or lacking in energy, and he took up his duties at Channon & Cie as if he'd been away for a long weekend.

On his return to Paris, he went almost immediately to see Dr Maisonfort. Brodie was requested to undress to his drawers and vest and he was then weighed, asked to touch his toes, his reflexes were tested with a rubber hammer and his heart and his lungs were listened to through Dr Maisonfort's stethoscope.

'You have gained an extra two hundred grams,' Dr Maisonfort said. 'That's good, no weight loss, that's a good sign.'

Brodie said that he felt very well.

'We made the right decision for you,' Dr Maisonfort said. 'Immediate rest, a regular diet, warmth, sunshine, tranquillity. It was very cold here in Paris while you were away in Nice, very. And no more haemorrhages? Spitting blood?'

'Nothing.'

'Excellent. You know, I have a patient – consumptive like you – who just celebrated his seventy-eighth birthday.'

'That's encouraging.'

'But of course your English poet, Kaytes?'

'Keats. John Keats.'

'He died from his tuberculosis at twenty-five. It's unpredictable.'

'Yes. At least I'm older than he was.'

Dr Maisonfort prescribed him a tincture of camphor to be taken in dilution twice a day. It was vital to avoid overwork and over-exercise. Ten hours' sleep a day – siestas at every opportunity. Brodie said he'd be especially careful. Dr Maisonfort booked him in for another appointment in a month. Brodie felt – though he knew it wasn't true – that, in a sense, however, he was cured. His life could begin again.

Two days after his appointment he regulated and tuned the piano for Karl-Heinz Nagel's recital in the Théâtre du Châtelet. Unlike most virtuosi, Nagel seemed to take a genuine interest in what Brodie was doing to his new Channon, almost marvelling as he watched Brodie shave off the hammer-heads with emery paper.

'I mean, you don't even take off half a millimetre,' Nagel said. 'Will it make any difference?'

'You'll see the minute you begin to play,' Brodie said. 'What I do to the hammers is my special trick, if you like. You're lucky I'm letting you see what I do.' He picked up his needle and loosened the felt, then shaved it down a touch.

Nagel chuckled. 'Magic arts, eh?'

'Something like that.'

When the tuning was finished Nagel invited Brodie to accompany him on his Scandinavian tour in the summer. Brodie was flattered but cautiously replied that it would depend on Mr Channon and what was going on in the business. There were many upcoming tours that he had to organize – he wasn't sure if he could get away.

'Are you still tuning for Kilbarron?' Nagel asked.

'Ah, no. Mr Kilbarron and Channon have separated,' Brodie said. 'They didn't renew the contract.'

'What a shame,' Nagel said, smiling. 'Have a think about my proposal, Mr Moncur. I'll make it worth your while.'

Brodie took a cab back to the shop and called for Benoît.

'Well?' he said, impatiently, when Benoît appeared. He had sent Benoît to the Kilbarron apartment in Saint-Germain on some footling errand.

'It was empty,' Benoît said. 'No one was there apart from the servants. They said they thought Monsieur Kilbarron was in Germany.'

'What about Mademoiselle Blum? Where is she?'

'I didn't ask.'

Lika hadn't replied to his last letter – with his Russian declaration of love – and Brodie wondered and worried whether he might have gone too far. After the shop closed he took a horse tram to Saint-Germain.

The dozy manservant answered the door, recognizing Brodie after a second or two of blank staring. Brodie explained that on his last visit some months ago he had left some sheet music behind – in a green folder – and he wondered if it had been kept safely aside somewhere. He now had need of it.

The manservant said he knew nothing of any sheet music and no specific instructions had been given.

'You can understand, sir, in a house like this – the place is full of music.'

'Perhaps Mademoiselle Blum has it.'

'She is in Weimar, appearing in *Le Roi d'Ys*.'

There was the sound of a soft, gruff bark and a little dog trotted into the hall. Brodie recognized it – Lika's dog – and felt his spirits rise. She was clearly coming back to Paris after her Weimar engagement. He crouched and the little dog came and sniffed his fingers. He scratched behind its ears and the dog immediately rolled over onto its back. Brodie stood.

'That's Mademoiselle Blum's dog, isn't it?' he said to the manservant.

'Yes, sir.'

'What's its name?'

'César. He's a good dog.'

'César, that's right.'

The dog César had righted himself and now wagged his short curved tail vigorously.

'When is Mademoiselle Blum returning?'

'I have no information, sir.'

'Is she well?'

'Very well.'

'Please give her my sincere good wishes when she returns. Tell her I was asking for her.'

'Certainly, sir. What's your name?'

'Monsieur Moncur.'

The only unusual aspect about Brodie's return to Channon & Cie, he realized, was that he saw little or nothing of Calder Channon.

There had been an impromptu encounter on the stairway one morning that gave rise to a brisk handshake and an insincere 'Very glad to have you back with us, Brodie', but that, apart from a few glimpses around the shop, was the extent of the welcome. If he had known any better he'd have said Calder was trying to avoid him.

He came out of his office one day and saw Calder turn and scuttle back up the stairs to the first floor. This is ridiculous, Brodie thought, what's going on? He knocked on Calder's door and was, after a pause, invited in. Calder seemed almost sheepish, embarrassed. He offered him a glass of vermouth – Brodie accepted – and asked him a flow of questions: how was his health? How was Nice? Was the weather good? Was there a hotel in Nice he could recommend? Brodie answered them all until they dried up. There was a silence. Brodie sipped at his vermouth.

'So that should be the end of it,' Calder said. 'Your illness, I mean.'

'No. Unfortunately there's no "end" to tuberculosis. One hopes to keep it at bay by this means or that.'

'Goodness,' he said, seemingly genuinely surprised. 'That's a heavy burden.'

'It's not like getting over influenza,' Brodie said. 'These capsules are there in your lungs, growing very slowly, one day one of them might make an artery or a vein burst, or not. It's a lottery.'

'A bad business,' Calder said vaguely, reaching for his horrible little pipe.

'Is everything all right, Calder?' Brodie asked directly.

'Yes . . . Dmitri has done pretty well in your absence. The Nagel tour is booked; the Sauter tour is going well. The tuning diaries are full to bursting.'

'And sales?'

'Sales are through the roof.'

'Why do I sense something's wrong, then?' Brodie said, emboldened. 'Why do I feel you're avoiding me?'

Calder wouldn't meet his eye, concentrating on thumbing tobacco into his pipe bowl.

'My father will be here the day after tomorrow. He'll explain everything.'

Brodie didn't go into the shop the next day, sending a note to say he had toothache and had to see a dentist. He ate a solitary lunch in the *pension* and then, having a sudden urge to leave the city and see some countryside, took a train to Saint-Denis. He wandered away from the village to discover that the fields and hamlets and woods of the Paris environs were dominated by massive low reinforced stone bastions with gun-emplacements and watchtowers, Les Forts Détachés. He strolled on and came across other redoubts, regularly spaced, realizing that Paris was encircled both by huge ramparts and these mighty fortresses. They stood there, brooding – implicit with violence, somehow – with their moats and glacis slopes, scarps and cordons, destroyed in the war of 1870–71, but since rebuilt, ringing the city, north, south, east and west. It rather shook his impression of Paris – the City of Light, of pleasure, beauty, of artists and self-indulgence – preparing for future conflicts. His trip to the countryside was less than uplifting. Then it started to rain.

That evening he went to the Gare de l'Est and enquired about the price of a ticket to Weimar. For a mad few moments he had thought about taking a train to Germany, finding the opera house in Weimar and surprising Lika. But what if Kilbarron was with her? . . . He returned to his quartier and drank too much brandy in the Café Americain, his thoughts endlessly returning to Ainsley Channon. What could Ainsley have to say to him? What could have provoked Calder's strange evasive mood? His own mood darkened as he speculated. Whatever it was it wouldn't be welcome, he felt sure, and he wandered homewards feeling very sorry for himself. The imminent Ainsley confrontation, the absence and silence of Lika, and the permanence of his tubercular state cast him down thoroughly. What had the Russian doctor said to him in Nice? It wouldn't be a real life without complications.

Ainsley Channon had changed again since their last encounter. His hair was cut *en brosse* like a Prussian officer and his sideburns were gone. The moustache was wider and waxed into horizontal points. He wore a cerise waistcoat and mustard-coloured ankle boots with his usual blue suit, shirt and tie. His visits to Paris were obviously still having a transformational effect on him.

They were sitting in Calder's office but there was no sign of Calder. Ainsley had brought a bottle of malt whisky with him from Edinburgh and he poured Brodie a small dram before he took his place in Calder's seat. His demeanour was calm and thoughtful – he was not his usual jolly, amiable self. There was some polite conversation about Brodie's health, about the delights of Nice and Monte Carlo, the best hotels there, but both men knew this was only postponing the crucial moment.

Ainsley tapped his fingertips together.

'This is very difficult for me, Brodie. I hope you know that.'

'I'm completely in the dark, sir.'

'Aye, but I'm not. I now know what's been going on.'

He opened a drawer and took out a sheaf of papers with columns of figures written on them.

'Thibault Dieulafoy has got to the bottom of your little scheme.'

'What scheme?'

'What shall we say? "Repairs in transit"? "Degeneration in shipping"? "Damage owing to transportation"? Many innocent, vague phrases have been used . . . Of the . . .' He consulted the papers. 'Of the four hundred and eighty-three pianos we have shipped and sold since Channon opened in Paris, a remarkable two hundred and sixty-three required repairs owing to "damages in transit", or however you would have it.'

'With great respect, I don't know what you're talking about, sir. This is absolutely—'

Ainsley held up his hand for silence and continued.

'Sometimes it's no more than a few pounds and a few shillings – cracked veneer replaced, new brass castors required – sometimes it's considerably more: new sounding board, new lyre, replacement of all ebony keys, total restringing of the instrument. Tens, twenties, thirties, occasionally hundreds of pounds. It all adds up to two thousand four hundred and thirty-five pounds.' He patted the documents. 'That's where our precious profits have gone – on your chimerical repairs of mysteriously damaged pianos!'

'What has this to do with me?' Brodie said, feeling sweat break out on his body.

'All these repairs were authorized by you.' Ainsley's voice was now raised, intemperate. 'All these dockets from the Saint-Cloud warehouse – which you advised us to set up – have your initials on them. B.M.'

'Who is making this accusation?'

'Thibault Dieulafoy and Calder. They scrutinized all the accounts while you were away, convalescing. They noticed that in your absence there was – surprise, surprise – absolutely no damage to pianos being shipped, not a single repair docket issuing from the Saint-Cloud warehouse. It roused their suspicions. It was very clever, Brodie, small amounts, random, nothing drawing attention to itself. Just a drip-drip-drip of embezzlement. But your own illness gave you away. Revealed the culprit. A bitter irony for you, no doubt.'

Brodie closed his eyes. He knew what was coming next.

'This is all desperate calumny,' he said, trying to keep the tremble out of his voice. 'Where are the corresponding figures for the tuners and the workshop? Where is a record of the savings made by the establishment of the Saint-Cloud warehouse? How many sales have been generated by the Channon Recitals – something I inaugurated? I've not stolen money from this firm, sir – I've made thousands of pounds for this firm. Thousands. I think you know that in your heart. Someone else has been stealing from you and has made it seem my responsibility – it's a terrible lie and a slander!'

'There's no need to shout, Brodie. I have the evidence in front of me.'

'You have the evidence but I am not the guilty party. The culprit is elsewhere.'

'The culprit is sitting right opposite me,' Ainsley said with a certain lack of conviction.

'Then call the police,' Brodie said, confidently. 'Let's have some lawyers in and do a proper investigation. I'll not submit to this Star Chamber. I know my rights as someone falsely accused.'

'There's no need for that,' Ainsley said, all composure leaving him and suddenly looking a bit flustered. 'For your own sake I'm going to draw a line under this matter. I appreciate some of the things you've done for this firm – I really do, Brodie – that's why this . . .' he searched for the words, 'this very unfortunate business will go no further than this room. My lips are sealed and I hope yours will be also.' He reached into the drawer again and took out a banker's draft. 'This is a year's salary. I give it to you in lieu of notice. You are dismissed from our employ.'

He pushed it across the desk. Brodie could see his hand was shaking.

For a moment Brodie thought of taking it, tearing it up and hurling the pieces in Ainsley Channon's face – but he knew that only he would be the victim of such a dramatic, foolhardy gesture. He picked up the draft.

'Can we speak candidly, Mr Channon?'

'Of course, Brodie. Of course.'

'We're not being overheard, I hope.'

'No, certainly not.'

'Well, in that case, you know as well as I do who the thief is. The thieves, I should say, are Calder and Dieulafoy. They're the two with their hands in the till, not me.'

There was a silence. Ainsley inhaled and exhaled loudly. He looked at his hands, looked at the ceiling, looked back at Brodie, abashed, rueful. He stayed silent for a few more seconds, frowning, as if weighing up the consequences of what he was about to say. He sighed and managed an apologetic smile.

'Aye. You're absolutely right. Calder's been feathering his nest ever since I sent him here.'

'So why am I being dismissed? The injustice is—'

'Brodie, Brodie, you're not being dismissed, you're "resigning".'

'Oh, I am, am I? That's very good of you.'

'Think about it . . . Calder's my only son. He's the father of wee Ainsley, my only grandson. What am I to do in these ghastly circumstances? He comes to me with incontrovertible "evidence" of your guilt. He swears on his child's head that he's done nothing, that it was all you – wily, thieving Brodie Moncur. He then hands me a sheaf of dockets with your initials on them.'

'Initials are not very hard to forge, I would argue.'

'I'm not a fool, Brodie. I kept smelling a rat so I sent George McIver from the bank down here from Edinburgh. It was while you were away in Nice. But before he could go to work Calder popped up with the evidence.' He shook the papers in the air. 'A father can't call his only son a fat brazen lying bastard to his face without that relationship between father and son ending. Forever. Do you see where I stand?' He spread his hands helplessly. 'It was either you or Calder that had to go. It was a pretty straightforward decision, however unjust, however unfortunate.' He smiled bitterly. 'Calder won't be stealing from me again, that's for sure. And I'll be showing Thibault Dieulafoy the door very shortly. But I don't suppose that's any consolation for you, the man who has to carry the can.'

'No. It's no consolation at all. I like my job. I like being here in Paris.'

'Ah. But the great thing about your job, Brodie, is you can do it anywhere. You've got a year's salary; you can set yourself up anywhere. You'll be fine, I know that.'

'Thank you for your confidence.'

Brodie stood up. It was over. Ainsley walked him to the door, his arm around Brodie's shoulders.

'I would say you've been like a son to me, Brodie. All these years at the firm, all your hard work, all your bright ideas. But at the end of the day you're not my son – you're my valued employee whom I have to sacrifice for the sake of my wretched real son. I'm very sorry it's come to this. But give it a couple of years and slip by and see me again, discreetly. We'll see how the land lies then.'

'Thank you, Mr Channon.'

He shook Brodie's hand firmly and closed the door on him. His Channon days were over.

14

Pension Berlinger
Paris

2 May 1898

My dearest Lika,

Are you back? Are you in Paris? I need to see you. I have been dismissed from Channon – on trumped-up charges but there's nothing I can do. It's a scandal but the real culprit is a member of the family, so he is protected and I am the scapegoat. I've been given a year's salary so at least I can live an independent life of sorts for a while. I am still at my old address above or you can contact me through Channon – through Dmitri or Benoît if that seems more circumspect. I hope and pray you received my letter from Nice. Please write to me and tell me what your plans are.

I kiss your beautiful hand,
Brodie

*

Brodie slowly succumbed to a form of despondency. He felt listless, bored, nothing gave him particular pleasure. Even the thought of a year's salary gaining interest in the bank seemed an irrelevance in the face of the vast injustice he'd experienced. He contemplated the idea of waiting outside Calder's apartment and accosting him one morning on his way to work. To try to shame him, he supposed; to make him confess. But he realized such a ploy would only end badly. Then there was Dieulafoy, Calder's semi-invisible accomplice who had furnished the forged and damaging documents, no doubt, the dockets and the repair slips – could he be exposed somehow? Was there a professional body of accountants – some league or syndicate – who could be approached and a malpractice complaint made to have him disbarred? But all these plans and questions ran into the same quicksand of inertia. He decided that anything he attempted to do to right the wrong he had suffered would probably only bring more discomfort on his head. Maybe accepting Ainsley's banker's draft would look like evidence of culpability. Perhaps he should have refused it – walked away and then mounted his campaign for retribution against the firm, his integrity uncompromised . . . But what to do, otherwise? How would he have lived? And there was always the overriding matter of Lika. Lika and Brodie. Brodie and Lika . . .

Despite his low mood he filled the days somehow. Like a tourist he took omnibus and tramway-car drives, sitting on the top deck, being transported to the Madeleine, the Bastille, the Jardin du Luxembourg, the Panthéon. One day he managed a great sweep of the 'new' boulevards, not even fifty years old, planned and constructed by Haussmann: Strasbourg, Sébastopol, Saint-Michel, de Magenta, Voltaire. He kept his distance from Saint-Germain. Sometimes he descended when the traffic became impossible and had a *petit café* in the various establishments on the avenues that bifurcated from the wider roads. Then he would walk and pick up another omnibus and continue his meanderings. He managed to fill the days, though his mood didn't lighten.

Some ten days after his 'resignation' – it seemed more like a month – Benoît appeared at the *pension* with a note. Brodie gave him two francs and opened it. It was unsigned:

> *Go to the Grand Hôtel des Etrangers, rue Racine, 6ème, on Monday and book a room in the name of Beaufils. Take a suitcase. I will come to you in the evening.*

*

So, as Monsieur Beaufils, Brodie made a reservation at the Grand Hôtel des Etrangers in the rue Racine. It had four narrow floors and twelve rooms and he was given the only available room on the top floor under the eaves. The bed sagged in the middle but the linen was clean. He placed his empty suitcase behind the door, put his hip flask of brandy on the bedside table and settled down to read Guy de Maupassant's account of his voyage along the Mediterranean littoral, *Sur l'Eau*.

At six in the evening there was a brisk rap on the door and the receptionist showed in Lika, also with an empty suitcase. She strode confidently into the room, tall and limber, and Brodie felt his guts squirm as he stood up, overcome.

'Here is your Madame Beaufils,' the receptionist said, trying to keep the smile off his face.

'Hello, darling,' Brodie said. 'Was your train late?'

The receptionist closed the door on them and they stood looking at each other for several moments, Brodie sensing almost overwhelming emotion – an urge to shed tears, his chest tightening, then filling, feeling enormously strong then limply weak – considering all that had happened since they had last been alone together. He straightened his back, squared his shoulders. He stepped towards her and put his arms around her. She adjusted his tie minutely and scrutinized his face.

'You don't look ill,' she said. 'I'm surprised.'

'I'm not ill. I'm cured.'

She was wearing a short crushed-velvet buff jacket and a long black skirt with a front fold. White, laced bootees, he noticed, and her hat was a jaunty pseudo-military style with a peak in black leather. She took it off and threw it on the bed. A thick lock of her hair tumbled free. Brodie now felt weak with desire.

'Will you give me the Lika-kiss?' he asked, taking off his spectacles. 'I've been dreaming about it for months.'

'Of course, my darling,' she said, and she pressed her face to his, nose to nose, lip to lip, chin to chin – still and unmoving until her tongue began gently to probe.

They lay in bed, naked, in each other's arms, warm, snug. Brodie moved his hand to cup a breast and bent his head to take her nipple in his mouth, tonguing it hard. She kissed his brow. He kissed her neck, marvelling that they were here together again, all these months on . . . All the nagging doubts that had always troubled him – that he would never be alone with her again, that their affair would fizzle out, unfulfilled – disappeared. He reached down and touched her, his fingers on the thick blonde furze of her pubis, cupping it under his palm. He felt hugely aroused again, massively potent. He—

'Brodie?'

'Yes?'

'When I die will you come to my funeral? If I die before you, of course.'

'You're not going to die! You're young, full of life.'

'But if it happened, would you come?'

'I'm not going to answer that question.'

'It would make me pleased to think that you would be there.'

'Don't talk like this, Lika.'

'Would you say some words about me?'

'There's going to be no funeral.'

'I would come to your funeral, if you died. I'd speak about you, if they'd let me.'

'Lika, please! Stop this!'

He sat up in bed and poured brandy from his flask into a tooth glass. He had a sip and handed it to her.

'What made you choose this hotel?' he asked, keen to change the subject, all potency gone, now.

'It was the first hotel I stayed in when I came to Paris. I liked its name. Full of foreigners. They can't tell us apart so it's very discreet. Russian, German, Swiss, Italians – we're all the same to them. I had a nostalgia for this hotel.'

'I see.'

'And John Kilbarron will never come to the Latin Quarter – so it's safe, also.'

'What's he doing? Where is he?'

'He's in Russia with Malachi. Talking to some impresario about a tour, I suppose.'

Brodie thought about this.

'Why Russia? Where in Russia?' he said.

'He wouldn't tell me. They went two days ago, by train. It's a long journey – I've done it myself many times.'

'But Russia? It doesn't make sense. The money isn't there – it's here. Germany, Austria.'

'Oh, no, you're wrong. There's plenty of money in Russia. And he needs money.'

'Does he?'

'Yes. Things are very difficult. I think we may have to leave Saint-Germain.'

'He should have signed for Channon for another six months – he would have made thousands.'

Lika reached over him for his cigarette case on his bedside table, her breasts hanging free for a moment. He picked up his lighter and lit her cigarette. She pulled the sheet up to her chin, suddenly demure.

'He knows he should have signed,' she says. 'And it makes him angry. I think he blames you.'

'Why? I advised him to sign.'

'He has to blame someone.'

'Then blame Malachi – he was the one who turned it down.'

'No. He'll never blame Malachi for anything.'

'Why? Malachi can be a fool.'

'I don't know. Some childhood secret. Perhaps some pact they made together. They are very close, extremely close, even for brothers. It's strange.'

'I don't want to talk about John Kilbarron.' He took the cigarette from her fingers and stubbed it out in the ashtray. 'In fact I don't want to talk about anything any more.' He reached for her and they kissed.

Over the next weeks Brodie waited patiently for Lika's notes – now sent directly to the Pension Berlinger. He structured his life around their meetings at the Grand Hôtel des Etrangers, both arriving with their empty suitcases under the futile pretext that they were trying to catch a few hours of sleep before their train was due. The manager, the various receptionists and the porters seemed to enjoy the pretence and started greeting them warmly: Monsieur and Madame Beaufils, welcome back! How was your journey? A pleasure to see you again. Twice they stayed a whole night together. Then John Kilbarron returned from Russia and the encounters ceased for a while. Brodie resumed his long promenades of Paris and its environs. He was content, he realized, caught in a kind of benign limbo. He had no job but he was in love and in the full conspiracy of a covert affair with the woman he adored. In the hours they contrived to spend together they made love with regular and shared enthusiasm. He felt blessed but he knew this benediction couldn't last forever. Something would happen, he knew, and then everything would change – possibly for the better. With luck it might even allow him and Lika more time together. That, he was somewhat shocked to realize, was all he actually cared about in life.

Then, after a long gap, a note arrived. 'BEAUFILS. 10 July.'

Brodie took a tram to the Latin Quarter and went to the Grand Hôtel.

'Monsieur Beaufils – a great pleasure. It's been a while but we have your usual room for you, I'm happy to say.'

'Excellent.'

'And Madame Beaufils, is she well?'

'Very well, thank you.'

'And she will be joining you later?'

'Yes. She's arriving by train from . . .' he thought of a place, randomly. 'Poitiers.'

'A most beautiful town.'

'So I believe. She has a cousin there,' he improvised.

He paid for the room in advance, took his key, declined any assistance with his suitcase and headed up the stairs to 'their' room.

His suitcase was no longer an empty prop. It contained food and drink, should the opportunity arrive for a more protracted stay. He unpacked a bottle of red wine, two glasses, a tea towel, a *saucisson sec*, a clasp knife, a small jar of gherkins and a fresh baguette and laid them out on the tea towel.

Half an hour later Lika arrived. They kissed, then Lika sat on the bed and broke the baguette in two.

'I'm starving,' she said. Brodie began to slice the sausage. 'But I can only stay an hour,' she said, munching. 'Now John's back it's difficult. He thinks I've gone for an audition.'

Brodie began to undress, throwing his boots across the room. He helped Lika off with her jacket and began to unbutton her skirt at the back.

'Oh yes,' she said, her mouth full. 'And he wants to see you, he said.'

'Who?'

'John.'

Brodie stopped his unbuttoning and straightened, alarmed. Lika stepped out of her skirt.

'Don't look so stern,' she said. 'It's nothing to worry about.'

'Why does he want to see me?'

'I don't know. He went to find you at Channon and they told him you didn't work there any more.'

'He can't be suspicious about us, surely?'

'No, no. I said I had met you in the street one day – quite by chance – and you had given me your visiting card.'

'It didn't make him suspect anything?'

'Brodie. I know you. He knows I know you. It's a coincidence – in a city people bump into people they know.'

'But it's not a coincidence, that's the point.'

'He thinks it's a coincidence. You'll find a letter waiting for you at the *pension*, I'm sure.'

She was naked now. She ran her fingers under the crease of her breasts and wiped the sweat on the coverlet.

'Phoo! It's hot in this room under the roof. Hurry up. Take your clothes off.'

John Kilbarron poured him a glass of champagne.

'What're we celebrating?' Brodie asked, cautiously. They were alone in the salon of the Saint-Germain apartment.

'The answer to our problems, I hope,' Kilbarron said, and clinked glasses with him. Kilbarron seemed in good spirits. The lines on his face seemed deeper, more obvious, like the creases in his dirty linen shirt. There was a French phrase that summed up his look perfectly, Brodie remembered: *visage buriné*.

'I hear you've parted company with Channon.'

'Yes. It was a . . . misunderstanding. But it was impossible for me to stay on. They've been very generous.'

'Something to do with that lazy fat sot, Calder, I'll wager.'

'Yes.'

'Well so much the better for me – and for you, young Brodie. Your lucky day has arrived!'

He went to search for one of his cigarillos and some matches. Brodie felt very uncomfortable – very conscious of his hypocrisy, his subterfuge – praying that Lika wouldn't come in. Kilbarron returned, puffing smoke.

'Sit, sit – and I'll tell you what's happened.'

Brodie sat and Kilbarron paced the room, smoking and drinking, recounting what had transpired. He had a new sponsor, he said – an extremely rich Russian woman, a philanthropist, who wanted him to come and be the virtuoso-composer-conductor at her own private theatre in St Petersburg.

'Stacks of money,' Kilbarron said. 'Barns full of money. Doesn't know what to do with it all. But,' he whirled round, 'she's a music lover, bless her. She wants to do something for Russian music and I'm her man.'

'Congratulations.'

'I have to give a few concerts, write some masterworks, devise a season or two of great Russian music for the good folk of St Petersburg and she'll pay for everyone.' He smiled. 'Including my entourage. Malachi, Lika and – if you've a sensible bone in your lanky great body – you.'

'St Petersburg . . .' Brodie said, playing for time.

'We'd all have to go and live there – for a while, like. A year or two, just to get the whole show up and running. What do you say, Brodie, my lad?'

'Who is this woman?'

'Her name is Elisaveta Somethingovna Vadimova. Her late husband – now sitting on the right hand of God Almighty – was Russia's fourth-richest man, so I'm told. Or third – who cares? Rich as the tsar, by all accounts. Iron, ships, coal – you name it, he profited mightily from it. And now old Mrs Vadimova controls the family fisc. And being such a music lover she's decided to become a patron of the arts. Built her own theatre, hired her own orchestra – all she needs is a bona-fide star of the European concert hall.' Kilbarron gave a little bow. 'Just to add the final touch of credibility.'

'Where do I fit in – to your entourage?'

Kilbarron held out his right hand. It was trembling.

'It's got worse, see. I need you, Brodie boy, to work your Moncur magic on the pianos I'll have to play. I insisted you were part of the *équipe*. Och, aye. Insisted. I can't play more than twenty minutes otherwise. And the pain is getting . . . intense.' He flexed his fingers, his eyes tightening with remembered agony. 'It's a fucking nightmare.'

He turned away and crossed the room to fill his champagne glass with brandy. For some reason it was only now that Brodie realized Kilbarron was actually quite drunk.

'But the Channon was perfect for you,' Brodie said. 'I regulated it so precisely. Bespoke, tailor-made.'

'Alas, alack, I had to sell the Channon. Damn shame – but I got a very good price for it, you'll be pleased to hear. I was in a temporary financial bind, shall we say. It was me or the piano, if you catch my drift.' He wandered back over to him, picking up the champagne bottle as he approached. 'So, are you with me?'

'I suppose I'm free, but—'

'Whatever they're paying you at Channon's I'll double it – or rather Madame Vadimova will double it. And free accommodation, by the way. Everybody's on a salary – Malachi, Lika. Then there's the concert fees on top. It's the golden goose, Brodie, I tell ye.' He topped up Brodie's champagne. Brodie had noticed how Kilbarron's accent thickened as he grew more drunk. The golden goose again . . . Brodie wondered at the prevalence of this particular fable in his life. It didn't augur well, he thought, all this talk of golden geese. But he didn't need to think further. If Kilbarron went to St Petersburg then Lika would go with him. And Brodie had to go where Lika went – it was as simple as that.

'Count me in, Mr Kilbarron. I'm very grateful to be asked.'

Then, as if on cue, Lika came into the room. She was wearing one of the newly fashionable tea gowns, full, diaphanous and swirling, a pale apricot colour embroidered with scarlet flowers.

Brodie stood. Tense.

'Miss Blum,' he said. 'Delighted to see you again.'

'Mr Moncur. A great pleasure.'

They shook hands. Brodie squeezed hard. He felt a blush creeping from his neck to his cheeks, as if his betrayal of Kilbarron was written on his forehead. When he thought of his last encounter with Lika – what she had done to him; what she had asked him to do to her . . . And now there she was, calmly accepting a glass of champagne, standing opposite him in her tea gown.

'Brodie is to come with us to St Petersburg,' Kilbarron announced. 'I managed to persuade him.'

'That's excellent news,' she said and raised her glass. 'Here's to our new life in Piter.' She wandered round behind Kilbarron and pointed to herself as if to say it had been her idea. *Mon idée*, she mouthed.

Brodie turned away and forced himself to listen to what Kilbarron was saying. He was complaining: he had to compose, not just perform: Madame Vadimova wanted a 'World Premiere' – a symphony, a concerto – most tiresome. Brodie nodded, encouragingly he hoped, but all he could think about was that he was going to St Petersburg with Lika, that their clandestine love affair would continue somehow in Russia, come what may. But, as the three of them stood there – the cuckold, the lover and the mistress – in the Saint-Germain apartment, drinking, enthusing, he had a sudden dark premonition that life in St Petersburg was going to prove more dangerous than Paris.

PART III

St Petersburg

1899

I

Apartment 4b
Malaya Morskaya, 57
St Petersburg
Russia

17 May 1899

Dear Lady Dalcastle,

Please forgive the epistolary silence but the picaresque travels of Don Brodie Moncur continue. I have quit Channon (amiably enough – a long story) and Paris and have been engaged as 'secretary' to Maestro John Kilbarron, the famous pianist. He has taken up an appointment in St Petersburg that is contracted for some five years. So here I am and here I will stay for a while.

Kilbarron's patrons are a mother and a daughter – the Vadimovas – heirs to an immense fortune and who have built their own theatre on an island in the bay of St Petersburg (or 'Piter' as the locals call it). They plan to offer a season of concerts, concentrating on Russian music, that will be organized by John Kilbarron who will very often perform himself. The repertory is his to choose but the excitement in the city is palpable. Great things are expected. My role is to give advice (hardly required) and to regulate and tune his piano (very important). I am, I blush to report, being exceptionally well remunerated.

Furthermore – the Russian bounty knows no end – I have been given free use of a vast apartment owned by the Vadimov family in a street just off Vosnesensky Prospekt, one of the city's great thoroughfares. Think of Edinburgh's Princes Street transposed to Russia and double the width. Shops, apartments, grand hotels – and there are three of these great boulevards radiating out from the Admiralty complex of buildings on the southern bank of the Neva river. Perhaps Piter's Champs-Elysées might give you a better sense of the huge scale of these streets. My apartment has seven rooms and I have a couple – Nikanor and Fyolka – who cook and generally look after my every need. I have to travel with John Kilbarron when he gives concerts in Russia and abroad and these last few months since arriving I have been to Stockholm, Moscow, Kiev, Berlin and Prague. But, for the main part, I reside here and this will be my address for the duration of my stay.

Petersburg is an astonishing city with a great river dividing it and then dividing it again into a kind of delta filled with islands crossed by innumerable bridges. My guidebook says that the buildings (very large) are somewhat 'monotonous in style'. I don't agree. They are painted in bright colours – yellow, pink, pale green, pale blue, ochre, terracotta. Imagine Edinburgh (or Peebles!) similarly bedecked – it would change everything.

It's a large city of over 2 million people. There are 10,000 Germans living here and 2,000 British, astonishingly. French will easily get you by in most bourgeois or intellectual environments. The locals may speak a few words of German or French but no English at all. Consequently I am trying to learn a few elementary Russian phrases so I can communicate with Nikanor and Fyolka but it's a d—nambly difficult language, Russian, what with its different Cyrillic alphabet (33 letters) and nouns that decline, like Latin. Progress is slow. Thank goodness I can speak French.

By the way, it is best to write to me care of my bank: the Russian and English Bank, Nevsky, 28, St P.

Wishing you good health, wealth and happiness (as they say in Russia).

Affectionately yours,
Brodie Moncur

*

Brodie came through to the dining room in his dressing gown with a scarf at his throat. As he had shaved he felt he had a cold coming on – his throat was scratchy and his chest felt a bit constricted and of course that always gave him cause for worry. He had survived an entire Russian winter in St Petersburg without the trace of a cold or sniffle – let alone any haemorrhage. It was face-numbing, eye-watering, snot-freezing winter cold of a sort that he had never encountered, even in the remotest Scottish glen – a ringing, shivering cold, almost audible, as if some vast ice gong had sounded, freezing the earth. He had managed to explain to Nikanor that he needed warmth and so Nikanor had obligingly lit the stoves in every room of the apartment, stoking up a winter-long fug of heat – tended assiduously all day by Fyolka – and consequently when Brodie was at home he basked in a near-hothouse atmosphere, often removing his jacket for more comfort. There was no question of the fuel expense involved in keeping the apartment thus heated – the Vadimovas' largesse seemed limitless. But now summer was arriving the stoves went unlit and perhaps the unfamiliar cool had brought on this irritating little cough. He was also suddenly aware of damp. The apartment was old and he suspected he was its first tenant in many years. Certainly Nikanor and Fyolka seemed delighted that he had moved in and that they actually had someone to look after and fuss over.

Brodie pushed open the door to the dining room and saw that his place had been laid out at the end of the huge table – it could seat twenty, easily. In the far corner in a wooden armchair sat Kyrill, reading a newspaper. Kyrill was an elderly man in his sixties with a thin, always smiling face, clean-shaven, almost bald, smartly dressed in a threadbare suit, a clean white shirt and tie. He spoke a little French and was a useful interpreter. Brodie had no idea who he was or what function he served but he seemed to live in the apartment, somewhere in Nikanor and Fyolka's quarters. He was often to be found in various rooms, reading or playing an elaborate form of patience with two packs of cards. He was an entirely benign, inoffensive presence. Like a plant in a pot, Brodie thought, moved from room to room.

'Bonjour, Monsieur Kyrill,' Brodie said and sat down.

'Bonjour, Monsieur Moncur,' Kyrill said in reply and returned to his newspaper.

Fyolka emerged from the kitchen with a tray and spoke to Brodie in garrulous Russian. She placed a glass of milk and a plate of cold herring in front of him and left. Why had she given him milk today? She had given him tea at every breakfast she had served him. He didn't want milk; he needed something hot for his throat.

'Fyolka?' Brodie summoned her back through the small door that led to the kitchen and their living quarters. He had never been through that door.

'*Du thé?*' he said. Kyrill had sworn that she understood some words of French and German. Fyolka said something in Russian back to him. She was obviously not familiar with *thé*. He looked round for Kyrill's aid but the man had silently slipped out of the room. What was the German for tea? He had left his small transliterated English–Russian dictionary in his room and couldn't be bothered going back for it. He remembered the German for tea.

'*Eine Tasse Tee, bitte.*'

No reaction. Where was Kyrill when you needed him? He mimed pouring from a teapot and stirring a cup of tea and then drinking from it. Fyolka disappeared and returned a minute later with a cup of coffee. At least it was hot. Brodie asked for bread and jam in French and German and handed her the cold herring to take away. She brought him a greyish bread roll and some gooseberry jelly. It was progress of sorts, he supposed. He ate his breakfast, bumped into Kyrill who was returning to the dining room for his newspaper, went back to his room, dressed and headed out into St Petersburg to his office.

Strolling though Piter to work always invigorated him – it was exciting: he couldn't quite believe it was he, Brodie Moncur from Liethen Manor, walking along these broad quays by the wide Neva, only recently thawed, past the coloured cliff-like facades of these huge ornate buildings with their spires and cupolas and countless flags flying, moving through these crowds, two-thirds of whom seemed to be in some kind of uniform. Some of them were military or naval types but it appeared to Brodie that having a job that required you to wear a uniform of sorts was somehow every Russian's dream. And almost everyone favoured the same style of hat – a variation of a forage cap made of felt, he assumed it was, with a little leather peak. He was aware of being very much the foreigner – his clothes, his shoes, his hat and coat seemed to shout 'I am not Russian!' and he could spot the other foreigners as he passed them and they too spotted him. It was an odd kind of solidarity amongst strangers. St Petersburg was meant to be Russia's most European city but, to Brodie, it always seemed very Russian indeed. He had come to feel at home in Paris, unreflectingly occupying and using the city like a Parisian. He doubted he'd ever experience something similar in Piter.

Brodie crossed Nikolaevsky Bridge, then Tuchkov Bridge, before arriving at what was known as the Petrograd Side and turned left until he came to the beginnings of Petrovsky Park where the New Russia Theatre was situated. His office was in the theatre building itself. The theatre had been built only two years previously, a 500-seat auditorium with stalls and two galleries, made entirely of wood (painted white) and fitted with electric power. His office, however, was something of a misnomer – a very small room on the top floor with a skylight. It had a desk and a chair and an empty pine filing cabinet. His name was on the door in Russian and English. He suspected he had been furnished with these modest premises as a result of Kilbarron's negotiations with the Vadimovas. In truth, he wasn't Kilbarron's secretary at all – he was his piano tuner, his piano fixer – but in order to seem like a secretary, and justify his salary, he had to be provided with minimal secretarial facilities.

Elisaveta Ivanovna Vadimova, like many a rich music lover in St Petersburg (Count Sheremetyev, Boris Liskov, Mikhail Berkesh), had her own theatre and her own orchestra. She was therefore in a position to establish tastes and advance reputations, all in the cause of celebrating the genius of Russian music. Brodie now knew that she had seen Kilbarron's recital at the *soirée russe* in the Théâtre de la République where she had been so overwhelmed by his playing of the Rimsky-Korsakov concerto and then by his own 'paraphrases' of Borodin that she had decided that, despite the fact that he was Irish and his star was dimming somewhat, he was the ideal person to be the guest artiste-cum-conductor-cum-composer of her New

Russia Theatre in Petrovsky Park, St Petersburg. Money was the least of her concerns – anything Kilbarron wanted he seemed to be instantly provided with. Brodie wondered if it had been the on-going negotiations with the Vadimovas that had made Kilbarron so bullish with Ainsley Channon. He could ask Ainsley for 200 guineas a concert, take it or leave it, because he knew he had Elisaveta Vadimova in St Petersburg ready to grant him anything.

Brodie closed the door to his office and sat down at his desk. He took off his spectacles, polished the lenses, replaced his spectacles and took out the novel he was reading from his desk drawer – *The Master of Ballantrae* by Robert Louis Stevenson. He had read a great deal since his arrival in St Petersburg because there was practically nothing else for him to do until a new concert was forthcoming. The concert piano at the New Russia Theatre was a three-year-old Zollmeyer. Though he didn't regard it as a marque of the top rank, Brodie had voiced and regulated it for Kilbarron in the same way he had regulated the Channon, carefully weighting the treble octaves for his ailing right hand. Once that was done there was nothing to do but await Kilbarron's summons. Kiev, Prague, Berlin or wherever he might be off to – a concert here, a recital there – as he prepared for the inaugural season at the New Russia. In any other circumstances, after a few months, Brodie would have resigned, such was the sheer lassitude and boredom of his existence – but he couldn't resign. Only by being present in St Petersburg did he have a chance of seeing Lika. And so he had to stay, however tedious his days were – he would never leave her.

Lika lived with Kilbarron – and Malachi – in what seemed a semi-palace on Nevsky Prospekt. It was an entire house with stabling and kitchens on the ground floor and a grand sweeping staircase in a separate foyer that led you up to the public rooms and the living quarters on the four floors above. Malachi had his suite of rooms on the third floor. The *piano nobile* contained two drawing rooms – one large, one small – a billiard room, a dining room (seating up to forty) and a small ballroom with a minstrel gallery. Above on the second floor were Lika and John Kilbarron's spacious apartments – two bedrooms, dressing rooms, a sitting room, a bathroom. Staff were plentiful: doormen, chambermaids, a coachman and grooms, a butler, a cook and numerous kitchen maids were all laid on, courtesy of Elisaveta Vadimova. Kilbarron revelled in the luxury and splendour. The problem for Brodie was that he could hardly ever be alone with Lika.

They had travelled to Petersburg in September the previous year – delays in leaving Paris were inevitable as the Kilbarron brothers made frequent trips to Petersburg to meet the Vadimovas, mother and daughter, and sort out the fine details of this job of jobs. And, while Kilbarron was away, Brodie and Lika availed themselves of the freedom of the Grand Hôtel des Etrangers. It had been perhaps the happiest period of their relationship – all fear of discovery absent – and one week they spent three uninterrupted days together. But now they were in Petersburg everything became highly complicated again. Brodie kept a running calculation: from September 1898 to May 1899 – no sexual congress with Lika. They had managed the odd seized kiss and carnal fumble in corridors and theatre dressing rooms but nothing more. And Brodie was often away himself with Kilbarron on his concert and recital tours. The frustration mounted steadily as Brodie, when he was in the city, saw Lika several times a week but always in Kilbarron's company. Masturbation was only the briefest consolation. Somehow they would find a way, Brodie knew, but Petersburg wasn't Paris, everything was different, more complicated.

He had slipped her a note once – 'Meet me in the Hôtel d'Angleterre tomorrow, room 113. I'll be there all day.' He waited, slept the night there, but she never appeared. In the few whispered moments when they were alone she had said, just be patient, something will work out – I'm thinking, planning. It was scant solace that she was missing him also. But whenever Kilbarron left Petersburg Brodie left with him, Lika staying behind. It was a maddening conundrum. What had seemed like the perfect solution – they would be together constantly in Petersburg – was proving incredibly disheartening.

He put down his novel at midday and went out to find something to eat.

The Restaurant Français Dominique had, at least, a French maître d' and Brodie liked going there if only to speak French and drink expensive French wine with his pike in the Jewish fashion, stuffed eel or boiled bream with horseradish (the Dominique specialized in fish dishes). There was a small garden at the back and, as the weather warmed, they laid out tables there. The maître d' – his name was Zéphyr Dommecq – greeted him familiarly and said they had some excellent Chablis, just arrived. Brodie didn't even ask how much it cost and ordered a bottle. He was, by his standards, richer than he'd ever been. His accommodation was free and he was earning double the amount that Channon had paid him – and yet he had little to spend his money on. In Paris the days and nights at the Grand Hôtel had diminished his savings severely. But now his account at the Russian and English Bank had several hundreds of pounds in it, untouched.

He sat down at his table in the garden and looked around, lighting a cigarette. He could hear that two other tables were occupied by Germans. The May sun warmed his thigh and the Chablis was ideally cold. Here he was in St Petersburg eating an expensive lunch with an entire bottle of wine to himself. Life was good, he supposed, except . . . As he sat there waiting for his first course – a cherry soup with buckwheat – he realized that personal happiness was such a fickle, fragile thing. He should be happy, yet he was unhappy because he couldn't be with Lika, the woman he loved beyond all reason. But to quit Piter and leave her would only make him more unhappy. Desperately unhappy. So, he told himself, better to be less unhappy, however unhappy that made him. He was trapped in a maddening cycle of strange unhappiness. He ate his soup and Zéphyr promptly brought him his boiled carp with red wine and topped up his glass of Chablis.

'I can recommend the sour cream pie for dessert,' Zéphyr said. 'Completely delicious.'

Brodie wandered back to the theatre after lunch feeling full and a bit wine-numbed. Perhaps a whole bottle of Chablis was somewhat self-indulgent, however mildly unhappy he happened to be.

He went into the theatre through the stage door to find it full of young women – tiny young women in the corps de ballet come for rehearsal. They quickly parted to make way for him – this strange giant – and fell silent. As he left the foyer he heard them erupt in giggles and laughing chatter, like a gibberish of songbirds. The ballet season was starting at the New Russia so, for him, it was even quieter than usual. More time for RLS.

But in his office he found two notes on his desk: one from his doctor reminding him of his appointment, and the other from Malachi Kilbarron announcing a meeting at the Nevsky Prospekt house at six o'clock that evening. Brodie's mood lifted – suddenly his day was full and he would probably catch a glimpse of Lika.

2

Dr Varia Alexandrovna Sampsoniyevskaya sat down at her desk and said he could put his shirt back on. She was in her late thirties, Brodie estimated – this was only their third meeting – and she had a bony handsome face with a strongly hooked nose. But it was an unsmiling severe face as if Dr Sampson, as Brodie referred to her, had little joy in her life. Perhaps she was as mildly unhappy as he was. She spoke excellent French and had studied in Paris for a year under Théophile Roguin. She was wearing a knee-length white cotton coat over her suit and her hair was held up in a loose bun secured with many hairclips.

'You have some congestion in the right lung,' she said. 'Just a cold, I would say. I'll give you a camphor inhalant to clear your throat and nose. Keep warm.' She scribbled something down on a notepad and sat back, looking at him as he buttoned up his shirt.

'So – you had no problems this last winter?'

'No. I felt well. Now that it's spring I feel ill.'

'You're very lucky. Next winter I advise you to leave Piter. Go to the south of Europe – or even North Africa. Lisbon, Seville, Marrakesh, Algiers, Biarritz, Nice. Wait until the Neva thaws before you come back.'

'I've been to Nice,' he said. 'That was my French doctor's recommendation.'

'Well, if you know somewhere agreeable I would book yourself a room from December to May.'

'I don't think my employer would permit such a long absence.'

She shrugged. 'Then you will have to "trust to luck".' She said the last three words in English. 'Is that the right expression?'

'It is. But isn't that life for us all? Trusting to luck?'

'You can always try to give luck a helping hand,' she said and pulled out a drawer to take out a cigarette case and opened it to offer him one. He saw they were Russian cigarettes – yellow paper with a long cardboard filter.

'If you don't mind,' Brodie said. 'I'd prefer one of my own.'

'What do you smoke?' Dr Sampson asked.

Brodie explained. 'They're called Margaritas, imported from the United States of America.'

'May I try one?'

They both lit up a Margarita and sat there savouring the American blend, doctor and patient. Brodie felt the mood shift in a subtle way – from professional rectitude to a kind of amiable curiosity.

'This is the first time I've smoked American tobacco,' she said.

'It's the best,' Brodie said.

'Do you like it here in Piter? Are you enjoying the city?' Dr Sampson asked, picking a shred from her tongue tip.

'Yes. Very much. It has its frustrations but so does every where.'

'And you're a musician.'

'I'm the secretary to a great pianist – John Kilbarrron.'

'John Kilbarron! Yes, I've heard of him. The "Irish Liszt".'

'That's him.' Brodie explained about the move from Paris to St Petersburg. 'Are you a music lover?' he asked.

'Of course. I'm Russian.'

'Then I must invite you – as my guest – to one of Kilbarron's recitals. He's extraordinary. They'll be starting up at the end of the summer.'

'Thank you, that's very kind,' she said. 'I'd like that very much.' Her face transformed itself briefly as she allowed herself a genuine smile.

There was something oddly attractive about Dr Sampson, Brodie thought, as she walked with him to the dispensary. In another life, a life without Lika, he might have been drawn to her handsome melancholic reserve and would have enjoyed the challenge of trying to break it down. She left him at the dispensary as his powdered camphor was being measured out and thanked him again for the invitation.

*

The butler, Sergei, showed him up to the main drawing room of the Nevsky Prospekt house on the first floor. Kilbarron had had it redecorated in varying shades of red. There were red velvet curtains, a maroon carpet and vivid scarlet Chesterfield sofas. He had also hung a large collection of ancient exotic weapons on the walls – swords and sabres, falchions and scimitars, claymores and axes, shields, halberds, pikes and lances, flails and morning stars. Helms and helmets were displayed on the occasional tables. It was not a comfortable room to be in, Brodie always thought: the assorted weapons, their blades polished and gleaming, hinted at a barely suppressed anger, the hues of red affected your mood, strangely, put you on edge. There was no piano in the room, nor any pictures. One would have thought it a military museum. Brodie had never found the time to ask Lika what she felt about it.

Malachi Kilbarron welcomed him. Brodie hadn't seen him for some weeks and, to his eye, Malachi appeared distinctly bulkier. It wasn't so much that he was corpulent – he just appeared to carry more weight, took up more space than most men – a block of solid flesh. He offered Brodie vodka but he declined, still feeling the effects of his lunchtime Chablis.

'Wonderful stuff,' Malachi said, pouring himself a small tumblerful. 'You can drink it any time of the day.'

'That's what they say about whisky,' Brodie said, considering that if you were so inclined you could justify drinking anything at any time of the day.

Then John Kilbarron came in – Brodie sensing instantly that he was not sober at all. He was perfectly steady as he crossed the floor but there was something unfocussed about his gaze, as if what was going on in his head was more interesting than what might be available in this room.

He shook Brodie's hand warmly, a two-fisted shake, and clapped him on the shoulder, as he accepted Malachi's offer of a cut-crystal glass of vodka. Kilbarron sat down carefully. Brodie saw there were food stains on the front of his jacket.

'We're going on a trip,' he said. 'Tomorrow. Elisaveta Vadimova has given me a dacha.'

'Has loaned you a dacha,' Malachi corrected.

'We're going to be *dachniki*!' Kilbarron exclaimed excitedly, almost shouting. 'Why aren't you drinking, Brodie? Get him some vodka, Malachi, we don't take no for an answer in this house.'

Malachi handed him a glass with an inch of vodka in it. Suddenly Brodie was grateful for more alcohol. The mood was febrile. He took a sip and his lips burned.

'You can have your own room, Brodie,' Kilbarron yelled at him. 'Summer is a comin' in and we'll have our own house in the country. Going to be country folk! Gentry!'

He hauled himself to his feet and went to refill his glass. Malachi sidled up to Brodie as Kilbarron went searching for his cigarillos.

'We need to talk about the New Russia programme.'

'Of course.'

'John says he wants to conduct, not play.'

'I think he has to play,' Brodie said. 'We're sold out.'

'Well you'd better work some magic on the piano,' Malachi said. 'He can barely last five minutes.'

Brodie thought: maybe he should stop drinking so much. Maybe he should stop injecting himself with his 'painkiller'. However, the concert season was still months off. Perhaps country life was the answer – peace and quiet, plenty of time to rehearse. Brodie switched his mind away from the prospect – it was Malachi's problem, not his.

And then Lika came in.

'Mr Moncur, what a pleasure to see you.'

'Likewise, Miss Blum.'

They shook hands, Brodie squeezing hers as hard as he dared. He felt the pulse-race, the oxygen-need. It was astonishing the physical effects her presence wrought on him.

'May I have another glass, Malachi? You're right, it is wonderful stuff.'

'We're all going to the dacha tomorrow,' Kilbarron declaimed. 'Ten o'clock, the Warsaw station.'

Lika turned her back to Kilbarron and Malachi and mouthed to Brodie, 'You must come.' Then she turned back.

'What fun,' she said. 'Our very own place in the country.'

3

It took only thirty minutes by train from the Warsaw station to Dubechnia, the nearest stop to Nikolskoe, the Vadimov estate, south of Petersburg.

A short journey, Brodie thought, a bonus. Kilbarron, after the exuberation of the day before, seemed taciturn, morose – and he didn't look well. Brodie sat opposite Lika in the train and from time to time would press his foot on hers while taking care to be looking out of the window, or at Malachi puffing on his thin cheroot. The compartment soon filled with smoke as Kilbarron roused himself to light one of his cigarillos. Brodie offered Lika a cigarette and they both lit up. Smoke was the best way to combat smoke.

The train slowed – today it was clearly going to be more than half an hour to Dubechnia. Brodie took out his *Blue Guide* from his bag and read about Dubechnia. The station (third class with a buffet) was just over a verst from the small town that boasted five hotels (two 'very bad' and another one under the management of Poles, so the guidebook said), six churches, eight schools, a nunnery and a library with a free reading room. But, when they arrived at the station twenty minutes late, it transpired that it was another hour to the estate by coach and horses. They were met by the estate manager, Philipp Philippovitch Lvov, a heavily bearded, reserved man. He had with him a four-horse carriage and, once boarded with their luggage on the roof, they were trundled through the town on its unpaved main street, past a few stone houses and then many wooden ones and then past a steam flour mill, an abattoir, a rope mill, a tannery and many warehouses before they reached open country.

They travelled fairly comfortably along dirt roads through growing rye fields towards a place that was called Maloe Nikolskoe – 'Lesser' Nikolskoe – the dacha that Elisaveta Vadimova had lent to

Kilbarron. Kilbarron himself perked up on the journey as Malachi passed around a hip flask of vodka. It was a sunny May day with a thin baggage of clouds hurried by a brisk breeze. Warm air flowed by him through the open window. From time to time Brodie's knees bumped against Lika's – she was opposite him in the carriage – and they stared at each other whenever the two Kilbarrons were in conversation. Brodie's eyes were saying – I want to be in bed with you, naked. Lika toyed provocatively with her hair and at one stage deliberately touched her lips with her forefinger for a good minute, her tongue licking out from time to time, driving him almost insane with desire, his erection a buckled L behind the straining barrier of his buttoned flies.

'Where is César?' he managed to ask, as innocently as possible, at one stage.

'Oh, I left him behind,' she said. 'I have to see what dogs they have here. They might eat him alive. I know these farm dogs – monsters.' She turned to Philipp Lvov and spoke to him in Russian.

'Yes, he told me that they have half a dozen dogs at the farm,' she said. 'A city dog like César would stand no chance.'

The day was warm and both Lika and Kilbarron fell into a doze as the carriage progressed steadily through the countryside. Brodie looked out of the window and felt that he might have been driving through the Borders of Scotland. Rye fields, valleys, copses, wooden bridges over small rivers dense with riverine trees and shrubs. It was only the villages they passed through that made the landscape strange again – made it Russian – with their thatched wooden shacks, small gardens with picket fences, the occasional stuccoed, onion-domed church. Then he was reminded that he was a thousand miles from home – but at least he was only three feet away from the woman he loved. Malachi was speaking to him.

'What's that? Sorry?'

'What're you smoking there, Brodie? I've always meant to ask.'

Brodie explained, offered him one and Malachi lit up.

'Very nice, very smooth,' Malachi said. 'There's no burn. You could smoke these all day long.'

Brodie told him about the shop in Edinburgh: Hoskings in the Grassmarket. Mr Hoskings would send anywhere in the world, but cash with order. Malachi took a little notebook from his pocket, unscrewed his pen and wrote down the details.

'You're a mine of useful information, Brodie Moncur. I shall be ordering from Mr Hoskings.'

He peered out of the window.

'Nearly there, I think. I wouldn't like to do this road in winter, begod, I'll tell you that for nothing.'

Maloe Nikolskoe was actually quite a large house made of green-painted planks with a rusty corrugated-iron roof. There was a fancy four-pillared porch over a wide veranda with an elaborate gingerbread verge-board and a mezzanine floor above, similarly over-decorated, with a disproportionately large weathervane. It was, so Philipp told them in his halting French, the house of the old estate steward, converted and improved. Behind it was a wide farmyard fringed with various wooden barns, storerooms and stables, where the farm animals were kept and where the servants slept. It was fenced off with high palings so it could not be seen from the house.

They clambered out of the carriage and their luggage was carried into the main house by a couple of lackeys that Philipp had summoned from the house. Brodie stretched and walked to the edge of the gravelled driveway. Here a small river had been dammed to create a large pond – more of a semi-lake – fifty yards across with a bathing house and a jetty with a boat tied to it. Through a copse of silver birches on the far side he could make out the roofs of the buildings of a small village half a mile beyond. Turning, he could see the dense woodland behind the main house, whence the small river flowed. Dogs barked, roosters uselessly crowed, cows moo-ed. The sun shone down. He felt, surprisingly, very at home. However much he enjoyed his urban existence, he was, he realized, still a country boy at heart.

Set beside the lake, not far from the bathing house, was a two-storey wooden cottage, also made of planks, also painted green. Philipp Lvov told them that the 'big house', Nikolskoe itself, was about two versts away, through the woodland. Having looked around they all went inside.

They found simple, airy rooms, sparsely furnished. Rugs on polished wooden floors, sofas and armchairs and bare wainscoted walls except for a small icon in one corner. The main thing, Lika declared, was that it was clean. No bugs, no cockroaches. They were each apportioned a room – or at least he and Malachi were. Lika and Kilbarron, it transpired, were to sleep in the cottage by the pond.

'I'm getting a piano shipped in,' Kilbarron said to Brodie. 'You'll need to get it regulated for me. I've got a devil of a lot of work to do.'

'What work?' Brodie said without thinking.

'I've got to write a fucking symphony in three months,' Kilbarron said. 'It's part of the contract, remember?' He smiled a dead smile. 'Busy summer for me.'

Philipp introduced them to the staff: the housekeeper, the cook, her assistant, two maids, two lackeys and the coachman who would transport them here and there. Outside there were gardeners and farm labourers. Maloe Nikolskoe had everything that might be required.

'And now lunch is served,' Philipp said and opened the door to the dining room.

In a significant way the arrival of Maloe Nikolskoe in the life of John Kilbarron and his entourage made everything worse for Brodie, he realized. Kilbarron decided that he and Lika would live there, not in Piter, much to Brodie's frustration. He was invited out at weekends, along with Malachi and various other friends and associates, and a form of Russian *dachniki* house party would ensue. A lot of eating and drinking, charades and games – there was a croquet lawn and a tennis court – walks and bathing. Brodie hoped these weekends would distract Kilbarron and allow time for him to be with Lika but it proved incredibly difficult to be alone with her – there was always someone hovering or sitting nearby or opening doors. Their fear of discovery made them ridiculously prudent – the occasional two-second kiss, tongues deep in each other's mouths; a brief, fervent holding of hands. Otherwise Brodie had to be satisfied with staring at her across a busy conversation-filled room or brushing against her as they passed on the croquet court. It was beginning to drive him mad. Then one day he had an idea.

It was their third weekend at Maloe Nikolskoe. In fact 'weekend' was something of a misnomer. True, the weekends would start on Friday afternoon with guests arriving from Piter, ferried in from Dubechnia, but the stay was open-ended and usually drifted on to Tuesday or Wednesday before the party finally broke up. Annoyingly, Kilbarron didn't seem to want to leave – and he insisted Lika stay with him. He had weeks before the New Russia concert season would begin and until then, he said, there was nothing to take him away from the country. Here lay inspiration and less distraction.

Brodie's idea took shape when, one sultry Friday afternoon, he spotted some fishing rods in the 'games room' of the dacha. He prepared his rod and reel, tied on his three hooks, dug up some earthworms from the dunghill in the farmyard and wandered up the river along a brambly path looking for a large enough pool where he could fish, glad to be away from the house and its rowdy guests.

The river – he should ask what it was called, he thought – was shallow but slow-flowing, nothing like the rushing, burbling Liethen Water. As soon as he left the farmland the vegetation thickened round it – aspens and birches, tall grass and thistles grew densely on the banks and made the going tricky. Flies buzzed around his head and the sun was hot on his face but he felt a familiar happiness settle on him. This was a world he knew and was at peace in. After about half an hour he found a place where the river made a big swerve and where a deep pool had formed. Here the slow river's lazy chestnut sprawl turned lithe as it poured over some rocks into a deep shadowed pool. There was no willow, but a tall ash tree leaned over the turbid dark water casting useful shadows. He baited his fine small hooks. There was a slight breeze and the coins of dappled sunlight on the water's surface shifted and merged. He walked up to the head of the pool where the running water slowed and deepened. He cast his line out to the head of the pool and let the current bumble the line and the worms downstream into the pool. He stripped off lengths of line from the reel, rod balanced in his hand, and let the line run free, floating the worms down with the current into the shadow cast by the ash. Blue damsel flies hovered over the watercress and ferns that edged the pool. A bite! He jerked on the line, turned the reel – not a big fish, he knew at once – and landed a small gudgeon, or so he thought. He wet his hands in the running water and unhooked it and threw it back in.

He set his rod down and lit a cigarette, taking a short stroll around, getting his bearings. Bushes and trees, many saplings, grew close to the river here but, under the ash, was a turfy green patch where you could spread a blanket and picnic, he thought. Or spread a blanket and make love . . .

That night during dinner he slipped Lika a note with a small map, detailing the route he had taken up the river. The pool with the ash tree was underlined. 'I go one way. Thirty minutes later you go another. We meet by the ash tree pool.'

The next day after lunch – the other guests playing croquet, lying in hammocks reading, or sitting drinking and smoking on the veranda – Brodie picked up his rod and fishing basket and announced he was off to catch their supper. Nobody gave him any notice and, anyway, Kilbarron had retreated to his cottage to sleep off lunch, soused on wine. Brodie imagined that in twenty minutes or so Lika would idly go off for a walk with César. César was now allowed to visit Maloe Nikolskoe as the farm dogs were mostly confined to their yard and, anyway, seemed uninterested in Lika's little dog.

In his fishing basket Brodie had a cotton tablecloth snaffled from the kitchen linen cupboard. When he reached the ash-tree pool he spread this on the grassy patch under the ash and sat down and waited. Thirty minutes later he saw Lika coming – but from upstream, to his surprise, emerging from a copse of silver birches. He stood up as she advanced through the high blond grass. She was wearing blue-lensed glasses against the sun and as she made her way towards him she left thistle-floss trailing, dancing in her wake. For him it was a wholly numinous encounter. Standing by this small river in the dense, natural countryside, on a hot day in June, seeing this vision of the woman he loved picking her way through the teazle and thistle clumps, her straw hat in her hand, her hair down, caught by the erratic warm breezes, César straining at his lead.

'Well, hello,' she said. 'Fancy meeting you here.'

They kissed. The Lika-kiss – and then they tore at their clothes. Lika hauled up her cotton skirt; Brodie hauled down his trousers and drawers, his erection craning free. And then they went to it – César's lead knotted to a low branch of the ash as he looked on, panting, bemused.

Later they stripped naked and swam in the pool. They moved the tablecloth into the sun and lay there, drying off, until they felt like making love again.

'We're like Adam and Eve,' he said. 'The Garden of Eden.'

'Where's the serpent?'

'In a drunken stupor sleeping off his lunchtime wine.'

Brodie touched her face and she kissed his fingertips.

'We're actually alone, Lika. Can you believe it?'

'We can come every day, every afternoon.'

'No, no! We have to be careful. I'll tell you when. Nobody must suspect. And you can't just go for a walk every day with César . . . I'm fishing – so you have to do something. Sketching, watercolours. Collecting wild flowers.'

'You're right,' she said, thinking, frowning. 'Malachi will be watching us.'

'Malachi? Why would he be watching us?'

'Because . . . It's in his nature. He checks up on me.'

Brodie held her damp pale body in his arms and kissed her breasts – thrilled in an obscure, unfathomable way to be naked on this riverbank with her. It seemed even more daring, somehow, more exciting than a room in some second-rate hotel. She hunkered into his side and reached down, taking his thickening penis in her hand, loosely.

'You've missed me,' she said, 'haven't you? . . .'

Later when they dressed they elaborated their plans. If Kilbarron was really drunk then there would be no problem; but if he was still at the lunch table when Brodie went fishing they would have to be more heedful. Brodie would leave with his rod then Lika should wait an hour before she set off herself. And then they had to come back separately, again divided by a significant period of time.

Brodie kissed her goodbye as she was about to set off homewards with César. He would fish on for another half an hour, he said, and try to come back with some sort of convincing catch.

'You know I never asked you,' he said, suddenly remembering. 'After all this time. How did the audition go?'

'What audition?'

'The Handel. *The Triumph of Time and Truth* – or whatever it was called.'

'Oh . . . Yes. A disaster. I couldn't sing.'

'Not even our little song?'

'I made a mess of everything. I was so nervous.'

'Never mind. Here we are. That's the main thing.'

'I think I was too terrified – singing in English, you know.'

'Do you still have the music?'

'What music?'

'The sheet I wrote out for you.'

'No . . . No, I left it at the theatre. I wasn't thinking. In a state. Why do you ask now, for heaven's sake? It was such a long time ago.'

'I don't know. It came into my mind. Anyway – it doesn't matter. I suddenly remembered, for some reason. I can write the song out for you again one day, if you want.'

'I think my career is slowly dying. Best not to try and revive the corpse.' She kissed him once more, touched his nose with a finger and wandered off back to the dacha, glancing back twice before she disappeared into the birches.

Brodie picked up his rod. He looked at the river where a flimsy smoke of caddis flies wavered in a sunbeam. He shivered, feeling a contentment fill him, like a powerful liquor; like some ambrosial, aphrodisiacal tonic invading every blood vessel and capillary in his body – his skin prickling with a sense of well-being, of unimprovable tactile happiness.

4

Like all practised lovers their subterfuges became more sophisticated as the summer wore on. Lika returned from a trip to Piter with sketchbooks and watercolours. Brodie paid Pyotr, a kitchen lackey, fifty kopeks to place four or five fresh fish in his fishing basket each time he went fishing so he never returned from their trysts empty-handed. In her room Lika would make sketches and drawings of notional rivers and woods, flowers and ferns. She had no talent for drawing and her ineptitude made each scene equally badly homogeneous. Kilbarron asked to see her sketches one day (she had returned later than Brodie, as planned), looked at them and said: 'Charming – but you've a long way to go, my dear.' The key fact was that the fishing trips and the *en plein air* sketching seemed entirely authentic.

As June progressed into July they managed to visit the pool by the ash tree at least once every weekend, sometimes twice, keeping scrupulously to their timings and artifice. They became familiar lovers once again – like the days of the Grand Hôtel des Etrangers – rediscovering the nuances of their lovemaking. There were some days when Lika said no – not today. She had a terrible fear of conceiving. Her menses were exceptionally regular – she said she knew precisely which days to avoid. On those days she would masturbate him with particular care and attention, stopping and starting, allowing the session to be drawn out over ten minutes or so (or as long as Brodie could contain himself), both of them naked on their blanket – they had moved on from their tablecloth.

'I could get a *capote*, if you'd prefer,' Brodie said. 'To be on the safe side.'

'I have some,' she said. 'Good idea. I'll bring one next time.'

She had some . . . This set Brodie thinking.

'Do you fuck with Kilbarron?'

'No. Not any more – not for the last two years, more or less. He's too drunk. He tries but he falls asleep. And of course now he's injecting himself with this coca.'

'But you sleep in the same bed.'

'We have a bed – but there's another bedroom. He snores so loudly the plaster falls from the ceiling! I get into bed with him but when he's asleep I go to the other bedroom.'

It consoled him, this information. He wondered if it were true.

'So why do you stay with him?' he asked one day, a little cruelly.

But she took the question seriously, thinking about it.

'In the beginning it wasn't too bad. And, I must admit, without John, in the early days, you know, I'd have had no career. He was incredibly helpful – got me all my first jobs. Malachi told me – John will make all the difference, just you wait.'

'Malachi?'

'Yes . . . I knew Malachi before I knew John, you see. Malachi introduced me to John. Didn't I tell you?'

She seemed suddenly uncomfortable with these memories and started talking about other matters. Brodie didn't pursue this line of questioning but logged away the fact that Malachi had been in Lika's life, in some capacity, longer than Kilbarron had. What did that signify? How had that happened?

One day when he was coming back down the river, stepping through the high grass in the water meadows that led down to Maloe Nikolskoe he saw Malachi – out with a shotgun with two of the yard dogs running around trying to set up birds.

They approached each other. Malachi was wearing a long fawn canvas duster coat that seemed to increase his bulk somehow, making his heft and presence more physically palpable, as if he were displacing extra volumes of air. He broke his gun and took out the cartridges, slipping them in his pocket.

'Thought I might set up some snipe or a partridge,' he said. 'Fat chance. How about you? Any luck?'

He tapped the wicker fishing basket slung over Brodie's shoulder. Brodie undid the buckles and showed him the four gleaming fish lying there – Pyotr's fifty-kopeks' worth.

'Looks like tench to me,' Malachi said.

'Gudgeon,' Brodie corrected.

'I'll take your word for it,' Malachi said.

'They're always biting upstream,' Brodie said. 'I don't think anyone fishes this river apart from me.' He smiled, though his mouth was dry. He worked his tongue to make more saliva.

'Have you seen anything of Lika?' Malachi asked, casually. 'She seemed to head out your way, I thought, to do some more of her terrible drawings.'

'No,' Brodie said. 'I just stuck to the river.'

Malachi looked at him.

'What is it?' Brodie asked.

'You might drop in on John if you've a moment. I think he wants a word.'

'Right,' Brodie said. 'I'd better head back then.'

'I'll come with you,' Malachi said. 'These dogs are rubbish.'

They headed back through the meadows towards Maloe Nikolskoe, the dogs bounding around them in the long grass. Malachi seemed brooding, thoughtful, and Brodie had no idea what to say to him. He remembered walking back with Callum towards Liethen Manor, that last afternoon he'd gone fishing in the Liethen Water – it seemed like another world, another life, centuries ago. He closed his eyes for a second conjuring up the memories of that day, the peace he'd felt. Malachi was saying something.

'Sorry?' Brodie said.

'I was wondering . . . How do you find Lika? As a person, I mean.'

Brodie was suddenly wary.

'I think she's very nice,' he said, glad of the bland adjective. 'Very easy to talk to.'

'She's a very special person,' Malachi said, almost fiercely, as if Brodie had said something uncomplimentary. 'She's a precious person.'

'Precious?'

'To John, I mean. John relies on her more than he realizes, I think.'

'I see.'

'She gives him confidence.'

'I don't think John's short of confidence,' Brodie said, suppressing a laugh.

'No, I mean, because she's there in his life he can concentrate on his work. It reassures him, if you know what I mean. Without Lika he would have gone to pieces. And if John had gone to pieces it would have been a disaster. For me as well – I owe everything to John, everything.'

'I see,' Brodie repeated. It wasn't making much sense to him. It was as if Malachi was working out some personal argument in his head through this baffling conversation.

'You knew Lika before John did, I believe,' Brodie said, unguardedly.

Malachi stopped.

'Who told you that?'

'I think John must have mentioned it – casually, in conversation.'

Malachi looked down at his feet.

'I knew her, yes – a little,' Malachi said, his voice suddenly almost inaudible. 'She was very young – eighteen, nineteen. Then John heard her sing and saw her talent. He was the one that saw her . . . her promise.'

'She has a lovely voice,' Brodie said, keen to get off the subject. Malachi seemed to be in some sort of turmoil and Brodie wondered if he suspected something and was deliberately trying to make him blunder into an error, give a crucial detail away.

'We'll have fish for supper,' he said, lamely.

'What?' Malachi looked up. 'What're you blathering about?' The old Malachi had returned.

'Supper. Fish. I've caught our supper.'

'You can catch fish. You can tune pianos. You're not entirely useless, Moncur.'

They turned around the edge of a copse and Maloe Nikolskoe lay before them.

Back at the house, Brodie put his rod away and took the fish to the kitchen. He went to his bedroom and smoked a calming cigarette before wandering over to Kilbarron's cottage. There was no sign of Lika, he was glad to notice: still out sketching.

Kilbarron had shipped a grand piano out to Maloe Nikolskoe – a Bösendorfer – and had it set up in the middle of the modest but high-ceilinged salon in the cottage. Two bedrooms and a small study led off the central room. Kilbarron was practising more, now the date of his inaugural concerts was approaching. He could be heard playing from the veranda of the main house.

All was quiet as Brodie knocked and pushed the door open.

'Mr K?' Brodie called. 'Are you there?'

He stepped in. Kilbarron was sprawled in an armchair, his feet on a stool. There was a glass of vodka on the table beside him.

'The piano's out of tune,' he said. His voice was hoarse, slurred.

Brodie went to the piano and played his usual octaves. It was perfectly in tune. He noticed a handwritten title and some manuscript pages set on the music rack. 'Der Tränensee'. What did that mean? He'd have to ask Lika.

'Is this your composition?' he said. 'For the concerts. A sonata?'

Kilbarron sat up and thought for a moment, coming to his senses slowly.

'It's a tone poem,' he said. 'I'm going all modern.' He stood and swayed over to the piano, snatching the manuscript off the rack. 'Work in progress,' he said.

'I'll retune the piano later,' Brodie said, diplomatically. 'Malachi mentioned you wanted a word.'

'We're going back to Piter on Monday – you and I. We have to set up the New Theatre piano. I'm getting rid of the Zollmeyer. I want a new piano – and you can go to work on that. To perfection, mind. Absolute perfection. I think I know my programme now. And of course I have to make a grand show of it.' He flexed his right hand and held it out, trembling. 'Except this bastard's not doing what it's told to any more.'

'I'll sort the piano, sir,' Brodie said. 'Don't give it another thought.'

'Soapsuds.'

'Feather-light.'

'Snowflakes.'

'Light as air.'

Kilbarron laughed at this and put his arm round Brodie's shoulder.

'What would I do without you, Brodie, boyo?'

At rare moments like these when he sensed Kilbarron's affection for him Brodie felt the sharp bite of his betrayal. He tried not to think of what he and Lika had been up to a couple of hours previously.

'Now – you're going to have a drink with me, Brodie, me fine fella,' he said, turning to look for the vodka bottle. 'And, by the by, we're all going up to the big house on Sunday. She who pays the piper has summoned us.'

On Sunday a carriage took them – Kilbarron, Malachi, Lika and Brodie – the mile or so to Nikolskoe. It was early evening and the light was rich and golden as they were driven through the beech and birch woods. They rounded a corner into the park and saw the house sitting on its small bluff behind the glassy stretch of its reflecting lake. Mirrored palaces. It had a high portico with four-yard-thick Doric columns supporting a tympanum crowded with mythic figures in bas-relief. Flanking the portico long symmetrical wings stretched to each side. The facade was white stucco with the wooden window embrasures picked out in forest green. It was at once imposing and unreal, almost like a vast stage flat set down in these cleared, manicured acres of countryside. Behind the house, Malachi explained, was a hamlet of the usual outbuildings – stables, kitchens, storerooms, servants' quarters, and, for good measure, a Chinese pavilion, a grotto at the foot of a plashing artificial series of waterfalls, a neo-Gothic chapel and the family mausoleum – bigger than the chapel.

The carriage pulled up and uniformed lackeys opened the doors. Tall braziers burned palely at the foot of the twenty wide steps that led you up to the massive brass doors which gave onto the hall. Like entering a cathedral, Brodie thought. He felt transported back in time – to the era of Catherine the Great, or Great Peter himself – yet he knew Nikolskoe was only fifty years old. This house and its clutter of extravagant outbuildings, its thousands of acres of forests and farmlands, was the realized dream of a bourgeois millionaire who wanted to let the world know that Nikolai Sergeevitch Vadimov had well and truly arrived.

Brodie followed the others into the towering hall, two storeys high with a domed ceiling. Marble was everywhere – white, black, beige and rose, veined and pure – whole quarries must have been emptied. He looked left and right and saw an enfilade of rooms disappearing into their own perspectives.

More liveried servants showed them up the curving white marble staircase into the main drawing room. Champagne was available at the door, served by tray-bearing waiters. They joined about twenty other guests – local landowners and neighbours, an important painter, lawyers and bankers and their wives from Piter. Kilbarron was the guest of honour – there was a little ripple of applause as the maestro entered. Brodie held back, feeling his tie and stiff collar choking him, and looked around for Lika, hoping for a glance of collusion and understanding, but she had already been led away and was talking animatedly to someone she appeared to know. She looked very beautiful, he thought – once again in a variation of her 'vision in white' style. Her hair held up by jewelled pins, her waist cinched tight, her décolleté perfectly poised on the border of decorum and allure.

Brodie saw that people were smoking so he took out his cigarette case and lit a Margarita. He drained his glass of champagne and looked around for a waiter. Maybe the answer to this evening was to become pleasantly, persistently drunk.

'May I please to trouble you for cigarette?'

The question was in English, heavily accented with Russian.

Brodie turned to find a small, slim young woman in a formal midnight-blue suit. She was wearing spectacles.

Brodie offered his case and explained about his foreign cigarettes.

'Do you speak French?' she asked.

Brodie repeated himself in French. He lit the small woman's cigarette.

'I am Varvara Nikolaevna Vadimova. You must be Monsieur Kilbarron's secretary.'

'I am. Brodie Moncur.'

They shook hands. She had small close-set eyes that were oddly offset by full, painted lips, and a frowning, serious demeanour, he thought, that said do not take me lightly, despite my painted lips, for I am rather formidable. Large emeralds were clipped to her earlobes. Money and intellect.

'Come,' she said. 'Let me introduce you to my mother.'

Brodie followed her through the room to find a small plump woman in her fifties with a dramatic badger's white stripe in her blue-black hair. This was Elisaveta Ivanovna Vadimova, the patron who was paying for everything. Brodie gave a small bow and smiled as Varvara introduced him. Madame Vadimova was polite but soon turned away – she wasn't that interested in the employees.

'You're not important enough, you see,' Varvara said candidly. 'Why would she speak to Kilbarron's secretary when she can speak to Kilbarron himself?'

'Fair enough,' Brodie said. He didn't care, anyway.

'But at least you can say that you've met her.'

'Something for the grandchildren to ponder.'

Varvara smiled.

'I'd rather talk to you. I find "great" men very disappointing on the whole. So predictable. Have you ever met Tolstoy?'

'Not yet.'

'You haven't missed a thing, I promise you. No, I'm much more interested in who these paragons choose to be around them. You gain more insight. You're sitting beside me at dinner, by the way. We'll talk then.' She wagged her finger at him, then smiled and drifted off to talk to someone else. Brodie lifted another glass of champagne from a passing tray, depositing his empty one. Yes, steady inebriation was the only solution.

The dining room was in a long, barrel-vaulted chamber, bright with many chandeliers and with walls crowded with portraits – mythical Vadimovs from centuries past. The ceiling was decorated with putti sporting amongst pink-hued clouds. They ate several courses – starting with *pirozhki* stuffed with smoked fish, crayfish tails in aspic, fried snipe, roast venison, a cress salad, then a cream *plombir* for dessert. Along with the wine, many flavoured vodkas were offered: clove, anise, cinnamon, caraway. Brodie tried everything and began to enjoy himself more as he struggled to keep up with Varvara's somewhat intense conversation.

'You know my grandfather built this house,' Varvara said. 'It's not old at all.'

'Yes, I had heard that.'

'It was in the 1850s. I find it pretentious.'

'Well, I think if you've got all that—'

'He was a simple engineer – a talented engineer – who built bridges. That was his speciality. He built more than four hundred bridges, all over Russia. The railway expansion, you know.'

'Goodness.'

'He made a lot of money. Then he bought coal mines and made another fortune and so purchased this estate. He demolished the old house and built Nikolskoe.'

'What you might call a monument to his success.'

'Then he bought ships and became even richer.'

'Amazing.'

'Before the emancipation – of the serfs, you know – there were two thousand servants in this house. Two thousand "souls". He built a theatre and plays were put on. It's astonishing isn't it? Just forty years ago – to think life was led in this way.'

'Nothing stays the same.'

'And now we have only two hundred servants.'

Brodie – such was the mood the cinnamon vodka was encouraging – immediately thought of five witty rejoinders but was still sober enough to say something bland.

'You've kept up the grand style, all the same. Extraordinary. I must say I—'

'Have you worked with many virtuosi, like Kilbarron?'

'Ah, yes,' Brodie said and mentioned a few names: Firmin, Sauter, Nagel.

'Fascinating. Would you come and give a talk at my salon? This is what fascinates me, you see. The oblique view – the view from the side, not face on. Not the view the world thinks it sees, or the view we're presented with: the official view. I'm not interested in the "official" view of anything.'

'Yes.'

'It's far more revealing – the view askance, you might say. My guests will find it fascinating.'

He wished she would stop using that word. Fascination wasn't really in his repertoire.

'I haven't ever spoken at a salon,' he said. 'I'm not sure I'll be able to—'

'It's very informal. You introduce yourself and people – sympathetic, intelligent people – will ask you questions. In French, of course – and you speak excellent French, may I congratulate you. Think of it as a conversation. A conversation with one subject. You.' She rested her hand on his arm for a second. 'We meet at my apartment in Piter. After the summer is over, of course. It's very congenial.'

'I'd be delighted,' Brodie said, weakly.

'I'll be in touch.'

'Let me give you my visiting card.'

'I have all the information, Monsieur Moncur, don't worry.' Now she squeezed his forearm. 'I very much look forward to consolidating our new friendship.'

5

Three days later Philipp Philippovitch Lvov dropped him at Dubechnia station. Brodie was sure he was still feeling the ill effects of the Nikolskoe dinner and the truly hill-cracking hangover it had engendered. After the meal, the guests had moved into another smaller salon where coffee was served along with more flavoured vodkas – something called Crimean vodka was pressed on people – along with Holland gin, cognac and arak. Brodie tried everything and paid the price. Even today his mouth felt oddly dry and he was mildly photophobic – the watery sun seemed unduly bright. He was returning to Petersburg to regulate the new piano that had arrived at the theatre, a Steingraeber, to make it ready for Kilbarron and Kilbarron's season. Lika had slipped a note into his hand as they had said their formal goodbyes (there had been no chance for another meeting at the ash-tree pool). As Philipp turned the carriage out of the Maloe Nikolskoe driveway, Brodie opened it. It was in Russian. 'Как я хочу, чтоб ты всунул в меня твой большой хуй.'

'Can you translate this for me, Philipp?' Brodie asked, handing it over. Philipp spoke reasonable French.

Philipp glanced at it, looked away, glanced at it again and blushed through his beard.

'Someone is playing a joke on you, sir.'

'No, please – just translate it.'

'It's very indelicate, sir.'

'I asked for it to be copied from a book,' Brodie said, improvising. 'Someone told me it was an old Russian saying.'

'Oh, no, I don't think so. It's extremely . . .' He paused. 'Extremely explicit. It must be a joke.'

'We're two men alone, Philipp. What have we to be embarrassed about?'

'All right, sir. If you insist. It says . . .' He concentrated. Coughed twice. 'It says: "I long to feel your very enormous penis inside me soon." ' He cleared his throat again and looked up at the sky.

Brodie took the note back from him and slipped it in his jacket pocket. They rode on the rest of the way in silence. Brodie couldn't help breaking out in a smile from time to time. Lika Blum – irrepressible – that was why he loved her so.

At the station Brodie was informed that the Petersburg train was running two hours late because of repair work further down the line, so he decided to wander into Dubechnia – about half a mile from the station – to see what the town was like.

He sauntered down Dubechnia's main street. Low houses, some with small mezzanines with dormer windows, were set behind front gardens with white picket fences, split paling fences, wicker and willow hurdles or irregular, diagonally laid logs between thin uprights. Brodie was struck by the variety of fencing on show in a small Russian town. Poplars and lilacs were planted on the roadside – a dirt road, beaten rock hard by the summer sun. He was glad of his straw hat. As he approached the crossroads that formed the modest square at the centre of town the road began to be paved with wood – thick oak planks set flush in the dirt – that rumbled loudly as carriages passed over them.

Here at the crossroads there was a small white wooden church with a pale blue cupola, the town hall and the best hotel (there was another inn – 'tolerable' his guidebook said – on the outskirts by the road north to Piter). Brodie read its name slowly, deciphering the Cyrillic: the Evangelical Society Hotel. He was finally making some progress with his Russian, but could that be correct? From the outside it looked well maintained – there were window boxes full of blue flax on the first floor – but, stepping inside, it seemed less appealing. There was an overriding smell of cooking fat and everything was brown. Brown walls, brown rugs on stained brown floorboards. Even the huge stuffed bear by the reception desk was brown – though it was becoming piebald as time advanced.

Brodie wandered into the dining room set off to one side of the brown foyer. Half a dozen locals, all wearing their various hats, were sitting drinking, talking, playing dominoes. Brodie found a table by a window and asked the pot-boy for vodka and bread and gherkins. He looked around. There was a huge samovar on a table and a small cluster of icons behind it. Bunches of dried flowers were tied up against the cornice that was painted black to distinguish it from the general brown. His order arrived surprisingly swiftly accompanied by a small plate of rusks and crackers. Perhaps the hotel was better than his first impressions suggested. He munched at his dry cracker and sipped his vodka, an idea forming in his head. He wandered back through to reception. Behind the desk he saw a row of keys with heavy pear-shaped weights hanging from them. Six rooms, he thought: there must be at least one good one. He spoke in French to the clerk who appeared – French didn't work. He tried his rudimentary German.

'*Das beste Zimmer, bitte,*' he said. Comprehension was achieved.

He was taken up the creaking stairs and shown into a large three-windowed room on the first floor, the one that had the flax window boxes. There was a wide wooden bed with a plump, soft eiderdown. The walls were pine, planed smooth and painted brown and there were Tatar rugs on the bare floorboards. It seemed clean enough. His plan was taking shape: he was beginning to see the Evangelical Society Hotel in Dubechnia as the Russian equivalent of the Grand Hôtel des Etrangers in Paris . . .

He went back to the taproom, finished his vodka and gherkins and paid – an exhilaration filling him. Lika would approve of this idea, he felt sure. It was safer, that was the main thing, away from prying eyes, far from Kilbarron and Malachi. Everything was falling into place.

Brodie crossed Dvortsovy Bridge heading for Varvara Vadimova's apartment on Nevsky Prospekt. He was a bit late – held up at the theatre. There was a large crowd gathered in front of the Admiralty for some reason, so he ducked down to the canal and swept round Moika Street. Varvara's apartment was about halfway down the Prospekt – he'd be there in ten minutes.

He was stopped by a row of policemen, barring the way. There had been some sort of an incident. Over the heads of the curious onlookers he could see a droshky turned on its side, a visible wheel shattered, and the horse lying still, immobile on the ground. There was a curious smell in the air, smoky, like a burning fabric, and not far off he could hear women, wailing.

He found someone – an official in his uniform, wearing a top hat – who could speak French and he was informed that a bomb had been thrown at a Cabinet minister who had just left the Ministry of Finance. He was alive, it seemed, but gravely wounded along with a few innocent passers-by. The bomb-thrower had been arrested.

Brodie doubled back and cut through Mikhailovskaya Place until he reached the Fontanka canal and rejoined Nevsky there. Traffic was moving slowly up the wide boulevard as if nothing had happened – another day, another bomb. He looked for the number of Varvara's apartment and found it opposite the public library. He composed himself and then rang the bell on the main door. He had absolutely no idea what he was letting himself in for.

Varvara greeted him as he handed a lackey his overcoat. She looked quite different: her hair was down, thick, a lustrous auburn, and she wore a vivid yellow blouse over a black skirt. Red shoes with high heels – she was significantly taller – completed the ensemble. Her yellow blouse was satin, like a second skin, and very clinging and Brodie felt ashamed as his gaze was instantly drawn to the way it revealed the shape of her breasts. He quickly looked her in the eye and smiled.

'I'm late, I know – I apologize. There was a problem up by the Admiralty, some kind of bomb went off.'

'You're not late because tonight you are the timekeeper,' she said, then, adding in English, 'Everyone is here, Mr Moncur, drinking, eating, having a wonderful occasion.' She led him down a dark corridor to a large drawing room that contained about thirty people, most of them women, Brodie noticed instantly, and most of them young – in their twenties and thirties, he estimated. He did spot one elderly gent with a shock of white hair smoking a pipe.

'Is your mother here?' Brodie asked.

'No, no! She disapproves of my soirées – she thinks they're decadent.'

Decadent? Brodie thought to himself as Varvara gripped his elbow and steered him towards a table with a punchbowl. He was served with a glass of punch by a white-jacketed waiter, took a sip and turned to see – with a sudden depression – that a chair had been placed on a dais at the end of the drawing room. Beside it was a small table with a carafe of water and a glass. Sofas and armchairs had been pushed back against the wall and a semicircle of wooden seats faced the dais. Varvara introduced him to smiling enthusiastic people – everyone seemed to speak French – but he was taking nothing in, in a mild daze of panic, trying to ignore the auguries of defeat and humiliation that were crowding in on him, cursing himself for agreeing to subject himself to this ordeal.

Brodie emptied his punch glass, set it down and smoked a Margarita as quickly as possible, muttering pleasantries, smiling and nodding at these people who seemed unusually keen to meet him. He must have shaken a dozen hands before Varvara left him and went to the dais, clapping her hands for silence. She then spoke in Russian for a minute or two, very fast, Brodie understanding nothing except the mentioning of his name and Kilbarron's. Then Varvara turned towards him and held out her hand.

'Je vous présente Monsieur Brodie Moncur!'

Brodie stepped on to the dais to an enthusiastic round of applause and sat down. He prayed to the gods of improvisation and, at Varvara's urging, began to tell the semicircle of rapt listeners what it was like to work for a man of unquestionable genius like John Kilbarron. He managed five minutes or so and sensed himself floundering so switched his speech to the mysterious art of piano tuning, talking of his apprenticeship and then his career, mentioning the names of all the master-pianists whose pianos he had tuned in Edinburgh and Paris.

A hand was raised in the audience. Brodie's relief was intense – the focus had shifted.

A young woman whose hair was so blonde it might have been white asked him what exactly he did when he tuned a piano for someone like Kilbarron or Karl-Heinz Nagel. Bless you, lovely blonde woman, he thought, as he launched into a potted description of his métier.

After that the questions began to flow and he began to relax. Also the audience began to debate amongst themselves. They were particularly intrigued by what he didn't disclose.

'So you have magic powers, then,' the white-blonde woman teased him.

'Let's say I have a few special tricks, known only to me,' he said, using the word *astuces*. 'If I told you what they were then everyone would copy me – and I'd be out of a job.'

There was laughter at this and, as he seemed to relax, so too did the mood in the room, as if the serious intellectual import of the evening was over and now people could concentrate on enjoying themselves. After a few more questions Varvara clapped her hands for silence again and thanked Brodie for his most fascinating disquisition. Fascinating – that word again . . .

He stepped down, acknowledging the applause, feeling his shirt damp, clinging to his back, and headed for the punchbowl. Varieties of vodka were now being served as well and canapés of blinis and caviar. He was congratulated on every side. He drank some orange-flavoured vodka and smoked another cigarette, Varvara standing beside him almost as if she owned him, somehow. He was aware of Varvara being congratulated as well.

'It was ideally relaxed, ideally informal and full of insight, Monsieur Moncur,' she said in an aside. 'This is more unusual for us. It was intimate. Personal. Most evenings it is rather forbidding and serious.'

'I hope I haven't lowered the tone,' Brodie said. But he sensed the social temperature in the room changing, now the business of the evening was over. Intimate was the right word. Suddenly there seemed more men in the room – late arrivals? – and the noise level rose and the laughter increased. And it was laughter of a certain recognizable sort – licentious, fun-filled – unmistakeable. He saw hands being held, hands being kissed, hands going round waists, men whispering in women's ears. It was contagious.

Varvara left his side for a moment and he turned to look at a picture on the wall behind him. It was of a river in winter, its banks flooded, stark, leafless trees silhouetted in a silver light. It reminded him of Maloe Nikolskoe – of the river he fished in and beside which he and Lika fucked. Maybe it looked like this in winter . . . The ash tree bare. He suddenly missed Lika with a palpable ache. How could he contrive to go back to Maloe Nikolskoe? They had to set their plan in motion.

Varvara was back at his side.

'Do you like this picture?' she asked.

'Very much.'

'It's by a painter called Levitan. He's a genius. I have a better one in my study – would you like to see it?'

'Well, if it's not too much trouble.'

'Follow me.'

Varvara led him through the parting crowd of guests up the dark corridor and into a room next to the apartment's hallway. It was a study: neat glassed-in bookshelves, a desk, a daybed, many pictures on the cream-papered walls. Varvara was pointing to a particular picture. He approached and saw the canvas was of a vast expanse of flat steppe and a thin, chalky cart-track disappearing into the distance where bulging clouds massed on the horizon, blue-black with rain. Some rooks were flying low to the ground above the yellow grasslands. He could almost hear their raucous yells.

'Very impressive,' he said.

'It's called *The Gathering Storm*.'

'Goodness. Extremely well painted. I must—'

Varvara had flung herself at him, grabbing his head between her palms and flattening her lips on his, her tongue pushing through his parting teeth searching for his tongue, their spectacles clashing so fiercely that Brodie's went flying. They kissed fiercely like this for a full minute then broke apart, panting. Varvara was a misty blur of yellow satin.

'My glasses,' Brodie said. 'I can't see a thing. Sorry.'

Varvara found them and handed them to him. Focus returned. Trepidation arrived.

'You will disapprove of me,' Varvara said, smiling modestly, unperturbed.

'Look . . . It's . . . There are moments . . . Sometimes . . .'

'Are you betrothed?'

'Yes,' he said immediately, inspired. 'There is someone. In Scotland.'

'Then it doesn't matter. You're here in Russia. It's so far away. She might as well be on the moon.'

She took both his hands and drew herself close to him, looking up. Then she placed his hands on her breasts and held them there. Brodie felt her breasts yield slightly through the yellow satin. 'Come tomorrow,' she said softly. 'Eight o'clock. We'll dine here, just the two of us.'

'Miss Vadimova, I should tell you—'

'Call me Varvara.'

'Varvara. I'm not well. I have tuberculosis.'

This took her aback and she let go of his hands. He let them drop to his side, welcoming his opportunity, boldly.

'I'm seeing a doctor here in Piter. They have high hopes, I'm glad to say. I'm being treated.'

'I know the best doctors. We'll talk about this. I can help you.'

But the mood had changed as suddenly as it had erupted. She looked at him intently, differently.

'You have a line across your lenses.'

'They're called Franklin spectacles. Two lenses of different focus. One for close work, one for distance.'

'Most interesting. I think this could be useful for me.'

She was walking to the door. Brodie followed.

'Shall we have some more vodka?' she said. 'And talk about optics?'

'I think that would be an excellent idea.'

They walked silently down the long corridor approaching the surging noise emanating from the drawing room. It was almost strident, swelling. Astonishingly, there seemed almost more people present. Where had they come from? Brodie now had the sense that the talk and the salon were simply the pretext to set an entirely different evening in motion. Varvara looked at him sadly, squeezed his arm and went to chat to other people. Brodie felt a terrible exhaustion descend on him. If only Lika were here; if only he could somehow summon her here in a second from Maloe Nikolskoe. He pushed all thoughts of what had happened away and edged through the throng, making for the punchbowl.

'Most interesting talk.' The compliment was in English. Brodie looked round.

A tall young man, gangly, balding, with a receding chin, a neat fair moustache and amused, twinkling eyes stood there.

'George Vere,' he said, holding out his hand. 'I'm at the embassy here in Piter. I'm an old friend – which is to say a new friend – of the impulsive Varvara.'

They shook hands.

'Did she jump on top of you?' Vere asked.

'No. Not at all.'

'Lucky you. I had to tell her I was married with four children back in England.'

'Are you?'

'God no. Confirmed bachelor, actually. But, you know, in a crisis, necessity being the mother of invention and all that.'

'It's quite a salon,' Brodie said. 'If it can be described as such.'

'Fair point. Anyway, you set the tone admirably,' Vere said. 'It's usually deadly dull and serious. But look at the fun everyone's having tonight. Can I invite you for lunch one day? We could go to the Imperial Yacht Club if you don't mind being surrounded by diplomats. French chef.'

'Thank you. I'd like that.'

Vere took his visiting card out of a slim flat silver box and gave it to Brodie.

'You can always get me at the embassy on Dvortsovaya. If not, they'll know where to find me.'

*

Nevsky Prospekt, 23 (1a)
St Petersburg

Dear Mr Brodie,

Please excuse my appalled English. Thank you for last night. You were, without any doubting, our most cherished speaker so far in two years of salon. And I liked our kiss. Did you not also like? 'And where a kiss may lead may one not permit to follow?' I think this is English saying. Please come to dinner at my apartment on Sunday 16th. There will be six or eight guests. Sehr gemütlich.

With affection,
V. N. Vadimova

Brodie made an excuse by letter, by return. He was needed at Maloe Nikolskoe with Kilbarron, many abject apologies. And, as July progressed, Kilbarron indeed seemed reluctant to leave the estate. He practised every day for at least four hours, as if he had suddenly realized the demands of the inaugural concerts – in early September – of the Kilbarron Season. As Brodie walked by the cottage he could hear Rimsky-Korsakov, Balakirev, Mussorgsky, Borodin, Tchaikovsky. From time to time he was called in for further tuning and voicing. Kilbarron's weak right hand was proving a liability. 'Thank God for my painkillers,' he would say, closing his eyes.

One afternoon Philipp Lvov returned from Dubechnia with a package for Kilbarron. Brodie was alone on the veranda and there was no sign of Malachi. He knew these were scores sent for from Piter: Kilbarron, despite his assurances, was still fretting about the programme for his inaugural concert.

Brodie sauntered across the patchy lawn towards the cottage. No sound of music emanated. Kilbarron had drunk his fill at lunch and was no doubt sleeping it off, Brodie thought. But the front door was ajar and peering through the gap Brodie saw that the piano was closed. He pushed the door open and slipped through, placing the package of scores on the piano stool, and turned to tiptoe out.

'You're just a fool,' Brodie heard. 'A stupid young fool. Why should I do anything for a fool?'

He stopped, thinking he was being addressed, then heard Lika bravely reply.

'You've always said I was a "fool". What's the difference now?'

Brodie froze, realizing that Kilbarron and Lika were in the bedroom. He felt sick.

'The difference,' Kilbarron said, 'is that I've got a job to do. An enormous demanding task in front of me – I can't be worrying about you and your foolish dreams.'

'I don't care what it is but I need to sing something, anything. I haven't sung for over a year. I need to—'

'So what?' Kilbarron suddenly shouted. 'Who gives a brass farthing for you? You're a third-rate chorus singer perfect for a third-rate chorus. Go and sing in a church choir if you want to exercise your vocal cords. I haven't got time to get you a job. Why do you want a job – you've got a salary. You're my musical assistant, for fuck's sake! A well-paid musical assistant. People would kill for your job. Cut off their right hand to work with me, John Kilbarron. But instead it's all me, me, me! Lika this! Lika that! Don't you ever give a thought for what I have to do? For what I stand for here in this country? What my responsibilities are? No – you're besotted with yourself and your thin little squeaky voice.'

At this Brodie heard Lika begin to sob, helplessly. He thought he might faint and took some steps to the door. He should never have stopped to listen. Overhearing like this was a shock – too raw, too unguarded, too private and personal. Slowly he pulled the door open, hearing it creak on its hinges and, to his consternation, heard Kilbarron suddenly pleading – his voice childlike, wheedling.

'Lika, darling, darling, don't cry, my lovely. I'm a horrible man. Horrible, shameful. A shameful monstrous drunk old man. I love my Lika – come to me my Lika-lovely. I'm so sorry, I should never have said that. I'll get you a job, I'll get you a role, whatever you want, an opera, an oratorio, we'll have a recital just for you, show the world what a beautiful person with a beautiful voice you are – I'll look after you, my darling.'

Brodie closed the door behind him and walked briskly away, feeling a shiver of disgust run through his body. He forced himself to think of Lika – poor Lika, what she had to go through, what she had to suffer. No one should have to endure this sort of humiliation. He felt his resolve solidify: he was going to find a way to free Lika from John Kilbarron. They had to escape, both of them, one way or another.

That evening before dinner he managed to snatch a moment alone with her. Her eyes were red, her face slumped from her crying.

'What's the matter?' he whispered. 'What happened?'

'My mother's not well,' she said. 'I had a letter. It made me upset. Stupidly.'

'Right,' Brodie said, realizing that secrets were being kept.

'I'll be all right. It's not serious. I'm being oversensitive.'

'Are you sure? There's nothing else you—'

'We'd better go in.'

They decided – mutually – that it was wise to be even more cautious about meeting by the river, Brodie claiming that he sensed that Malachi thought something was afoot. So, some days Brodie went fishing as usual and Lika stayed at the house, playing croquet and reading. Some days she went off sketching and Brodie made a point of being seen by Malachi mooching around the pond or practising his casting on the lawn. In any event they both felt the riverbank encounters were coming to an end, their days of sun-favoured lovemaking over. And the weather was proving less than perfect that summer as it continued: sudden thunderstorms drenching them and then a few days of unseasonable coolness before the timid sun appeared again.

There was one odd moment that confirmed this prudence had been right. He was returning from the bathing hut after a swim in the pond and he saw Malachi and Lika down at the foot of the orchard, in conversation, Lika with a basket full of windfalls on her arm. Brodie saw Malachi – who was talking intently to her – suddenly reach forward and take her free hand. Lika snatched it away and said something brusque to him. Malachi turned and marched back to the house, rebuked in some way, eyes fixed ahead. Brodie heard the door to his room slam. What had happened in the orchard? What had Malachi said and why had he taken her hand like that? Had he accused her of something – something that angered her? Brodie sensed he'd get no answer from Lika – what went on between her and the Kilbarron brothers was not something she ever seemed to want to reveal to him.

Brodie's new plan had taken firmer shape and Lika was aware of its intricate details. He had instructed the manager of the New Russia Theatre to send him a telegram on a certain day, a week hence, saying that he was urgently required to restring the bass section on the new concert piano. The telegram duly arrived and Brodie informed the Maloe Nikolskoe household that he had to go back to Piter for a few days. The following morning he was taken in a pony and trap to the station at Dubechnia and from there he walked into town and checked into the Evangelical Society Hotel and was shown to the *beste Zimmer* on the first floor. In his halting German he told the manager that his wife would be joining him the next day.

Brodie had a spare evening in Dubechnia. At dusk he went for a stroll, turning off the main street at random. He passed a club – he could hear the click of billiard balls, laughter and some music playing – a milliner's, a shop selling bagels. Then he found himself in a surprisingly kempt and tidy park with a small rushing river flowing through it, planted out with sick-looking saplings lashed tightly to stout raw pickets. At one end of the park behind a high wall was a substantial stone mansion that he was told was the governor's house. A hawker selling various types of brooms and dusters engaged him in conversation but they could not communicate. He tried to enter the largest church in Dubechnia – the 'cathedral', so-called – but it was locked. There was a beggar outside the main door, asleep.

He turned away and spontaneously selected another street that, very quickly, he saw brought him to the edge of the town. Here the mud road was thickly rutted and on either side were the meanest lean-to wooden shacks with their collapsed thatched roofs, boxy hovels with turf and plank roofs, a blackened smoking stove pipe protruding. Animals – dogs, hens, pigs – sniffed, picked and rummaged at steaming rubbish heaps and the few people he saw looked like aborigines, burnt black by the sun or their skin darkened by accumulated filth, their bulky clothes cut from some sort of thick felt or leather. Half-naked children stared at him – their eyes white in their bronze faces – as if he were a visitor from some distant planet, standing there in his suit and tie with his polished shoes. Brodie raised his hand in vague salutation – they were fellow human beings after all – and quickly retraced his steps. An old woman, draped in rags, bent double, bared toothless gums at him and tried to grab his sleeve. He threw some coins on the ground and strode away, managing to find his way back to the hotel where he dined on mutton chops with a caraway sauce followed by apple *kissel*, a kind of moulded pudding thickened with potato starch, that he thought delicious. He went to bed and dreamt of Lika.

On Lika's side the deception was meant to commence a good twenty-four hours later so that Brodie's departure seemed long gone and unconnected with her own. A nagging toothache – she had better see her dentist in Piter. So she too was taken to Dubechnia and deposited at the station. Once the Petersburg train had left she made her way into town and the Evangelical Society Hotel where her lover was waiting impatiently.

Brodie told the concierge that his wife wasn't feeling well so they would like some food sent up to their room. They were sent a cold roast capon, bread rolls and a green and white bean salad. They asked for wine but there was only Ukrainian champagne available. Brodie and Lika ate their food naked in bed, setting out their feast on a towel between them. They toasted each other and congratulated themselves on their clever scheme. It was so different being in a hotel with a bed – like Paris – a whole night together.

'What will we do, Brodie?'

'What do you mean?'

'What will become of us?'

'Let's not think about anything until this first concert season is over. Kilbarron knows I can't stay here forever – there's practically nothing for me to do.'

'What then?'

'We'll leave. Go away – back to Paris, anywhere. We could go to America. You can sing; I can tune pianos.'

'It's easy for you to say,' she said, reaching for the bottle. 'It'll be harder for me to leave.'

'Just tell him it's over. These things occur. Love dies, all that.'

'And then it'll be a new century,' she said, thinking and frowning as if the idea troubled her in some way.

'What's that got to do with anything?'

She pulled the soft centre from a bread roll and munched on it.

'I mean – what will it be like, the twentieth century? Will we even notice? Will it seem that nothing has changed – just a date in the calendar?'

'Automobiles,' Brodie said, thinking about the twentieth century. 'There'll be no more horses in a few years, I bet you. No horse trams or horse cabs. Our children will be amazed that we needed horses to get from here to there. Millions of horses. That the streets of the grandest, richest cities in the world stank of horse shit. It'll seem like a fantasy.'

'And there will be no more wars,' Lika said. 'No diseases.'

'Well, I'm not so sure about that,' Brodie said. He thought further: 'People will travel the world in balloons, giant balloons – I read about them in a newspaper.'

She lay down, resting her head on his knee. He leaned and kissed her forehead.

'I know one thing the next century will bring for sure,' she said in a quiet voice.

'What's that?'

'Our deaths. We will die in the twentieth century, Brodie, you realize.'

'Please don't talk like that!'

'But it's true. We'll both die in the twentieth century.'

'Everybody has to die at some time. Everything dies – trees, animals, stars . . .' He cupped her sweet, troubled face. 'Don't think about that, Lika. Think about us, here in this room, now. This is our world. Time has stopped. That's all that matters.'

In the morning, Lika said: 'Let's stay one more night. Let's not leave this room the whole day.'

Brodie thought about it.

'It might be risky.'

'I'll send a telegram – say I have to have a tooth out.'

'How can you send a telegram from Dubechnia to Dubechnia?' But Brodie was thinking hard – perhaps there was a way . . .

He dressed and went out to the post office. On the telegraph form he wrote, *'Complications avec dent. Revenir demain. L. V. Blum.'* He asked the postmaster if there was a commissionaire in Dubechnia who could deliver the form to Maloe Nikolskoe. The postmaster, a thin man with a truly massive moustache, looked at him sadly.

'This is not Petersburg, sir. We have no commissionaires here.'

'I would pay a rouble for someone to deliver this to Maloe Nikolskoe.'

'There's a boy who could deliver it. I'll see to it.'

'Oh – would you stamp the telegram?'

The postmaster reached for his stamp and banged it down on the form. Brodie handed over the rouble, folded the telegram and wrote 'J. Kilbarron, Maloe Nikolskoe.'

He then handed another rouble to the postmaster.

'With thanks for your trouble, sir.'

He walked slowly back to the hotel pondering this duplicity. Another night – they should be safe, then Lika would reappear at Maloe Nikolskoe, toothache cured. He would wait a day and a half and return himself. Why would anyone suspect anything? Just more comings and goings amongst the constant comings and goings. And then guests would be arriving for the next weekend. He bounded up the stairs to their room, two at a time.

They stayed put all day, as Lika wanted. They ordered a lunch of forcemeat *pirogi* and a bottle of vodka. They drank too much and smoked cigarettes. They made love when they felt aroused. They chased flies round their room. They looked out of the window at the good people of Dubechnia passing by and speculated about them, making up stories. As dusk arrived they felt hungry again and ordered more Ukrainian champagne, blinis and pressed caviar. Then they extinguished the oil lamps and lay in bed in the darkness, holding each other.

'I'll never forget these hours, here,' Brodie said. 'Never.'

'Neither will I.'

'Our time in the Evangelical Society Hotel.'

'It's been . . .' She thought. 'Enchanted.'

Brodie decided it was time to make his declaration.

'You know I love you, Lika.'

'Yes. Yes, I do, my darling.'

'I want to spend my life with you. I can't be without you any more. I can't imagine ever being without you. We have to find a way to—'

'Stop! Don't say any more, Brodie. It's very complicated, my situation – you've no idea. Our situation is complicated as well. There'll be times when we have to be apart – you know that.'

'Then we should uncomplicate it. It'll be hard – there'll be bad feeling and we won't be forgiven. But you see what it's been like these last two days together. Imagine if this was the way it always was – no hiding, no lying. Just you and me. Free.'

'It's a nice dream, Brodie. Let me dream about it.'

They slept in each other's arms under the soft eiderdown, facing each other, her head on his shoulder, knee to knee.

And then in the night he felt cold and reached for the eiderdown to pull it over him – and it wasn't there. He opened his eyes to see a candle burning and beyond its halo of orange light stood Malachi Kilbarron.

Brodie knew he wasn't dreaming. He sat up, his hands quickly concealing his groin. Malachi kicked the bed and Lika woke. She gave a little scream, covering her breasts with her arms.

'Well, well, well,' Malachi said, unpleasantly. 'The happy couple.'

He stared at Lika and she avoided his gaze.

'Pretty as ever, my sweet,' he said. 'Those lovely titties.'

Lika tore the sheet from under her and wrapped it around her body. Malachi turned to Brodie.

'I'll see you downstairs, Moncur. In two minutes. Get your cock and balls into a pair of trousers. Make yourself decent.'

He strolled out of the room.

Lika could hardly speak. She seemed in a strange kind of shock, dry retching, coughing as she dressed as quickly as possible. They hugged each other before he went downstairs to confront Malachi.

'You know,' Brodie said softly, trying to calm her, 'maybe this is for the best. Everything has to change now.'

'No,' she said in a small voice. 'You don't know Malachi. Everything will become worse now. Everything will be bad.'

Brodie kissed her and went to meet Malachi Kilbarron.

6

Lika had been right: everything was indeed worse than before, but in varying degrees. Sometimes it seemed, for a minute or two, as if nothing had changed. But then a remark would be tossed into a conversation, or a statement made, or a look deflected, that reminded him how life had been better before the awful discovery.

Downstairs that night in the taproom of the Evangelical Society Hotel, Malachi had sounded surprisingly reasonable as he had laid out his terms – his conditions for remaining silent. He was drinking vodka and didn't offer any to Brodie. Brodie was aware of Philipp Lvov lurking in the lobby, also. Malachi said he wouldn't tell Kilbarron – poor brother John – about this betrayal as it would destroy him. And particularly at this moment as he prepared for his inaugural concerts and the opening of his first season – and every reward attending on it – such a revelation would be devastating. So, Malachi said, condition one: the Brodie–Lika 'affair' was over. Condition two: Brodie and Lika had to do everything Malachi told them. There was to be no independent activity or initiative, everything had to be referred to Malachi.

'You are my creatures,' Malachi said, straightforwardly. 'Got that? My creatures henceforth and until I tell you that you are released. And you will do my bidding. Understand?'

Brodie could only agree to the terms and Malachi went away, leaving instructions. Lika was to return to Maloe Nikolskoe in the morning. Brodie was to wait the day out and return in the evening.

Brodie felt he had to ask a question.

'How did you know? How did you know we were here?'

Malachi smiled.

'I recognized your handwriting on the telegram. The way you do your "C" and your "R". I thought – hello? Brodie Moncur's sending us a telegram from Piter about Lika's teeth. Funny. Then I looked at the stamp. Dubechnia. It wasn't difficult to find you.'

All so simple, Brodie thought. If only he'd asked the postmaster to write the telegram . . .

What did change was John Kilbarron's attitude. Malachi had said he wouldn't tell him but Brodie felt Kilbarron was suddenly noticeably cooler towards him. Just a nod of the head when they met and he seemed to want to keep his distance. But, on the other hand, nothing appeared changed between Kilbarron and Lika. She sat beside him at meals; she slept in his bed at night, or so Brodie assumed. He calculated further that Malachi had probably said something vague to his brother – along the lines that Brodie was not to be trusted – hence Kilbarron's *froideur*. Brodie survived on the margins for a few more days as guests came and went. There was another dinner up at the big house but Brodie wasn't invited this time – only Kilbarron, Malachi and Lika.

Because of the pressure they were under he only dared risk a few snatched conversations with Lika. She seemed calmer.

'He doesn't know,' she said. 'I'm absolutely convinced. But he's on edge, tense, because of the concerts. In fact he's being quite sweet to me.'

For the first time in their relationship Brodie regretted that he and Lika had to converse in a second language. His good French wasn't quite good enough to make clear the nuances of his suspicions. Surely Lika sensed something, he asked. Has he said anything about me? No, she replied: *'Il est absolument comme d'habitude.'* It wasn't enough. And Lika's reassurances were also troublingly bland. 'I've seen him like this before. It's always the same when he prepares for big concerts.' But Brodie wasn't reassured. Their shared language was at variance.

Three days after the Malachi confrontation Brodie walked past the cottage and could hear Kilbarron practising – Brahms, he recognized, the 'Paganini-variationen'. The technique was flawless but he could tell at once that the piano was slightly out of tune and, before lunch as they gathered in the dining room, he mentioned this.

'It's fine,' Kilbarron said. 'It serves its purpose. Doesn't bother me.' He looked searchingly at Brodie and Brodie wondered again what it was that Malachi had told him, sensing Kilbarron's orchestrated concentration of his antipathy.

'Are you all right, Brodie? Fit and well, I hope?' There was something taunting and sneering about his enquiry – not concern.

'Yes. Very well, thank you.'

'Good. I want you to go back to Piter tomorrow. I know my programme now. I'll be coming back for first rehearsals soon. Feather-light on the treble octaves. Feather-light, mind.'

'Of course. But tomorrow – are you sure?'

'Yes. First thing. I want everything ready. Tip-top.'

He turned brusquely and walked away. Lika had come into the dining room and he took her hand and led her out. For Brodie that confirmed everything: Malachi had concocted and told his brother some story or other that reflected badly on Brodie. Brodie Moncur was no longer in the inner circle – he was being banished from Maloe Nikolskoe.

Brodie couldn't sleep that night – trapped in a delicate balance of indecision and misgiving. It would be his last night at Maloe Nikolskoe, he assumed. His mind was alive, running through possibilities, probabilities, the future, what to do – and where in the world would he and Lika go? He left his bed as dawn approached, dressed and packed up his few belongings.

He stepped outside. Not even the kitchen staff were stirring and no smoke rose from the brick chimney in the farmyard. He walked up the path by the lake in the nacreous light, glad of his hat and overcoat. This was the track that Lika would take to the ash-tree pool. Out of sight of the house, it curled its way round the farm buildings and disappeared into a wood of silver birch. In the leaf-linked darkness of the wood there was an eerie silence, as if Brodie were the only breathing creature alive in the landscape. He stepped out of the gloom into the lacy light of dawn, confronted by the swelling contours of a harvested wheat field. At the side of the field was a two-horse reaper-binder, its reel-slats damp with dew. Brodie glanced at its gearing and wheels and chains, marvelling at the solidity and heaviness of agricultural metal. Somehow this machine cut the corn and miraculously laid the stalks behind it in tied sheaves. He'd seen them at work on the bigger farms of Liethen Valley.

Brodie looked around – he was entirely alone in the thinning dawn light and felt he was in a painting by – what was his name? – the one he had seen in Varvara Vadimova's apartment. 'Dawn at Nikolskoe' . . . The wheat field's empty acres undulated easily to the fringe of trees. The wheat had been cut, the sheaves stooked then carted away, winnowed, and the rest used to make a hayrick somewhere. The stubble glittered as if dusted with frost in the angled early-morning light – maybe more magical machines would be brought for harrowing, he wondered. The field harrowed, left, then ploughed up before the winter frosts made the ground iron-hard and—

Brodie froze.

A hundred yards away a young deer was eating the green shoots of emerging grass growing between the stubble. Delicate, nervy, it would eat for a second or two then look up sharply and scan the field, alarmed for a second. Then, all well, it would resume eating – then repeat the process. Brodie stood motionless. The deer looked up and turned its head to him. If he didn't move or make a sound he would be registered as just another immobile feature in the landscape. For long seconds the two of them held their positions, the deer constantly looking up, seemingly staring straight at Brodie. Brodie rigid, staring back. The deer seemed a thing of absolute perfect natural beauty, he thought, quiveringly alive, both fragile and athletically graceful on its slim legs, its pelt glowing like caramel as the first rays of sun hit the wheat field. Why would anyone want to shoot a creature as beautiful as that, Brodie found himself wondering? A wood pigeon made its husky fluting call from the birch wood and suddenly – perhaps some scent of human on the breeze – the deer was off, leaping away in great bounds until it reached the safety of the trees and disappeared. Brodie felt both oddly stirred and shriven by the encounter. He had been perfectly still but the animal had sensed something was amiss and had bolted.

The moment seemed freighted with symbolism – but a symbolism that was lost to him. An omen, then, perhaps – a bad omen.

Brodie turned and walked solemnly back to the house. The staff were stirring now – a clatter of pans, the gong of a ladle on a pot coming from the kitchen in the yard, the dogs barking at the cocks crowing. In the empty dining room he asked a sleepy serving maid for a pot of coffee and confirmed that the trap that he had ordered would be there in half an hour to take him into Dubechnia to catch the Petersburg train. He realized, with a sudden whelm of chagrin, that he wouldn't be able to say goodbye to Lika.

7

Brodie did exactly what Kilbarron asked. He spent a day on the new concert grand – the Steingraeber – now set firmly on centre stage, the ballet season over. He retuned the piano, then worked on every hammer-head with his needles and hammer-irons, and weighted the treble octaves with his thin sheets of lead – an operation of elaborate precision – so that the tiniest pressure delivered by the brush of a finger would produce a clear, true note. With his miniature India-rubber bellows and his own mixture of dry lubrication – a concoction of talc, graphite and, his special touch, finely ground molybdenite from Norway – he dusted the rollers and the key bed. The piano was ready, perfectly set for Kilbarron's touch. It wasn't the ideal instrument for him, as the old Channon had been, but it was close. He would be pleased, Brodie hoped.

As he was leaving, the manager of the theatre showed him the proof of the poster announcing the Kilbarron Season. Here were the details of the inaugural concert. First up was Kilbarron's own composition – 'Der Tränensee – Tondichtung für grosses Orchester'. Then Tchaikovsky's Piano Concerto No. 3, then Balakirev's 'Islamey'. A heavy evening for Kilbarron – bravura stuff, but exhausting – but designated a night to remember, clearly. He might have to retune at the interval, he realized. Kilbarron had asked for three full days of rehearsal with the orchestra – there was a lot at stake.

He had lunch with George Vere at the Imperial Yacht Club. The walls were heavily overhung with clustered photographs of yachts and yachtsmen, trophies and pennants. The tables were crowded and the style was French – crisp white napery, ostentatious 'good' service, by tail-coated waiters. During lunch Brodie came to realize that, actually, he liked Vere – he had an easy smile and that Englishman's feigned air of polished self-deprecation and absent-mindedness that, in fact, just failed to entirely disguise a shrewd and observant mind.

'Are you all right, Moncur?' he asked after their first course. 'Bit under the weather?'

For some reason Brodie felt the need to unburden himself of his problems.

'An affair of the heart,' he said. 'I'm in love and it's not going well.'

'Do I know the young lady? No need to tell me, if you don't want to.'

'She's not Varvara Vadimova, if that's what you were wondering.'

'Well, that's a bonus. But I'm no use to you on that score,' Vere said.

'I'm experiencing feelings of impending doom,' Brodie said. 'I have this horrible, growing conviction that everything is going to turn out very badly and I don't know what to do.'

'Funnily enough, that's exactly my state of mind when I wake up every morning.'

Brodie had to laugh.

'I assume she's married,' Vere said.

'No. But there is another man in the picture.'

'Well, seriously, anything I can do to help,' Vere said in a genuinely kindly way. 'If things get really bad, just let me know, if you want.'

There was a quiet knock at his bedroom door. Brodie was reading Lady Dalcastle's gift of Swinburne's poems, musing over the lines, thinking that Swinburne was a bit florid and verbose and wondering if he was too rich a dish for his current mood. He closed the book, called 'Come in' and Kyrill's smiling face appeared.

'A boy has delivered a note, sir.'

Brodie took it from him. It was from Lika.

'We are coming back,' it said. 'Write to me at Poste Restante, General Post Office, window 43.' It was unsigned.

'Is there a reply for the boy?' Kyrill asked.

Brodie fished in his pocket for some kopeks and handed a few coins over.

'With respect, sir, this is too generous. Ten kopeks is enough for a boy.'

'You decide, Kyrill. Buy yourself a drink with the rest.'

'You're extremely kind, sir.' He was about to withdraw then paused. 'We enjoy having you here, sir.'

'Thank you, Kyrill.'

Brodie immediately wrote to Lika.

Malaya Morskaya, 57

23 August 1899

My darling Lika,

It's perhaps too risky to try and meet at the moment, but let us make plans to leave Piter as soon as we can – perhaps after the first concert. I have plenty of money and will withdraw the cash from the bank so we're properly ready to travel. We can go anywhere – Paris, Buenos Aires, New York. Just let me know and I will organize everything. Once this concert is over – and the money begins to flow in – Kilbarron won't care about us any more.

I love you, my darling.
Your Brodie

On the Monday following he went to his office at the theatre as usual. He could see the orchestra arriving for what must be the first rehearsal. Could Kilbarron be back already? They were professional musicians hired on contract for this New Russia Symphony Orchestra, as advertised. There must over a hundred, Brodie calculated – Kilbarron wanted huge volume, apparently. But there was no sign of the maestro himself; Brodie assumed he must be somewhere in the building, however. An hour later in his office he could hear the orchestra tuning up – now Kilbarron must be there, conducting from the piano. He wandered down backstage but found the door to the amphitheatre locked. He tried another, also locked. He went to find the manager – an amiable fellow called Ardeyev – and told him that, mysteriously, all the doors into the theatre were locked. The man looked abashed.

'Yes, it's Maestro Kilbarron's instructions, sir.'

'I understand. But I work for Maestro Kilbarron. He will need me for the piano.'

'I think a new tuner has been employed, sir.'

Brodie took this in. The exclusion was becoming a totality.

'All the same, I would like to hear the rehearsal,' Brodie said.

Ardeyev looked at the ground. His fingers twitched with embarrassment.

'I'm afraid you're not allowed, sir. The doors are closed against you. It is a specific demand.'

Brodie went back to his office, waited ten minutes then walked calmly along the corridor, up a flight of narrow stairs and through a small unlocked door (he had to crouch) that led to the fly-tower high above the theatre's stage. He closed the door carefully behind him. It was dim up in the fly-gallery, light only came up from below, and all the backdrops from the ballet season were hanging there like huge curtains, adding to the gloom. He waited, letting his eyes grow accustomed to the near-darkness. Webs of tight hemp ropes secured with cleats held the backdrops like so many clothes in a giant wardrobe. Ahead of him he could now make out a narrow catwalk stretching across the grid-deck filled with wooden battens that weren't being used.

Slowly, he inched forward along the catwalk and steadily, below him, his view down on the orchestra and the stage was revealed. He could see Kilbarron, sitting at the piano, an interpreter beside him. Kilbarron was speaking but he couldn't make out what was being said. The smell of the hemp ropes was powerful – he felt he was high in the rigging of a tall-masted ship looking down on the deck below.

He had reached the middle of the catwalk and he sank down on his knees. Kilbarron was back at the piano again and gave the time to the orchestra. The sound of the music rose up to Brodie in the fly-gallery – prodigious, palpable, rich and romantic. He didn't recognize it and Brodie realized they must be rehearsing Kilbarron's own composition, the tone poem. A bit like Richard Strauss, Brodie thought, or even Wagner – remembering Kilbarron's own words: 'I'm not a composer, I'm an arranger.'

And then he heard the orchestra take up the central melody, massed strings and French horns only – the refrain.

It was 'My Bonny Boy'.

Then it was strings only, and then the piano joined and took over the melody at the crucial juncture. Brodie felt the tear-itch in his eye, spontaneously. Tears of shock, injustice, of massive betrayal. He felt a kind of treacly loathing clot his throat. He wanted to spit but he knew he couldn't. He closed his eyes and swallowed the bile.

He stayed in the fly-tower for forty minutes or so listening to Kilbarron take the orchestra through his tone poem, stopping and starting, going back to the beginning, concentrating on certain passages. It was masterfully done – the adaptation, the transfiguration – he had to admit, every emotional stop pulled out to the full, the final minutes a marked diminuendo leading towards a final reprise of the ballad's simple melody – piano, strings, French horns – the dying fall of the conclusion – and his key sequence of notes played on the piano, solo. G flat major to D flat major and then the surprise shift to D flat minor ninth. Plangent, moving, overwhelming. And not a dry eye in the house, he would wager . . .

He saw Kilbarron halt the rehearsal and leave the stage. Brodie sensed now was the only time for a confrontation. Back in his office he quickly packed up his few possessions – his blotter, the theatre's notepaper, his pen, his novel – stuffed them into the Gladstone bag that contained his tuning tools and implements and walked downstairs to the floor where the dressing rooms were. He felt surprisingly calm – though he knew the feeling was possibly very temporary.

'*Oui, entrez*,' he heard Kilbarron call in response to his knock.

He pushed the door open and found Kilbarron stretched out on his divan with a bottle of brandy on the table beside him. He was very surprised to see Brodie.

'What're you doing here, Moncur?' he said, sitting up and swinging his legs off the divan. 'I haven't got time to talk to you.'

'It won't take long,' Brodie said. 'I just heard your tone poem – despite your best efforts.'

'Oh, yes? What did you think?' He wasn't smiling.

'Congratulations – it's wonderful. There's only one problem. A big problem.'

'And what's that?'

'You stole it from me.'

'Don't be ridiculous.'

'It's my song. "My Bonny Boy". You heard me play it in Paris. You sat beside me at your piano and played it yourself.'

'I've no memory of that. Sorry.'

'I wrote the words and the music down for Lika.'

Mention of her name seemed to rile him.

'Well maybe I heard Lika sing it.' He knew at once he shouldn't have said that. 'Or maybe not,' he added quickly. 'In fact it's based on an old Irish folk tune, if you'd like to know – "Cailín fionn". I don't need to steal anything from the likes of you, Moncur.' He looked at Brodie, his anger at being caught out now beginning to distort his face. He stood up.

'Mon Cur,' he said. 'My cur. You dog. You mongrel whelp. How fucking dare you! You fucking dog, get out of here!'

'You can't play without me,' Brodie said, his voice trembling now. 'You need your dog. Otherwise you'll be a one-handed pianist in a month.'

'You're just a piano tuner, Moncur. They're ten a penny. I've got a new one, a Russian. He's done an exceptional job on the piano. Makes you look like an apprentice.'

'I'm afraid that's impossible. There's no one better than me. No one.'

'Vainglory!' Kilbarron shouted. 'You vain little cretin! The world's full of piano tuners but there's only one John Kilbarron!'

Kilbarron stepped up to him and Brodie could smell the brandy on his breath.

'Fuck off out of my life, you dog, you insect. Fuck off and die somewhere, miserably.'

Brodie closed his eyes. Opened them.

'When you crawl back to me with your useless hand and you beg me – beg me – to tune and regulate your piano for you, know what I'll do, Kilbarron? I'll spit in your face.'

'But I don't care any more because after this concert I'm stopping playing. You stupid fucking idiot!' He was yelling in triumph now. 'I'm going to conduct.' He made grotesque conducting movements like a man in front of a marching band. 'One and two and three and four! Yes, I'm going to beat time like Mahler and Weingartner and Bülow. Any fool can do it and make a fortune. This is going to be my last concert. And you're not invited!'

He reached to grab Brodie, but Brodie stepped back and Kilbarron stumbled and swayed, regaining his balance. Brodie turned and slammed the door behind him as he left. He walked out of the New Russia Theatre into a fine rain. He knew he'd never be back.

8

Brodie decided to walk home, he was in such a turmoil, needing to clear his head. He was thinking: was it Kilbarron who had stolen the sheet of music he'd written down for Lika? Was that how it had really disappeared? He thought back to that afternoon in the Saint-Germain apartment, remembering how intrigued Kilbarron had been with the song and how he had so skilfully analysed how its effects were achieved. 'I'm an arranger, not a composer,' he always said and, hearing the song, he had seen an opportunity. Brodie had unwittingly provided him with the key to his tone poem. 'Der Tränensee' . . . It came to him now: 'The Lake of Tears'. Of course, the evidence was there in the title. He had a horrible feeling it would make Kilbarron's name.

He crossed the Neva on Nikolaevsky Bridge. It was a chilly day for late August. Autumn not far off and winter hard on autumn's heels. He paused in the middle of the bridge, aware of a slight tremble in his body. The shock, he supposed, all the raw emotion of the encounter, the insults, the threats. He looked across the water at the wide quays of the city's magnificent waterfront – the Admiralty, the Winter Palace, the Hermitage – as the light tarnished and thickened with evening coming on. Then he saw, in the distance, a flight of geese, a dozen or so, flying low over the river, coming towards him in a loose chevron – just feet above the grey choppy water, their heavy wings beating in near-unison. The flight rose slightly as the geese reached the bridge and they flashed over, almost within touching distance of him, the sound of their wings audible – *whoomph, whoomph* – effortlessly occupying the air. He felt moved and overwhelmed and turned to watch them disappear into the coppery sunset, heading for Vasilievsky Island.

He leaned on the parapet, feeling the hard stone on his elbows, and looked at the dark flowing water below him, thinking of his future and how precarious it was, how everything now depended on Lika.

And then he felt something stir in his chest and rise to his throat. He had time to grab his handkerchief and he coughed fiercely into it, feeling a loosening in his lungs. He knew what he would find when he opened it – bright blood. A growing tubercle had eroded an artery branch and blood was flooding his lungs. He cursed John Kilbarron. The thieving bastard. The bastard thief. All this agitation, the unseemly malice and hate had made his body break. He spat blood into the Neva, trying to breathe calmly, evenly, throwing his red soaking handkerchief into the water and watching the current carry it away. The haemorrhage was over – a short one, thank God. He should go home, have something warm to eat, go to bed, think about leaving, think about leaving Petersburg with Lika.

Malaya Morskaya, 57

28 August 1899

My darling Lika,

I have broken with Kilbarron. We had a terrible confrontation – very bitter, very unpleasant – and I have left his employ. The trouble is I have no idea how long I can stay in this apartment. No doubt Kilbarron will have Elisaveta Vadimova evict me as soon as he remembers. The only good news is that he seems to know nothing about us. Obviously Malachi has kept his mouth shut for the moment – but, I'm afraid, not for long.

Come away with me, my love. Leave him. He's insane – destroying himself – and he'll destroy you. I've withdrawn all my money from the bank. We can live comfortably for a year – travel, be together with no concerns. Free yourself, my darling. Come with me.

I love you.
Your Brodie

*

Fyolka set the dish of fried calves' feet with brown sauce in front of him.

'Danke schön,' Brodie said.

'Das ist gut,' she said. *'Wunderbar. Magnifique.'*

'Merci infiniment.'

Fyolka was excelling herself in the kitchen, spoiling him with new dishes every day since his haemorrhage. He had asked her, through Kyrill, for robust hot meals to build up his strength. It was almost as if she knew he was going to be leaving and wanted to provide him with fond memories of her Russian cuisine.

He began to eat the calves' feet – surprisingly tasty with a sauce that was both honeyed and sour, somehow. It was very hot, that was the main thing. He went quickly to his room and poured himself a glass of vodka from the bottle he kept there and returned to his meal. Hot food and the burn of vodka – he was feeling better already. But something nagged at him as he ate his calves' feet, something Kilbarron had said during their bitter row.

'I've got a new tuner, a Russian. He's done an exceptional job on the piano. Makes you look like an apprentice . . .'

But what could another tuner have done that he hadn't done already? Who was this Russian prodigy? Brodie knew how much care he'd put into regulating Kilbarron's piano for the inaugural concert. The tiny calibration of the minute weights on the keys of treble octaves. Slivers of lead cut to fit the underside of the keys giving the lightest possible down-weight. No piano in existence had such light action. Then his precise positioning of the dampers and the elaborate preparation of the hammer-heads, softening or hardening as required with his pins and the damper-iron. The dry lubricant. What could any tuner do that was better? What expertise could excel his?

Brodie knew the concert was now just a few days off: on Friday at four in the afternoon. There was some time left for him to find out.

On Thursday evening Brodie stood in the shadows opposite the New Russia Theatre watching the last of the musicians and the stagehands leave. He waited another half-hour and no one emerged. He crossed the road and headed for the stage door, Gladstone bag in one hand and several feet of rolled-up piano wire in the other. He knew all the men who manned the reception desk at the stage door: Boris, Radislav, Mstislav. And it was Mstislav on duty when he rushed in, flourishing the wire.

'Disaster. A real crisis!' he said in French. Then repeated it in German. *'Katastrophe. Eine echte Krise!'*

Mstislav – a simple, earnest man – saw the roll of wire, jumped to the correct conclusion, hurried him into the theatre and switched on the lights. Brodie opened the piano, hauled out the action and flipped apart his Gladstone bag, laying out his tools like a surgeon about to operate.

'Thank you, Mstislav,' he said. 'It'll take me half an hour.'

Mstislav left and it took Brodie twenty seconds to realize that nothing was different. No one had touched the workings of this piano since he had regulated it for Kilbarron days before. This was his handiwork; all his little *astuces* were present. The graphite in the lubricating dust from his bottle still gleamed on the rail and the levers. He played some octaves, notes in unison – perfect. He began to suspect there was no Russian tuning genius at all – it was simply a way of scoring another malign point, another perverse slap in the face.

Brodie felt a sudden nausea. A bitter sickness of real resentment, of betrayal, after everything he had done for Kilbarron: how he had extended – maybe even saved – his career as a virtuoso pianist of the very first rank through his finesse, his expertise as a tuner. Any other pianist might have been forced to retire . . . As he slid the action back into position he had an idea – now he was here, alone with the piano, unobserved, not likely to be interrupted – and he tugged the action out again.

Brodie brought to mind a saying that his old teacher and mentor, Findlay Lanhire, had told him: namely that of all the miraculous mechanical components that went into the superbly sophisticated machine that is a modern piano, the most remarkable is the 'repetition action'. Discovered and patented in 1821, it was an arrangement of levers that allows a note to be repeated without the key returning to its position of rest. The ability to strike a note, the same note in rapid succession, and have it sound true and discrete each time it was struck was what had transformed the instrument entirely. Pianists like Liszt, Thalberg and Kilbarron could strike the one note six times in a split second, such was their virtuosity. But it was the complicated assemblage of pins, screws and jacks beneath the hammer, all controlled by the tension in the repetition spring, producing the necessary torque, along with minute movements of the component parts, that allowed them to do so – that allowed the note to be played in apparently effortless repetition and that permitted the virtuoso's brilliance and dexterity such easy display.

With the tip of a fine screwdriver he tapped and pushed out the brass centre pin on the jack of note D in the fifth octave so it extended a tenth of an inch – loosened inevitably therefore from its snug tight hole – so it was just touching the adjacent note. Then he ran in the entire action, tested the note a few times – sounded normal – and closed the piano with the fall.

The jack pin was now touching the adjacent lever of the action of the next note, E. Vibrations caused by any fortissimo passage would cause it to jam up against E and when it jammed up, and then bent under the pressure, it would bind to the next note so that when you played D, you would actually sound two notes, D and E, and then moments later both notes would stick. It would be impossible to continue.

It would take, he reckoned, around fifteen or twenty minutes of John Kilbarron's playing before the strain on that tiny pin would become acute and effectively make the piano malfunction irreparably. The beauty of the little sabotage, he thought further, was that it showed no sign of tampering. Alas, under the extraordinary pressure of fortissimo concert performances, these sorts of accidents occurred from time to time, inevitably. It was highly complex machinery – and highly complex machinery could go wrong. Why would the jack pin on the D action work loose? Who could say? *Force majeure*, filthy rotten luck – just desserts.

'Thanks, Mstislav,' Brodie said as he left, giving him a smile and pretending to wipe his brow in relief, *'alles ist in Ordnung.'*

9

Brodie was back in position opposite the theatre the next afternoon – it was a gusty day with sudden showers – standing in his mackintosh and with trilby pulled low watching the carriages arrive and the dignitaries hurry into the theatre. *Le tout* Piter was present for John Kilbarron's inaugural concert to launch his season of Russian classical music, all excitingly led off by the world premiere of Kilbarron's own composition, the tone poem 'Der Tränensee'. The excited laughter and chatter carried to him across the street. The carriages, barouches and landaus were backed up as far as Tuchkov Bridge. Once everyone was inside and the concert about to begin, Brodie went home to his apartment and finished packing his belongings into his two cabin trunks. He had received no reply from Lika to his last letter so he wrote her another and took it to window 43 in the central post office, the Poste Restante window. On his way back he waited an hour outside the house on Nevsky Prospekt and then realized that, of course, she would be at the New Russia Theatre herself, no doubt with Malachi at her side, observing the apotheosis of John Kilbarron.

It was in the French-language *St Petersburg Gazette* the next day.

> The inaugural Kilbarron concert was abandoned after ten minutes owing to a sudden technical malfunction in the grand piano (manufacturer Steingraeber). The full concert programme will take place in a week's time. All ticket holders are cordially invited to present themselves at the box office if a refund is required.

There was more. Apparently, after approximately ten minutes of 'Der Tränensee' Kilbarron had abruptly stopped playing, stood, bowed briefly to the audience and left the stage, leaving the orchestra and the audience baffled. In the midst of the general consternation, a manager had appeared and had made an announcement. It was impossible to continue for technical reasons – a defect in the piano – and the concert would reluctantly have to be postponed. There were some boos and programmes had been thrown and the audience had dispersed, reluctant and displeased. There had been no further comment from John Kilbarron nor the concert season's sponsors, Elisaveta and Varvara Vadimova.

Reading this, Brodie felt a simultaneous thrill of pleasure and a deeper twinge of alarm. The dog – the cur, the mongrel whelp, Moncur – had had his day. But, Brodie knew, it wouldn't end at that. In any other circumstances he would have left Piter instantly, caught a train to Paris – that very evening, if at all possible – but he couldn't leave without seeing Lika. All plans included Lika. Lika Blum was anchoring him to St Petersburg until further notice.

In the morning he went to keep his appointment with Dr Sampsoniyevskaya. They both lit cigarettes as they discussed his case and the recent haemorrhage.

'It was more like a large ball of blood,' he said. 'Not the full haemorrhage that I had before. More like spitting blood, but from deep down, you know.'

'I think you'll be spitting more blood, I'm sorry to say,' Dr Sampson said, smiling ruefully. 'And winter is coming. I think it's time to fly south to the sun.' She frowned. 'I tell you in all honesty, Mr Moncur, that the only cure – the only cure I really believe in, though I prescribe many cures, many various cures – is warmth and rest. If you've started spitting blood then Piter is the last place you want to be. You've been to Nice, you told me?'

'Yes, I spent some months there.'

'Go back to Nice for the winter. Or Biarritz. Do you know Biarritz?'

'No.'

'Very popular with wealthy Russians and English royalty. I know a doctor in Biarritz whom I can recommend.' She scribbled his name and address on a piece of paper. 'Come back to Piter next summer and we'll meet again,' she said, handing it to him.

They shook hands and Brodie felt that sad premonition that farewells bring – that this would be their last one. He was reluctant to let the moment go, for some reason, hesitating to say a final goodbye to this stern but warm physician.

She smiled, led him to the door and patted him reassuringly on the back.

'Good luck,' she said. 'All will be well.'

Brodie walked homewards in low spirits, unconvinced by her optimism. More blood-spitting, she had said, and despite her assurances and smiles he had a sense that she had foreseen the inevitable progression of his disease. How much time do I have? Brodie asked himself. A year? Two years? A decade, a quarter of a century? . . . It was too depressing to contemplate; it made everything fragile, everything was now no more than a vague possibility – all probability and certainty had gone from his life. But then he reflected further: when had probability and certainty ever played a reliable part in the human condition?

As he let himself into the apartment he heard – bizarrely – a dog bark. More like a yap. *Yap-yap-yap*. He stepped into the sitting room and saw Lika was there with César, who was barking excitedly at him. Nikanor was serving tea.

'Hello,' Brodie managed to say, as if seeing Lika in his own sitting room was an everyday occurrence. 'I can't tell you how pleased I am that you managed to drop by.'

Nikanor left and they kissed. He hugged her to himself – suddenly everything was all right again. It was miraculous how it happened, he—

'He's thrown me out,' Lika said, bright-lashed with tears, then flowing. She was in a state, he saw, febrile, panicked.

'Kilbarron? Why?'

'Malachi told him about that night he found us in the hotel in Dubechnia.'

Part of him was exulting but he said, 'But why, for God's sake? Why would he do that now?'

'Do you know – I think it was to distract him from the fiasco of the concert. To make him think of something else. Anyway, he was horrible, called me the foulest names. Of course he's been drunk for twenty-four hours.'

'My God . . .' Brodie was thinking.

'My trunks, my luggage, are in your room. I've left so much behind, but he gave me no time. Your man – Nikanor? – was most helpful.' She paused and took his hand. 'I had to come to you Brodie. I couldn't stay, couldn't reason with them.'

'This is the best thing,' Brodie said firmly. 'The very best. We're free, Lika, my darling. No ties any more. It's over. He's gone. We leave Kilbarron to his miserable fate and go away and make our own life.'

'But . . .' She paused. 'He wants to see you,' she said. 'He insists. That's the last message he gave me. You have to go and see him tonight. You have to.'

'I'll do no such thing. He can go to hell.'

'Or else he'll go to the police and have you arrested.'

'On what charge, for God's sake?'

'I don't know. He just kept talking about the police,' she said, taking his hand. 'You'd better go.'

Brodie stood uneasily in Kilbarron's red drawing room, hung with its arsenal of ancient weapons. He had refused the offer of a drink from the butler and instead was smoking a cigarette, avidly, drawing the smoke deep into his lungs. He thought he was prepared for anything – insults, tears, fisticuffs. This, he hoped, was the last time he'd ever see John Kilbarron. He was only here because of Lika – time to make his final brief farewell.

But it was Malachi who came in, smiling, almost swaggering, somehow on show in a lurid emerald-green waistcoat, as if he was going to a costume ball. He looked neater: his hair and beard were trimmed – for the concert, probably, Brodie thought. He didn't offer his hand.

'Well, I almost have to give you a round of applause, Moncur,' he said. 'I didn't think you had it in you. But you buggered us up well and truly, royally buggered us up, you devious rascal, you.'

Brodie wasn't fooled by the pseudo-jocular tone – it was underpinned by Malachi's high-tension aggression.

'I don't know what you're talking about.'

'We know everything. Mstislav confirmed it – the man at the stage door. Your emergency repair job.'

'I was just checking to see all was in order. The man barely speaks any German. He must be confused.'

'Of course you were – and your hand slipped.'

'Why don't you ask your new tuner? The Russian genius. He'll tell you these accidents sometimes happen to the best pianos. Wear and tear.'

'Because there is no "new" tuner. You stupid arse.'

Brodie turned to see it was Kilbarron who'd spoken. Raging drunk, Brodie also realized instantly, swaying slightly.

'I was just trying to get your goat, boyo,' Kilbarron said, leeringly. 'And I succeeded. How did I succeed!'

'Look,' Brodie said, coldly, brazening himself. 'You know what you did. You know what you stole from me. We both have – what shall I say? – grievances with each other. You can hardly—'

'Grievances!' Kilbarron shouted. 'Oh, yes. Let's start with my grievances, if I may. Here's one. What about you topping Lika Blum when I wasn't looking, you filthy whoreson urchin. I assume she's come running to you. You're welcome to her.'

'Keep Lika out of this. This is a personal matter—'

'I can go to the police, you fool,' Kilbarron said crossing the room unsteadily towards him. 'Deliberate sabotage. I have witnesses. Cause and effect. Evidence.' He stopped by Malachi and rested his hand on Malachi's shoulder for support. 'Do you know how much your little act of vengeance has cost us? Madame Vadimova is most displeased. It's a perfect Petersburg scandal – everybody's talking, laughing behind their hands – which is hardly what she wanted.'

'Say what you have to say and I'll leave you alone,' Brodie declaimed, a little self-consciously. 'I don't think Madame Vadimova would like to hear of your act of plagiarism, either. That might dent the reputation of her wonderful Maestro Kilbarron. The world premiere of his tone poem.'

Kilbarron was in front of him now; his gaunt pale features were limned with a fine sweat. He looked ill. The dew of ill health.

He slapped Brodie's face – hard, stingingly.

'That's my challenge to you, you Scottish guttersnipe. I demand satisfaction. Get your seconds to talk to Malachi. You have twenty-four hours. Otherwise I go to the police and have you prosecuted for sabotaging my concert.'

He swayed out of the room banging into the doorjamb as he left.

'What's he talking about?' Brodie said, rubbing his smarting cheek. 'Challenge? Seconds? Has he gone mad or is it just the drink?'

'He's challenging you to a duel,' Malachi said reasonably. 'And he's not joking.'

IO

'It's completely absurd,' Brodie said. 'Here we are four months away from the twentieth century and he's challenging me to a duel. It's insane.'

George Vere shrugged and made a face. 'His brother told me that Kilbarron has actually fought two duels – one in Ireland and one in Germany – and he's made a dozen challenges over the years. He's a bit obsessed with the whole ritual. You know: reputation besmirched, debts of honour repaid – man-to-man stuff. *Un vrai bretteur,* as they say in French.'

'But I can't go through with this, seriously.'

Brodie had asked George Vere to be his second. He felt it presumptuous as they hardly knew each other but Vere said he'd be delighted. Very grateful. He seemed genuinely excited by the prospect.

'I think you can relax, Moncur,' he said. 'His brother – what's his name?'

'Malachi.'

'Yes, Malachi says you just have to participate in the rigmarole. This is modern duelling. There are two options: you can make your peace "under the gun" as they say – shake hands at the last minute and leave. Or you deliberately shoot to miss. This is what happened before in Kilbarron's other duels, apparently. You both fire in the air – and go your separate ways. Symbolic, you know.'

Vere was pacing about the sitting room in Morskaya Street. Brodie sensed he was looking forward to this absurd sham duel.

'The thing is – at least this was the drift I caught – is that if you don't go through with this duel, however preposterous it seems, then he will go to the police. Don't tell me anything, by the way. All I know is some accusation of sabotage – a concert ruined. Shame and humiliation pouring down on everyone.' He paused to light a cigarette. 'I think this ritualistic settling of scores is the answer. Very Russian, of course.'

'And neither of us is Russian. As it happens. A Scotsman and an Irishman fighting a duel. It's preposterous.'

'Fighting a duel in Russia, though – here we live – we're all under the influence.'

Brodie thought on unhappily. Nothing was clear: no solution, no alternative, presented itself.

Vere was talking again.

'The other issue, as Mr Malachi Kilbarron quietly pointed out, is Madame Vadimova. She's a very powerful woman, very influential. And if you were to find yourselves in the hands of the authorities – the police – detained, say, even charged. A court case. She might make it very awkward and difficult for you.' He spread his arms. 'Play his game, Moncur. Act out this duel fantasy. That should end the matter. Kilbarron – Malachi – assured me that no one wants to get hurt.'

'So what happens next? If I play his game.'

'We meet at dawn tomorrow in the Yelaginsky Park. I'll pick you up here at five thirty. It'll take us half an hour to get there.'

'Don't I need two seconds?'

'I'll bring someone along from the embassy. There's an arbiter, also. Colonel Somebody. It's all very proper. Every aspect observed. I think that's part of the satisfaction.' Vere said he had to go and Brodie walked him to the front door where they shook hands.

'Think of it as a strange adventure,' Vere said, consolingly. 'Something to tell your grandchildren. "I fought a duel in the Yelaginsky Park in St Petersburg in 1899." I'd swap places with you if I could.'

Vere left and Brodie went back to his room. Lika was there, smoking, jittery, waiting, César sitting at her feet. He saw Brodie and ran to him and Brodie picked him up, unthinkingly.

'That dog likes you,' Lika said. 'I can't think why – you hardly know him.'

'Maybe I smell nice.'

'Do you like dogs?'

'I've never really thought about it. I suppose so.'

He told her what was going to happen – this pretence of a duel that was going to take place at dawn in the Yelaginsky Park.

'Let's just run away, Brodie.'

'Then he'll go to the police and I'll be arrested – at the very least. This is the quid pro quo. This is the only way we can be free, be rid of him.'

'But I just don't like it. It makes me worried.'

'Malachi has assured my man, my second – he's from the British Embassy, by the way – that it's a gesture. It's something Kilbarron does, or needs to do in some perverse way.'

He sat beside her and kissed her neck. Already he was seeing the dividends of all this *Sturm und Drang*. He and Lika were together, now. She lived with him, now, not Kilbarron.

'Your servants have made up a bed for me in the room across the corridor.'

'That's fine. I'll creep in later.'

'Who's that elderly man that sits quietly in the corner of every room, it seems?'

'He's called Kyrill. I've no idea why he lives here.'

Lika went to her bedroom with César. Brodie waited half an hour and then slipped out of his room.

'Good evening, sir.' Kyrill was walking through the hall, newspaper in hand.

'Good evening, Kyrill Denisovitch. I'm just going to see if Miss Blum has everything she needs.'

'A delightful young lady. I wish you goodnight, sir.'

Lying in bed with Lika, Brodie could tell there was something troubling her.

'What're you thinking?' he asked softly. 'What's wrong?'

'I'm thinking about John Kilbarron and tomorrow,' she said.

'It's just a "show", a harlequinade, to satisfy him. Then we can leave and start our life together.'

She hunched into him, holding him close.

'No,' she said. 'I think he really wants to kill you.'

II

Brodie was waiting outside the apartment on Morskaya Street. The air was chilly and he wore his hat and overcoat and wished he'd brought a scarf. It was five o'clock and he hadn't slept at all and it was still dark, more or less, a tarnished moon-sliver in the sky, the street lamps glowing brightly down Morskaya, no one stirring. He had felt nervously alert all night. And now that he had to be fully awake he felt tired. He heard horses' hooves and then saw a landau approaching. It stopped and Vere jumped out, followed by another man.

'This is your other second,' Vere said. 'Michael Rubenstein, a colleague from the embassy.'

Brodie shook hands with Rubenstein and thanked him for coming. They climbed into the landau and headed off.

Brodie felt anxious, subdued, but Vere and Rubenstein were in fine spirits.

'There's a duel in Tolstoy, of course, *War and Peace*,' Rubenstein said.

'And Dostoevsky . . . And Lermontov and Turgenev, come to think of it,' Vere added. 'And there's a Chekhov story called "The Duel". Not forgetting poor Pushkin, of course.' He smiled sadly at Brodie.

'There's a duel in the novel I'm reading, coincidentally,' Brodie said.

'What novel's that?' Rubenstein asked.

Brodie told him about the Stevenson, *The Master of Ballantrae*. The disturbing thought came to him that he might never finish it.

'Pistols?' Vere asked.

'Swords.'

'Well, you're spared that,' Rubenstein said. 'A blessing.'

'You could say,' Vere mused, 'that, looking at it from one angle, you're having an amazing Russian literary experience.'

'Or you could say,' Brodie responded, 'looking at it from another angle, that I'm a stupid benighted fool for going through with this. What am I doing? What am I playing at?'

'It's a full stop,' Vere said. 'Think of it that way. Kilbarron has his fun and games. All talk of police and lawsuits is over.'

'I could sue Kilbarron myself,' Brodie said with sudden anger, 'for plagiarism.'

'What do you mean? What's he stolen?'

'It doesn't matter,' Brodie said, slumping down in his seat. 'The whole thing's a farce. I just want it to be over.'

He looked out of the window of the landau as it crossed the Neva on Nikolaevsky Bridge and then rumbled over Tuchkov Bridge as they headed for Yelagin Island and its so-called park. It was an untamed wilderness as far as Brodie could see. Dawn was silvering the view as they reached the outermost limits of the city and there were no street lamps here on the wooden road they were trundling over. Vere spoke to the driver in excellent Russian confirming their route and soon the landau turned off the road and progressed down a dirt track. They stopped at the edge of a grassy meadow flanked with mature beech and silver-birch woods. Beyond the meadow was a narrow strip of lake and beyond that what looked like forest with no sign of human habitation. They could have been in the vast hinterlands of Russia, Brodie thought, feeling sick as he stepped out of the landau and buttoned his greatcoat tightly around him. It seemed colder here on Yelagin Island, cold and damp.

Vere had spotted the others standing round a trestle table in the lee of some huge pines and he and Rubenstein wandered down to meet them. Brodie, following slowly, took his spectacles off and polished them, thinking for the thousandth time that this was possibly the most ridiculous act that anyone could commit in their lives. What did Kilbarron gain, what satisfaction did he achieve by going through this charade? He repeated to himself: in half an hour it will be over. You and Lika will be free. You'll be with Lika, the woman you love. You can make your life with her anywhere you want. You have enough money; you have your skills; you're twenty-nine years old and all your life is ahead of you. The incantations appeared to work. He put his spectacles back on and felt a new vigour in his body. Let's get this nonsense over and done with, he thought, and went to join the small group at the meadow's rim.

Brodie saw Kilbarron and Malachi and another man whom he didn't recognize. The second second, he assumed. He was introduced to a moustachioed man in a dark suit: Colonel Vladimir Vladimirovich Ilyichov, he was told – the duel's arbiter.

The colonel led him to the table where three sets of long-barrelled, single-shot duelling pistols were on display, snug in their velvet moulds, set in their chestnut coffers. Kilbarron was staring at him intently; Malachi was smoking a cigar, its reek rancid and unpleasant in the crisp dawn air.

'Choose your weapon,' Vere whispered to him.

Brodie tapped one of the pistols at random and Vere selected it, checked that it was loaded and that the percussion cap was properly in place and told Malachi that he was satisfied. He handed the gun to Rubenstein, who glanced at it and handed it on to Brodie. Then Kilbarron chose his pistol.

Colonel Ilyichov had two sabres. He advanced into the meadow – the grass was knee-high – contemplated the direction of the rising sun (so that no one would be blinded), skewered one sabre into the turf, and strode out another fifteen paces before pronging the other sabre into the ground.

He summoned the duellists and addressed them in heavily accented French.

'You will be fifteen paces apart, and you both will have one shot when I drop my handkerchief. Is that understood, gentlemen?'

Brodie said yes, feeling somewhat faint, again overwhelmed by the ridiculous formalities of this game Kilbarron had chosen to play. Was it the theatricality that he relished? Somehow feeding off the gathering tensions and animosities concentrated in this archaic ritual? To think, Brodie reflected, that for centuries quarrels and affronts had been settled like this. It defied belief – and yet here he was participating in this burlesque role-playing. It struck him that for Kilbarron the very fact that he had him here and was putting him through this ridiculous palaver – that Brodie Moncur, his enemy, was doing his perverse bidding – was maybe enough to make him feel he had won.

Brodie told himself to stop thinking – no more questions – become an automaton. This would all be over in a few moments and they would climb into the landau and be driven to Morskaya Street. He would kiss Lika and they would go to the Warsaw station and their new life would begin.

'Positions, gentlemen!' Ilyichov called.

Brodie walked, as in a dream, towards his sabre planted in the turf. It was an old sabre, he saw, its blade badged with rust, the leather binding of its hilt mildewed and worn. He looked up to see Kilbarron, fifteen paces away, arrive at his sabre. The rising sun flashed off its cage-guard, a sudden dazzling sunburst that made Brodie blink.

The seconds consulted for the last time. Vere and Rubenstein came over to him, clustering close.

'When the colonel drops his handkerchief, simply raise your pistol and fire into the air,' Vere said. 'Kilbarron will do the same. You'll shake hands – if you want, no obligation – and we'll go off for a slap-up breakfast at the Hotel Astoria. I've booked a table.' Vere winked at him. 'Everything's going to be fine.'

'Hear, hear,' Rubenstein agreed.

Then he and Rubenstein stepped away and left Brodie alone by his sabre that had now begun to cant over somewhat. He felt the gun heavy in his hand. Preposterous, ludicrous, shameful.

Colonel Ilyichov stepped into view, a white handkerchief in his upheld hand.

'On the count of three,' he said. 'One, two, three.'

He dropped the handkerchief.

Brodie raised his arm vertically and fired his shot, sending his ball of lead high into the pale blue immensity of a St Petersburg dawn sky. He felt quite a recoil, juddering his elbow and shoulder.

He looked over at Kilbarron who still had his pistol held low by his thigh. Then he pointed it directly at Brodie's face.

'No, sir! This is unacceptable!' Brodie heard Vere shout – a split second before Kilbarron fired.

Brodie felt something tear at his left ear, tugging at it, and he spun round in a reflex, clapping his hand to the side of his head. Blood! His hand was slick with blood. He could see the blood dripping from his torn ear, like a tap left running. The blood pattered onto the dry blond meadow-grass of summer. Faintness overcame him and he fell to his knees, then his hands and knees. He could hear shouting and sounds of a scuffle. Malachi and the other second were holding back Vere and Rubenstein. Colonel Ilyichov was shouting furiously in Russian. Brodie shook his head, causing more blood to fall and looked around. Kilbarron was walking over to him, standing over him. He threw away his pistol and reached into his greatcoat and drew out another, cocked. Brodie felt the muzzle press against the back of his head. Cold for a second. He tried to turn.

'Don't do it,' he said to Kilbarron, over his shoulder.

Kilbarron was smiling. Two rows of teeth.

'I'll deal with you first, you Scottish bastard, and then I'll deal with that bitch-whore of yours.'

There was nothing for it. Brodie turned quickly, squirmed round and shot Kilbarron square in the chest with Lika's hotel-gun, her little Derringer – both barrels.

PART IV

Biarritz – Edinburgh – Nice

1900–1902

I

'Bonsoir, Monsieur Balfour. A demain.'

Brodie said goodbye to Madame Grosjean and heard her close and lock the front door of the shop behind him. He crossed the place de la Liberté and headed for Biarritz's central post office. It was early May and finally, he saw, workmen were taking down the strung bunting from the lamp posts, last vestiges of the centennial celebrations. May 1900, he thought: it still seemed strange to be in a new century. It should feel different, he imagined, but it didn't. He still felt trapped in the nineteenth century, somehow. It would not let him go.

He presented himself at the Poste Restante window, gave his name and was handed a small packet wrapped in brown paper – this was what he was waiting for – and, to his surprise, a letter. The packet changed his mood absolutely. He knew what it was, a pound of Margarita tobacco blend from Hoskings in Edinburgh. He had run out some weeks ago and, to his vague self-disgust, had found himself searching the crevices of his jacket and trouser pockets in the hope that he might retrieve enough rivelled strands that had fallen there to furnish the slimmest of rolled-up cigarettes. He had been successful. Of course he smoked other cigarettes and used other tobaccos – but his heart belonged to Margarita.

The letter, however, was unexpected. Talk about the nineteenth century, he thought, looking at the Russian stamps – here it was pursuing him. It was addressed to 'Monsieur B. Balfour, Poste Restante, Biarritz, Pyrénées-Atlantiques, France'. Brodie wandered back to the Café Terminus-Olympia by the railway station right in the heart of town, found a table in the shade, ordered an anisette, rolled and lit a cigarette and opened the letter. It was from George Vere.

St Petersburg

27 March 1900

Dear Balfour,

I was very glad to hear from you after these few months. Excuse my many errors on this typewriter and the absence of a signature at the end. I know you'll understand my discretion.

Here, as you requested, is my account of the aftermath of the events in the meadow at Yelagin Island. After you left with Rubenstein to seek medical aid, I reminded Malachi Kilbarron and his second that all the people involved in this unfortunate incident were British citizens and that, in St Petersburg, I was their representative on earth. Therefore they would be well advised to do what I said. As far as I could see, I told them, this was as clear-cut a case of self-defence that could be presented in any court of law. I, Rubenstein and Colonel Ilyichov would all testify to that effect. Equally the late JK was guilty of a premeditated act of attempted murder. Again, we would all testify to that effect. I gave Malachi twenty-four hours to come up with an explanation for the demise of his brother – otherwise I would go to the police. He and his second would certainly be arrested as accessories to this attempted murder. It was clearly an elaborate plot to kill Mr Brodie Moncur. They seemed to register the intent and force of my message, though Malachi was in something of a state of shock (JK's body was lying ten feet away covered in a greatcoat). Colonel Ilyichov vouchsafed the same opinion though I sensed he was more outraged at the violation of ancient duelling codes rather than the loss of life. He was incandescent and incredulous.

In due course Malachi and his second removed JK's body to their carriage and drove it away. Somehow, by some means, the body was transported the eighty or so versts to the estate of Maloe Nikolskoe. And it was from there, two days later, that JK's death from a heart seizure was announced to the world. It was widely reported in Piter and Moscow but not, I believe, in any British newspapers. I imagine you are ignorant of this official 'cause of death'. It was in everybody's interest that it should be so described. From the Petersburg perspective there was and is only sadness and mourning – no hint of scandal, no suspicion of anything underhand. JK died prematurely, melancholy and true, but all too typical of human mortality. I think you can assume, as far as you are concerned, that the matter is closed.

The only irony – and one you won't appreciate – is that two months after the death of the composer there was a memorial concert in the New Russia Theatre featuring 'Der Tränensee'. It was a monumental success. There have been other subsequent performances and the sales of sheet music have been very impressive. Word is spreading throughout Europe where other concerts are planned. Funny old life, one is tempted to say.

I think you and Mrs Balfour can consider yourselves safe. The matter has been completely hushed up. Please stay in communication. I am always pleased to afford any assistance I can.

Wishing you the best of good fortune,

Yr obt servant,
G

Brodie rolled another cigarette, thinking back to that terrible morning when he'd killed John Kilbarron . . . He felt a retrospective horror cool him suddenly and his hand went unreflectingly to his torn, diminished ear. Kill or be killed, he reminded himself sternly, though he noticed how the flame of his lighter trembled as he held it to his cigarette's end.

Brodie thought back. Forced himself.

Kilbarron's face was animate enough after the impact of the two bullets in his chest to register his utter shock. His mouth gaped, he staggered, dropped his own gun, and fell to his knees and then toppled slowly over on his side, apparently dead. Brodie heaved himself to his feet and saw Colonel Ilyichov, Vere, Rubenstein and Kilbarron's second holding Malachi pinioned. He was bellowing incoherently. He saw Vere then hissing words in Malachi's ear and very quickly he quietened and was led away a few paces by the other second. Vere, Rubenstein and Ilyichov then came over to see how Brodie was. His shirt collar and shirt front were sopping with blood from his wounded ear. He was given two handkerchiefs and held them to the wound to stop the bleeding. He felt no pain worth speaking of. The absurd thought came to him – who would have guessed that an injured human ear could bleed so much?

He was led shakily to the landau, asked the name of his doctor and then he and Rubenstein – leaving Vere behind to sort out the mess – made their way to Dr Sampson's consulting rooms.

'So,' Dr Sampson asked neutrally, as she cleaned the wound on his ear, 'what happened?'

'I . . . Ah. Yes. A hunting accident. A foolish, careless mistake. Hunting rabbits at dawn. It's the best time. I tripped, fell, the gun went off.'

'Mmm, really?' Her scepticism was manifest. 'Lucky escape.'

'Yes. Indeed.'

She stitched his left ear up – his lobe had been shredded – and wound a length of bandage round his head. She stepped back to admire her handiwork.

'You look surprisingly romantic.' She handed him his spectacles and he put them on. 'And there I was never expecting to see you again.'

'You never know in life,' Brodie said. 'Strange things can happen.'

She helped him into his jacket. While Brodie had been attended to by Dr Sampson, Rubenstein had gone to Lika to tell her what had happened on Yelagin Island. When Brodie arrived back at the apartment she was still crying with relief. She held her body tight against his, as if she was trying to meld herself to him.

'Is he really dead?' she whispered.

'Yes.'

'I warned you didn't I? I knew he wanted to kill you.'

'Thank God you gave me your gun. He was going to shoot me in the back of the head like an animal.'

'You see – I knew it, I knew it about him.'

She turned away and with the heels of her hands crushed tears from her eyes. What must it be like for her, Brodie wondered? Kilbarron dead – killed by her lover. All this terrible information.

'What about Malachi?' she asked, not turning.

'What about him?'

'Is he dead?'

'No, of course not. He was the second.'

She stepped back and turned now, her face an odd half-crying, half-smiling grimace.

'You should have killed him too.'

'How could I possibly have done that?'

She seemed suddenly galvanized.

'We have to go. We have to leave this place, now.'

'Go where? Why?'

'Because Malachi will come looking for us. We have to leave Piter, now.'

Brodie didn't argue. There was a strange determination about her as they swiftly completed their packing.

'Where are we going?' Brodie asked.

'To Narva. We can catch a train to Riga and Warsaw and Berlin from there.'

'Why Narva?'

'Because he'll be looking for us here in Piter and he won't find us in Narva.'

'Who?'

'Malachi! Believe me, Brodie. This is how we escape.'

'Listen, Lika, my darling, there's no hurry. Vere told me. Everything is under control.'

Lika closed her eyes as if she was talking to an imbecile.

'We have to go to a police station. Have you your passport? Your certificate of residence?'

'Of course.'

'Then we go. We pay for the stamp and then we wait in the police station and then we go to Narva. Just listen to me – I know what I'm doing.'

It took most of the rest of the day to have their documentation authorized, passports stamped, forms filled in, money paid (five roubles, fifty kopeks) for the foreigner's travel permit. It seemed odd, as a British citizen, to have to ask official permission to leave St Petersburg and go home, but this was Russia, Brodie realized.

Their documents in order, they returned to the Morskaya apartment and Lika sent Nikanor to find a troika that would take them the three hours to Narva. The troika secured, Nikanor, Kyrill and Fyolka helped them load their cases and trunks in the rear, where the driver roped them down.

The sense of something being wrong, seriously amiss, underlaid all their banter and chatter. Kyrill seemed almost tearful and Fyolka was very concerned about Brodie's bandage around his head.

'Tell them we're going to Riga and we'll be back in a month,' Brodie whispered.

'Good idea,' Lika agreed and told them so. This seemed to make the mood ease, somewhat, and the final exchange of handshakes and a kiss for Fyolka appeared to normalize the farewells – though Brodie's kiss on Fyolka's cheek sent César into a brief barking fit before Lika silenced him with a slap.

And then they boarded the troika, the driver gave a crack of his whip and they set off with a lurch on the beginning of the long journey that had brought them across Europe all the way to Biarritz.

Biarritz . . . Brodie paid for his anisette and looked at his watch. Lika wouldn't be home for an hour yet so he wandered down to the Grande Plage. The tide was out and the small perfect crescent of sand was as large as it would ever be. Brodie stepped down to the beach beside the row of bathing huts set in front of the salt baths with their strange Moorish architecture. There was quite a crowd on the terrace; tricolours flew from every flagpole. La Belle France, he thought, consoled by Vere's letter. Perhaps the nineteenth century was finally loosening its grip on him.

The crash and fall of the heavy surf also soothed him as he walked down over the softly yielding sand to the waves' edge. He believed, more and more, that it was important to acknowledge and recognize these moments in your life – these moments of absolute calm and security – however long or short your lifespan might be. Brodie realized that, now they had escaped from Russia and the Kilbarrons, now that he and Lika, although unmarried, were living as man and wife, he had actually never been as happy in his life before.

He trudged back along the beach towards the casino on its

bluff – a useful source of income to them both and handily placed, a mere ten-minute walk from their apartment. He climbed the steps up towards the Grand Hôtel and idled. Thinking about the duel had reminded him and he detoured to a shop on the rue Broquedis next to the Anglican church, St Andrew's. It was called 'Rochefoucauld. Chasse-Pêche'.

Inside, the walls were lined with glass cabinets full of shotguns interspersed with stuffed hunting trophies from land and sea. The head of a wild boar beside a six-foot-long basking shark. A polished turtle shell next to a ten-point antler. A chalk-white whale's jawbone sat on the counter like a strange piece of sculpture. Monsieur Rochefoucauld was glad to see him and said his order had arrived over two months previously. Brodie apologized, paid what he owed – rather expensive, he thought – and Monsieur Rochefoucauld, a tall, unsmiling man with a neatly trimmed grey beard, unwrapped the rag that contained the cleaned and oiled Derringer and then took a small cardboard box out of a drawer and handed it to him. Brodie read the English label: '.41 Short Rimfire. Oilless non-Mercuric Cartridge. Navy Arms Company'.

'How many are there in the box?'

Monsieur Rochefoucauld wordlessly pointed to the number fifty circled in each corner.

'I don't need all these,' Brodie said. 'Can you sell me ten?'

'*Hélas*, no,' Monsieur Rochefoucauld said. 'I'm afraid you must pay for the full order.' He shrugged. 'After all, what would I do with forty bullets for a muff-pistol?'

Brodie pocketed his small gun and his bullets and walked homeward along the rue Gambetta, pausing to look in shop windows, then past the covered market until he reached the junction of their street, the rue Duler. They had rented two floors above a milliner's shop. They had a small kitchen, a flushing toilet and bathroom and above that, on the top floor, a sitting room and a bedroom. Lika had decorated the rooms with bright fustian curtains – banana yellow – and had placed pots of flowers and houseplants on windowsills and occasional tables. Brodie began to feel a typical petit bourgeois and rejoiced in it.

He heard César give his short welcoming bark at the sound of Brodie's key in the lock and he pushed the door open and picked the excited little dog up, scratching him behind his ears as César tried to lick Brodie's face. Lika would be home soon, her lessons usually ended at five in the afternoon. He set César down and raked up the coals in the small range and set the coffee pot to brew. Perhaps they would go to the casino tonight after supper and make a few francs. He heard Lika's step on the stairway coming up from the shop floor below and went to open the door for her.

2

17 bis, rue Duler
Biarritz
Pyrénées-Atlantiques
France

15 January 1900

Dear Callum, brother, silent one, hopeless correspondent,

I thought you should know that I have left Russia and St Petersburg and am now back in France, living in a town on the Atlantic coast, not far from the Spanish border, called Biarritz. Get your atlas out! I have a job in a piano shop and I'm also tuning, of course, building up a little business. Write to me Poste Restante, Biarritz, Pyrénées-Atlantiques, France – but address your letter to 'Monsieur BALFOUR'. That is the name I am currently living under. It would be a long and complicated story to explain why but there is nothing to worry about – it's just a precaution.

I am in love with and living with a young Russian woman. For the sake of decorum and a quiet life we've established the pretence that we're married – Mr and Mrs Brodie Balfour, if you please. She's a lovely girl – you would adore her and congratulate me enviously. One day we'll be married but – alas – elements of her previous private life make that currently impossible.

I look forward to hearing from you. Yes, I do. Give my fondest wishes to the family (excluding Malky).

Yr affect. bro.,
Brodie

*

Madame Grosjean managed a faint smile as Brodie said goodbye and that he would see her tomorrow, *comme d'habitude*. Madame Grosjean was a recent widow – a widow of two years. She was a severe sharp-faced woman who spent more time than was necessary reminding people that her husband was dead. Two years on she still wore black and her bitterness over the death of her husband, Norbert (aged sixty-seven), had shaped her features: it was as if his death were a personal provocation. She seldom smiled, her regular expression one of stoic suffering. Brodie had never known Monsieur Grosjean and so was incapable of estimating the scale of the loss. The Grosjeans' one son, Fabrice, was a pharmacist in Rennes and had no desire to take over the family business of selling and repairing pianos.

Brodie had noticed the shop on the place de la Liberté as he had wandered about Biarritz when they first arrived in early October 1899. It was positioned between a tailor's called 'Henry' – with a sign in the window that said, simply, 'English' – and a photographer's. Above the small parade of shops – there was a patisserie and a *tabac* – ran the upper terrace of the Café Terminus-Olympia that also had an entrance on the railway station behind. The place de la Liberté was a bustling busy rectangle with newly planted plane trees and, at certain angles, a view down streets to the creaming surf of Atlantic Ocean beyond, a fact that added to its particular charm.

He had entered the shop, asked for the proprietor and duly met Madame Grosjean – who immediately informed him that she was a widow and her husband had passed away two years previously. He offered his condolences and told her he was a fully qualified piano tuner and repairer who had worked for Channon in Edinburgh and did they have any work going? Madame Grosjean asked him to wait ten minutes. He went up to the terrace of the Terminus and had a coffee. When he returned to the shop Madame Grosjean said he could start the next day. There was a workshop in a yard at the back and a list of twenty-four pianos in and around Biarritz needing to be tuned. Brodie wondered what had happened in the ten minutes that he'd been absent to encourage Madame Grosjean to make this impulsive decision. Had she swiftly sacked the man he was replacing? The place had the air of being suddenly vacated. Had she communed with the shade of Norbert Grosjean?

No matter, he wasn't complaining: he had a job that paid at the rate of a hundred francs a week and, several months later, was thoroughly established. Not for the first time he gave thanks to the universal nature of his profession. Wherever there were pianos he could find work, one way or another.

Lika, for her part, made inroads into Biarritz's sizeable Russian population. She had a visiting card made, in Russian and French, advertising her services as Madame L. V. Balfour, teacher of French and of singing. She posted advertisements on the noticeboard of the Russian Orthodox church, in the hallway of the Franco-Russe Club, and in Biarritz's Russian-language weekly newspaper, the *Russkii biulleten' Biarritsa*, a four-page news-sheet that circulated amongst Biarritz's Russian community during the season. She was almost immediately taken up by one Princess Marie Petrovna Stolypina and offered a job, two hours a day, Monday to Friday, teaching her two children French. This aristocratic connection, in turn, led to other tutoring.

So, between them, they made a modest living, supplemented by their nights gambling with the martingale system in Biarritz's casino. Their mainstay, and the source of their petit-bourgeois existence, was Brodie's job at Piano-Grosjean. He knew how important he was to Madame Grosjean – every week brought more responsibilities; he was wondering when would be the right moment to ask for an increase in his wages.

He left the shop, bought a week-old edition of *The Times* and went upstairs to the Café Terminus-Olympia's high terrace and found a table by the balustrade with a distant view of the Grande Plage and the Hôtel Palais on its small promontory. Biarritz was a town of many levels and winding streets that doubled back on themselves. It was easy to forget that high, distant perspectives were often surprisingly on offer. He ordered a Dubonnet, lit a cigarette and opened his newspaper. An anarchist had shot at – and missed – the Prince of Wales in Belgium, the Olympic Games were about to start in Paris, and the Automobile Club of Great Britain had completed a

1,000-mile trial run from London to Edinburgh and back. Sixty-five motors had started and fifty-one were still running by the time they reached Edinburgh. Mr Rolls's Panhard had reached a speed of 37 mph.

Brodie thought of Edinburgh and Channon's – the life he'd lived once. He called to mind images of Liethen Manor and his family, feeling no nostalgia or melancholy. Something about his new life – his life with Lika – convinced him that he would never return home, never return to Scotland. And then he did feel a moment's sadness: thinking of his brothers and sisters and their circumscribed conditions. Here he was on a terrace of a café in the south of France looking out at the breakers of the Atlantic Ocean. Escape, flight, freedom – that was the only solution. Perhaps he'd write to them and urge them to leave.

Brodie finished his drink and strolled home, pondering the letter he'd compose. To Callum, he thought, then Callum could pass it round to the others. Perhaps it was what they needed. A jolt, a catalyst – the prospect of new horizons.

When he stepped into the apartment Lika was already there – and he knew instantly something was wrong. Her face was set, her chin buckled slightly as she tried to control her emotions.

'What is it?' he sat down beside her at the kitchen table and took her hand.

She pushed a newspaper at him. It was the Russian weekly, the *Russkii biulleten' Biarritsa*. She pointed to an advertisement at the bottom of the first page.

'I'll translate for you,' she said, running her finger under the headline. 'Significant Inheritance!' she said. 'We are seeking the whereabouts of Mademoiselle Lydia V. Blum. She is the recipient of a large inheritance from a benefactor. We will offer a reward of 20,000 roubles to anyone who can inform us of Mlle Blum's whereabouts. Please contact Monsieur M. Kilbarron, 33 boulevard Beaumarchais, Paris IIIème.' This last address was in Russian and French.

'Malachi Kilbarron,' Brodie said. He stood up, feeling sick. He went to the kitchen sink and ran the tap, drinking water from his hand. He turned. 'How did he know we were in Biarritz?'

'I don't know. We've been so careful. Maybe he's putting advertisements everywhere. Everywhere where there are Russians.'

She stood up and began to walk around the room, clenching her fists and then shaking her fingers, as if they were sore.

'I knew he'd find us,' she said harshly. 'I told you. I told you that you should have killed him as well.'

'But *how* did he find us?' Brodie said, ignoring her last remark. 'In the whole of Europe. How?'

'There are agencies. Ex-policemen. They search for missing people. Maybe he hired one.'

'It doesn't make sense. We left no trail. You don't need a passport in France. We haven't even registered with the Préfecture—'

'It doesn't matter,' she said, closing her eyes and bracing her back. 'We have to leave. We have to go far away. He's after us, following us. Like a hell-hound. And if he finds us . . .' She came over to him and he took her in his arms.

'He wants to kill us, Brodie,' she whispered. 'He won't give up.'

3

Brodie looked out of the train window. It was raining and the Borders landscape was drab, drenched and barren-looking as the line crossed a stretch of treeless khaki moorland. Beyond, unhedged, unwalled, sheepless hillsides climbed to meet the enfolding grey-flannel sky. Scotland at its most uncompromising. He felt weak, unmanned somehow, as if a more craven, helpless Brodie Moncur had parasitically occupied his body and spirit. It doesn't matter, Brodie told himself, they're only your family, that's all – people you can leave and forget if you've a mind to.

'How much further?' Lika asked. She was eating a sugar bun, the last of three she'd purchased at Waverley station.

'Half an hour, maybe less. But then we have to get to the village.'

She popped the last of the bun in her mouth and licked her fingers free of stickiness. They had been living in Edinburgh for five months now and Brodie could see the physical changes wrought in her – she had put on pounds. The tall rangy girl was growing plump. He didn't mind – she still looked beautiful; in some ways even more voluptuous and alluring in this larger, fleshier incarnation. And he knew why she was eating so much – fear, worry, uncertainty.

'Are you happy, my darling?' he asked suddenly, reaching forward to take her hands, now she'd stopped eating.

'Of course I'm happy. I'm with you.'

'You don't mind that I brought you with me, on this trip?'

'I wanted to come. I want to meet your family – your father, your sisters and brothers.'

'We'll only stay one night – maximum two.'

'Stay as long as you like, my love. These are your people and you haven't seen them for years.'

Yes, he thought, and there the problem lay. 'These people' explained who he was, explained his life. He looked back out of the window at the waterlogged heathland, a few stunted elders bent sideways from the prevailing wind the only variation in a landscape that was almost entirely beige and grey. What was that expression? Yes, the 'pathetic fallacy'. This grim, bleak view summed up his mood perfectly.

They had left Biarritz for Edinburgh in September. Brodie handed in his notice to Madame Grosjean, apologizing for his abruptness and inventing some story about his wife's inheritance and how they were going back to Russia. Madame Grosjean's absolute conviction that the world was an unfair and unjust place increased an iota or two. Lika told her Princess Stolypina she was returning to Russia also, hoping the word would spread. Brodie experienced retrospective relief that they had adopted the Balfour pseudonym. All this subterfuge was to throw Malachi Kilbarron off the scent should he or his agents ever come to Biarritz and start making enquiries.

They took the train to Le Havre and caught a ferry to Harwich. From there it was another train journey to Edinburgh. They spent two nights at the North British Hotel at the end of Princes Street before Brodie found some acceptable furnished rooms in the basement of a house in the Dean Village district of town. They registered themselves as Mr and Mrs Moncur, dropping Balfour for the return home. Brodie knew too many people in Edinburgh – a nom de plume would only draw attention. It was strange being back in Edinburgh, however. To Brodie it seemed a defeat, somehow – this unwanted return a symbol of how things could so easily go wrong in life; of careless fate, an unknown destiny buffeting you, heedlessly, mocking your own petty plans and fond dreams of a life that you might lead. He tried not to let Lika see what he was feeling as she herself experienced something of a nervous decline. But as the weeks went by, and the new rhythms of their new life established themselves – and the fear of Malachi's pursuit receded – their days became more equable. A kind of cautious happiness returned.

In Dean Village their basement apartment consisted of a large sitting room with a fireplace, a small kitchen and WC (no bath) and a damp bedroom that gave on to a dark, sunless yard. Small ferns grew in the cracks of the paving stones. They had the services of a housemaid three days a week, a lumpy girl with bad skin but a nice nature called Joyce McGillivray. In the yard there was a coal shed and a privy. César was let out there to '*faire pipi*' when required but, for some reason, he didn't like being in the yard, growling, bristling, no tail-wag, always scratching at the back door, wanting to return inside. Perhaps a previous lodger's dog had been there before, Brodie wondered, and left his noisome spoor impregnated in the bricks and mortar.

Thus settled anonymously – Brodie made no contact with his family or any old friends or acquaintances – they resumed a reduced Scottish version of their Biarritz life, minus the casino. Brodie sought part-time work piano tuning, piano repairing and even piano teaching. He found a job one day a week at a small preparatory school in Corstorphine.

Lika joined a choral society – mainly to improve her English – as there seemed little or no demand for French or Russian lessons in Edinburgh. She sang the role of Hélène in an amateur production of Offenbach's *La Belle Hélène* and received a good notice in the *Scotsman*: 'Mrs Lydia Moncur was outstanding as Hélène, demonstrating a lyric gift rare in our native productions of contemporary opera.' Brodie was busy enough – he could always earn a living – but Lika, he noticed, was often alone at home with César, bored. For all her efforts she found learning English difficult. When he suggested they talk English at home they managed a stuttering five minutes before they relapsed into French again. She began to cook large meals for them in the evening – stews and pies, compotes and puddings – and she started baking, also – tarts, cakes, biscuits. It seemed to Brodie that, as he crossed the threshold at the end of the working day, the first thing he was required to do was eat.

'Are you happy, darling?' he asked her every now and then.

'Stop asking me if I'm happy!' she would remonstrate. 'I feel safe. I like it here in Edinburgh. I like being Mrs Moncur.'

'Why won't you marry me, then?'

'Why do we need to be married when everyone assumes I'm already married to you?'

'It would . . . It would cement our union. I love you. I want you to be my wife, my legal wife.'

'Our union doesn't need cement, Brodie. I don't need a marriage certificate. This little brass ring I wear is perfect.'

He gave up raising the matter – they would marry in due course, he assumed, once they were finally decided on where to live and felt safe – and they settled in for an Edinburgh winter. In the New Year Brodie wrote to Callum.

15, Danube Street
Stockbridge
Edinburgh

15 January 1901

Dear Callum Moncur,

Do you have a brother called Brodie? If so, he would like to inform you that he is now residing in Edinburgh at the above address with his lady wife. He suggests a visit to the family home at some stage in the near future to introduce said wife to his siblings and his horrible father, Malky. Do please communicate if you think this is a good idea – or not.

Sincerely yours,
Yr affect. bro.,
Mr Moncur (Brodie)

*

At Peebles station Brodie was astonished to see an automobile parked close to the diligences and dog carts that usually acted as local cabs. There was a sign leaning on its rear wheel. 'Ten times faster – same price.' Brodie and Lika stepped aboard – to boos and catcalls from the other cabbies – and asked to be driven to Liethen Manor. Brodie asked the name of the vehicle and was informed that it was a De Dion-Bouton 'Motorette'. Brodie sat beside the driver and Lika sat facing them on a small padded bench opposite. The thing was steered by a kind of central column with a brass handle. The driver of the motor was a young man with a strong Glaswegian accent. He wore a reversed tweed cap and goggles and his name was Jamesie, he said. He started the motor by cranking a handle at the rear and jumped aboard. The noise wasn't insufferable and he put the motor in gear and they chugged out of the station yard, picking up speed at they made their way down the high street. They were out of the town within a minute, living up to the brag of his advertisement.

'I'll gie you my visiting card,' he shouted. 'Have you a telephone in your house?'

'I don't think so,' Brodie said.

'If you can avail yourself of a telephone, sir, just make a call to the station. The stationmaster knows me. I can be at your house in an hour or less.'

'What language is he speaking?' Lika asked in French, leaning forward.

'Are youse foreigners?' Jamesie asked.

'Yes,' Brodie said. 'We are.'

He thought his mood couldn't descend any lower but it could, and did, as they were driven into Liethen Manor. He saw that the Howden Inn was closed, its windows boarded up. An old woman in a dirty pinafore shouted and shook her fist at the De Dion as it puttered past. Apart from her the village seemed deserted.

Lika was looking around her, fascinated.

'It reminds me of Russia, this place,' she said.

'Really?'

'Yes. I feel I could be travelling through a Russian village, so isolated, you know? The mood, the landscape. These small, low houses. The poverty. It's different, of course, but somehow it makes me feel back home.'

Brodie left it at that, not picking up what she was responding to – or maybe his own familiarity with Liethen Manor made him unaware of its particular, unique nature that was at once apparent to others. Home is somewhere you never really know, Brodie thought gloomily, as the De Dion pulled into the driveway of the manse. Brodie felt that he was returning to some abandoned dwelling, an untenanted arena of some other life that someone else had lived.

'How many brothers and sisters do you have?' Lika asked. 'Remind me.'

'I've six sisters and two brothers.'

'You see, it's very Russian.'

'It's very Scottish.'

They stepped out of the motor, paid Jamesie and bade him farewell. Brodie looked around, it had been years since he had last stood here and the place looked the same – only the season and the weather were different. The same couldn't be said for him, he realized, thinking about all that had occurred in his life since his last poisonous exchange with Malky, here on this driveway. Perhaps the garden was more unkempt: the lawn was tufty and weedy under the conifers and the monkey-puzzle trees. Yet, now he was here, memories crowded in – it seemed as if he'd been here last week, not over six years ago. You may leave home, but home never leaves you, he thought darkly.

The front door opened and Doreen stood there, smartly dressed, her hair quite grey. She kissed Brodie and then Lika and they went inside to meet the rest of the family.

Brodie could tell that Lika was very nervous. Who wouldn't be, he thought? They had gathered in the drawing room before dinner and Brodie knew his almost desperate need for a calming cigarette would be shared by Lika. They were all waiting for Malky. Doreen, Ernestine, Aileen, Edith, Alfie, Isabella and Electra. Only Callum and his wife and child were absent. Brodie was very struck by Electra, now almost twenty, pretty, with a round alert face, tall and darker than the others, like him. If she didn't leave the manse soon she'd be lost, Brodie thought, like the three 'Eens', old before their time, old maids betrothed to Malky Moncur, domestic potentate. He looked around – there was no sherry or Madeira on offer either, and the butler's pantry was locked.

'Could I offer anyone a cigarette?' Brodie asked, casually. 'I've just picked up a new supply of Margarita – you know, my blend.'

Brodie's entire family was pleased to accept the offer as he passed round his cigarette case, lighting their cigarettes one by one. Lika gave him a heartfelt look of thanks.

'We're at home,' Doreen said, fetching and dispersing ashtrays. 'We set the proprieties,' she added as if responding to some unspoken rebuke.

'What's wrong with smoking?' Electra said.

'Nothing. As long as you don't do it in public.'

'Or they'll think you're a hure,' Alfie said. 'This is an excellent smoke, Brodie.'

'Alfie!' Ernestine snapped, reprovingly.

'Not every loun smokes,' Electra said. 'And not every woman who smokes in the street is a loun.'

'Can we change the subject, please?' Doreen said. 'What must Lika be thinking of our conversation?'

'I'm not understanding this word,' Lika said, in her heavily accented English. Her voice sounded unbelievably exotic in this room, Brodie thought, admiringly, like a refreshing breeze on a hot day.

'Just as well,' Aileen said. 'We can always count on Alfie to lower the tone.'

'Oh, yes, we've a letter for you, Brodie,' Ernestine said. 'It came some weeks ago.' And she darted out of the room, returning moments later with a small envelope. Brodie tucked it in a pocket.

'Why isn't Callum here?' Brodie asked. He and Callum had met briefly for a drink in a pub in Edinburgh two weeks previously to discuss this visit. Callum seemed unwell and said he'd been suffering from influenza. He drank three glasses of hot rum. They agreed he would be present if only to dilute the Malky effect.

'There's a message. You're invited to dine with him tomorrow night.'

'He's become very grand since he married,' Electra said. 'We're a bit infra dig here at the manse, for Mrs Moncur.' Nobody contradicted her, Brodie noticed.

The tobacco had relaxed them all. Edith and Ernestine started talking to Lika. Alfie wandered over and asked him what Paris was like. Electra joined them.

'But why did you leave St Petersburg?' Electra asked. 'I'd kill someone to go and live in St Petersburg.'

Brodie swallowed. Coughed.

'Professional reasons,' he said.

'Callum tells us all your news,' Alfie said. 'When we see him, that is. We follow you around Europe.'

'Take me with you, Brodie,' Electra said quietly. 'I beg you.'

There was a thumping on the ceiling.

'That'll be Papa,' Doreen said. 'I'll go and get him. He's ready to come down.'

Brodie was pleased to see that everyone continued smoking. Brodie crossed the room to stand by Lika. He took her hand behind their backs.

The door swung open and the Reverend Malcolm Moncur entered the room.

Brodie was shocked. His father was gaunt, half his usual size, walking with two sticks, dewlaps of flesh hanging on either side of his ragged moustache, now mouse-grey. His wasted body made his head seem larger, more gargoyle-like. He looked at his family, gathered in a semicircle facing him, blinking as if surprised, then his watery eyes settled on Brodie.

'Have you come back home after all these years, you black bastard?'

'Very good to see you, Father. May I introduce my wife, Lydia.'

Malky shuffled over towards them both.

'You're still as black as the earl of hell's waistcoat.' He turned to Lika. 'He's no son of mine, madam.'

'Everyone calls her Lika.'

'Why did you marry this octaroon, my good lady? Was there nobody else in Russia but this swarthy dog?'

'That's quite enough, Father,' Brodie said stepping in front of Lika.

'Yes,' said Doreen, taking Malky's arm. 'You come away into dinner, now.' She led him into the dining room.

'Welcome to our happy family, Lika,' Electra said.

They all filed into the dining room, following Malky and Doreen.

'Sorry,' Brodie whispered to Lika. 'At least I warned you.'

'I feel I'm back home,' she said. 'In a funny way I'm very glad to be here.' She smiled at him. 'And I feel I know you better now.'

Doreen had placed Brodie and Lika at the far end of the table, away from Malky. Malky was able to feed himself but Doreen cut up the slices of mutton on his plate and poured the gravy. He muttered to himself as he chewed laboriously and sent Ernestine out for some brandy and water to ease his food down.

'What happened to him?' he asked Electra who was on his left.

'About two years ago he had a bad fall and he knocked himself out. We found him on the landing upstairs, unconscious.' She told the rest of the story, quickly. Malky was carried to bed, a doctor called, but before the doctor arrived he came round. 'He said he had tripped and fallen. But we think he had some sort of infarction. He's never been the same since.'

'No more sermons.'

'No.' She lowered her voice. 'And I think we're in financial difficulties. But Doreen won't tell us.'

'But he made a fortune from those sermons.'

'You'll have to ask Doreen. She controls what money there is.' She leaned closer to him. 'Take me away with you, Brodie. I like Lika – she's very beautiful. I could be your housekeeper, your secretary – all I need is board and lodging.'

'I would, like a shot,' he said. 'But I've my own difficulties – financial and professional. I don't even have a job, everything I do is part-time.'

'What are you two darkies whispering about down there?' Malky bellowed furiously. 'I'll have no whispering in my house!'

Everybody went silent.

'We're talking about . . .' Brodie hesitated, then improvised. 'Our dead mother. Your late wife.'

He knew that would silence him and Malky returned to his mutton, forking a portion into his mouth, eyes focussed on the salt cellar in front of him. Everyone seemed stunned by Brodie's audacity – and its effectiveness. He suddenly felt – and it was not a comfortable feeling – as if the others were beginning to look at him as head of the family, the baton passed on, now Malky's infirmity was so evident. Brodie drank some water, composing himself. Then he asked Ernestine for some brandy and she silently fetched the decanter. Malky watched him make a drink of brandy and water but said nothing. Some small victory had been won here. The conversation levels rose. The brandy decanter was passed around. After pudding – an apple pie – Doreen led Malky away to his bedroom. He did not say goodnight.

Later, lying in bed with Lika, in his old bedroom – a gentle rain falling steadily outside – Brodie thought about the dinner and registered it as one of the strangest and most significant experiences in his life.

'You don't know what it was like growing up in this house with that man,' he explained. 'And for me to be here, now, married, with you, lying in this room, in this bed with you. And he can say nothing. It's wonderful for me.'

'Remember we're not actually married, Brodie.'

'All right, not officially – but in all but name. Even better, in that case.'

'He's a very frightened man, your father. I can see it in him, the fear. That's why he attacks you all.'

'It's not as simple as that. He needs us but he resents us. So he tries to dominate us, shape our lives, to prove he has power over us.'

'But not you.'

'No. Not me – and that's why I think he hates me because I never did what he wanted. And now he's just a sick angry old man. He's going to die soon and he knows it. And he knows nobody's frightened of him any more.'

When Brodie was dressing the next morning he remembered the letter he'd slipped into his pocket the previous night. He found it and tore it open. It was from Ainsley Channon. He would have sent it to Liethen Manor, knowing the connection with Lady Dalcastle, Brodie realized.

Channon & Co.
48, George Street
Edinburgh

5 January 1901

My dear Brodie,

Notice has reached me from the piano-tuning world that you are back in Edinburgh. I'm offended that you haven't found the time to drop into the shop and see me. However, all will be forgiven if your good self arrives in the shop in George Street as soon as is feasible for you. We have something important to discuss.

Cordially yours,
Ainsley Channon

This made Brodie somewhat apprehensive: 'something important to discuss' . . . They had parted in Paris on rueful but unhappy terms – but now the mood was jaunty and unconcerned. Had he really no idea of how wounded Brodie had felt at his unjust dismissal? Or had he simply forgotten?

Brodie, still pondering how best to respond to this invitation, went down to breakfast with Lika. Only Alfie was present and then Isabella arrived. There was a kedgeree served in a chafing dish on the sideboard and, after they'd eaten – there was also tea and rolls, butter and jam – Brodie went through to see Mrs Daw in the kitchen. She kissed his cheek, tears in her eyes.

'I never thought to see you again, Brodie. Never, ever,' she said. 'And here you've gone and married a Russian woman, they tell me.'

'She's very lovely. Come and meet her.'

'Oh, no, that's not my place. No, no, I wish you all the best, however.'

'I told you I'd be back.'

'Aye, but for how long? You're not one for staying put, Brodie.'

Brodie assured her he was back in Edinburgh for a good long while and would be a regular visitor to the manse, and went to rejoin Lika. They put on their hats and coats for the short walk to

Dalcastle Hall. Brodie had sent a note on ahead when they'd arrived. Lady Dalcastle was expecting them.

'Why don't you go yourself?' Lika suggested. 'I don't mind staying here.'

'No. I want the two of you to meet. It's important to me.'

As they walked past the lodge through the gates and entered the shadowed drive down through the beech avenue, now bare-branched, that led towards the house the roadway seemed more eroded, puddled and potholed and, as the house itself came into view, Brodie saw more windows were boarded up in the keep. It almost had a derelict air. Some untethered sheep were munching grass on the front lawn.

At their knock the door was opened by a surly young lad in a green apron who seemed unable to close his mouth. He led them upstairs to the small sitting room and left them to find Lady Dalcastle. Brodie saw the tremulous flame-fidget of a neglected fire and pokered it into more vigorous life and they both sat there in silence, waiting for Lady Dalcastle.

'Doesn't this seem like Russia to you?' Lika asked again. 'This old house falling down, this servant boy?'

'I don't know,' he said. 'I can't see it through your eyes. I know it too well.'

Then Lady Dalcastle came in, clinging to the young lad's arm. She was like a wisp, as if a gust of air could carry her away and fling her against the wall. She was still wearing her bright clothes – an ultramarine silk jacket with a tartan shawl and a dark maroon woollen dress. She clasped Brodie's face between her claw-like hands and stared at him, repeating his name softly.

'Brodie, Brodie, Brodie Moncur, as I live and breathe. I never thought I'd see you again.'

She turned her bright blinking eyes on Lika.

'And who is this young lady?'

'This is my wife, Lady Dalcastle. Lydia – whom we all call Lika. Lika Moncur, *ma femme*.'

Lika gave a little curtsey and smiled as Lady Dalcastle advanced on her, as if she were seeing some kind of ghost.

'Enchantée, enchantée,' Lady Dalcastle spoke to her in her politely accented Scottish-French. *'C'est un très grand plaisir.'* She turned. 'Where's that stupid boy? He's old Broderick's great-nephew. Call for him Brodie, his name is Lennox.'

Brodie stepped out into the corridor. Lennox was sitting there on a stool picking at his fingernails. Brodie ordered tea and returned to the room. Lady Dalcastle was talking to Lika about Paris.

'J'adore Paris. Mais elle est dangereuse.'

Tea was brought in on a tray and served, just warm – Lennox had clearly been well trained by his great-uncle. Brodie gave Lady Dalcastle an edited version of his travels.

'And where did you two get married, my dear?'

'Biarritz,' Brodie interrupted quickly. 'The English consul.'

'How romantic!' Lady Dalcastle clapped her hands in pleasure. And young Lennox appeared.

'What do you want?' Lady Dalcastle asked him, crossly.

'I thought you summoned me, my lady.'

'Well, we'll have some cake, seeing you're here.'

'There is no cake, my lady.'

'Some shortbread biscuits, then.'

'I don't think the shortbread biscuits will do, my lady.'

'We're not hungry,' Brodie said. 'We've just breakfasted.'

They stayed another twenty minutes, the tepid tea growing cold in their cups. Lady Dalcastle reminisced about her times in Paris with her late husband, Hugo.

'And that was in the last century,' she said to Lika. 'I never thought I'd live to say that. Never.'

As they were leaving, Lady Dalcastle resting on Brodie's arm – like a straw on his sleeve – she drew him out of the corridor into her study.

'J'ai une commission à faire,' she explained to Lika.

Her study was lined with empty glass-fronted bookshelves. Here and there were small stuffed animals mounted on plinths – a marmoset, a capercaillie, a red squirrel. Her desk was heaped with mounds of papers. She searched a drawer and took out a book of cheques.

'I've sold all Hugo's library,' she said. 'Quite a tidy sum. I couldn't believe how much they paid me for them. I had an antiquarian bookseller up from London – none of those Edinburgh thieves. I've got enough to last me two years, now. If I survive, that is.' She laughed gaily at this prospect. 'Darling Hugo, finally did me a favour. Silly, worthless man, who'd have thought?' She sat down and wrote out a cheque for £100 and handed it to Brodie.

'You know I can't accept it,' he said.

'It's your wedding present,' she said. 'Cash it fast while there's money in the bank. The creditors are waiting to pounce.'

Alfie had managed to find a man with a neat, sprung gig cart in the village who would take them into Peebles for a shilling and deposit them at Callum's house. Brodie and Lika made their farewells to the sisters. The mood was untypically emotional – tears were shed and wiped away quickly – and when he kissed Electra goodbye she whispered in his ear, 'Send for me, Brodie, I beg you.' Brodie whispered back that he would try but he could sense her despondency.

He and Lika were about to climb into the gig when Brodie suddenly asked where his father was.

'In the garden,' Doreen said. 'He takes a short walk once a day. Doctor's orders.' She smiled. 'Don't worry, I'll say your goodbyes for you, he's not in the happiest of moods.'

'That's never put me off before,' Brodie said and, telling Lika to wait a moment, went to find him.

He wandered round the side of the manse into the darkness of the garden, the evergreen leaves seeming to suck up the meagre winter light. The sagging conifers were heavy with night dew, still dripping. The damp smell of mould and rotting leaves was strong. He saw Malky with his two sticks tottering along a gravel path, muttering to himself. He was wearing an old homburg and a rust-coloured tweed coat that hung nearly to his ankles.

'Father!' he called, and crossed the lawn to him, wetting his boots. 'We're away. I've come to say goodbye.'

'Away with your Russian whore.'

'She's my wife,' Brodie said. 'And mind your language, if you please.'

'She's as much *my* wife,' Malky said. 'Do you take me for a damn bloody fool? I can tell. I know lust. I know fornication. I know the reek of the harlot.'

'Of course you think you do, speaking as an old fornicator yourself.'

'How dare you!' Malky half-raised his stick as if to strike him and thought better of it. 'You're not welcome in this house any more, you black swine. Take your painted bawd and go to hell.'

Brodie drew his fist back and, for a split second, was fully prepared to punch his father in the face. Then he stopped himself, and smiled.

'The leopard never changes its spots,' he said evenly, though his heartbeat was reverberating in his chest. 'You've lived as a miserable bastard all your life and you'll die one.'

Then he kicked one of Malky's sticks away and watched him keel over onto the path, slowly.

'I hope your death won't be too painful,' Brodie said as Malky swore vilely at him and threw his other stick at him, wildly, sending it clattering off the trunk of a fir. He rolled onto his back struggling vainly to get up. Brodie leaned forward. 'And I'll never see you alive again.'

Brodie walked away as Malky began to bellow for Doreen. He stored this final image of his father in his memory – supine, raging, impotent – and didn't look back at him.

On the way into Peebles Brodie told Lika what had happened, word for word, moment by moment.

'My God,' she said, nodding, taking it in. 'Just as I keep telling you – it's completely like Russia.'

15, Danube Street
Stockbridge
Edinburgh

17 March 1901

Dear Callum,

Please don't take offence at this letter. I am your older brother and your best friend. Everything I write down I would say to you face to face.

I can't tell you how much I was looking forward to introducing you to Lika. So, to find you drunk at 2 p.m. was the first unwelcome shock. The second was your appearance. When we met you said you'd been ill – I now know it's dipsomania. It seems you've aged twenty years since I left.

I thought your Sheila was delightful and I was sorry that little Randolph had the croup. A pretty child, nonetheless. But think what that child is storing in its memory. To see his father, unwashed, unshaven, unsteady – bumping into chairs, cursing like a dragoon. We grew up with Malcolm Moncur – we know what a domestic monster is and I think that the saddest aspect of our visit to you at Edenbrae was for me to see you following in his noxious footsteps and having the awful premonition of like father, like son.

Moreover, how can you talk to Sheila like that in front of strangers? How can you order her around like a kitchen skivvy? And why is your language so persistently foul? Fucking this, shit and shite and fucking that. I know it's the drink talking but that doesn't excuse the stream of profanity we endured. And to address the little serving maid in the way you did was deeply offensive to me and to Lika. Lika thought she was coming to meet my beloved brother, about whom I've told her everything, my soul's companion. Yet you sat there, soused, a cigar burning by your plate, complaining about the food, calling out your cook to upbraid her like some medieval tyrant. It was as well you took yourself off to your bed, carafe in hand. Sheila was sweetness itself, trying to make excuses, apologizing, explaining that you had lost your job at the Writer to the Signet's office and were depressed to be looking for work. She made as good a gloss on your behaviour as was humanly possible. You have a sweet devoted wife, Callum. That is your good fortune – don't destroy it.

But if that wasn't enough, Lika, going down to breakfast, finds you on the stairs in your nightshirt, still drunk, practically bare-arsed, bellowing for your chamber pot and cursing the little maid who was bringing it to you in the most revolting terms.

You are turning into a drunken bully. Yet we are the sons of a drunken bully. Look what he did to our poor mother, driving her to an early death. Look at the despotism he inflicts on our poor suffering sisters, his daughters. We have always been disgusted with Malky Moncur. I don't want to be disgusted by his son, Callum.

By nature you are a funny, generous and affectionate person. Return to that state, to the old Callum – throw this ugly doppelgänger out of the door. It's not you, brother, and I was sick at heart to witness it.

Well, I've stated my case. My conscience is clear. Read this letter as a love letter, sent by someone who loves you. Write and tell me that you have listened to its message and that the old Callum will live and thrive again.

I am your faithful brother,
Brodie Moncur

*

Brodie and Lika went round the corner to their neighbour, Mrs Dalmire, who had agreed to look after César during their short trip to Peebles. Mrs Dalmire slipped César's leash and he rushed to Brodie, jumping up so Brodie had to catch him, writhing in his arms as he desperately tried to lick Brodie's face.

'See, he loves you more than me,' Lika said, laughing.

For the first time since he'd left Callum's house Brodie felt his mood improving.

'I'm so sorry about my family,' he said as they walked home, César trotting happily between them.

'I think that's now more than two hundred times you've apologized since we left Peebles.'

'But I'm shocked. So embarrassed. It was so horrible.'

'Your sisters are charming. Alfie is a fine young man.'

'What's happened, though? Malky unrepentant, revolting. Yes. But Callum?'

'It's life, unfortunately,' Lika said. 'I had an uncle who shot himself. A devoted wife and five children, a good job as a collegiate assessor, second class. He brought ruin and misery down on everyone. Families. I hate to say it but yours is more normal than you think.'

They went down the worn stone stairs to their little flat in the basement. Soon a fire was reddening in the grate and there was the smell of soup coming from the kitchen. César jumped up onto his favourite armchair and rolled onto his back, wanting his stomach scratched.

'We're home,' Lika said, carrying in a steaming tureen and setting it on the small dining table. 'Everything is fine now.'

'I'm going to go and see Ainsley Channon next week,' Brodie said, serving them soup. 'I wonder what he wants . . .'

4

It was strange being back in the Channon showroom – nothing had really changed. The same dour portraits, the same motionless flock of gleaming pianos in the display area. Brodie had walked past the place a few times since his return to Edinburgh, but always on the far side of George Street, sufficiently distanced from it. It was an important chapter of his life that had ended badly, unjustly. But here he was, back, climbing the stairs behind Ainsley's new secretary (Mrs Grant had retired). Ainsley himself stood at his office door waiting to greet him, whiskers grey, regrown, beaming, arms spread in welcome.

'Brodie Moncur. Brodie, Brodie, Brodie. How happy I am to see you!'

They shook hands warmly and Ainsley led him in, arm round his shoulders and sat him down, then immediately headed for the ranked decanters to select a suitable whisky to celebrate their reunion. He poured; they clinked glasses.

'The prodigal returns,' Brodie said.

'No! Not at all. I won't hear it. You know the unfortunate circumstances, Brodie – I was very candid with you. No blame apportioned, no bad feelings between us.'

'Of course not,' Brodie said, sipping his whisky, feeling the reassuring hot glow.

'Which brings me to the matter in hand,' Ainsley said. 'There have been a few changes.'

He explained in more detail. Calder had been 'removed' from Paris a year ago and was now living in Perth running the small shop that Channon had opened on Mill Street.

'Your young fellow, Dmitri, is acting manager in Paris. He's doing a fine job but his heart isn't in it, if you know what I mean. And he's not exactly part of the family as you were – are.' He sighed.

'Calder has . . . Let's say Calder has now reached his perfect level of competence, running a small shop in a small provincial town. I should never have set him up in Paris. Too many temptations. My mistake – and I paid the price.' He smiled benignly at Brodie. Brodie didn't know how to respond.

'So. Brodie.'

'So – what, Mr Channon?'

'Would you go back to Paris? But this time as manager.'

Brodie felt his face go cold – then warm in a blush.

'Don't say anything!' Ainsley entreated him. 'Let the idea germinate awhile. Think about it. Take a day or two – take a week. The job's yours. Same salary as Calder had.' He stood up and replenished their glasses. 'Quite apart from the benefits your presence in Paris would bring to the firm I would, personally, see it as some sort of tardy recompense for the unfortunate nature of your dismissal. It would make me very happy if you were to accept our proposal.'

Brodie could see, as if in a vision, a Parisian life for him and Lika. Solvent, a very good salary, a nice apartment. He didn't go any further.

'I'll need twenty-four hours, Mr Channon. I have to talk it over with my wife.'

'A wife? So you're a married man, now, Brodie. Congratulations.'

Ainsley chatted on. Calder's old apartment in the sixteenth arrondissement was also available. And everything Brodie had set in place while he was working there was still functioning well. The tuners he'd trained; the Channon recitals, the tours – they still had Sauter and Nagel on their books. Dmitri handled that side of the business very skilfully.

'You see these were all your smart ideas, Brodie. That's what we need more of.'

'Yes, I think I—'

'Talking of your smart ideas – terrible news about John Kilbarron, dying so suddenly like that.'

'What? Yes.'

'A sudden heart attack, his brother was telling me.'

'His brother?'

'Yes. What's his name? Malachi – that's right. Malachi Kilbarron. Said John dropped dead like that.' Ainsley snapped his fingers, dramatically. 'Dead before he hit the floor.'

'Have you seen Malachi Kilbarron?'

'Saw him last week. Sitting in the very chair you're sitting in.' Ainsley leaned forward. 'He presented himself very well, all smiles. But he was after money, oh yes. A fishing expedition for money, let's say. He claimed I owed money to his brother.' Ainsley laughed. 'He realized he had as much chance as a snowball in hell.' He frowned. 'Weren't you working for John Kilbarron?'

'I was – but I'd left his employ. In fact I'd left Russia before he died.'

'Well, you never know when the grim reaper will come a-calling.'

Brodie looked at his hands. They were perfectly still.

'Did you tell him – Malachi – that you were meeting me?'

'He asked after you – most cordially. I told him I'd written to you but at that stage I hadn't had a reply.'

'But he knew I was in Edinburgh.'

'Yes, I think so. Everything he said seemed to imply that you were in town – somewhere.'

Brodie stood up, feeling the dull, leaden weight in the chest that disappointment and awful apprehension brings.

'I'd better be getting along, sir. You'll have your answer in twenty-four hours.'

'A positive one, I hope, Brodie, my boy. I'm sure the little lady at home would be drawn to Paris, no? *Merci beaucoup!*'

Brodie agreed and said he was just going to pop downstairs to the workshop and say hello to Lachlan Hood. He shook hands with Ainsley, who was issuing more positive views of a move to Paris, but he wasn't really listening. As he descended the staircase he felt a distinct trembling in his legs. Malachi Kilbarron in Edinburgh . . . How could he have known? How had he been able to follow him first to Biarritz and then Edinburgh? He felt a bolus of nausea in his throat and paused to swallow and regain some calm. He wasn't going to leave by the front entrance as he was sure that Malachi would have paid someone to watch the shop, having given a description of Brodie. Follow him home, would have been the injunction. He might be observed going in but there would be no sign of his departure.

Lachlan Hood was obviously pleased to see him but tried to hide it, acting as if Brodie had been absent on a day off rather than for nearly seven years.

'You're looking well, Brodie. How's life?'

They smoked a cigarette for old times' sake and Brodie told him something of his travels.

'I heard you'd got the chop in Paris,' Lachlan said. 'Fingers in the till or something.'

'I was the scapegoat for fat Calder. All's forgotten and forgiven, anyway. By the by, Lachlan, can I step out the back?'

Lachlan led him through the storeroom at the rear of the shop and out into a cobbled mews lane behind. A fine wind-shifted rain was falling.

'Bailiffs after you?' Lachlan said.

'Something like that. You haven't seen me if anyone asks.'

'My lips are sealed, Mr Moncur.' Lachlan winked at him and then frowned.

'You all right, Brodie? You've gone awfy pale.'

Brodie leaned against the wall and vomited a pint of warm blood onto the damp cobblestones.

Dr McDaid peered at Brodie through thick-lensed spectacles. His eyes seemed enormous.

'How many haemorrhages have you had?' he asked.

'Three. Three bad ones. There's a bit of blood-spitting sometimes.'

'Aye, aye. Yes, yes, yes. Hmmm. Well, there we are, there we go.'

Brodie shifted away in the bed a bit. Dr McDaid was sitting too close, making him feel hot.

'What do you recommend?'

'Well, I'd leave Edinburgh as soon as possible. Get out of this country. We're in a Scottish winter. Go somewhere warm.'

He seemed to sense Brodie's discomfort at his proximity and

stood up, stepping away from the bed. He was a tall thin man in his forties, Brodie estimated, with dark yellow hair glossed back like metal and slicked behind his ears. He was Ainsley Channon's doctor, hence his presence in the Dean Village basement.

'I can give you medicaments – inhalants, rubs – but it's the cold, the damp, the wet that'll do for you. The "warm South" is what I'd recommend,' he said. 'And a touch of the "blushful Hippocrene" from time to time to improve the mood. Yes, yes. Aye. There we go. How old are you, sir?'

'Thirty-one, give or take.'

'You'll make forty, I'm pretty sure.'

'Thank you, Doctor. How much do I owe you?'

'Nothing at all. Ainsley Channon told me to send my bill to him. He's most concerned, naturally. I'll see myself out. Book yourself a ticket to the Mediterranean, Mr Moncur. I wish I could come with you.'

He left the room and Brodie could hear him in the parlour talking to Lika, then the front door closing. He felt not too bad, considering. It was shock more than anything, he reckoned. Malachi-shock. It hadn't been his worst haemorrhage – a blessing of sorts – but he would not become manager of the Paris shop, that was evident. Malachi Kilbarron destroying his future again. He saw that dream disappear, a bright bubble bursting.

Lika came in with a steaming cup of hot milk and set it down on the dresser by the bed, leaned forward and kissed him. She took his hand.

'The doctor said it was not so serious. Lots of rest, he said.'

Brodie sipped his milk. He had decided not to tell her of Ainsley's offer of the Paris job.

'There's bad news,' he said. 'Malachi Kilbarron's in Edinburgh. Looking for me.'

She recoiled with such force that the milk slopped in the wide cup in his hand. She covered her face with her hands for a moment, taking this in.

'Oh, no,' she said quietly, her back straightening, dropping her hands. 'How did he know we were here?'

'I've no idea,' he said. None at all. First Biarritz and now here . . . He was at Channon's last week.'

'May God protect us.'

'He's not the Devil, Lika.'

'Oh, yes he is. I know him better than you.'

'I just can't think how he can follow us like this. How does he find us?'

'What're we going to do?' she asked in a small hopeless voice.

'Go away – again. Far from Malachi Kilbarron. Go somewhere hot and warm.'

5

Brodie lit a cigarette and looked up at the dark night sky, star-rich, star-powdered by the Milky Way. It was both warm and cool – perfect Nice weather. The palm trees around him gave their muted wooden rattle as the leaves were stirred and shivered by a breeze coming off the Mediterranean. Lika took the cigarette from his fingers and had a discreet puff.

They were standing outside the Rosanoff concert hall in Cimiez, home of the Conservatoire Russe des Alpes-Maritimes. It was the interval and many of the audience had stepped outside to enjoy the balmy evening while they waited for the second part of the programme to begin.

'How do you feel?' Lika asked.

'Nervous. I can't help thinking back. That hellish day.'

They had listened to Balakirev's *Tamara* and Glinka's 'Souvenir d'une nuit d'été à Madrid' and now, after the interval they were going to hear 'Der Tränensee' by John Kilbarron, played by the conservatoire's excellent orchestra. Lika was rehearsing *Rusalka* at the conservatoire and had told him about the concert, having seen it advertised on a poster in the foyer. Brodie knew instantly that he had to hear it just once more in his life. He felt strangely neutral and numb, however, trying to come to terms with what he was about to listen to and his fraught memories of John Kilbarron and what had occurred that morning over two years ago in Yelaginsky Park in St Petersburg. All the excuses, all George Vere's wise words about self-defence, were valid. But at the same time he knew that his hot rage at Kilbarron's theft had made him decide to sabotage the world premiere concert. It had been his personal act of revenge, a way of settling his scores and Lika's, and one thing had led to another. If only he had walked away, simply resigned himself to the world's injustices. But would Lika have come with him? Of course she would, he told himself. There was no doubt about that. He turned and smiled at her.

'Why are you smiling at me like that?' she said. 'I thought you said you were nervous.'

'I was just thinking how much I love you.'

'Poor silly man!'

A commissionaire appeared on the steps of the theatre and rang the bell to announce the end of the interval.

'Are you sure you can do it?' Lika asked, carefully.

'Yes, yes. Well, I'll try.'

They went inside.

The piano is in tune, Brodie repeated to himself as the opening bars of Kilbarron's tone poem softly echoed through the concert hall. The piano is in tune – and playing my tune. The music built and then came the key transition – the suspensions, the unresolved tonics, that moment of the surprising chord. The strings, the French horns, the piano – it was highly affecting and, glancing side to side, Brodie saw women dab at their eyes with handkerchiefs; men clench their jawbones and inhale. Of course its reputation had preceded it but listening to 'Der Tränensee' did actually make you cry. It was working. Lika had sensed it, experienced it first, and Kilbarron had seen his opportunity to make his name and perhaps his fortune.

'I have to go,' Brodie whispered to Lika. 'I can't listen to it any more.'

He left his seat and sidled out past irritated concertgoers. He strode quickly up the central aisle where a frowning attendant held the door open for him. He heard the soaring orchestra behind him almost as a personal affront.

He smoked three cigarettes waiting for Lika, trying to clear his head of memories of that morning in Yelaginsky Park. The muzzle of Kilbarron's pistol pressed cold and hard against his skull. And then Kilbarron's moment of horror as he realized what Brodie had just done to him . . . Self-defence, Vere had said. He was one second away from shooting you like a dog. You're vindicated. Any court in any country in the world. You'd be a dead man. You had no choice . . .

Secrets, Brodie said to himself, hearing the applause and the cheering from the concert hall. Secrets inside eating at him like his tubercles . . . He roused himself: Kilbarron's tone poem, his posthumous monument, had ended. Brodie thought with rueful bitterness: Kilbarron's posthumous revenge, also, on the man who had killed him, set to echo down the decades in concert halls the world over.

Lika came out. He saw her looking for him and he signalled to her from the edge of the terrace. She kissed him and took his arm.

'It does make you cry,' she said. 'Just like the first time I heard you play it.'

'Yes. But they're cheering John Kilbarron.'

They decided to walk down from Cimiez to the town, drawn by the complicated embroidery of a city's lights shining brightly on its gentle bay below them. Maybe have a bite to eat and then go back to the Pension Deladier where they had the best suite of rooms on the first floor: a drawing room, a bedroom, a dressing room and a bathroom of their own. They had been there ten months now, taking their meandering, precautionary time to arrive in Nice, their old itinerant life re-established, Brodie once more a patient of Dr Roissansac. His health was restored and they were making their modest living – Brodie tuning and repairing pianos; Lika teaching singing and French to the Russians in town. There were more Russians in Nice than in Biarritz, so she was doing well. In the summer, the off-season, they resumed their martingale system at roulette to make ends meet, gambling in Nice, Beaulieu, Villefranche-sur-Mer and Monte Carlo. There was no need to patronize just one casino here on the Côte d'Azur. They weren't rich but they led their familiar comfortable life, easily able to afford the Deladier. If they ever needed more money they simply increased their visits to the casinos. They called it the Martingale Benefaction.

It was easy going, strolling down from the heights of Cimiez, down the winding road towards the city in the warm night, arm in arm. They walked for a while in silence. Both of them thinking back, Brodie supposed, each with their respective memories of John Kilbarron.

'Lika – I've a question for you. A difficult question.'

'You can ask me anything, Brodie. You know that.'

'Right . . . Can you remember that time when you said you wanted to sing "My Bonny Boy" for the audition?'

'Not very well. I think I wanted to sing something in English.'

'Exactly. You asked me to come and see you and write down the words and the music . . .' He paused. 'Was that your idea or John Kilbarron's?'

'My idea. It was an excuse – I wanted to be alone with you. And I knew he was going to be away.' She kissed his cheek. 'I wanted you, Brodie. So I contrived a way that we could be alone. The song was the perfect pretext. And you didn't suspect a thing, did you?'

'No. But you knew how I felt about you.'

'I'm afraid it was very obvious.'

'So what happened to the manuscript – the music and the lyrics?'

'I left them at the audition. Stupidly forgot them. I told you.'

'Could John Kilbarron have got hold of them somehow?'

He was troubled and she sensed it.

'What're you trying to say, Brodie?' She was angered now at his implicit accusation. 'I have to tell you: John Kilbarron didn't need your manuscript to steal your melody. He would have it all stored away after listening to it once. He had that kind of brain. You saw him. He even played it. Analysed it. He had it all then – all of it, in his head.' She stopped them and looked him in the eye, stern, unabashed. 'He didn't need me to be his accomplice, if that's what you're thinking.'

Brodie took her in his arms, hugged her and kissed her cheek.

'I'm sorry, my love. Hearing it tonight has shaken me up, disturbed me. And of course it brought all the bad memories back. That terrible day. Jesus . . .'

They started walking again, Lika taking his arm.

'There was nothing you could do, my darling. He was set on his course.'

They ate in a small brasserie on the rue de France – oysters, a sole with a bottle of wine – and sauntered back to the *pension*, Brodie calmer now, reassured. They went upstairs to their suite. Brodie came out of the dressing room in his nightshirt to find Lika sitting on the bed, naked. Her hair was down and the solitary light was casting sickle-shaped shadows under her small heavy breasts. She uncrossed her legs.

'Take that nightshirt off.'

He slipped it off and they lay beside each other. He kissed her, kissed her neck, her breasts.

'You believe me, don't you?' she said, easing herself round so he could lie on top of her.

'I'd believe you if you said the earth was flat and the moon was made of cheese.'

'What kind of answer is that?' she said, reaching down for him and guiding him inside her. Sometimes, Brodie thought, wordless, this was the best moment, this simple conjoining of two bodies, this linking, one inside the other, better than *la petite mort*. He looked down at her face, her sleepy-lidded eyes, her little strong chin. She frowned and licked her lips as he eased himself in a little deeper, and lowered his brow to touch hers.

'Of course I believe you. I believe everything you tell me. I'm your slave.'

She laughed at that, hoarse in her throat, delighted.

'Ah-ha. Good. Well, in that case, slave – fuck me.'

Three weeks later they were breakfasting in the *pension*'s dining room, smiling at each other, in a benign morning stupor, taking their time. Everybody knew them, all the staff. Madame Deladier had just introduced them to some new guests as 'Monsieur et Madame Moncur, *nos habitués*'. Sometimes Brodie thought they should rent their own apartment and Lika occasionally returned with offers from some of her Russian clients to look after their houses for the off-season but neither of them thought of Nice as their permanent home – they sensed that would be elsewhere – and Brodie was more and more aware of Lika talking about a return to Russia, to Moscow, where her mother lived. She would suggest buying a small dacha – they could easily get a mortgage – and pictured the simple life they could live there as *dachniki*, much cheaper than France, she said, moving between Moscow and the country. Brodie said nothing – nodded and smiled. He was uncertain about returning to Russia.

Lika went off to her rehearsal at the conservatoire and Brodie, having no tuning appointments until the afternoon, wandered down to the main post office on the place de la Liberté in the centre of town to see if any letters had arrived. Callum had started writing to him again – never referring to the letter of admonishment. According to Callum nothing was amiss in his world. He had a new job; Sheila was pregnant again; Malky was now bedridden but still clinging on to life. It was as if Brodie had invented that distressing twenty-four hours at Edenbrae.

At the Poste Restante window he was handed a small brown paper parcel. He smiled: good old Mr Hoskings in Edinburgh sending his pound of Margarita blend tobacco, as requested. Timely, as he was running low and now Lika smoked only Margaritas as well. He wandered down to the place Masséna, bought some cigarette papers in a *tabac* and found a pavement table at the Café Marmot. He still wasn't used to the change in the street noise – the old hubbub of traffic: the rumble of metal-rimmed wheels, the clip-clopping of horses' hooves, the bells of the trams and the omnibuses – but now it was transformed with the admixture of the throaty chugging of automobiles, the warning claxons, more and more. Here in Nice there were more automobiles than in Edinburgh and the streets were growing steadily noisier.

He ordered a Dubonnet with ice, and unwrapped his parcel, keen to roll a fresh cigarette. There was a rare note included from old Hoskings, he saw – usually it was just a receipt with a 'Paid in full' stamp. Brodie unfolded the note to see what news there was from Edinburgh.

Hoskings Ltd
21, West Port
Edinburgh

2 March 1902

Dear Mr Moncur,

Herewith your latest order and my thanks for the banker's draft. I wish all my customers were as assiduous as your good self when it comes to the matter of 'cash with order'! Here we are suffering from continuous gales racing down the Firth of Forth – a good two weeks now – you are best placed to be in clement foreign climes in La Belle France. At least the news from South Africa is better. It seems we will win this needless war after all.

Do not hesitate to order more Margarita if required. My agent in the United States assures me he has plentiful supplies. However, I doubt you'll be needing any in the immediate future. Your good friend, Mr Kilbarron, who always asks after you and your whereabouts, tells me he will be sending you his usual package by way of thanks for your introduction. He is a regular and valued customer now and I had the pleasure of meeting him last year when he called into the shop.

With my thanks and sincere good wishes,
Lamont Hoskings

Brodie sat still, unmoving, unlit cigarette held poised as – like some sort of gaming machine or automaton – the separate realizations settled into their place, *click, click, click,* like a series of bolts locking into their sockets. He felt a creeping nape-of-the-neck apprehension. Yes, back in Russia, on the first journey to Maloe Nikolskoe, he remembered telling Malachi about Hoskings' shop in Edinburgh, how it was possible to order supplies to be sent abroad, cash with order. Malachi wanted to order some, himself, so taken was he with the taste. What had he said? 'You could smoke these all day long.' And Brodie had supplied the address.

He sat there in a stupor, stunned at the unanswerable logic of his argument, realizing what had happened. He had been the hapless, unwitting agent of his own discovery. There was nothing diabolic about it, as Lika feared. It was that simple: that was how Malachi had known he was in Biarritz, and then in Edinburgh. And now he knew he was in Nice . . . Brodie looked at the date on the letter. It had taken just over three weeks to arrive and Hoskings seemed to imply that Malachi already knew . . .

Brodie threw some coins on the table and hailed a cab to take him back to the *pension*. When he arrived he saw Lika was back from her rehearsal – no room key on its hook.

'Oh, Monsieur Moncur,' the receptionist said. 'Your friend was here again this morning, about two hours ago. I told him monsieur and madame were both out. He said he would come back again.'

'Did he say when?'

'No. Just another time.'

'Did he leave his name?'

'No. But he was an Englishman, I think.'

'Thank you, Clothilde.'

Brodie ran upstairs to their suite. Lika was sitting in an armchair embroidering a blouse.

'What's wrong?' She could see his panic.

'Malachi was here. Two hours ago.'

He saw the sudden pallor in her face. An instant, pure shock.

'It's impossible,' she said, standing slowly. 'Impossible,' she repeated incredulously. 'Again? How, in God's name?'

'I've realized how he tracks us. I'll tell you later. Pack a few things, we just have to leave, get out of here, this *pension*. Then I'll think about what we can do – where we can go. We'll be safe from now on. Now I know how he finds us.'

Lika said nothing, staring at the carpet, still in shock. Then she stood and took a portmanteau from the cupboard.

'We won't be away long,' Brodie said. 'We just have to disappear for forty-eight hours while I think of something.'

6

By the end of the afternoon they were installed in a double room in the Hôtel Royal & Westminster on the avenue Félix Faure just off the Promenade du Midi in Menton. An hour by train from Nice; very close to the Italian border. They went for an agitated walk in the *jardin publique*, César greatly intrigued by his new surroundings, and Brodie explained in further detail about the Margarita revelation.

Everything made sense now, and in a way, he said, it was the best turn of events. They now had it in their power to disappear totally, as far as Malachi Kilbarron was concerned, simply by stopping the despatch of parcels from Edinburgh. Or, even better, sending parcels to Stockholm or Nicosia, Cairo or Cape Town, to lead Malachi astray. He felt more reassured, he said, now the whole of Europe could be their hiding place – anywhere in the world – and they'd never be found again. The initial shock began to recede. Lika, by contrast, seemed still flustered and tearful. They wandered back to the hotel and, once in their room, Lika said she needed to go out to a pharmacy to buy something to 'calm her nerves'. She left César with Brodie and went out, returning half an hour later with a paper bag full of pills and sachets. She made herself a drink of a powder in solution and she seemed calmer now.

They dined in the hotel, speculating about where they could go next. Brodie was in favour of Italy, seeing as they were so close to the frontier – the south of Italy, even Sicily, perhaps. Lika suggested that large cities were the best place to lose yourself: London, New York, Shanghai – somewhere you could live completely anonymously. After their main course – a copious *daube de boeuf* – she said she felt chilly and Brodie went upstairs to fetch her shawl.

'We'll be all right, won't we?' she said when he returned.

'Of course. Even now – look, he's in Nice, we're in Menton. He has no idea where we are in the world – we're completely safe. And that's how it'll be from now on. I'll send a message to the *pension* and tell them to pack up our things. Then we decide where to go and our old life starts again.' He smiled, trying to reassure her – despite her potion she still seemed nervy and insecure. 'But this time he'll never find us.'

In bed, later, they lay in each other's arms. Brodie felt unusually tired, yawning constantly, a fact that he put down to the unusual stresses of the day.

'Have you ever thought,' Lika said, 'how you'd like to die?'

'Lika, please, don't—'

'No, seriously. I was thinking about it today. How I'd like to go. Tell me.'

'All right. Like this, simultaneously, in your arms.'

'No, I mean, do you ever imagine how it would be, that final moment?'

'My God, Lika, why do you keep—'

'I swatted a fly today with a rolled-up newspaper, while I was waiting to go into rehearsal. *Thwack!* And I thought: that's how I'd like to go – like a swatted fly.'

'Please. Let's not spend time imagining potential deaths before we go to sleep.'

'And then you'd make a wonderful, moving speech at my funeral, and break down in tears. And every year on the anniversary of my death you'd come to my grave and lay flowers.'

'I'm stopping this conversation now. I'm very tired. Go to sleep. We've a lot to do tomorrow.'

Brodie woke, his eyes struck by a thin ray of bright sunshine slicing through a gap in the drawn curtains. He felt ill, his tongue thick and dry. He slipped on his spectacles and looked at his watch. Ten minutes to twelve! It was practically midday. He sat up. No Lika. César was tied by his lead to the radiator, tail wagging, ready for the day's excitements.

Brodie tried to gather his thoughts, sitting on the edge of the bed, staring at the sunlit pattern of the rug at his feet, feeling as if he had a terrible hangover. Lika must have gone down to breakfast. He stood up, swayed and sat down. It was if he had been drugged – and now a mild headache was beginning to thump at his temples. Where was Lika for God's sake? César, frustrated, gave a little yap. Brodie turned to look at him – something was odd. There was a folded piece of paper tucked into his collar. Brodie retrieved it, unfolded it, and saw Lika's handwriting.

My darling Brodie,

I have gone away, gone away with Malachi Kilbarron. It was always me he wanted, not you, and I can't continue this endless flight from him, on and on in terror, ruining your life. So I have gone to him and you are free. I leave you César as a token of our wonderful times together. This is the only solution my love, believe me. I have known the Kilbarron brothers very well. I know their ties of blood, what bonds they have between them. Malachi would kill you, yes, but only to have me back. Without me, you are free, free to live your life. I will never forget you,

Your Lika

PART V

Paris

1902

I

Brodie sat in the middle of the curved banquette at the far side of the Café Riche. Through the big plate-glass window he had a perfect view of the large door, with a smaller door contained in it, of the apartment block (number 33) on the boulevard Beaumarchais. It was strange being back in Paris – somehow he had thought he would never see the city again. But such was life: never say something will never happen; nothing stays the same – two of life's many implacable rules. He had a newspaper unfolded in front of him, a notebook and two novels and he ordered regular *petits cafés*, giving as good an impression as he could of a writer in the throes of composition or inspiration. He spent many hours a day in the Riche covertly watching the door to number 33 and the staff were beginning to greet him as a regular, pleased also with the generous tips he left after deciding his day was done and it was time to return to his modest hotel.

Sometimes a whole morning and afternoon would go by without his seeing either Lika or Malachi Kilbarron; some days he'd see them on several occasions, either together or singly, emerging from the apartment block. He watched, he made notes: he was waiting for his moment. In his jacket pocket Lika's Derringer was snug – and now loaded with the bullets he'd purchased from Rochefoucauld Chasse-Pêche in Biarritz.

It was nearing lunchtime, so Brodie ordered an anise and water and a plate of lentils with ham. He sat and ate his lunch thinking back to that morning in Menton. He spent a lot of his time in the Riche reflecting. Seeing the two of them together shocked him: Lika and Malachi, Malachi and Lika. Now he had to try to come to terms with thinking of them as a couple, however distasteful that was to him; a couple, moreover, who seemed entirely content together, chatting, smiling, secure in their utter normality of being.

Although he was observing them secretly he felt he was looking at two people who were in a world that had never contained Brodie Moncur. How could they be so at ease? How could Lika smile back at Malachi as she climbed into a fiacre? It made no sense in the context of the life that he and Lika had led together for those years – it was as if he'd dreamt their existence, that it was a fond fantasy concocted to console and delude himself.

When he had read Lika's note several times, he drank two pints of water and washed his face and, slowly, the turbid heart-pound of dread started to diminish and his brain began to work. Lika had drugged him somehow – no doubt with some sleeping potion she'd purchased when she went out to the chemist's – and she had probably poured it into his wine when she asked him to go up to their room during dinner to fetch her shawl. Then, while he was still comatose, she left in the morning with her few things, leaving the 'Ne pas déranger' sign hanging on the outside of their door. Brodie had dressed, paid his bill, and with César trotting by his side had gone to the station in Menton and caught the first train to Nice.

Yes, they told him at the Pension Deladier, Madame Moncur had indeed left some hours ago accompanied by a friend, the Englishman who had called the day before. She had informed them she had to go away for a few days but that Monsieur Moncur would continue to occupy their rooms.

Monsieur Moncur, and the dog César, did occupy their rooms, and they both went for long walks along the Promenade des Anglais, one of them thinking hard. Brodie was trying to formulate and come to terms with this new appalling situation – Lika Blum and Malachi Kilbarron. He could not fathom it; it remained beyond his wildest cogitations. Yet he began to recall certain statements Lika had made: that Malachi 'checks up' on her; that Malachi had known her before she knew John Kilbarron. Was there a clue there, he wondered? And what did John feel about Lika's earlier relationship with Malachi, whatever that had been, and how had that impinged on their relationship? What secret history had she kept from him? What hold did Malachi have on her? What time had they shared together? The tormenting questions never ceased. A new focus came to bear on his recent history; new significances revealed, slowly. He brought to mind that day he'd encountered Malachi at Maloe Nikolskoe, out with his gun, asking him if he'd seen Lika, and their walk back to the house. How strange Malachi had been that day, and the odd questions he'd asked. He had thought that Malachi was simply being his brother's keeper but perhaps there were other jealous forces operating in him. And there was that moment in the orchard when Malachi had taken Lika's hand. What level of intimacy did that imply? And, as he thought further, he remembered that night in the hotel in Dubechnia when they'd been discovered – how Malachi had looked at Lika's nakedness and how almost physically sick she had been. What had he said as he'd stared at her breasts? 'Pretty as ever . . .' What import did that have, that throwaway remark? It clearly meant, Brodie now assumed as his self-interrogation continued, that he had seen Lika naked before. He began to understand, began to enumerate the multiplying complications. When Brodie and Lika had started their affair she was betraying not only John Kilbarron but his brother . . .

Now he felt his own growing despair as his deliberations made a dawning sense. But what sort of a person could do that, he asked himself? To move from one man to his brother? And with these questions came a disturbing sadness. What did he really know of Lika Blum? Really understand? And the answer followed: only what she had wanted him to know. It didn't matter how well you thought you knew someone, he realized. You saw what you wanted to see or you saw what that other person wanted you to see. People were opaque; another person was a mystery. Maybe he was as much a mystery to Lika as she was to him . . . And because he had no real answers, he found, as the days went by, that his mood remained in a strange kind of limbo. He would feel bereft and then, moments later – he felt mystified and angry instead. He didn't weep and wail – because he assumed, logically, this disorder in his life would return to order in due course once the conundrum was solved and Lika came to her senses. His only working explanations were dreadful threats and abiding fear of Malachi and what he might do to her. Or had she always been lying to him?

But there was no escaping the bitter facts that faced him: Lika had left him to go away with Malachi, that much was certain. But where? St Petersburg? Dublin? . . . Something was nagging at him and in due course he remembered. Somewhere Malachi had given an address where he could be contacted. Somewhere . . . It took him a while of concentrated recall but eventually it came to him. The advertisement in the Russian newspaper in Biarritz.

Brodie and César changed trains twice before they arrived at Biarritz where he presented himself at the offices of the *Russkii biulleten' Biarritsa* and asked if he could see some of their back numbers. There was a scrupulous archive and the date was relatively easy to remember: sometime in the early summer of 1900. The newspaper was a weekly so it took Brodie no time to find the relevant issue and there, on the front page at the bottom, was Malachi's advertisement – in Cyrillic but with the contact address in the original French: 33 boulevard Beaumarchais, Paris IIIème. Brodie was convinced that this was where he would find the couple. He returned to Nice, quietly confident, and settled his affairs there, making up some story about joining Madame Moncur in Paris when she returned from Russia. Madame Deladier was sorry to see him go. Dr Roissansac advised still warmer climes – Algiers, Palermo, Ajaccio. Brodie caught the train to Paris three weeks to the day after Lika had left him.

And his surmise proved to be right. After a fruitless couple of days at the Café Riche he saw Lika and Malachi emerge from number 33 boulevard Beaumarchais and climb into a cab. Now he had confirmed where they were living, all he had to do was decide when and how the confrontation would occur.

He scratched his cheek unthinkingly and was startled for a second by the bristles. He sometimes forgot that he had grown a beard. After years of beardlessness he suddenly decided he needed a change of appearance, a disguise of sorts, even if the disguise would only last seconds. He wanted a different Brodie Moncur to appear before Lika and Malachi, whatever he decided to do, when he confronted them and made Lika face the brute facts of her betrayal, never mind the consequences. His beard grew well but was already – alarmingly – flecked with grey. He shaved its edges carefully each morning, shaping it on his cheeks and under his chin. It struck him that growing a beard did not free one from the labour of shaving; his shaving, if anything, was even more finical now he was bearded. Still, when he caught sight of himself in a mirror it gave him pause. He looked so much older, he considered, and more of a force to be reckoned with. All boyishness about him had gone; his beard gave him gravitas, he thought. He saw the older man he might become one day, if he was lucky.

He ordered yet another *petit café*. His gaze swept the room, idly, and then refocussed on the view through the big window. Malachi Kilbarron was heading out of the apartment block, crossing the avenue and making for the Café Riche. Brodie stiffened. He slipped his hand into his jacket pocket and his fingers briefly gripped the small curved butt of the Derringer. He rested his head on the palm of his other hand, as if absorbed in his novel, and, through his fingers, watched Malachi come into the bar and give his order. As he waited, Malachi glanced round the café. He looked a bit slimmer, Brodie thought, now he could see him close to – and more prosperous, somehow. He was wearing a dark grey frock coat and one of the new low top hats. He had a pearl stud on the foulard-stock at his throat. He had ordered a cognac and drained it in one go. He paused to light a cheroot, tossed some coins on the zinc bar, sauntered out to hail a passing cab and was soon lost to view.

Brodie sat there, frozen, then began to tremble slightly; he felt his bowels move and clenched his sphincter hard. They had been twenty feet apart. When Malachi had looked round the Café Riche his gaze would have swept without pause across the bearded man in the corner reading. But for Brodie this encounter was a catalyst: no more watching and waiting – time to act. Seeing Malachi so close, being in the same room, had shaken him, rendered concrete the fact that Lika had left him for this other man. He knew enough, now, of Lika and Malachi's routines – when they usually left the building and when they tended to return. Now was the moment for confrontation and reckoning.

He walked homewards to the Grand Hôtel des Etrangers in a strange mood. In his room César welcomed him with his usual manic tail-wagging enthusiasm. César jumped on the bed and rolled on his back so Brodie could rub his stomach. Later Brodie took him out for a walk and then he had a solitary meal in a small bistro, César lying silently, content, under the table. He was a good little dog, Brodie thought, and he was glad of his company. César was his connection to Lika and he knew she had deliberately left him behind for a reason. Was it a message of sorts, he wondered: don't forget me, don't leave me, come and find me? Or was it: my life with you is over – I leave you my dog as a symbol? He found his mood vacillating again between hope and sour resentment. He had decided how to initiate the next day – tomorrow – but he had no idea how it would end.

2

Brodie sat in a cab, a fiacre, with the hood up, parked by the side of the boulevard Beaumarchais, forty yards away from the entrance to number 33. Whoever emerged first – Lika or Malachi – would determine his course of action. And, ten minutes later, he saw that it was Lika, wearing a long cape and a small black boater, who stepped out of the door. She waited while the concierge went running to search for a cab. Two minutes later she climbed into a landau.

Brodie tapped his driver on the shoulder.

'Follow that landau, if you please. Thank you.'

The driver flicked his whip and they pulled away into the traffic of the boulevard.

'Not too close,' Brodie said.

'I've done this many times, sir, please don't worry,' the cabbie said. 'I assume the lady is your wife.'

'Yes. Just don't lose her.'

They clip-clopped across Paris in the landau's wake, finally heading down the rue du Faubourg Saint-Honoré past the grand shops and boutiques. At the corner of rue Matignon the landau stopped and Lika stepped down and paid. Brodie told his driver to keep going and, as they went past, he saw her enter a small shop between two larger ones. She opened the door with her own key.

Brodie paid off his driver and waited five minutes, crossing the street to gain a better view. He saw a curved display window beside a wood and wrought-iron door, and above that a glass sign that read: 'LIKMAL. Magasin de Broderie'. He crossed the road. He saw in the corner of the sign, in small copperplate, the words: 'Prop. Mme L. V. Kilbarron'.

This made him draw up and he felt the physical pain, the muscle-anguish inside, as his gut spasmed reflexively. He didn't delay and pushed open the door, hearing the heavy tinkle of a sprung brass bell on the door frame as he entered. A young woman assistant stood behind a counter. The shop was piled high with bedspreads, quilts, tablecloths, elaborately tasselled cushions, bolts of linen, tulle, chambray, felt and calico. There were glass cabinets full of needles and scissors, piles of hoops and frames of different sizes, great racks of bobbins with multicoloured threads.

'Can I help you, monsieur?' the assistant asked. She had an accent – Russian.

'I'm looking for the proprietor,' Brodie said.

'She's busy, I'm afraid.'

'I'm an old friend – she'll want to see me. Monsieur Moncur.'

The assistant left and Brodie heard stairs being climbed and then descended.

'She will see you upstairs, monsieur.'

Brodie went up the narrow stairs, they had a steep turn in them, and he paused for a moment outside the door on the landing, hand on the wall for support. He felt a kind of weightlessness, as if he might collapse, boneless. Then a snatching fear of awful rejection. He took in great lungfuls of air and pushed the door open.

She was sitting behind her small desk, covered with paper, patterns and fashion magazines. There was a ceramic bowl full of freesias in one corner.

'Hello, Lika.'

'I wondered how long it would take you,' she said, apparently wholly unsurprised to see him. 'Sit down, sit down.'

Brodie drew a wooden chair up to the desk and sat down, gratefully. He looked around. Lika's new world seemed to have been in existence for years; she appeared entirely at home, as if she'd never left it.

'I like your beard,' she said. 'Suddenly you look a bit Russian.'

She was very calm – and Brodie strove to match her calm, outwardly, though inwardly he was a mass of competing afflictions: ardent love, bafflement, anger, impotence, yearning, despair. He wanted to kiss her – he wanted the Lika-kiss – and then he wanted to hold her in his arms but now, bizarrely, he felt it would be importunate, a liberty. An importunate act with this woman he knew so intimately . . . It was astonishing how quickly life could change, how the ground moved beneath you and the landscape you thought you were living in turned out to be entirely different. Like waking up after an earthquake. It was as if their years together had never happened.

He offered her a Margarita – just to do something while his brain settled. She accepted, he lit it, he lit his own.

'The Margarita,' she said, pluming smoke out of the side of her mouth. 'Our downfall.' She smiled ruefully. 'How is little César?'

'What? He's fine. He seems happy.'

'He was always meant to be your dog. He loves you, you know.'

Brodie wasn't going to let chat about César deflect him.

'Why does it say . . .' Brodie was glad he was composed enough to mention the words, 'Propriétaire Madame Kilbarron?'

'Because . . .' And now he saw emotion overcome her.

'Because he bought this shop for you? Paid for you to have your own shop in the Faubourg Saint-Honoré?'

'Because he's my husband. I am Madame Kilbarron – Mrs Kilbarron,' she added in English.

Brodie stared at her, wondering, wordless.

'You're *married* to him?'

'Yes.'

'So quickly?'

She closed her eyes and spoke in a monotone without opening them.

'I married him when I was eighteen. I've always been married to him.' Now she opened her eyes. Lash-moist, tear-bright.

Brodie stood up, then he sat down, there was no room to pace about in the tiny packed room.

'I don't understand.'

'I was in a touring opera's chorus. Malachi saw me, met me, thought I had promise. He offered to help, said his brother was a famous musician and could help me also . . . I was overwhelmed. And then . . . Then we married.'

'But what about John Kilbarron? How did you end up with him?'

'Malachi and I were having difficulties. It wasn't easy being together – and he was very dependent on John. I was thinking about leaving him. But John was attracted to me. Very attracted.'

'So what?'

'John always got what he wanted. And Malachi would have gone to hell for his brother,' she said simply. 'He appears very confident, Malachi, very sure of himself, but he was always in the shadow of his brother. It was John who achieved everything – the renown, the adulation, the money – and he brought Malachi along in his train. Without John, Malachi was nothing. I think, in fact, he was awe-struck and at the same time frightened. It can be a dangerous combination. Malachi would do anything for John, anything.'

'Including sharing his wife?'

'It wasn't sharing.'

'Ah. A kind of loan. You like her? Please try her for size.'

'That's unkind, Brodie. It wasn't like that. Malachi stepped back, in a manner of speaking, and John stepped forward.'

'Brotherly love.'

'I think for Malachi it was also a way of keeping me close . . .' She made a face – frowning, hurt. 'Perhaps I shouldn't have done it – but I did. You only saw John at the end but when I met him he was one of the most famous musicians in Europe, in the world. And when a man like that notices you, wants you by his side, it's difficult to resist. Malachi and I had separated, effectively. And John Kilbarron was there. It was very complicated, Brodie. John was a complicated man.'

'I know. Too complicated for my simple mind.'

'Not everybody thinks in simple, logical ways like you, Brodie.'

'It's perverse.'

'It's human, I'm afraid to say. We do these things – and sometimes we don't really know why. Some need in us, I suppose. And it happens more often than you think, this kind of thing. How people move from one person to another. How a love can die and another love replace it. Amongst artists. Amongst artistic people.'

'I've led a sheltered life, clearly. So our love died and you rediscovered your love for Malachi.'

'Our love hasn't died, Brodie. But Malachi would kill you if I stayed with you. I told you: I did this to make you free.'

He stubbed out his cigarette noticing that the ashtray on her desk was full of cigarette ends – she was obviously smoking more than ever.

'Well. At least now I know why you wouldn't marry me.'

'I couldn't marry you. I was married already.'

They sat silent for a while.

'It's all very sad,' she said. 'I did love Malachi once, in a way, at the beginning. He was different then.'

'And the man he's become is now the man for you.'

'I don't see that. But I know him better than you do. Knew him better, long ago, let's say.'

'But what was wrong with you and me?'

'Nothing. It was wonderful. But it couldn't continue. Malachi was always going to come after me and would ruin everything one way or another. I realized that in Nice. I realized we had to stop running. He'll kill you, Brodie. Or he would have. He could bear that I was with John but he couldn't tolerate that I was with you, the man who had killed his brother. It was eating him alive. And that's what I realized in Nice: I had to leave you to make everything stop. That's the only reason. I know him – I know what he would do.'

'But we could have escaped.'

'No. He would always find us. One day. I did it for you, Brodie. For us. I decided it was best—'

'Best to be the proprietor of an embroidery shop in Paris.'

Now she stood and came over to him. She touched his cheek and made to sit on his knee so he eased his chair back and she sat down, straddling his lap. His arms went loosely around her. He thought he might faint. He found breathing difficult. What was it about this woman?

'It's so good to see you. To be close to you,' she said.

'But why Malachi?' He groaned. 'I just don't understand.'

'Try to imagine me as an eighteen-year-old girl in an opera chorus with dreams of being a great singer. Put yourself in my place – imagine what it was like for me. To be part of John Kilbarron's world made everything possible. But it began to change. And then I met you.'

'I still don't understand.'

'Look at your love for me. It's blind. You don't see me as I really am. All the many nuances of Lika Blum. The light and the dark. You just see the light. You just see what you want to see. And when I met Malachi I was the same.'

'That's just love – not blindness.'

'Malachi sees me for what I am – and he still wants me. It's me he wants, not you. If you got in the way he would remove you. It was because of me that he followed us everywhere. Now he has me again you're free.'

'I don't want to be free. I can't live without you.'

This simple declaration made Brodie want to cry, to bawl like a baby, but he controlled himself, somehow.

'I worry that he might harm you. Take out his anger at me on you,' he said.

'He'll never harm me – now that he has me. Never. I promise you that. You're free now.'

'I don't want to be free.'

'Yes, you do. This is the only way.'

She took his spectacles off and placed them on the desk behind her. Then she gently touched her forehead to his and he knew what was coming. The Lika-kiss. He closed his eyes and she pressed her face against his. Lash to lash, nose against nose, lips to lips, for seconds. The sound of their breathing like a wind in his ears. He counted: eight, nine, ten, eleven . . . Then he felt the flicker of her tongue and they kissed.

Then she stood up abruptly and he rocked back on his chair. She sat behind her desk again and handed him his spectacles. He put them on.

'Remember when you said you were my slave?' she smiled.

'Yes. I was. I am.'

'So you have to obey me . . .' She paused. 'Go away, Brodie. You're free. A free man, not a slave any more. I've freed you.'

'I don't want to be free, I've told you. I can't live with the thought that I'll never see you again.'

'But you *will* see me again.' She leaned forward, intently. 'I promise. Write to me, here at the shop, only here, and tell me where you are. I'll never reply but I'll always know where you're living. And one day I'll come to you.'

'When?'

'I don't know.' She picked up a skein of yarn from the detritus on her desk and tied it round her fingers as she talked. 'I just have to live out this bit of my life. We're young, Brodie. Let me live out this bit of my life and one day I'll come to your door wherever you are and we'll be together again.'

Brodie looked up at the ceiling, sensing that weakness invade him again. It was something, he supposed. Something to hold on to.

There was a knock on the door.

'Madame, you're needed down here, excuse me,' the assistant said, remaining outside. It was over.

They had time for one more feral, furious kiss, a clash of teeth and tongues, causing his spectacles to clatter to the floor.

And then she was gone, off down the stairs. Brodie retrieved his glasses and put them on. He waited until his breathing calmed and then walked slowly down to the shop floor to see Lika talking in Russian to a severe-looking woman in black, accompanied by her maid.

Lika turned, smiled and raised her hand to him, casually, as if he'd come to repair a broken window.

'Mille mercis, monsieur. Au revoir.'

Brodie smiled back and said nothing. *Au revoir.* To the re-seeing. Until we see each other again. He heard the heavy tinkle of the sprung brass bell as he closed the door behind him and he thought to himself: every time I hear a bell I'll think of you, Lika. Every time.

3

It took two days of patient waiting in the Café Riche before Brodie spotted Malachi Kilbarron again. He saw nothing of Lika's comings and goings and, for a while on the second day, began to wonder if there was some rear entrance to the building that they used or if they had both gone away somewhere, but then, after lunch on the second day, at about 3.30 he saw Malachi appear – in overcoat and top hat – and go striding off down the boulevard. Brodie left some francs on his table and darted out after him.

He followed Malachi carefully – always a good thirty yards or so behind him, always ready to turn his back or veer away – as he walked briskly by the northern side of the place des Vosges and then cut down to the river to the quai de l'Hôtel de Ville. He was setting quite a pace and Brodie's breathing began to labour as he strove to keep up with him.

Then Malachi went into a building on the avenue Victoria and Brodie had a chance to get his breath back. Once Malachi was safely inside, Brodie approached to see many brass plates beside the doors – doctors and lawyers in the main. Some sort of business meeting? Health issues? . . . An hour and three cigarettes later, Brodie saw Malachi emerge and continue his march westwards, along the quays until he turned up to the rue de Rivoli. There he went into a *salon de thé* for some refreshment and Brodie lingered under the arcades, easily keeping out of sight. Half an hour later he sauntered out, at a slower pace, entering the Jardin des Tuileries at the place du Carrousel.

The late afternoon was shifting into evening and there was a hazy golden light developing in the sky over the city. For a moment the idea struck Brodie that Malachi was going to walk all the way to Lika's shop but it seemed from the way his pace slowed to a meander that he was simply killing some time in the gardens. He bought an ice cream and consumed it; he bought a newspaper and sat on a bench and read it for ten minutes. Then he resumed his perambulations.

The population of the gardens was thinning as the light dimmed and the air became noticeably chillier. Infants were being ushered or wheeled home by nannies – though he could still hear excited cries and shrieks of children playing somewhere out of sight – kiosks were being closed up; a puppet show's finale entertained an audience of three. Malachi now picked up speed, as if he had remembered an appointment somewhere, taking a side path lined with pleached chestnuts that would take him down to the riverine extremities of the gardens. For a moment the two of them were alone in the gravelled *allée* – thirty paces apart – the sound of their shoes crunching on the sharp pebbly sand almost as if they were marching in time. Malachi now seemed to be making for the Orangerie and Brodie assumed he was going to cross the river at the Pont de la Concorde. This corner of the gardens was quiet and virtually deserted. A man cycled by on a white bicycle; they passed a painter folding up his easel. Malachi paused to light a cigar and Brodie darted behind a chestnut. Malachi tossed his spent match away and set off again, the long perspective of the *allée* stretching in front of him. Now was the time. He quickened his pace and began to gain on Malachi.

When he was ten yards or so behind him Brodie reached into the pocket of his overcoat and eased out the Derringer, holding it loosely and half-concealed in his right hand. He felt alive with peril, like something about to explode. He had no intention of shooting Malachi Kilbarron in the back – no, he was going to call his name, and force him to stop, turn and confront his nemesis. Then he would advance on him and shoot him in the chest – both barrels. Simple as that. He didn't need to say anything or insult him – Malachi would know why he was there and what he was about to happen. Finis.

Brodie matched his paces exactly with Malachi's – he had no idea what he would do after administering his *coup de grâce*. Perhaps just walk down another path and leave the body there to be discovered.

Or turn on his heel and run in the other direction. A running man might look suspicious, however – people would have heard the shots. Best to appear unconcerned. But he couldn't seem to force his mind to function beyond the immediate task he had set himself – something spontaneous would come to him. Then he had the idea that he might go to Lika's shop. Let the hue and cry erupt in the gardens and break the news to Lika that she was free, once and for all. That they were free, once and for all.

He glanced around – no one in sight – just a distant chestnut vendor pushing his chariot up a side alley, heading away. Two women with black umbrellas up (for some reason) looking at a statue a hundred yards off. Brodie gained a couple of paces more, testing the tension of the triggers with his forefinger. There was Malachi's broad back beneath the gabardine of his coat; there was his creased bull neck beneath the brim of his topper. What should he shout? Malachi! Or – Kilbarron! What would make him stop instantly and turn?

They passed through a small crossroads in the pathways, with a little lead fountain in the centre plashing water into a stone basin.

'Monsieur! Aidez-moi!'

Instinctively, Brodie slowed and glanced round to his right where the shout had come from. A figure was lying on the ground, waving feebly.

Malachi had heard nothing – the patter of water from the fountain intervening – and walked on, his pace unchanged.

Brodie stopped. The man was waving at him, calling for help, plaintively.

Brodie pocketed the Derringer and walked over to him. He was a small man with a soft, untrimmed moustache and a middle parting. Bizarrely, he was wearing two overcoats, the top one with a fur collar, and it was the bulk and weight of the two, plus his obvious grogginess, that was preventing him from clambering to his feet. Brodie helped him up and dusted the gravel off his coat. His hat – a homburg – had rolled some way off and Brodie retrieved that also.

'Thank you, sir. You're very kind,' the man said. 'Two girls, bowling hoops with sticks, racing along, made me stumble and fall.

And I banged my head.' He carefully touched his brow where a small egg-shaped lump had formed, the skin stretched but unbroken. 'I think I blacked out for a few seconds. I couldn't move. I thought I'd had a heart attack or something. For a moment I thought I'd died. Yes I did. I was convinced I was dead and this was the afterlife. Exactly like the one I'd left.'

Brodie could see the man was a little – what was the word? – hysterical. He handed him back his hat.

'Better go and see your doctor, sir. You may be concussed. I have to rush, excuse me.'

Brodie ran back to the fountain. He thought he could just make out the figure of Malachi leaving the garden by the gate that led to the place de la Concorde. No following him now . . . Brodie felt something heave and catch in his chest and for a moment thought he might be on the verge of a haemorrhage but he suddenly calmed.

The little man in the two overcoats was approaching.

'I feel I should offer you something, sir, for helping me. A reward. A meal, a drink, some money.'

'Absolutely no need,' Brodie said, watching Malachi disappear from view. 'Happy to be of assistance.' He tapped his hat brim with a finger.

'These young girls – running out of the shadows like that. I never saw them. They shouldn't be allowed to run wild with their hoops. It was most disconcerting. They fly by you heedless, shouting, shrieking . . .' He pulled on a pair of yellow leather gloves.

'I did hear children playing,' Brodie said vaguely. 'Perhaps it was those girls with the hoops.'

'Well, if it's only my gratitude you'll accept then be assured my gratitude is copious. Extravagant.'

'Thank you,' Brodie said, shaking the man's proffered, yellow-gloved hand. 'Keep to the side of the pathways if I were you.'

'Excellent advice. Are you an Englishman, sir? The accent . . .'

'I'm a Scotsman.'

'I've never met a Scotsman. Until this very day. How extraordinary! And how fortuitous that you came to my rescue, a Scotsman. I'll never forget you, kind sir. Immensely grateful.'

He pottered off, flicking at bits of grit still sticking to his outer overcoat.

Brodie felt a depression settle on him as he turned and retraced his steps eastwards. He felt a kind of fizzing in his head, then a hot flush overwhelmed him to such an extent that he had to find a bench and sit down.

What was happening to him? Was he going insane? Had he really planned to gun down Malachi Kilbarron in the Jardin des Tuileries like some anarchist assassin and just wander away? The flush now gave way to a violent perspiration. His new beard was damp. He took off his hat and ran his fingers through his slick hair. A bead of sweat dropped from the tip of his nose. He was having some kind of fit, he thought. A fit of remorse, of incomprehension, of losing Lika. A mad fit. He had gone mad for an hour or two, he decided. He breathed deeply. Lucky that little fellow in the two overcoats had brought him to his senses.

He left the garden and crossed the quay to the Pont de Solférino. He walked out to the middle of the bridge and turned to face upstream. He could see the immense curved glass vault of the Grand Palais burning gold as the setting sun turned its thousands of panes ablaze with light. He reached into his pocket, found Lika's little Derringer and, casually, so he didn't draw attention to himself, threw it into the Seine.

He heard its faint splash as it hit the water and thought: the fit is over. I am calm. Time for my new life to begin. Time to leave Paris forever.

PART VI

Geneva – Vienna – Graz – Trieste

1902–1905

I

It was the seventeenth letter he had written to Lika since he had left Paris.

27, Via San Michele
Trieste
Austria–Hungary

29 November 1905

My darling Lika,

I am still in Trieste and, as you can see from the address, I am still in the same place. But I have moved up one floor and I now have a decent-sized room in this gentlemen's lodging house (all bachelors, plus, new arrivals, a couple of widowers). I have almost two rooms if you count a bed-space behind a curtain as a room. Two leather armchairs in front of a fire, a table and chair. Pets allowed – César is in good health. My health, after the near-catastrophe in Graz, seems stable. My job is secure, I'm eating well, I like this city. But my life is incomplete: I think about you every waking hour. I wait for your knock on my door.

With my undying love,
Brodic

'I think about you every waking hour.' It was the constant refrain of his letters. Most sleeping hours, also, he thought. Lika made a regular appearance in his dream life, but so too did the Kilbarron brothers and he consequently slept less well these days. He often felt unnaturally tired and wondered if this was a sign that his tuberculosis was growing more chronic, his lung capacity diminishing as the tubercles continued their secret growth.

He sealed the envelope, addressed it to the Paris shop, affixed stamps and slipped it in his jacket pocket. He filled César's bowl with water and set it down on a German newspaper on the floor by the unlit fire. This room was all he really needed, he thought, given his meagre possessions. He had the use of a bathroom and lavatory at the end of the corridor outside. As with all the lodgings he rented the assumption he made was that he'd occupy them for a few weeks at the most, a month or two, but in fact he'd been at this address on the Via San Michele for well over a year, now, since he'd arrived in Trieste in September 1904. And now it was November 1905 . . . The room also had a view of the Castello from its solitary window and he was only a ten-minute walk from his place of work.

He patted César goodbye and pulled on his greatcoat, setting his old felt trilby on his head. As he left the building, he paused and looked up and down the street, casually, but searching for anyone lurking, watching. It was a reflex now, something he did automatically, having been followed, one way or another, through the various European cities he had lived and worked in over the past few years. But he saw nothing untoward. Carriages and wagons and a few automobiles – another crisp, sunny autumn day in Trieste, this curious Austro-Hungarian city, full of Italians, nestling at the top of the Adriatic Sea. He was just another foreigner in a city of foreigners – Italians, Germans, Austrians, Hungarians, Slovenes, Greeks and a dozen other nationalities all drawn to this vast port – the Hamburg of the Mediterranean. If there was a perfect city in which to find anonymity – to disappear – then Trieste was ideal.

He posted his letter in the yellow letter box, adorned with its imperial black double-headed eagle, and strolled on towards Nicolo-Piano where he worked part-time. It was owned by Gabriele Nicolo, a plump energetic man in his fifties, who sold and repaired pianos in a shop on the Via Malcantan behind the Piazza Grande. At the rear of the shop front on Via Malcantan there was a big roofed-in yard where the repair work was done and the pianos stored. In summer you could hear the bands playing in the piazza. Brodie had been working there for eight months now, principally repairing pianos, but he had introduced the idea of a tuning service and it was proving successful. Brodie was training up a young apprentice called Gianluca Geppa – a skinny, studious lad – and was contemplating hiring another, such was the demand.

He pushed open the rear door to the yard, smelling the wood, the glue and the resin, and realizing that these odours were a constant in his professional life. Amongst all the jobs that had begun and ended in Edinburgh, Paris, Biarritz, Nice, Geneva, Vienna, Graz and now Trieste, these smells had never changed. Same job, same smells – circumstances always unique.

In the corner of the yard was a small wooden shed with a stove that functioned as a rudimentary office and as a retreat for him, Gianluca and Ottavio the carpenter. Brodie's Italian was about as good as his German so communication was halting and heavily gestural, through broadly efficacious. Gabriele Nicolo spoke some French and wanted to learn English – he had enrolled at the Berlitz school in Trieste – and was happy to have employed an English-speaker as well as an excellent tuner.

Brodie removed his coat and hung up his hat, pulling on a brown overall, and went to look at the faulty pedal on an old upright. He was almost immediately interrupted by Gabriele who told him he was wanted urgently at the theatre. This was the Teatro Politeama Rossetti where Brodie also worked as an occasional tuner when concerts there required him.

'Brodie, they say going this afternoon. Any time.'

'Go this afternoon.'

'Go this afternoon.'

Gabriele asked him to correct every mistake in his English, however petty. Only this way, he reasoned, would he avoid bad habits and improve. He was a heavy-set, bald man, always smoking, always slightly sweaty and harassed. He lit a cigarette off the one he was finishing and asked how Gianluca was progressing.

'Very well. I sent him out on two jobs yesterday. On his own.'

'Be careful, Brodie. He is taking your position soon.'

'Will take my position.'

'Will take. Will take. Will take.'

Brodie went back to work and corrected the faulty pedal. Then he started on the rust-damaged dampers in a baby grand, a job that took him up to his lunch break. He wandered over to the Piazza Grande and found a table at a café where he ate a plate of gnocchi and drank a glass of Prosecco before strolling on to the promenade where he smoked a cigarette and stared at the ships in the bay, thinking about Lika Blum and how he missed her. Every now and then he would turn full circle and scrutinize the passers-by, the people strolling along the waterside, just in case he saw someone that seemed to be taking a particular interest in him. He was beginning to relax in Trieste; he was beginning to feel secure again after all these months. Maybe Malachi Kilbarron and his detective agencies had finally lost him. The trail had gone well and truly cold.

He had thought that leaving Paris, and leaving Lika to Malachi, would have been the end of Malachi's obsession with him. Lika had always claimed that *she* was the object of Malachi's relentless pursuit – not Brodie. But, Brodie wondered, now that Malachi had Lika, his thoughts might be returning to the man who had killed his brother. Maybe Lika was wrong – he wasn't free, as she'd promised: Malachi's resentment, his urge for some blood-for-blood recompense was still in ferment. Because in Geneva and Vienna and Graz – the cities he'd lived in since Paris – he had become aware of Malachi's continued search for him. He had left Graz clandestinely – unobserved, he thought, his next destination a mystery – but he could never truly be sure that it was over, he realized. Never.

He walked out on the long solid pier that was the Molo San Carlo, taking him some hundred yards out to sea from the city's edge, a favourite promenade for Triestines, enjoying the weak sunshine on his face, hearing the slap and slurry of the waves as they hit the wall, thinking about his peripatetic life over these last three years or so.

In Geneva, where he'd gone directly after leaving Paris, he'd stayed only a few months. He had used contacts from his old days of the Channon–Kilbarron tour to find jobs at theatres and music halls but having seen the same man watching his hotel for four days in a row he sensed he was being followed. There were many 'detective' agencies and organizations in Europe and Brodie suspected that Malachi had engaged one to track him down.

So he moved at once to Vienna, thinking that Austria–Hungary might be a better refuge. They were trying months: his English and French were little use and his German too rudimentary at that stage to gain him employment with German piano makers. He managed some private tuning and played the piano in cafés and bars but he was poor and out of sorts in Vienna – he never really settled.

And the dissatisfaction increased when he received a letter from Callum saying that a man had called at Edenbrae asking for him and his whereabouts. This man said he worked for Channon – there had been an accountancy error discovered and Brodie was owed a significant amount of back pay – but when Callum telephoned the Edinburgh shop they said they had no knowledge of such a person. Brodie replied saying that the rest of the family should be alerted and no one should tell any stranger anything about him. But the scare was enough to prompt another move.

He decided to set himself up in Graz, the provincial capital of Styria, a venerable small city, situated 120 miles or so to the south of Vienna. Graz was divided by the river Mur, surrounded by the high mountains of the eastern Alps and dominated by its own castle on a hill, the Schlossberg. It reminded him vaguely of Edinburgh – though the red-tiled roofs of the old town were a far remove from Edinburgh's presiding grey – and he began to feel at home.

He stayed in Graz for six months as 1903 moved into 1904, employed at a small piano manufacturer called Audritz und Stahl. He lodged in a villa in a suburb south of the city near the racecourse, on Castellfeld Gasse. There was one other lodger – a lecturer in engineering at the Karl-Franz University called Maximilian Scholz. Their landlady was a timid young woman, a spinster, who had inherited the villa when her parents had died. Fräulein Leopold must have been in her late thirties, Brodie supposed. She had a perfectly round face and a middle parting of incredible rectitude. She could not meet his eye when she talked to him, always addressing one shoulder or the other, yet it was her habit at night to walk naked about her rooms, curtains undrawn; rooms, moreover, that were directly opposite Brodie's suite. Was she trying to send him a signal, he wondered?

Consequently he kept his own curtains permanently drawn, day and night, to César's irritation, he felt sure, but it removed any voyeuristic temptation.

After three months, she managed to ask him if he would join her in her apartments after supper for a round of *Sechsundsechzig*. Brodie said he was unfamiliar with the game. Fräulein Leopold informed him it was very simple, requiring only a deck of cards and two players – she could teach him the rules in five minutes – it might be fun for him to learn a new game, no? Brodie apologized, saying he was very tired, and overheard her inviting Maximilian Scholz instead. For the first time since he had arrived, Fräulein Leopold's curtains were drawn that night.

Brodie began to feel secure in Graz but what made him leave was nothing initially to do with Malachi Kilbarron. In the early summer of 1904 he had another haemorrhage, a really severe one, as bad as his first haemorrhage in Paris. He woke in the night feeling his lungs flooding, almost to the point of drowning, and vomited blood all over his bed before passing out. He was found in the morning by the maid who had come to wake him for breakfast. Her screams could be heard the length of Castellfeld Gasse, reputedly.

He spent nearly two months in the Hasner Sanatorium on the slopes of the Plabutsch mountain, west of the city, an enforced stay that used up almost all of his savings. His doctor at the sanatorium advised him to go to the coast, to Trieste, where the climate was better, and recommended a colleague there.

When Brodie returned to the villa in Castellfeld Gasse to collect his few belongings Fräulein Leopold said that a friend of his had passed by a week previously looking for him. What friend? He was an American friend, Fräulein Leopold recalled. I told him you were ill and in a sanatorium. She assured Brodie that no more information had been passed on but that he had said he would be back, Fräulein Leopold added helpfully. If he calls again, Brodie said, would you kindly tell him I'm going to convalesce in France, in Nice, at the Pension Deladier? He scribbled the address on a sheet of paper. I'll be sure to pass the message on, Fräulein Leopold said. And Brodie caught the train to Trieste.

And that seemed to have covered his tracks, he felt. Arriving in Trieste, he had moved hotels three times in a fortnight before he'd found and settled in his lodging house on San Michele. He constantly asked his landlord and everyone he had business with to inform him if anyone – anyone – made enquiries as to his whereabouts. He tried to vary his routines – where he ate, where he wandered – and always kept up a form of regular surveillance, when he was out and about, looking for strangers who reappeared, changing the routes that he took to work and when he returned home. Slowly but surely he came to realize that there was nothing out of the ordinary going on, that nobody appeared to be looking for him. He hoped Malachi's agents were haunting the pensions and casinos of the Côte d'Azur searching for a tall consumptive Scotsman with a little dog. Only Lika knew exactly where he was and that secret was as secure as the grave.

He stood on the Molo San Carlo, hands in his pockets, staring out over the Adriatic with its silent migration of clouds. This was the view that inspired him, though he knew that if he turned round to look back at the city he would be confronted by the splendid panorama of the littoral. It was only the Adriatic, he was aware, but to him it looked like a boundless ocean, the distance-hazed horizon barely visible, the charge of light from the sea and the sky half-blinding him. He liked to think of his presence here on this jutting stone promontory as a symbol of his journey's end. Thus far and no further . . . He looked at his pocket watch. He'd better make his way to the theatre and see what they wanted him for.

The Teatro Politeama Rossetti was a twenty-minute walk away. It was Trieste's largest theatre, easily capable of seating an audience of more than 3,000, and attracted many a virtuoso coming on to Trieste after concerts in Milan, Venice and Vienna. Brodie had made enquiries and offered his services on arrival in the city and was told that he wasn't required. He left his particulars, nonetheless, and a month later was summoned with some urgency. The maestro playing turned out to be Karl-Heinz Nagel, giving a recital of Brahms and Mendelssohn, and a warm reunion ensued. Nagel's enthusiastic encomium had gained him regular employ afterwards.

Brodie sensed that, for the manager of the Politeama, his nationality and his fluent French, as much as his expertise, gave the theatre some strange cachet. Look who we have tuning our piano – a Scotsman who speaks French!

Brodie strolled up the Canale Grande and cut across the Via G. Carducci onto the Via Chiozza where the theatre was to be found, its huge facade soon visible. He went to the stage door and on to the manager's office. On his way he passed a poster for the next concert: Beethoven, Mozart and Mahler, he saw. However, there was no sign of the manager – instead his deputy sat at his desk in something of a panic. He was Bojan Kupitur, a Slovene, a lean, tense man who drank too much. Brodie liked Bojan – they were both outsiders in the theatre staffed almost entirely by Italians – but he also recognized his essential incompetence. He could see Bojan was in a state and could smell the liquor on him. Bojan spoke fast but broken French.

'He is Mozart, oh yes, Sonata in C, and no stupid shit piano ready. *Putain!* And the maestro is coming in two hours. Brodie, please you fix him for me, Brodie. *Subito! Subito!*'

Brodie went down to the basement store and selected the Bösendorfer that Nagel had used. It was old but the best piano the Politeama possessed. He found some stagehands and they wheeled it into the freight lift and up to the auditorium, settling it in the middle of the stage.

He opened it up, sat down, found the pitch and played his usual octave sequences. Not too bad. Fifteen minutes' work – Bojan could relax.

Bojan was pacing around, darting off from time to time to take a quick swig from whatever he was drinking in the wings.

'Who's the pianist?' Brodie asked him. 'I may need to make some final adjustments.'

'They don't tell me nothing.'

Brodie fetched his tools from his locker and went to work. When he had finished he played a few bars of 'My Bonny Boy' and, of course, thought of Lika. Every waking hour. That day in the Saint-Germain apartment . . . That song had been the catalyst of all the happiness in his life, he thought. He thought further: and all the unhappiness, also. Perhaps the very first playing of that song could even explain his presence here in Trieste, years later – a man on the run from his past – the causal chain stretched back to that moment, unbroken, when you analysed it closely. He had a sudden idea.

'It's done, I'm off,' he said to Bojan. 'You owe me eighty crowns.'

'No, Brodie, I beg you. Stay till they come. I give you one hundred crowns.'

Another fifteen shillings, Brodie thought. Every little helps. They went back to the office and Bojan poured him a glass of schnapps.

'Why, in the name of Jesus Christ, is Ricardo ill?' Bojan said, furiously, as if it were a personal slight, some sort of fiendish vendetta. Ricardo was the Politeama's manager. 'Today of all the days. *Putain!*' He swore again and topped up his glass.

They were interrupted by a boy who tapped on the door and said in an awestruck whisper, 'They are here, *signori*.'

Brodie and Bojan went up to the stage where they saw three men in smart suits looking around the auditorium. Members of the Orchestra Triestini were beginning to settle down in their seats and unpack their instruments and scores in readiness for the rehearsal.

Bojan said, 'Look, there's Banzo. I'll talk to him. Stay here.'

Brodie knew who Marion Banzo was – a local Triestine conductor who often rehearsed the orchestra before the star conductor arrived. In the group of three was a tall portly man with greying hair and, beside him, a tiny, lithe figure, bespectacled, in a pale brown three-piece suit and a bow tie. He was peering out into the gloom of the vast unlit auditorium, impressed. He spotted Brodie standing there and wandered over.

'It's huge,' he said in German. 'I had no idea.' He had wild hair and thin lips. His spectacles were rimless and set so close to his eyes they were almost invisible.

'Indeed,' Brodie said. 'We can fit five thousand in here, if we allow standing.'

'My God, that's a small town.'

'Do you speak French?' Brodie asked. 'My German isn't so good.'

'Oui, oui. Bien sûr. So, may I ask you a question? Why is there a piano in the middle of the stage?'

'It's for the Mozart. I tuned it myself an hour ago.'

'We're performing Mozart's Jupiter Symphony. So we have no need of a piano.'

Brodie noticed that the man's left leg had a curious pronounced twitch. There was a dull percussive thud of his heel vibrating on the stage's flooring.

Brodie urgently signalled Bojan over.

'It's a Mozart symphony,' Brodie said quietly. 'Not a piano concerto.'

'Wrong. No. It's Piano Concerto number twenty-one, in C.'

'Jupiter Symphony, number forty-one, in C,' the little man interjected.

Bojan swore to himself expressively in Slovene. He took Brodie's elbow and led him away a few paces.

'It's Ricardo,' Bojan said, desperately. 'His handwriting – it's impossible. I can't read it. Forty-one, twenty-one, thirty-one – is all the same.'

'Please remove the piano,' the little man said. 'We want to rehearse.' Then, aside to Brodie: 'I'm sorry to have wasted your time.'

'I'll still be paid,' Brodie said. 'It's some consolation.'

The little man was staring at his glasses.

'You have a line across your lens.'

'Two lenses. One on top of the other. The bottom for close work; the top for distance. They're called Franklin spectacles.'

'Fascinating. I could use this. Did you get them here in Trieste?'

'No. In Edinburgh. Scotland.'

'Ah. You're the Scotsman. They told me they had a Scottish piano tuner here.' He looked again at Brodie's spectacles. 'Are they efficient?'

'Excellent. I'd be blind without them.'

'Me too . . . Yes.' He paused. 'Blind as a worm. Is that what you say in English?'

'Blind as a bat.'

'A bat. Yes, that makes sense, also.' He smiled. 'Do you have a cigarette, by any chance?'

Brodie took out his cigarette case and held it open. The little man took a cigarette and Brodie lit it for him. In the background Bojan was supervising the stagehands removing the redundant piano.

'Very nice to meet you,' the little man said. 'Thank you for the cigarette.' He smiled, gave a brisk bow and wandered over to rejoin Banzo and the other man. Another impresario, Brodie assumed. He went down the stairs to Bojan's office and demanded his hundred crowns. Bojan was drinking and muttering about the shame and that *morceau de merde* Ricardo who hadn't learned to write his name properly. He opened his cash box and counted out the five twenty-kröne notes.

'Well, no harm done,' Brodie said, pocketing them.

'Oh, no,' Bojan said, gloomily. 'On the contrary – you wait. It's a disaster for me. The Italians will use it as an excuse to kick me out. They want me out. No Slovenes here.'

Brodie commiserated and then hurried home to compose his letter. He had decided to write to Dmitri at Channon's showroom in Paris. He told him to go to Lika's shop in the Faubourg Saint-Honoré and gave him precise instructions. It had been too long an absence; too long a one-sided correspondence. He needed news of her: he needed to communicate properly. He needed her.

Two days later, Brodie sat in the upper tiers of the Politeama listening to Mahler's Fifth Symphony. The response to the first half of the programme – Beethoven's Coriolan Overture and Mozart's Jupiter Symphony – had been very warm, verging on rapturous. At the end of the Fifth, however, the reaction was decidedly cooler. He saw people glancing at each other in puzzlement. There were a few shouts – 'Nonsense!', 'Rubbish!' – that were largely obscured by the general polite applause and the sound of people leaving in haste, as if keen to remove themselves from this modern cacophony.

Brodie had enjoyed the Fifth, particularly the fourth movement, the Adagietto. It reminded him in some way of 'Der Tränensee', but he assumed that was mere coincidence. It was almost impossible to imagine in what circumstances Mahler could have heard Kilbarron's tone poem. They were both swimming in the current of the new century's new music, he supposed: the zeitgeist.

He stepped out of the theatre into the chilly night. It was 1 December and there were stars in the sky above his head – a cloudless frosty night – and his breath condensed in front of him. He turned down a side street looking for an *osterie*. He needed a drink. A cognac, a schnapps, a slivovitz – something warming, at any rate.

He found a small bar on the Via del Tora, a side street on the way back to the quays. It was busy and smoky, full of people from the theatre, judging by the numbers with programmes in their hands or their pockets. There was a lot of talk about the music. He pushed his way through the crowd to the bar and wedged himself in a corner, ordering his plum brandy and lighting a cigarette. How he missed his Margaritas! He took a sip of his drink and someone jogged his elbow and made him splash brandy on his sleeve.

'*Mi dispiace molto. Mille scuse!*'

The accent was appalling and came from a brawny young man in a bashed tweed cap and who had a blunt, raw-boned, open, smiling face.

'No harm done,' Brodie said in English.

'No, no. I'll buy you another,' the young man replied in a strong Irish accent. 'But my brother has all me money.' He turned and shouted, 'Shem!' and at this another man joined them, two glasses raised high. He was tall, almost as tall as Brodie, in his twenties, Brodie thought, with thick-lensed spectacles and a strong-jawed, thin-lipped face. He handed over a glass of clear liquid to his brother.

'Sure, I've gone and knocked this chap's drink clear out of his hand.'

'It was just a drop. No bother at all,' Brodie said.

'Are you English?'

'Scottish.'

'What?'

'Scottish!' The noise in the *osterie* was almost overpowering – they had to shout to make themselves heard. The three of them settled in their corner. The brothers loudly reintroduced themselves, properly. Stan, the younger, and Shem, the older, the one with the spectacles.

'Have you been to the Teatro?' Shem asked.

'Yes.'

'What did you think of the Mahler?'

'Rather wonderful. I'd need to hear it again. Very modern.'

'You're in a small minority as far as I can tell,' Shem said.

'I heard this fellow say,' Stan interposed. 'He said the Mozart was "too rococo". And the Mahler was "beer-garden music". He liked the Beethoven, though.'

'How can you be "too rococo"? Rococo is too baroque, no?' Shem looked bemused. 'I thought he said it was "cynical" music. Cynical music, what in God's name is that?'

'I think he said "cyclical" music,' Stan said.

'Cycling music?' Shem said, not hearing through the din. 'Cynical, cyclical, cycling music. I'd like to hear that, all right.'

There was a group of people behind them talking in French. They were being disparaging about the Mahler, also. Brodie translated.

'This lot describes it as "insipid dancing music".'

'Well,' Shem said, 'the composer is always ten years ahead of his audience. If he's any good, that is.'

Brodie bought them all another round of drinks. He was enjoying speaking English to intelligent people. Shem and Stan accepted the offer of his cigarettes. The *osterie* was filling up even more – they could hardly hear each other.

'That's what I like about Trieste,' Shem shouted. 'Everyone arguing about music and getting drunk.'

They had both arrived in the city fairly recently, it transpired, Stan just some weeks previously. They were both teaching English. Earning a navvy's wage, Shem said.

Brodie said he was a piano tuner.

'Will you tune my old piano?' Shem asked. 'It's a bit of a wreck.'

'Delighted,' Brodie said. 'I'm not fussy.' He fished in a pocket for his visiting card with the address of Nicolo-Piano on it. 'I'm there most days – or leave word.'

Shem scrutinized it and handed it to Stan.

'My business associate will be in touch.'

A young woman with orange hair and red lips asked if she might be given access to the bar.

'Now, there's a beauty,' Shem said, allowing her to squeeze tightly past. 'A lady of the night, if I'm not mistaken. Not a rough edge on her, I can vouch for that.'

'I won't tell your wife about your vouching,' Stan said.

'You a married man, Brodie?' Shem asked.

'I'm engaged. But she's far away – in Paris.'

'Ah, Paree . . .' Shem sighed. 'I lived in Paris once.'

'Is she a Frenchie, then, your girl?'

'She's Russian, actually.'

'A Russian girl, now that would be something,' Shem said. 'Have you been to Russia, Brodie?'

'Yes,' Brodie said and told them something of his travels.

'Where are you from?'

'Edinburgh.'

'We're both from Dublin. Surprise, surprise.'

The mention of their home towns gave them all a moment of reflection.

'We're a long way from the motherland, that's for sure,' Shem said. 'Let's get another round in and drink to us exiles. Exiled Celts. Celts in exile. Celxiles.'

2

The day Brodie received his reply from Dmitri was the day he saw Malachi Kilbarron going into the Teatro Politeama. At least he thought it was Malachi – and his heart thought so too, such was the juddering thud that came with the recognition. A man leaving a motor taxi and walking into a theatre. Stout, bearded like Malachi, smoking a cheroot.

Brodie leaned back against the wall. Don't be a fool, he told himself: how many bearded cigar-smoking men are there in this city? Dozens, hundreds . . . He waited a few minutes and then went into the foyer and spoke to a commissionaire. A friend of mine just came in – English, with a beard, smoking a cigar. I saw no one like that, sir. Brodie didn't linger and put the delusion – the hallucination – down to his state of nerves. They were a week away from Christmas and bells were tolling in every belfry in the city – and every time he heard a bell toll he thought of Lika, of course. And therefore Malachi, of course. He was haunted by memories – and this was making him see ghosts, spectres, doppelgängers, that's all, he rebuked himself.

All the same, he counter-rebuked, it *was* disturbing, and this took him to the central post office up by the main station to see if there was anything for him at the Poste Restante counter and, sure enough, there was – it was Dmitri's reply.

Channon & Cie
Avenue de l'Alma
Paris

8 December 1905

Mon cher Brodie,

I received your letter, thank you. And I send you my good wishes in return. I went immediately to the shop you mentioned in the rue du

Faubourg Saint-Honoré but it was closed. In the window was a sign: 'Fermeture définitive pour cause de décès dans la famille'. *I asked in nearby shops and they said it had closed suddenly some weeks before – and they said the shop was for sale. I couldn't get any more information, I'm sorry to say.*

Please come back to Paris. We miss you. They have made me manager but I'm not very good at my job, I fear. Mr Channon is very patient and understanding.

With my sincere friendship,
Dmitri Kuvakin

'*Pour cause de décès dans la famille* . . .' A death in the family . . . He felt utterly confident that it wasn't Lika. Not at all. He knew that if Lika had died something in him would have died also, however far away he was from her. He would have felt something change; he would have felt the world alter in some minuscule but irrefutable way; a Lika-absence registering itself in the atmosphere – a change in air pressure, isobars acknowledging a shift in the nature of existence. Most likely it was her ailing mother, and that would have taken her back to Moscow. He considered further. But – had Lika left Malachi and Malachi had then assumed she was going to join Brodie? . . . Questions proliferated, hypotheses multiplied. Maybe he had seen Malachi at the theatre after all. Maybe Malachi had found his letters in the shop once it had been closed . . . But surely Lika wouldn't have been so careless to leave them in a drawer or a cabinet . . .

He wandered down to the quayside, and walked out onto the Molo San Carlo and looked out at the restless sea as if an answer might be found there. It was a cold blustery day and the water was choppy, waves dashing against the sides of the quay sending spray shooting high. A steamship belched smoke as it hove to, heading for the shelter of the harbour's breakwater. Was Malachi Kilbarron in Trieste? . . .

Hallucination or not, he thought, he would take extra precautions. He would change lodgings; he would ask Gabriele Nicolo to fend off any enquiries and feign ignorance; he would avoid the theatre for a good while, pretend he was ill. He walked back to his lodging house in a confusion of emotions. He liked Trieste – where would he go now? And he had to think of his health – he had to go somewhere warm. Crimea? Egypt? Constantinople? Perhaps leaving Europe was the answer. But then, he reflected, a solitary Briton abroad was all the more noticeable.

He gave his notice at the lodging house, paid the punitive fine of a month's rent and packed his bags. What meagre possessions he had for a man in his mid-thirties, he thought. A bag of tuning tools, a couple of suitcases of clothes and a small dog. César sensed something was wrong but for him that meant excitement, change – not alarm, not growing apprehension. For the first time he regretted throwing Lika's Derringer into the Seine. Perhaps he should arm himself once more . . .

He went down the passageway to the communal bathroom to collect his shaving kit and his soaps and towels. He locked the door and sat on the lavatory for a while making further plans. Tonight he would find a hotel and start looking for new lodgings at the weekend. Or maybe wait until the New Year. One solution might be to live outside Trieste in Grado or Capodistria. There were regular ferries to the city. He could regulate his work easily enough—

His eye was caught by a spider trapped in the bathtub. A small spider, a fingernail across, trying to climb the smooth enamel of the bath and falling back time after time. He watched it make two dozen vain attempts, admiring its doggedness in the face of such obvious, persistent failure and acknowledging that this was his Robert the Bruce moment. He smiled, thinking: what must it be like for a spider in that alien, eerie landscape? Towering unscaleable walls of white – a world of white, an immense canyon of glossy blankness. A spider nightmare. An insect that could climb up anything suddenly utterly impotent. Brodie glanced to his right. And yet the plug was in its plughole and its chain led upwards to safety and security. If the spider simply moved a few feet down the bath it could climb the chain to freedom effortlessly. He was tempted to help it out but decided it should learn the lesson itself. He stood, eased his shoulders, massaged his biceps and forearms. Time to go to work and warn Gabriele about strangers asking leading questions.

3

'Hello there. Remember me?'

A young man was standing leaning against the wall by the door of Nicolo-Piano. He was wearing a shiny, worn black suit whose trousers were so short they exposed the tops of his lace-up, unpolished boots.

'It's Stan, isn't it? The drink-spiller.'

'The very same.'

They shook hands.

'My brother wants you to tune his old piano. Fancies himself as a singer, you see. Wants to practise at home, God help us.'

'I can do that.'

'But there's a budget. Only twenty crowns, I'm afraid.'

'It's on the house. For the Celtic Exiles.'

'You're a scholar and a gentleman, Mr Brodie, sir.'

Stan waited while Brodie went into the shop to fetch his tools and explain to Gabriele what he was up to and when he'd be back. Then he and Stan wandered off through side streets in a southerly direction to the apartment where Shem lived with his wife. Except she wasn't really his wife, Stan explained – they hadn't got round to the marriage part of the matrimonial union. Married in all but name, Stan said. Brodie knew what he meant.

The apartment was in a building in a working-class district of Trieste next door to the language school where both brothers taught. They climbed three flights of stairs to the front door of the flat, passing on the way up a little girl sitting on a stair, naked apart from a ragged blanket around her. Brodie glanced around for a parent or a sibling but saw no one. Stan seemed unperturbed by the encounter and when Shem opened the door to them – still in his pyjamas and dressing gown – Brodie realized that the polite norms of bourgeois behaviour were redundant here.

Stan went off to make a cup of tea while Shem led Brodie to the piano. It was a battered upright, monstrously out of tune and most of the ivory had fallen off the keys leaving the wood exposed.

'How did you get it up here?' Brodie asked.

'It only had to come up one floor,' Shem said. 'An old chap died and his son sold it to me for twenty crowns and a bottle of moonshine.'

Brodie played his usual octaves and unisons again. The piano was dead.

'I can make it sound better, that's for sure. But I won't guarantee it'll stay in tune.'

'I bow to your astonishing expertise,' Shem said as a plump, bosomy young woman with a rosy-cheeked fresh complexion emerged from a back room, carrying a baby.

'Ah. Here's the missus, and the son and heir,' Shem said, adding his introduction, 'This is Mr Brodie . . .'

'Moncur.'

'A very decent Scotchman.'

'Who's tuning the piano gratis,' Stan added, coming out of the kitchen with a saucerless cup of tea.

'Well, good for you, Mr Brodie Moncur,' said Mrs Shem in a strong Dublin accent. 'I'm off to buy some scraps of food for supper. Will you be joining us, perchance?'

'I'll be long gone by supper,' Brodie said.

Then Shem and Stan also excused themselves and Brodie was left alone with the piano. He opened it up and went to work hoping to achieve an approximation of an in-tune piano before they returned. After an hour's work he played 'My Bonny Boy' and, relatively satisfied, closed the fall on the upright. It was certainly ten times better now, though the decent, proper act would have been to put the poor instrument out of its misery.

The brothers returned half an hour later and marvelled at the improvement. Shem went into the small kitchen and emerged with a bottle of eau de vie, so he said. Stan found some tumblers and they all toasted the transformed piano. Shem sat down and played and sang a song: 'I Dreamt That I Dwelt in Marble Halls'. He had a fine light tenor, Brodie noted.

'My concert career is now up and running, thanks to you, Brodie,' he said.

They talked about opportunities in Trieste, city of music. The brothers liked it better than Dublin, they said, but it was a devil making a living. The eau de vie went round again and Brodie found himself, under its influence, telling them something of his predicament, of how he was being followed by a vindictive, jealous man; how he was thinking of leaving the city, trying to cover up his movements – to escape, disappear, once and for all.

'The world's your lobster,' Shem said, enthusiastically. 'Don't go somewhere else in Europe or the Med. No, spread your wings, Brodie – take a leap.'

For some reason Brodie thought of the spider in the bath that he'd seen that morning – endlessly trying to scale the same unscaleable wall while safety and freedom lay three feet away. That was the lesson, he reasoned – move away from the standard plan, the obvious route: move laterally.

'But where?' Brodie said. 'Timbuktu? Serendip? Vladivostok? Tierra del Fuego?'

'Wrong approach,' Shem said. 'Rely on the aleatory – write that down, Stannie. Yes, Brodie. Hazard the haphazard.'

He poured them all another glass of the powerful liquor – as inert as water, it seemed, but with a fiery finish – and slipped away to another room. He returned with a child's globe and a pin.

'I spin the globe – you pin the pin,' Shem said.

Brodie accepted the pin and Shem placed the globe on the table in front of him.

'Close your eyes, Brodie.'

Brodie did so and heard the globe begin to turn rapidly on its axis making an erratic wooden rattling sound. He stabbed with the pin and let go, opening his eyes. Shem turned the globe towards him and Brodie saw that the pin had stuck in the open sea – in blue ocean somewhere between India and Burma.

'Can I have another go?' Brodie said, feeling suddenly intoxicated.

'No. No, look, you've hit something there. Fetch me my glass, Stan.'

Stan left and returned with a magnifying glass. Shem peered through it.

'Begod, there's something here, Brodie. You've hit your destiny, son. Square on. There are islands here, as old Archie Pelago would say. Here be islands.'

He handed Brodie the magnifying glass and Brodie held it over the pin, moving the glass slightly so he could see where the pin-point had impacted. Shem was right – he had landed on a small group of islands off the coast of Burma. He removed the pin and held the glass closer so he could read the tiny print.

'The Andaman and Nicobar Islands,' he read out. 'Part of the British Empire as well.'

'Don't let that put you off,' Shem said. 'It's a sign.'

Brodie looked at the two brothers, a strange exhilaration filling him.

'The Andaman and Nicobar Islands. That's where I'll go. To hell with it.'

Shem and Stan applauded him, delightedly, laughing, and Shem topped his glass up.

They toasted him. 'Brodie Moncur, adventurer.'

'God, I envy you,' Shem said with feeling. 'Lucky bastard.'

PART VII

The Andaman and Nicobar Islands

1906

I

Brodie left Deemer's Hotel and commenced his usual morning round, accompanied by César on his lead. Dogs were eaten in the Andamans, he had been advised, or were more often stolen to hunt pigs – or to breed with the mongrel dogs that hunted pigs for the natives in the jungle. He didn't want to take any chances with César, a pure-bred Jack Russell, and a dog of insatiable curiosity, who often darted off pursuing his own individual searches of whatever neighbourhood he might be passing through.

Brodie walked down the hill from the hotel towards the harbour at Port Blair, looking out over the Andaman Sea towards the invisible Malay Peninsula, many dozens of miles distant. He was wearing a white drill suit, a cork helmet and pipe-clayed white shoes – every inch, he thought, the old colonial. Even after three months in the archipelago he still found it strange that he was living here – strange in a dreamlike way – leading a normal life with a white suit to wear, a place to stay and a job to do, being paid. It was another warm and humid day. The temperature was always around eighty degrees, most of the year – occasionally slightly warmer or slightly cooler – and at some stage during the day it would probably rain for a while. Paul Deemer, the eponymous proprietor of the hotel where he stayed, had told him that the lowest temperature ever recorded in the Andamans was sixty-six degrees – a warm summer day by Edinburgh standards. All this heat and warm humidity was good for his lungs, Brodie reminded himself. He had never breathed so freely – perhaps he should have come to the tropics years ago.

He went to the harbourmaster's office and looked at the shipping manifests – ships that had arrived or docked in transit in Port Blair. He was looking for shipping lines that had a European origin. It was more a matter of intuition than logic as his journey to the Andamans had been very eccentric. First an Austrian-Lloyd steamer from Trieste to

Port Said. Very quickly, he found a berth on a P&O coaler to Aden then, after a week in Aden, he paid for a tiny cabin on an ancient tea clipper heading for Calcutta. He didn't care how he travelled – he felt it was important simply to be moving on. There was another frustrating wait in Calcutta until he secured a place on a ferry full of convicts making the 700-mile crossing to the Andamans. It had taken him nearly two months to make the journey to the place picked out by a pin in Shem's apartment in Trieste. Now he had reached his destination he liked to see what European-registered ships called in at Port Blair – not many, in fact – but every time one arrived it made him more alert.

After the harbourmaster he went to the general post office and asked for mail for Miss Arbogast, his employer, and also to see if there was any for him. He was still waiting for his first letter. Nothing from his family and nothing from Lika – no surprise there. But he was still writing to her, addressing letters to the old shop, asking on the envelope that they be forwarded – *Faire suivre, svp* – emboldened now by his distance from Europe. He could never know if they actually reached her but the impulse to write was emotional, not intellectual, not logical. He had a strange faith in a posted letter: one way or another, he felt, it would find its recipient, however long it took, thanks to the diligence of the postal services of Europe. The very act of writing made him feel in contact and he wanted to keep living with the idea that her promise could be fulfilled. If he didn't write and tell her where he was, how would she ever find him? How would she ever knock on his door one day? He had a letter to post.

Poste Restante
GPO Port Blair
Middle Andaman
Andaman Islands
Indian Empire

7 June 1906

My darling Lika,

I am still here and happier now that I have a job working for an American ethnologist called Paget Arbogast. When I answered the advertisement I assumed I was going to be interviewed by a man but in fact Paget Arbogast is a woman, in her early forties – a very strange woman but we seem to get along well. She broke her leg in a fall recently and had need of an assistant, advertised and I responded and was employed. Her research project into the Andaman aborigines will last another two years, she tells me, so I am gainfully employed for as long as I want and as long as she remains here. When the job ends or I grow bored I think I may move on to Australia.

I miss you, my darling. I think of you every waking hour. My latest news from Paris is over six months old. I didn't tell you in my last letter but I know your shop has closed. Do you not think it is safe to write to me now? I long to know what has happened. I'm staying in a small clean hotel called Deemer's Hotel. It has a billiard room, a tin shed 'for concerts' and a garden with enormous shade trees. It even has a telephone! But there are only two numbers that it can connect with – the customs house and the prison governor. However, I am comfortable, my health is better than ever and César is enjoying his new life in the Orient.

I send all my love, as ever.
Your Brodie

He handed his letter to the post-office clerk – a Sikh, judging by his turban – and, leaving, walked up Port Blair's busy, ramshackle main street heading for Miss Arbogast's house. Port Blair was founded as a penal colony and its huge prison still dominated the town – a vast panopticon structure with a central tower and seven radiating, three-storey wings of individual cells, like spokes in a rim-less wheel. He saw the first convict gangs emerging to do their day's unpaid labour. There were over a thousand convicts, men and women, most of them murderers from India and Burma who had been spared execution. Generations of prisoners, having served their sentence, were encouraged to settle and farm, or start businesses and, as more and more villages were established and the forest cleared for agriculture, so the Andaman aborigines and their hunter-gatherer culture came under threat. There were now thousands of 'born locals', as the prisoners' children and grandchildren and their descendants were known, steadily colonizing this chain of tiny islands that their forebears had been sent to rot in.

It was a most curious society, Brodie had come to learn, and a surprisingly peaceful place considering that a significant proportion of its inhabitants were progeny of murderous felons. There were a lot of British and Indian soldiers and police, of course. There was a substantial garrison in barracks on the outskirts of Port Blair and many supervisory British staff running this small far-flung colony. Add all the ancillary business of being a thriving port, with its transitory traffic of adventurers, speculators and ships' crews, it was no surprise that, despite the clutter and the haphazard nature of the buildings, the main street gave every impression of growing prosperity. General merchandise stores and grog-shops, ships' chandlers and lodging houses and, down by the harbour with its long coaling wharf and quays, cranes and warehouses, all the administrative paraphernalia of a busy port.

Brodie trudged up the gentle slope that led to Miss Arbogast's substantial wooden bungalow in its large neat garden. It had a long veranda running the length of its facade and its corrugated-iron roof was painted forest green. Stooping gardeners were cutting the tough grass of the lawn with long thin cutlasses. As Brodie walked up the path to the front door they stopped, stood and gave a little bow and then resumed their back-straining task.

Miss Arbogast deplored the practice of settling released convicts on the land. As she saw it, the Andaman tribes were being corrupted and pressured in every conceivable way. Soon, she said, we would know nothing about these ancient peoples who had been the most isolated on earth over millennia – all their culture, folklore and mythologies would be lost forever. Hence her ethnographical project, funded by her wealthy family and the Smithsonian Institute. She had been living in Port Blair for over two years now, making journeys into the dense forests of the interior, gathering facts and figures for her eventual book.

Brodie knocked on the door and was admitted by Lokima, her Andaman housekeeper. He handed her Miss Arbogast's mail and took a seat in the main room as he waited for Miss Arbogast to arrive. The floor was painted concrete – maroon – and covered with elaborately woven palm-frond mats. The walls were filled with photographs from field trips and ethnographic artefacts – bows and arrows, masks and ceremonial beaded skirts, shelves of wooden pots and, at one end, an entire fishing net stretched over the wall. The wooden sofas and armchairs with their brightly coloured kapok-stuffed cushions were surprisingly comfortable.

Several of the photographs featured a bald, lean man with intense staring eyes, usually standing beside Miss Arbogast in the company of naked tribespeople. This was Francis Bartkowiak, the eminent ethnologist, and the project leader. A year before he had nearly died of amoebic dysentery and, when partially recovered, had been despatched to a hospital in Madras. His health still poor, he had returned to the United States where he continued to convalesce. Miss Arbogast had taken over the Andaman project and had been running it alone – with the help of her Indian staff – since Bartkowiak's sudden departure. All had been well until her fall and the fractured leg. Brodie, she told him, was the 'godsend, sent by the gods of ethnology' to save her.

Brodie lit a cigarette and picked up a three-month-old copy of *Harper's Magazine* and started reading an article about Upton Sinclair's novel called *The Jungle*. He had been employed first as a general dogsbody while Miss Arbogast's broken leg slowly healed but now he was a fully paid-up member of her small ethnographic team. There had been a major problem that she had encountered that he had inadvertently solved. In the Andaman tribes men would often refuse to speak to a woman about certain subjects. Brodie was now invaluable as a transcriber of these male confidences. The 'born local' translators – most of whom couldn't write – would relay the tribal lore and Brodie would scribble down the details. Miss Arbogast said she didn't know how she had coped without him – vast tracts of Andaman society had been hidden from her because of this gender embargo. Brodie was glad to be of use: for the first time in his life his expertise as a piano tuner was wholly valueless.

Miss Arbogast limped in, leaning on her stick, which she

promptly disposed of, seeing him there. She was still in some pain, she complained, worrying that her doctor, Dr Klein (a German), hadn't set the fractured tibia properly. Brodie repeated his constant advice – rest, rest and more rest – but she wouldn't hear of it: there was vital work to be done. She was a skinny dark-haired woman with the palest blue eyes Brodie had ever seen. They were disconcertingly pale, he thought, and they added to the intensity of a manner that was already fairly intense. She did everything with absolute concentration whether it was buttering toast or climbing mountains, cleaning her teeth or taking photographs of savage tribes. For Miss Arbogast, he realized, life was an entirely controllable entity if only you made sufficient effort. Difficulties, setbacks, confusions and barriers were a sign of some deficiency in yourself; a way could be found to overcome anything if you sought for it with the required vigour. Her broken leg had undermined this adamantine certainty, somewhat. She reluctantly had to admit that *force majeure* existed, here and there.

'Brodie, good morning. There you are.' She shook his hand firmly as she did every day. 'How're things going?'

He enjoyed her American accent. She was the first American he had come to know properly, he realized.

'Everything's aboard. Though I still need to know our final numbers. Of our group.'

'Ah, yes. Good point. Colonel Ticknell has offered us four sepoy soldiers, as protection. They'll provide for themselves – food and drink, and so forth – but we'll need another tent for them.'

Brodie had been charged with organizing and fitting out a two-week expedition to the Nicobar Islands, part of the greater archipelago but eighty miles to the south and separated by a significant sound of water, the Ten Degree Channel. So close, but so different, Miss Arbogast had said. The Andamans were part of the Negrito race; the Nicobars were entirely different, closer to Malays and Burmese. She had to make a comparison to see if further study of the Nicobars would be an essential part of the eventual book.

She lit a cigarette – she smoked an American brand called Gypsy Queen – and they discussed when they might set off for Great

Nicobar, the largest island in the chain. Brodie had chartered an ungainly lumber schooner with a steam engine called the *Lau*. The *Lau* was an ugly boat with its funnel set aft and two gaff-rigged masts forward. He had hired it from a timber merchant called Deepmal Khan for ten US dollars a day.

He had told Miss Arbogast that there were two substantial cabins on board but she insisted that they make camp on Great Nicobar. The Nicobar tribes were reputedly both curious and friendly and only by making camp would they attract them and be led to their village settlements.

Brodie agreed with everything, half-listening, watching Miss Arbogast as she limped around her sitting room. She seemed much older than he was – wise, assured and infinitely more capable – but he realized that they were probably separated by only five or six years. She was wearing a khaki drill skirt that came down to her ankles and what looked like a man's shirt, navy blue, with patch breast-pockets and epaulettes. Her hair was tied up in a loose bun. Her face was suntanned from all her hours out in the field – tanned like a peasant, Brodie thought – which made her ice-blue eyes even more striking.

'How could I have done this without you, Brodie?'

'What? Sorry?'

'I couldn't mount this trip to Nicobar myself, not in a hundred years.'

'I'm sure you could.'

'I'm sure I could as well but it would cost me. Don't you get it? They see me coming. "Rich American Woman" – they try to rob me blind. I should have had someone like you the moment Francis left. Everything would've gone more smoothly.' She smiled at him. 'Hi-ho. You live and learn. Fiddle-dee-dee.'

'Thank you, Miss Arbogast.'

She sat down on the armchair beside him and stubbed out her cigarette.

'I think you should start calling me Page. Don't you? We've known each other long enough.'

*

Brodie sat beside the interpreter, Ram, on a mat set on the floor of the bachelors' hut, as it was known. Three near-naked young Nicobar men sat opposite, chewing betel nuts and talking freely to Ram, an ex-convict who farmed on Great Nicobar, who had married a native woman, and had learned the language of the tribe. His English was remarkably good, also. He had been a deputy station manager on the Bengal railway, he told Brodie. And then one day he had killed a beggar – beaten him to death with a metal stave – who had refused to leave the station platform after several warnings. Brodie thought it must have been the sheer reasonableness with which Ram recounted this event – wouldn't anyone have bludgeoned such a recalcitrant fool to death in these circumstances? – that had made the court spare the hangman's noose and send him to the Andamans instead.

From time to time Ram would hold up his hand for a pause and translate what he had been told into English and Brodie would summarize what he said, scribbling it down as fast as he could, in a ledger. Page had given him a list of specific questions to ask the bachelors. They all seemed to be about the sexual habits of the tribe.

'They say,' Ram recounted, unperturbed, 'that usually they do it in the yam-garden at night. For copulation, I mean, when they are young. When they are older they can bring the girl in here.'

Brodie duly wrote this down and looked at his next question.

'What is the position for the sexual act?'

Ram engaged in animated conversation and two of the young men happily demonstrated the preferred position, one acting the man, the other the woman.

Brodie wrote down: 'The man kneels and pulls the woman towards him, her legs apart. Holding her legs up with his elbows until penetration is achieved.'

There was more chatter.

'But,' Ram added, 'in this house, when others are sleeping nearby, they do it like this.'

The two men lay on their side facing each other. One man lifted his upper leg and laid it across the other man's upper leg.

'This way,' Ram translated, 'they are making less noise. Not disturbing the other men in the hut.'

Brodie duly jotted this down, made a quick sketch and looked down his list of questions.

'What about other positions?'

There was a lot of ribald laughter – clearly some sort of mockery was taking place.

'They say . . .' Ram coughed and for the first time his disinterested composure left him. 'They say that the white man does not know how to copulate.'

'How do they know this?'

'Many white men come to sleep with their women.'

'What do the white men do that is wrong – that's so amusing?'

Ram asked and more scurrilous laughter ensued. Ram listened intently and translated carefully.

'They say the white man bears down on the woman too heavily and she cannot respond.' One of the young men stopped Ram and spoke rapidly. Ram nodded. 'The white man is too quick. Nicobar man takes a long time . . .' He listened further. 'It is best to kneeling like this. This way you have good control over . . . Over the discharge of fluid.'

Brodie looked at his next question.

'Do they kiss?'

'They suck the lower lip,' came the eventual answer. 'They will bite each other, also. Neck, shoulder, cheek. The spit is flowing between the mouths.' Ram pointed. 'They will bite off the eyelashes of the loved one.'

'Really?' Brodie was intrigued.

'Both men and women will bite off the lashes. It is a sign of great . . .' Ram thought of the English words. 'Great emotion.'

There was more urgent conversation – the bachelors were clearly enjoying the interrogation. Ram gave his translation serious thought.

'As there is little contacting between the two bodies,' Ram said, thoughtfully, 'so, a handsome boy like him can fornicate with an old woman, and an ugly woman, where no love is existing.'

'Do they masturbate?' Brodie asked Page's next question.

'Only an idiot will masturbate,' was the blunt reply. 'Or an albino.'

When the session was over and they were about to leave, one of the young men took off the amulet on his wrist and handed it to Brodie, saying a few words. It was woven from a kind of leathery frond and was threaded through some seeds and a tiny cowrie shell. Ram rebuked him but the man persisted and slipped it over Brodie's wrist.

'He says – and forgive me, please, sahib – that he can see you have had no copulation for a long time. If you wear this charm, copulation will come to you very soon.'

That night in Page's tent, lit by two lanterns, he read out the transcriptions to her and she wrote them down in her own heavy leather notebook.

'This is fascinating,' she said. 'The women were saying something similar. They seem very sexually . . .' She thought and smiled. 'Free. Untroubled. As a society.'

'I know what you mean,' Brodie said, suddenly a bit uncomfortable.

'The women said that they like the men to "move on horizontally". At least that's how it seemed to be translated. I couldn't understand what they were talking about. Now I do – now I know about this squatting, kneeling position the men use. You say they hold the woman's legs up and apart with the crook of their elbows.'

'That's what they said.'

Page offered him a Gypsy Queen. The American blend reminded him of his old Margaritas.

'The women kept using the same expression: *Kubi-labala-ta*. Literally it means "a log lying on the ground, moving".' She gestured, moving her hand back and forth. 'When the context is fornication it's pretty obvious what they're talking about, wouldn't you say?'

'I suppose so.'

'And the women bite off the men's eyelashes also – during the sexual act. Fascinating. I don't really understand that one but it's meant to be the height of intimacy.' She laughed, a throaty deep laugh. 'I don't think that'll catch on back home, somehow.'

Every day of their short visit to Great Nicobar was occupied with these interrogations. Page with the women of the camp; Brodie with the young men. Page would give him her list of questions and Brodie and Ram would spend hours talking with the young men of the tribe in the bachelors' hut – a simple dwelling with a sloping roof of palm leaves erected on four poles, two long and two short. For some reason they didn't talk to the married couples or the older generation – only young, unmarried men and women – he assumed it must have something to do with the subject of Page's eventual book. However, Page's questions did cover other topics – daily routine, division of labour, domestic tasks, marriage, pregnancy, death rituals, taboos and myths of the spirit world – and steadily they built up a picture of the life of the tribe in all its complexity. Simple hunter-gathering and survival in the forest was overlaid with a complex of morality, rules, strictures, belief patterns that, in their own, way, Brodie thought, rivalled anything that millennia of so-called civilization had brought about. He developed a new respect for primitive *Homo sapiens*, even though he rather enjoyed the anomalies. The most offensive insult in this Nicobar tribe – one that might on occasion provoke a fight to the death – was the injunction: eat your own shit. Adultery was a capital crime. And personal hygiene was more of a virtue here on Grand Nicobar than it was in Edinburgh. Any foul odour was anathema.

Sometimes he would ask Ram to stop and he would take a break and step outside the bachelors' hut to smoke a cigarette. The village consisted of eight of these rudimentary structures, facing inwards and arranged in a rough oval. The centre of the oval contained a communal fire and was reserved for dancing – which, apart from fornication, appeared the sole leisure pursuit. Brodie would look for a patch of shade and light a cigarette and always find himself reflecting on and marvelling at the length and nature of his long journey. From smoking a cigarette outside Channon & Co. in rainy Edinburgh to smoking a cigarette while standing in a

Nicobar village, in the stirring leaf-shadows of the palm trees on the other side of the world.

He always drew a small crowd on these occasions, composed of girls and young women. The Nicobars and the Andamans were tiny, around about five feet tall. Brodie knew that he must seem a giant to them, a freak of nature. The women were naked apart from short skirts of grass fronds, their breasts always uncovered. They stood a discreet couple of yards away, in a semicircle, giggling and pointing at him, talking about him behind their hands, content to look on. He would smile and say 'Hello, ladies, good morning' – only provoking more giggles and whispered chit-chat. What were they saying about him, he wondered? Another mystery.

As he thought about the journey he'd made to end up here in this Nicobar village he contemplated his own tribe seen through his new ethnological lens. The despotic patriarch figure, Malky, served by his reluctant sons and daughters, trapped through penury in his privileged dwelling in their cold northern habitat. And, next door, the place of worship with its own rituals, its songs, its incantations, its readings and its own potent symbols – the tortured, naked man dying slowly on a wooden cross. It was good to gain some objectivity on a situation that familiarity had made stale. Your life was turned on its head when you thought about it in this way. If the Nicobars seemed strange and their beliefs outlandish, then so were ours, Brodie thought, seen from another perspective. Those girls had every right to laugh at him.

On their last day the questions Page gave him were all about death. In the mythology of this tribe – it was slowly revealed to him by Ram's translations – after you died you went to a place called the Island of the Dead. Here life was a replica of life on earth – only happier – and there was no old age. If you had loved many women the only one you would meet again would be the one you had loved most, your true love. This consequence applied to men and women. There would be no unseemly, embarrassing encounters between rival lovers. Brodie found this idea consoling and asked many supplementary questions to be sure he wrote down the details correctly.

In the evenings after supper he and Page would spend an hour or two collating their transcriptions. The subjects she had chosen all conformed with chapters of the book she was going to write about the Andamans, so she told him. Nicobar life and society – so geographically close – was turning out to be entirely different from that of the Andamans. This trip had been more significant than she had ever thought possible – she was truly grateful to Brodie for all his diligent noting-down. Brodie said he was glad to have been of real help.

'What's the title of your book?' he asked.

Page thought. 'I haven't really made up my mind,' she said. 'Our proposal to the Smithsonian was called *An Ethnographic Study of the Aborigines of the Andaman Islands*. Francis Bartkowiak's idea. A bit dry, don't you think? I always knew we'd need something more arresting.'

'You'll think of something.'

'I think I know the sort of thing – now we've been here, thanks to the Nicobars. Now we've learned so much more.'

'Oh yes?'

'Something like – *Magic, Ritual and Morality in the Andaman Islands*.'

'It has a certain ring to it.'

'Or – given our recent questions – *Male and Female Relations in the Andamans*.'

'I like that.'

'Or – *The Morality of Sexual Life in the Andamans*.'

'Why not?'

'Or, quite simply, *The Sexual Life of Andaman Natives*. Given our new focus.'

'That should bring hordes of new readers.'

She laughed – her throaty, unselfconscious laugh.

'Or I could just call it *Sexual Life*. Why beat about the bush?'

Brodie was fully aware what was slowly happening here. A shift had occurred in their relationship. He felt a tightening of his throat as Page's amused blue eyes turned upon him.

'I suppose there's a risk it might be banned,' he said. 'The book, I mean, not sexual life. Do you have any more of that bourbon left, by any chance?'

They always had a small glass of sour-mash whiskey after the evening meal and Brodie had a sudden craving for some liquor.

'Good idea,' she said. 'It's in that trunk there.'

She pointed to her camp bed, hung with a mosquito net. He crossed the tent and opened the trunk, finding the bottle. Page had set two enamel mugs at their places and was standing waiting for him. Brodie poured them each a dram and they clinked their mugs together.

'Here's to horizontal movement,' she said, taking half a pace closer towards him.

Brodie knew that she wanted him to kiss her but instead he smiled at the joke and turned away and strolled over to the open flap of the tent. He could see the lights of the *Lau* reflected in the dark lagoon beyond the beach. Discreetly he slipped off his fornication amulet and thrust it into his pocket.

He drained his bourbon and turned. Page hadn't moved.

'I think I'd better be off to bed,' he yawned. 'I'm fair wabbit, as we say in Scotland.'

'Goodnight, Brodie. See you in the morning.'

2

César licked his lips, then licked the plate that had contained his chopped chicken until it was entirely clean. Then he jumped onto Brodie's lap and put his front paws on his chest, staring at him intently as if to make sure it was really he and that he had returned. He didn't like Brodie going away and leaving him behind, and when Brodie returned he was given a display of dog affection that was both superfluous and heart-warming. Brodie scratched behind César's ears and the stumpy apostrophe that was his tail disappeared into a blur of enthusiastic wagging.

He thought of Lika and wondered what she was doing and where she was. Would she have received his latest letter? And then he thought maybe this was why she had left César with him – the little dog was a constant memory-catalyst. The César–Lika, Lika–César connection a daily reminder. But thinking about her these days brought melancholy in its train. More and more he was beginning to believe that he would never see her again and that to have come halfway around the world just to free himself of Malachi Kilbarron had been foolish, however effective. He was relying on some new occupant of her shop to forward letters on to the previous owner. Too hopeful? . . .

An unpleasant realization struck him: what if they were being forwarded to her Paris home? To the apartment on the boulevard Beaumarchais? Malachi would surely open any letter addressed to Lika, particularly if there was a foreign stamp on it. Brodie thought further: maybe he'd been too hasty . . . Maybe all he was doing was guilelessly providing Malachi with his new location. He should have asked Dmitri to make more enquiries, he realized. Perhaps it might have been more prudent to have written to Lika care of her mother in Moscow . . . He felt troubled and tipped César off his lap and reached under his bed for the chamber pot. He raked his throat and spat and saw, amongst the foam of his saliva, pink bubbles and a vermicular thread of glistening bloody mucous. His lungs stirring. From time to time his body seemed to need to remind him – to provide new evidence of the tubercles nestling in his chest, growing, ripening. He knew they were cavities, expanding holes of necrosis filled with dead tissue and pus – like cream cheese, one of his doctors had told him – but he imagined them instead as mouldy rotting plums set in the spongy tissues of his pleural membranes, the branching networks of bronchioles and alveoli.

There was a knock at the door and César barked once. For some reason Brodie felt suddenly apprehensive. It was dark outside, late.

'Who is it?' he called.

'It's me, Mr Moncur. I've a message for you, just delivered.'

It was Paul Deemer, the proprietor. Brodie opened the door and was handed an envelope with his name written on it.

He thanked Deemer, closed the door and ripped it open.

Wednesday night

Dear Brodie,

I need to speak to you on a matter of some urgency. Come to my house now, if you will – we can have some supper while we discuss the matter. See you soon.

Cordially,
Page

Brodie thought: what could she want him for that couldn't wait until morning?

3

Page reached forward and brushed back the long lock of hair that had fallen over his face.

'What happened to your poor ear?' she asked.

'Would you believe me if I told you that it was the result of a duel I fought in Russia?'

'Certainly not.'

Brodie leaned back from the ledger. The gesture had caught him by surprise with its intimacy. Page smiled at him, unperturbed.

She sat opposite him across the narrow table, one elbow hooked over the back of the chair, the attitude causing the cloth of her cream blouse to tighten and flatten her breasts. Wide flat breasts. Brodie thought of all the breasts he'd seen in the Andamans and the Nicobars – dozens and dozens. Hundreds. But innocently revealed, modestly revealed, not a trace of prurience. There was something markedly un-innocent and immodest about Page's pose, he thought, and stood up, stretching as if he were stiff and needed to ease an aching back.

'Well, it's true. A near miss. Took off my earlobe and a bit more.'

'So what happened to the other man – your fellow duellist?'

Brodie scratched his head and wondered if he should tell her.

'I killed him.'

Page laughed. Unconstrained, delighted.

'Come on! Quit fooling.'

She stood up as well and went to refill their glasses with bourbon. Her long hair was down, falling over her back and shoulders, making her look younger, less wiry and shrewd.

'Tell me you're joking,' she said, bringing the bottle over. 'You're no killer, Brodie Moncur.'

'I'm joking. I had a bad fall from a bicycle.'

'That I can believe. Cigarette?'

'No thanks.'

She poured their drinks into the glasses, the solitary oil lamp on the table thickly lighting one side of her face, like yellow paint. Cadmium. Butter. Honey.

She closed the ledger and put it on top of the pile of four others. Francis Bartkowiak's ledgers, all the work he had done in the Andamans before falling ill and being sent to India to recover in hospital.

'Can we do it, do you think?'

'I don't see why not. They seem perfectly legible.'

This was why she had called him over to her bungalow. She had returned from their trip to find a letter from Bartkowiak asking for the immediate return of the ledgers containing his fieldwork – he had left them in a suitcase in his lodgings. They were to be returned forthwith to him at Yale University where he had taken up a position in the Department of Philosophy. Brodie couldn't understand why Page was so agitated by the request.

'He had to leave so quickly,' she said. 'So he left most of his belongings behind. I have a mass of his stuff, clothes, books and pieces of luggage. I found the suitcase with these ledgers in them.'

'So why don't you just send them back?'

'He's going to write his own book, don't you see?' she said, almost angrily. 'He's going to beat me to it.'

'But can he?' Brodie said. 'You've been here twice as long as he was.'

'I would say no. But whoever publishes first usually wins in our game. We're a young discipline, ethnography. People are starting to peg out their territory and make their names.'

Page had suggested that they go through the Bartkowiak ledgers together and copy down anything that seemed relevant to her research as soon as they possibly could. The Andaman project was a joint effort – Francis Bartkowiak couldn't claim sole authorship. They would fillet – her word – his ledgers and send them back to him when they had the information they needed. But it had to be done quickly so he wouldn't be suspicious.

'Many hands make light work,' she said. 'Two heads are better than one. The faster we go through his stuff – the sooner we send it back – the less he'll suspect.'

Brodie said he was at her service. He didn't understand the manoeuvrings of this academic competition but he would do what he could – he was up for the challenge, he said.

His support made her relax, made her almost exultant, and she poured more bourbon to toast their enterprise. He had looked quickly through the ledgers. Bartkowiak had an easy hand – black ink, copperplate – it wouldn't take the two of them long to see if there was anything in them that would be valuable.

He began to spend every night at Page's house. They would have supper together and then go through the ledgers, Brodie checking with her for anything that could be valuable to her research. They would wind up the evening with a glass and a smoke on the veranda, looking out over the lights of Port Blair. Brodie left around midnight to return to his room at the hotel. Their regular hours together made their relationship change in subtle ways. In the field, during their days in the Andaman villages where they conducted their interviews, took photographs, made measurements, Page remained formal, issuing instructions, very much the research-project leader. But when night fell and he wandered over to her house to go through the Bartkowiak ledgers a kind of conspiratorial intimacy took over and he sensed the mood between them changing.

During their post-ledger moments on the veranda Brodie found himself telling her of his travels, of the journey he had made from rainy Edinburgh to sweltering Port Blair – and the name of Lika Blum inevitably came up, time and again.

'Why didn't you marry her?' Page asked.

'Because I discovered she was already married.'

'That can be a problem,' she said with surprising bitterness.

'Why aren't you married?' Brodie asked boldly, bourbon-stimulated.

'None of your business,' she said. 'I've not asked you about your amorous past, you may have noticed.'

'But I've told you about Lika.'

'You told me – I didn't ask.'

'All right, I apologize.'

'All right, if you really want to know,' she said, screwing up her face. 'There was a man – an older man – years ago. A long time ago. He was at Princeton. We had a "liaison". I didn't know it was doomed.'

'Because he was married?'

'Something like that.'

'What was his name?'

'What's that got to do with anything?'

'I just like to know these details.'

'Emerson.' She looked away. 'Turned out he was rotten at the core.'

Brodie stopped asking questions.

'He was nothing like you,' she said, turning to him, taking his hand, tenderly. 'In case that's why you were asking.'

'I wasn't. Wondering, that is. Just making conversation – asking questions.'

'You're much nicer. Sweeter.'

'Thank you.'

She let go of his hand and picked up her glass and looked at him searchingly over its rim.

'You're a dark horse, though, Brodie Moncur. Why, I almost believe you could have fought a duel. Was it over the woman? Lika?'

'It was over a piece of music, in fact.'

'Of course. And the moon is made of cheese.'

Brodie felt a sharp pang of memory at the phrase, remembering when he had said it before – to Lika.

She must have seen his expression change. She stood up and walked to the edge of the veranda and, in a businesslike voice, not looking at him, said, 'I was thinking. Why don't you move in here? We could rig up a room for you easily. There are three more bedrooms through that door.' She pointed. 'It would make everything easier. More convenient. You wouldn't have to be criss-crossing the town day and night.'

'What about my dog?'

'He's very keen on the idea. I asked him.'

They looked at each other candidly. Despite the airy, efficient tone, she was offering herself to him, Brodie knew: offering him the next developing stage in their relationship – employer, to friend, to lover. Suggesting a new arrangement that might lead somewhere, to another more permanent arrangement.

'I think,' he said carefully, 'it's probably better if I stay in the hotel. You know how small Port Blair is. Tongues would wag. People would talk behind our backs.'

'Who cares? Look what goes on in this town. It's a town full of murderers and criminals.'

Brodie didn't follow through and Page didn't mention it again. He said goodnight and walked back to Deemer's hotel thinking about what had been made overt by their last exchange. He knew it was a genuine proposal – Page Arbogast was that sort of person: that was how she dealt with issues in her life. They were to be solved, practically, swiftly, with the least fuss. He thought about it, wondered what marriage to Page Arbogast might mean and saw, that from one perspective, it would solve many problems. He liked her; she intrigued him, was beginning to arouse him, she was clever, laconic and funny. And he knew her family was rich. Her parents were dead and she had one brother, a lawyer in Washington DC. The Andaman project had another year or so to run then she would go back to her home in Connecticut and write her book. Brodie could go with her . . . he stopped himself. What about Lika? How could he even think about being with Page Arbogast when Lika Blum might knock on his door, one of these days? They had made a promise to each other. A promise was a promise.

4

Brodie helped Page out of the steam yacht after it was securely berthed by the wharf in front of the customs house. Ram supervised the coolies unloading their equipment and supplies. They had spent a fruitless forty-eight hours looking for settlements of the Jarawas, the Andamans' most elusive and reputedly most aggressive tribe. Colonel Ticknell's sepoys had been called upon and Page had even brought along her own gun – again supplied by the colonel – a revolver, an old .45 Adams Mark III she told him, powerful enough to stop a charging buffalo, she claimed. It had rained both nights when they had camped and he had been badly bitten by mosquitoes that had found a tear in his net. Brodie felt dirty and itchy and, for him, unusually tired. It had been a frustrating and exhausting field trip.

Page let go of his hand.

'I've got to have a bath,' she said, adding quietly, 'Have you, thought any more about my idea? We can take it very easily. Step by step. One night at a time . . .'

Brodie was suddenly tempted, thought – yes, maybe this is the new direction for him, that he should explore it – then he saw Malachi Kilbarron walk out of the customs house and disappear round the corner.

'Are you all right?' Page asked, seeing him flinch.

'I've just seen a ghost,' he said. 'I'd better get back to Deemer's. I'll come round later.'

She was perplexed, he could see. 'It's nothing,' he said. 'I'll come by later.' He picked up his bag and walked away.

At the hotel he asked Paul Deemer if there were any new residents. None, he was told. Anyone asking for me while I was away? No, was the same reply.

He was moderately reassured. If it was Malachi, then he must have only just arrived, he thought. He washed and shaved, telling himself repeatedly that he could have easily been mistaken. Stout, bearded, European men were hardly rare in the Andamans. There were the garrison officers, the Port Authority officials, the Cellular Gaol administrators, the superintendent's staff, not to mention any number of ships' masters and the crews of passing boats, plus the customs officers and the merchants – so why did he think this man was Malachi?

He sat down on his chair and hung his head, again feeling an untypical wave of fatigue overwhelm him. All he wanted to do was go to sleep but he knew that if it was indeed Malachi that he had seen then his best opportunity to confront him was now, before he had settled and begun to make enquiries. There were only a few suitable hotels and boarding houses where Europeans would stay in Port Blair. It wouldn't take long to investigate them all and see if he had been hallucinating or not. And if he found Malachi Kilbarron – then Malachi Kilbarron would have to be dealt with, once and for all. He wasn't going to be distracted again.

He walked over to Page's house. She was waiting, fragrant, bathed, wearing a dark navy dress with red shoes that he hadn't seen before. She was unusually excited, he thought, and then unusually disappointed when, after their supper of pork chops and beans, he had said he felt very tired and worried that he had a fever coming on. She felt his brow, agreed he looked pale, and left to find some sachets of quinine.

In the two minutes she was absent Brodie darted to her desk and found the Adams revolver. He knew which drawer she kept it in. It was fully loaded. He slipped it in his jacket pocket and slung his jacket over the back of his chair. He said goodnight and apologized again.

'Are you sure you're all right?' she said, taking his hand. She had started doing this almost regularly, as if unthinkingly, when they were alone. It was both intimate and unimportant. It perplexed him. 'Shall I call Dr Klein?' she asked.

'I just need ten hours' sleep,' Brodie said, reassuringly. 'Tramping through dripping jungle isn't what I'm used to.'

'Then sleep well. Come tomorrow evening if you feel better. We'll have a day off.'

Brodie left, his revolver-encumbered jacket heavy over his arm, and headed immediately down to Port Blair's main street. In fact he wasn't feeling well, at all – perhaps he did have a temperature – he could feel the hot flush of fever growing on him. It was strange: he felt weak and yet full of improbable energy all the same. He had a quarry to hunt. He shrugged on his linen jacket, tucked the revolver in his belt, and buttoned his jacket over it. All he had to do was find Malachi Kilbarron – there were a limited number of places where he could be at this time of night.

He found him in the third hotel he visited. It was called O'Malley's Grand Oriental Hotel and he supposed it was the Irish connotation that had drawn Malachi there. It was a shabby place with a go-down bar, hung with Chinese lanterns, full of prostitutes looking for sailors. There were a few rooms above a so-called chophouse with greasy chequered tablecloths where you could eat oyster pie, fried fish or pork chops – with plenty of watered-down beer and whiskey to aid digestion.

Malachi was eating on his own, turned away from the chophouse door, Brodie saw, as he stepped inside. He recognized the same broad back that he had followed in the Jardin des Tuileries. An opportunity missed. He was not going to be distracted tonight.

He unbuttoned his jacket so he had easy access to his revolver and made his way through the busy tables to where Malachi was enjoying his solitary meal. Brodie stood three feet behind him for a moment – Malachi entirely unaware of his presence as he shovelled some sort of steaming stew into his mouth.

'Kilbarron,' Brodie said softly.

No reaction.

'Malachi. I need a word with you outside.'

Nothing.

Brodie closed his right hand around the butt of the revolver and, with his left, tapped Malachi on the shoulder.

Now Malachi turned.

Except it wasn't Malachi. It was a pasty-faced European with a dark beard.

'Czy mogę w czymś pomóc?'

Polish, Brodie thought. Something about the accent.

'Mes excuses. Entschuldigung.'

He walked out of O'Malley's feeling a surge of unreal relief – exhilaration – mingled with odd shamefacedness. What was wrong with him? Was he going insane? He bounced off a wall, feeling suddenly unsteady and faint, pulse racing then thready. He slid down the wall, falling to his knees. Oh God, he said to himself. Here it comes. Oh God.

A big tubercle in his lung responded to the increase of pressure in his blood and the aneurism on the artery beside it burst and dark blood flowed from his mouth, endlessly.

5

Brodie knew he was very ill, as ill as he had ever been in his life. His lungs were on fire and he found breathing laboriously difficult even when propped upright on five pillows in Page's bed. He came in and out of his senses. Dr Klein had given him some sort of opiate that made him dream awake, it seemed to him, the room wanderingly populated with figures from his life – his brothers and sisters, his father Malky, Lady Dalcastle, Ainsley Channon, Calder . . . Then the world would clear and order itself and he knew exactly where he was: here was Page, concerned, loving. Here was Dr Klein, moustachioed, morose, with his soft clean hands taking his pulse. He would talk to Page, tell her he was feeling a little better and, the next minute, it seemed, John Kilbarron would walk into the room.

In his moments of lucidity the events of the past few days were explained to him. He had experienced a massive haemorrhage outside O'Malley's Hotel. He had been discovered, unconscious, but someone had recognized him and word was sent to Page. Dr Klein was summoned and then in the feverish semi-conscious days that followed he had developed pneumonia in his now damaged and depleted lungs. It was the pneumonia that was causing the pain and making his breathing difficult, that was causing the intense fever. The hallucinations were encouraged by the opiates Dr Klein provided to ease the fiery pain.

Brodie felt as weak as he ever had – almost without energy, concentrating on respiration: breathe in, breathe out. Page sat by his bed, holding his hand.

'What were you doing there?' she asked him softly. 'What was happening, Brodie?'

'I was looking for a man. A man who had come to kill me.'

Page smiled at him. He could tell she thought his feverish mind had taken over again.

And every time the door was opened César would sprint in and leap on his bed and lick his hand. Sometimes Brodie would know it was César, sometimes he would recoil in horror when Malachi Kilbarron was licking his hand.

One day he felt momentarily better, calmer. The pain in his chest, the molten bands of metal circling his lungs like hoops of a barrel, had eased.

Page asked, 'Why did you take my gun?'

'I saw somebody. Somebody who had been chasing me for years, for years.'

'Who, for God's sake? Who would come all the way here?'

'Malachi would. Malachi Kilbarron.'

'Who's Malachi?'

'A devil who wants to kill me.'

She smiled. He sensed she thought his clarity was going again. A devil, a fiend – a demon called Malachi.

'Never mind,' he said. 'In fact I was wrong. Just some Polish sailor.'

The next day he felt himself palpably weakening, diminishing, as if there were a tap in his body left running and his vital spirit was flowing out, freely, unchecked, until he barely had the strength to lift his arm from the sheet. He drifted in and out of consciousness. Page's face, Dr Klein's face – blurred, deforming – registering briefly in the contracting circle that was his vision.

He had a final moment of clarity. So clear that he thought he might magically be getting better. Then he realized what this moment of clarity signified.

He saw a shape, like the map of an unknown island, that turned into Lika's face. Then he saw the skein of geese flying low over the Neva river. He saw the deer at Maloe Nikolskoe look up from its grazing and stare at him. He saw Lika come through the door and walk towards him smiling. 'Brodie!' she called. 'I'm here!' And he felt tears fill his eyes – an eerie sense of happiness, of other-worldly well-being filled him.

Dr Klein was standing by his bedside. He had injected something into Brodie's arm.

'Where's Page?'

'She's sleeping. It's middle-night.'

'Leave her. Don't worry about me, Dr Klein,' Brodie said.

'What is? *Bitte?*' Dr Klein's English was rudimentary.

'I'll be fine. I'm going to the Island of the Dead.'

'Please. I don't understand. *Verstehe nicht.*'

'*Ich sterbe,*' Brodie explained.

'Oh, yes. Yes, I'm very sorry to say.'

Dr Klein stood up and rummaged busily in his bag and Brodie turned to see what he was doing but his spectacles were on the bedside table. He tried to reach for them, ordered his hand to move but it wouldn't. Dimly, blurrily, Brodie was aware of Dr Klein opening what looked like a bottle of champagne. A golden gleam of foil, its rip then a pause and a dull pop as the cork was removed. Brodie heard a tumbler filled. His fingers were fitted round it and it was guided to his lips.

'What is it?'

'Champagne. It is a German tradition. At the end.'

Brodie managed a mouthful of warm champagne. The bubbles fizzed around his teeth.

Page came into the room. At least a figure did, a woman. No, it was Lika, come to find him, at last.

'Thank you very much,' Brodie said. 'Thank you for everything.'

Epilogue

Poste Restante
GPO Port Blair
Middle Andaman
Andaman Islands
Indian Empire

2 September 1906

My dear Amelia,

I will be home in a month or three, I estimate. I'm winding things up, more swiftly than I should, probably, but life in the Andamans isn't the same since poor Brodie Moncur died.

The funniest thing was that every morning, when the doors of the house were opened, Brodie's little dog César went running to the graveyard, about a quarter of a mile away, and sat there by Brodie's grave all day. If I didn't send Lakima to collect him he would have stayed there all night. It was very strange and very affecting.

And then, this is extraordinary – last week a young Russian woman arrived. Blonde, attractive, with a servant in tow and many trunks of possessions, so obviously quite rich. She went straight to Deemer's Hotel, asked for Mr Moncur, was relayed the sad news and was then directed to me. Her name, she said, was Mrs Lydia Kilbarron. Of course, I realized this was the famous 'Lika'. I told her what I could of Brodie's life here in Port Blair. Told her as much as I wanted to, I should say – not everything. We walked to the graveyard and found César sitting there by poor Brodie's grave. The little dog was very happy to see her – he knew her, so it seemed.

I left her at the graveside for five minutes or so and then walked her back to the hotel. I could tell she had been weeping – her eyes red, her face quite collapsed – but she had pulled herself together, somehow. She told me that her husband – Mr Kilbarron – had died suddenly from a fall from a bridge in Paris. An awful accident. He was trying to retrieve her hat that had been blown off by a gust of wind and, in grabbing at it, had lost his footing and fallen from this high bridge. Grieving, she had decided to travel round the world, she said. She knew that her friend, Brodie Moncur, was living here in Port Blair and so had made a detour to visit him. I nodded, kept up the pretence, and said yes, how sad, how interesting, and so forth. She told me she was intending to journey further – to China and Japan and on and on if the mood took her. She asked if she might take César as a travelling companion and I said yes, of course. I was returning to the United States myself, I informed her, and César was Brodie's dog, not mine. And so we parted – everything unsaid, though perhaps nothing needed to be said. The lady left with the little dog.

I thought I had seen the last of her but the next morning she was back. She gave me some money – hundreds of rupees – and asked for a few lines to be carved on Brodie's headstone – wooden, like all of them here. She copied the lines out and I passed them on to a local carpenter who incised them – very neatly – into the wood. I don't know where these lines came from but they stand as an epigraph to poor Brodie's short life. He was only thirty-six years old and a gentle, lovely soul – or so I say, shedding a selfish tear, who knew him all too briefly.

Anyway, Lika, Mrs Kilbarron, left on her travels with her little dog. I felt very down for a few days after she had gone, I confess. Life is so unfair, so cruel and hard, sometimes. She and I had kept our Brodie Moncur secrets from each other. Two women with so much unspoken. Her visit disturbed me, I have to admit, and made me want to leave here all the more.

And so, I'll be home soon, my dear. The great adventure is over and now the hard work begins.

With love from your sad, grieving sister,
Page

PS. By the way, these are the lines she had inscribed on the headstone. Mrs Kilbarron – Lika – was very insistent and made me promise that they were nicely done. A promise I fulfilled.

My bonny man has gone tae sleep,
His journey o'er – he's heard the call.
Birth tae death is the shortest leap,
The grave is waiting for one and all.

Gratitude and Acknowledgements

The Musicians

Clive Ackroyd, Patrick Doyle, Chloé van Soeterstède, Patrick Neil Doyle, the estate of Ernst Sauter, Aleksandr Markevich.

The Tertulia

Professor Donald Rayfield, Dr David T. Evans, Sam M. Goodforth, Mélisande Sautoy, Dr Dermot O'Flynn.

Any Human Heart
WILLIAM BOYD

Every life is both ordinary and extraordinary, and Logan Mountstuart's, stretching across the twentieth century, is a rich tapestry of both. As a writer who finds inspiration with Hemingway in Paris and Virginia Woolf in London, as a spy recruited by Ian Fleming and betrayed in the war, and as an art dealer in sixties' New York, Logan mixes with the men and women who shape his times. But as a son, friend, lover and husband, he makes the same mistakes we all do in our search for happiness. Here, then, is the story of a life lived to the full – and a journey deep into a *very* human heart.

'Astounding. One of Boyd's greatest achievements'

Mail on Sunday

'A work of astonishing, ventriloquistic virtuosity'

Sunday Telegraph

'Thoroughly entertaining and enjoyable'

Guardian

The New Confessions
WILLIAM BOYD

Meet John James Todd: Scotsman, auteur, Rousseau fanatic – and 'subversive element'.

Born in 1889, John James Todd is one of the great failed geniuses of the last century. His reminiscences, collected in *The New Confessions*, take us from Edinburgh to the Western Front, the Berlin film world in the twenties to Hollywood in the thirties, forties and beyond.

Suffering imprisonment, a shooting, marriage, fatherhood, divorce and McCarthyism, Todd is a hostage to good fortune, ill-judgement, bad luck, the vast sweep of history and the cruel, cruel hand of fate . . .

'Brilliant. A *Citizen Kane* of a novel'

Daily Telegraph

'A magnificent feat of storytelling'

Observer

'Paced and plotted with sinewy, unfailing skill'

Sunday Times

www.penguin.co.uk